Hagley

By Mark E. D'Amico

Mrs. Wolk,
I hope you enjoy
the adventure.
Mark

Hagley Park
By Mark E. D'Amico

Copyright © 2016 by Mark E. D'Amico

Edited by Mark P. D'Amico

Cover design by Becky Gradisek

Printed in the United States of America

ISBN: 978-0-9971720-0-3

Acknowledgements

Were it not for the support of my family, Hagley Park would still be a dream. Instead, it has become a dream come true. I'm sure that my wife, Susie, wanted to ask me many times if I was ever going to finish it. But she never did. She didn't give up on me, and for that, I am grateful. Many thanks as well, to my sons Luke and Zach for believing in me.

I am most grateful to my son, Mark Philip, for not just believing in me, but also for believing in my story and in the characters. He deserves the most credit for tirelessly and patiently editing and helping me to self-publish this book. I want to also thank Becky Gradisek for the beautiful cover design.

Finally, I extend a special thanks to my good friend Tony Moon and his wife Arnna in New Zealand, who have waited patiently for a copy of the novel.

Contents

Chapter 1
Out of the Ashes

A wailing, warning-sounding horn blared from a train as it passed through the little town of Greensburg, Pennsylvania, breaking the silence of a sweltering August midnight. The horn faded as the slow-moving freight passed the old, once ornate, Jacobean-style train station and headed west, away from the city. A few blocks from the station, in a neat, tree-lined neighborhood of American four-square houses, at the residence of Albert and Marie Trane, an upstairs window fan strained to cool Albert's graying, ailing body as he stared out the window at the pole light illuminating the street corner below. He limped back to his desk, and once again reread the letter that he was typing.

The throbbing headache continued in spite of the pain pills. He grabbed a prescription bottle and emptied two more pills in his hand, washing them down with a glass of warm water. He stood up slowly and walked into his son's empty bedroom across the hall. The streetlight shed a faint shimmer of light on a Beatles Abbey Road poster and a Gardens of Versailles poster on the wall above the empty bed.

The stifling heat and the stabbing pains in his head and back were the usual reasons for sleepless nights this past summer. But tonight, he was thinking about his only son, Jack, who had returned to college to begin his junior year a few days earlier. The freshness of his son's spirit and optimism had evaporated from the house. He could almost hear Jack's laughter echoing off the walls downstairs, as he thought about something else that weighed heavily on his mind. Now was the time he wanted to tell Jack about the war, about the truth of what happened all those years ago.

"No more excuses," said Albert. "No more missed opportunities. I can't take the weight of injustice any longer. I want Jack to know the truth."

Marie pushed the sheets off her sweaty body, her hair wet with perspiration.

"Please come to bed, Albert," she insisted.

"I can't sleep. How can I tell Jack that we can't afford to pay for his college? No bank will give us a loan, and my medical bills are killing us. Who am I kidding with this part-time security guard job? We're broke! There's no more money from Ian. I can't take it anymore."

He nervously fidgeted with the pill bottle, trying to drop another into his palm as his hand shook. The pills spilled onto the floor, and Marie bent over to pick them up.

"Leave them," he said, as he grasped her hand. "I have to tell you something." The shaking stopped. "I finally did it, Marie. I sent him a letter."

"Sent who a letter?"

"Kettering. I told him that I'm going to expose him unless he pays me what I want."

"Oh my God! Albert, do you know what you've done?"

1

"You bet I do. That bastard was a murderer! He's the reason I live in pain every day. I got the blame on Guam. The lying coward pinned it on me. We're not living like this anymore."

"You can't do this, Albert. You can't tell Jack."

"Jack needs to know. I'm going to drive to the college tomorrow and tell him everything… about Kettering, about Ian and Sarah. It's time. He's twenty-one. He's a man now, something I should have been more of."

"You can't put us through this, not at this stage of our lives. Kettering will destroy us. It's been twenty-eight years since it happened, and you're not even sure of what you saw. It will still be his word against yours."

"All these years, I've denied what I saw… but I know he murdered them. He got away with it too. He even got decorated and promoted. And what did I get? I got nothing. No honor, no money, no nothing! I'm tired, Marie."

"You have Jack and me."

"And what if something happens to one of us? There's nothing for Jack. Don't you worry, Kettering will pay. And if he doesn't cooperate, I have the documents and a sworn testimony downstairs that I'm mailing to the New York Times."

"I'm scared, Al."

"He won't do anything to us, not with that letter. Marie, you and Jack are my reason to live. That's why I want to be rid of this burden. I want to live to see Jack graduate and become a landscape architect. I want to travel. I want to go to New Zealand. There's so much to live for."

"I love you, Albert. I love you as much now as I did when we first met on the Mercy."

She touched his face and gently stroked his cheek. Albert pulled her closer, and kissed her softly. He felt a surge of inspiration, a light and free feeling from the lifting of a lifelong burden. He fell back on the pillow and thought about Jack. Happy images of Jack filled his head… opening presents on Christmas morning, jumping in a pile of autumn leaves, crossing the finish line. They were a smattering of the happy moments in an otherwise uphill life.

Suddenly, Albert sat up. His sweaty, red face turned pale white.

"What is it, dear?" asked Marie.

"Do you smell that? It's gas! Marie, did you say there was a man from the gas company here today?"

"Yes, he said he was checking for leaks in the neighborhood. I… I didn't ask to see identification… I let him in the basement. He said everything was fine, and then he left. Come to think of it, I didn't see a gas company vehicle parked outside… I'm sorry, Al."

"Marie, get up! We have to get out of here… I love you, Marie—"

"I love you, Albert. Jack! He's in danger—"

The microsecond of silence after the gas ignited in the basement lasted an hour in God's time. There was plenty of time for Albert and Marie to touch their sleeping son, who lay peacefully dreaming in his dormitory bed. They spoke to him in his dream. They both kissed him on the forehead, and witnessed the promise of hope in their son's eyes. Then, the house and all its memories exploded, consuming their lives in a giant fireball. By the time the fire trucks arrived, the wood frame house had disintegrated into a pile of ashes.

Jack Trane awoke in his dorm room at exactly 3:00 a.m. on August 23, 1972, at the exact moment the miniature electronic timer ignited the gas regulator on the hot water tank. Jack sat up in his bed, his forehead dripping in a cold sweat. A feeling of inexplicable panic fell upon him. He thought he heard his parents calling to him, but he went back to sleep, convinced it was just a bad dream. At 4:30 a.m., he received an abrupt visit from his dormitory prefect, Brother Vincent.

"Jack, wake up," said Brother Vincent. "There's been a fire at your home. The police are sending a car to pick you up. They need you to iden... I mean, they want to talk to you there."

"What about my parents? Did they say anything about them?"

"I don't know."

Jack stood in front of the bathroom mirror, staring at his pale, white face. His hands shook so badly that he could barely cup them to splash water on his face. He hurriedly dressed, and sprinted halfway down the hallway before he realized he had forgotten his glasses. Moments later, he was staring out the rear window of the police cruiser at the sight of the peaceful-looking Saint Mark College campus, with its old, weathered, brick buildings nestled in the rolling Southwestern Pennsylvania hills. The last view before the college disappeared around the bend was the bright basilica bell tower, illuminated in the dawn sky tinged with a purplish hue of the waking sun above the distant Laurel Mountains.

An acrid, lifeless cloud of smoke emerged over the hilly Greensburg neighborhood. The odor made Jack sick. He held his breath as the police car descended the steep street that led to his home at the bottom of the hill. Fire trucks and hoses filled every square foot of the street in front of them. Fireman rushed about in a surreal scene of flashing red lights, floodlights, and smoke amidst the sound of police radio transmissions. The policeman squeezed the cruiser behind a fire truck. Jack jumped out before the car stopped, and he ran to the charred, wooden entrance gate, staring in disbelief at the smoldering remains of his family's house.

Rubbernecking neighbors across the street whispered predictions of the death toll and destruction. The smell of burned debris was unbearable. The fire chief met Jack at the gate, and handed him a dust mask as he led him to the rear of the house. He picked his way through the rubble in silence and in shock, unable to comprehend the disaster that descended all around him. The fire chief pointed to the charred remains of two bodies that were burned beyond recognition. The figures were noticeably locked in an embrace.

A police sergeant asked Jack if the bodies were those of his parents. Jack struggled to hold back the tears. His voice quivered as he pointed to the wedding ring on his mother's hand and nodded. A thousand feelings and images flooded his mind that morning… happy memories of his parents, and of his childhood spent in this home. But now, he felt completely alone. He had no brothers or sisters, and no other relatives except for his Aunt Sarah, who wasn't really his aunt. She was a professor at Saint Mark, but she was out of the country.

The coolness of the early morning gave way to the rising heat of another hot, sticky August day. Jack sat in the police car, staring at the neighborhood around him. He noticed a huge oak tree in the neighbor's yard behind the remains of his house. He was never able to see the whole tree from the street before. It was hidden from view by his house. Now, he could see the entire tree, with its branches reaching skyward and spreading out to almost touch the ground. He fell into a trance while staring at the tree, until the police sergeant tapped him on the shoulder.

"Son, there's nothing more you can do here. The fire marshal will do an investigation and issue a report in a few days. I'm sorry about your loss. I'll drive you back to the college now. Did you know your father wanted to be a policeman?"

"He never said much about it to me. I'm sorry, but I don't really feel like talking right now."

Neither of them said a word during the ride back to Saint Mark until they reached the entrance to the college.

"Do you want me to drive you to your dorm, son?"

"No thanks. You can drop me off at the gate. I feel like walking."

The car drove away in the sweltering heat, its tires smacking the mosaic of tar-covered cracks in the old concrete pavement. Jack watched the car disappear over the crest in the road as he slowly walked up the hill to the basilica. He found a shady spot and sat down on the cool, granite steps in front of the main doors. He stayed there all afternoon, staring at the distant mountains, unable to shake off the emotional numbness. Finally, around dinnertime, he entered the church and knelt in a pew near the altar until he fell asleep, just before 9 o'clock. Shortly after, the large, wooden entrance doors creaked open and woke him up. He recognized the familiar sound of leather sandals slapping the terrazzo floor. An imposing, broad-shouldered figure sat down next to him.

"You should be back in the dorm with your friends," said Brother Vincent. "They're worried about you."

Jack sat up and extended a handshake. Brother Vincent was not a conventional-looking monk. He was a soft-spoken, middle-aged man whose demeanor did not match his husky appearance and reputation for being the loudest, rowdiest fan at all the sporting events. He had a mop of curly, reddish-brown hair and a thick, brown beard. He was a Benedictine monk who had attended seminary twenty years earlier at Saint Mark. He taught economics and philosophy, and he and Jack shared the same dry brand of humor.

"I'm sorry about your folks. Try to be strong. We know not the hour of

4

our death, nor do we know when God will challenge us."

Tears welled in Jack's eyes.

"I'm scared, Vincent. I have nobody. No grandparents, no relatives… just Sarah."

"Have faith, Jack. I've already talked to the archabbot… the college will help you. Come on, I'll walk with you back to the dorm. You've prayed enough for tonight."

Chapter 2
Changing Course

Three days passed. It was the night before the funeral, and a somber Brother Vincent stood outside Jack's dorm room. He hesitated before knocking. The pained expression on his face would not easily leave him. He knocked once.

"It's open," said Jack.

"Hello, Jack. I hate to deliver troubling news, but I spoke with the police chief on the phone earlier this evening. He said the fire will most likely be ruled an accident. The explosion was caused by a faulty water heater." Jack stood up. "What's worse is we've learned that your parents had no insurance. Apparently, they cashed in their homeowners and life insurance policies last year, and they have nothing in the bank."

"Are you serious? You mean I don't have any kind of inheritance?"

"It doesn't look that way. Your parents were thousands of dollars in debt."

Jack sat back on the bed, as his face turned white.

"There has to be some kind of mistake. What am I going to do, Vincent? How am I going to pay these debts? How am I going to pay for the funeral?"

"The archabbot has agreed to cover the funeral costs, and I'm checking on some funds to cover your tuition for this semester. I'll do everything I can to help you."

"They left me nothing? I don't know how they got into all this debt."

"Don't worry about that right now. There is always a solution. God will provide."

"Oh really? And when is that, Vincent? What do I do in the meantime? Why is this happening to me?"

"Why, I should slap you! How do you know your parents didn't sacrifice for you? You better get yourself together. Life is not fair, but at least you have life, and you have your immortal soul. Be thankful for that! You get what you get from God. The rest is up to you. I suggest you stop feeling sorry for yourself."

"Thanks for your help, but I just want to be left alone."

"As you wish, but I would suggest you pray to the Holy Spirit for inspiration and guidance. I will pray for you too. You must be strong. Your parents would want you to carry on. Their love, in the form of prayer and intercession, flows through you, even after their deaths. Don't lose hope, and above all, don't lose faith. God's grace will sustain you in your hour of need. I'll see you at the funeral."

The next morning, Jack lay in bed thinking about the poignant reminder about God's grace from Brother Vincent. He was still groggy from a hot, sticky, sleepless night. He skipped breakfast and took a long, meandering walk to the basilica, arriving before anyone else. He stopped at the front steps to

6

look at the bell towers that glistened in the early morning sunlight, and then quickly disappeared as gray, threatening rain clouds rolled in. Soon, his friends and classmates arrived and joined him in the front pews. A few dozen of his parents' friends and neighbors filed through the broad, wooden entrance doors, and sat scattered in the pews. The vivid colors of stained glass depicting figures of the saints in the windows turned to dull tones as the sky darkened with rain clouds. A welcoming, cool breeze blew across the pews from the opened windows.

The parts of the mass seemed to pass quickly. Before he knew it, the priest was signaling for Brother Vincent to deliver the eulogy. That's when time slowed, as his thoughts wandered to his mother, who always seemed to be cheerful. She taught him a creative curiosity about life and nature. He chuckled to himself as he thought about the two of them watching *Star Trek* together. Aunt Sarah got them hooked on it, and they never missed an episode.

He thought about his father, who lived every day in pain from his war wounds. His father was a mystery that he couldn't solve, a troubled man who kept his memories and dreams inside, but periodically left signs that he wanted to open up to Jack. Unfortunately, it never happened. As the mass continued, Jack dwelt on what he knew best about his father… his courage and steadfastness in the face of his debilitations. He wished he knew more about the war, about what it was like to fight the Japanese. He wished he could have somehow eased his father's pain.

When the mass concluded, the pallbearers began to carry the caskets away, and Jack broke down and cried. For the first time in his life, he felt alone, frightened, and uncertain of his future. The funeral procession moved slowly toward the cemetery on the hill behind the college, and toward finality. The procession only lasted a few minutes before they arrived at the cemetery gate. Moments later, Jack found himself standing at the gravesite listening to Brother Vincent's final prayer. Then it was over, and the mourners departed, leaving the two of them alone.

"Thanks, Vincent… for everything. It was a beautiful funeral, a tribute to my parents."

"It was the least I could do. Now, come to the reception and be amongst your friends."

"If you don't mind, I'd like to stay here alone for a bit."

"Of course. I'll see you later."

Jack stood silently alongside his parents' graves in the drizzling rain. His usually untamed, thick, dark brown hair was matted down from the rain, and his glasses were smeared with perspiration and the foggy drizzle. He was quickly besieged with panic and fear. His eye began to twitch. He knelt on the wet grass and tried to pray, but he soon broke down into tears. Thoughts of loneliness and anguish tightened the grip of fear in his head, and he felt paralyzed.

This kind of fear was not a stranger to him. It was there when he was a child, when his parents argued about money, or about his father's unemployment. He hated the thought of it. As he went to stand up, a gust of wind shook the branches of a huge maple tree above him. Suddenly, a heavy branch snapped and plunged to the ground, just missing him. The wind was whipping the trees around him. He thought about the whims of nature, about his own mortality.

He stood up and leaned against the massive trunk of the old maple, looking off into the distance and staring at the rows of graves in the 120-year-old cemetery where the Benedictine monks were buried. The black iron crosses that marked each grave stretched across the field in front of him, along the horizon with the distant Laurel Mountains that were draped in gray mist, twenty miles to the east. Out of the corner of his eye, he caught a glimpse of a dark silhouette at the far side of the cemetery. The man walked through the iron gate and strode slowly toward Jack. As he drew closer, Jack noticed that he wore the dress blue uniform of a Navy serviceman.

"How's it going? I'm Chief Petty Officer Stan Driggers from the Navy Recruiting Office in Greensburg. You must be Jack Trane. I saw in the obituary that your father was a Marine Corps veteran, and I've come to pay my respects. I'm sorry to hear about your parents."

Jack at once felt bothered and confused by the stranger, who seemed to have dropped out of the sky. He was square-jawed, with blond hair and a threatening demeanor.

"Damn, what happened to you?" he asked, catching sight of Jack's mud-covered shirt.

"Thanks. I slipped over there. A branch almost hit me. If you don't mind me asking, why wouldn't they send a Marine?"

The man quickly fired back.

"We're all in the same Navy. Besides, there weren't any Marines available, so I volunteered. How do you like it here at Saint Mark? What's your major?"

"It's good. I study landscape architecture."

"So, you study landscaping and gardening?"

"No, no. It's about planning and the design of the land… parks, campuses, things like that."

"Oh, I see. Bet you'd like to travel the world and see some of the famous parks?"

"Actually, I still have two more years until I get my degree. Then I can think about travel."

"I bet it costs a lot of dough to go here. Did your parents leave you anything to help you pay for school, if you don't mind me asking?"

"With all due respect, I'd rather not talk about that. Listen, I've got to go. You're welcome to come to the reception."

"No can do. I have to get back to the office. Hey, maybe I could stop back and drop off some information for you. No obligation of course. I just want to show you a way you could pay for college and maybe see some of those famous places. It's something to think about."

"I don't know," said Jack. "I have a lot of things on my mind, but I will

8

think about it." Then Petty Officer Driggers closed the gate, and disappeared over the hill.

During the next couple of weeks, the weight of sorrow and financial stress overshadowed Jack's studies, and the strain began to wear him down. He had trouble focusing in class, and he spent less and less time in the design studio. On one particular Friday afternoon in late September, he took a detour from the usual route to class and headed through the woods to the Old Mill Coffee Shop by Saint Mark Lake. The leaf-covered path was spattered with drops of sunlight from the bright afternoon sun that filtered through the autumn woodland canopy. At this point in past semesters, he would have been completely immersed in a design project. Instead, he found himself in the middle of the woods, feeling angry and resentful, unfocused over the anxiety and instability in his life. A part of him wanted to walk away from this place.

He sat down in his usual corner table, ordered a strong coffee, and pulled out a stack of papers. One by one, he sifted through the pile of bills, bank statements, and legal documents. He wondered how he would pay all of the bills, or whether he'd even be obligated to. He was beginning to question the direction his life was taking. For the first time since he arrived at Saint Mark, he wasn't sure what he wanted to do. Then the door opened, and in the dim light of the coffee shop, he recognized the outline of Brother Vincent's hair.

"What are you doing down here? I thought you had a big design project due soon."

"Sorry, Vincent, but I don't really care about my project right now."

"Feeling sorry for yourself, Jack?"

"I think I'm entitled to feel however the hell I want right now. My parents are dead, my home is a pile of ashes, and I'm broke… and it looks like there won't be much help from the college. I'd say right now, I'm flat out of enthusiasm."

"Jack, you must pray to the Holy Spirit for guidance. You must pray for help to choose the right path. Life is not about chasing money. Our lives have no meaning unless we serve God… and through God, serve man. Service and love of your fellow man lead to the truth."

"Vincent, being broke really sucks. I'm beginning to think I need to be somewhere else right now. I'm not sure where. I need some time to think, away from here."

"Jack, please don't act impetuously. Pray for the path that God wants you to follow, and God will give you a sign. I'll see you later. Come to vespers this evening, okay."

"Maybe."

After Brother Vincent left, the waitress switched on a small television set on the counter. Walter Cronkite was reading the latest report of American casualties in Vietnam on the CBS Evening News. A Marine unit had been ambushed in the Mekong Delta. Five Marines killed. The pictures of bloody,

9

wounded soldiers disturbed him. Like most of his friends in college, he hated the war, but at the same time, felt sorry for the guys who got drafted and had to go. His thoughts turned to his father. He never had the chance to go to college, but he never complained about it. He wondered if he could walk in his father's shoes, if he could fight in a war and survive the terror of combat.

The news reports continued. A reporter discussed the nuclear arms race. President Nixon hoped for arms reduction talks with the Soviets before the end of 1972. An unnamed congressman declared that something had to be done to prevent nuclear annihilation. He asked the waitress if he could change the channel. *Star Trek* reruns were on. This particular episode was his mother's favorite. It was the one where the Enterprise was sent to a remote galaxy to prevent a rogue planet from developing a dark matter weapon.

As he fixated on the TV, he did not notice the two silhouettes of a man and a woman standing at the doorway. The man was looking around the room. He spotted Jack, and then the two of them shuffled toward him. The woman was partially hidden behind the large man, whose face was in shadow until he passed under a light. Jack recognized him instantly as Petty Officer Driggers, the Navy man from the funeral. A curvaceous, reddish-brown haired, twenty-something girl in tight jeans stepped from behind him.

"Hey there, Jack. I thought I'd stop by with that information. How are you faring these days?" They shook hands.

"Mr. Driggers, right?" asked Jack.

"That would be me. This is Petty Officer Cindy Carter. She's a radioman on leave from her station in Naples, Italy. We were in meetings at the Federal Building in Pittsburgh earlier today, and I asked her to come along to talk to you about the Navy."

She shot a coy smile at Jack, and shook his hand.

"Do you mind if we join you? Or better yet, why don't you let me buy you dinner? There's a nice Italian restaurant near here. Are you hungry, Cindy?"

"Famished," she replied.

"Well, I suppose so," said Jack. "It's Friday night."

Driggers led them to his car outside the coffee shop; it was a brand new ocean-blue Dodge Challenger.

"Wow, nice car," said Jack.

"Thanks. Navy pay is pretty good these days."

At the restaurant, Cindy purposely sat close to Jack. Driggers ordered a round of beers.

"Jack, Cindy says she's traveled throughout Europe while stationed in Naples. Isn't that right, Cindy?"

"Oh yes. I've been to Rome, Florence, Paris, and London. I especially enjoyed the Gardens of Versailles in Paris. I used my thirty days paid leave to explore Europe, especially the art and architecture. It was all so beautiful; a great experience, thanks to the Navy!"

"That's what I wanted to tell you, Jack. The Navy has a program where you can serve two years of active duty, and then spend a few years in the

Reserves. In just two years, you could be back here finishing your degree on the GI Bill. I'm sure you could… ah… use the money, and I bet you'd like to visit some of those places Cindy mentioned."

"Versailles gave me goose bumps," said Cindy, as she squeezed his hand. "Another beer, Jack?"

Jack fumbled with his glass and dropped his napkin. Driggers winked at Cindy, and ordered another round.

"You should think about it, Jack," said Cindy. "The Navy might just be the answer to your problems."

"So, will you allow me to leave some information about careers in the Navy with you to read over the weekend?" asked Driggers. "I think you'll see we offer some pretty valuable benefits to help you with your education costs."

"Yea, sure. I guess if I enlisted in the Navy, I would sort of be honoring my father's memory. I could travel and see the places I've read about. But wait a minute. I have no idea what the hell I would do in the Navy. What kind of skills do I have?"

"Don't worry, they'll train you," said Driggers.

"You should be a radioman like me," said Cindy. "Then, you'd have a better chance of getting shore duty in Europe. You could visit me in Italy."

"Wouldn't that be nice?" asked Driggers.

"Yes, I suppose so. What do you do, Stan?"

"I was a SEAL in Special Forces for a few years. Now I'm a communications technician. Snooping and behind-the-scenes stuff is my deal."

"Stick to being a radioman like me," said Cindy. "It's a lot safer. You'll go to school in Bainbridge, Maryland." She put on fresh lipstick, licked her lips, and then smiled at him. "Yes, it's a real nice place."

She leaned back in Jack's arms, as Driggers went off to pay the bill. He returned a few minutes later, and glanced at his watch.

"Well, it's getting late. I better get you back to your dorm. Cindy has a plane to catch tomorrow too."

"Ah, that's too bad. Will I see you again, Cindy?"

"I hope so, but not unless you enlist and come to Europe. You really should think about it."

Driggers left Jack and Cindy alone on the porch outside the restaurant while he went to get the car. She pressed her body against his chest, and then she kissed him.

"You should join the Navy, Jack," she whispered in his ear, as Driggers pulled alongside them. "You should do it soon." They both slid into the backseat. She sat close to him as Driggers sped along the winding road on the way back to the college. A few minutes later, they were back on campus. Driggers down shifted the Challenger and revved the engine, as the car pulled up and screeched to a halt in front of the dormitory.

"Say, Jack," said Driggers. "You probably don't get much action here, huh? This is an all men's college, right?"

"Well, there's a women's college near here—"

11

Cindy giggled, and touched his thigh.

"Opportunity is knocking. Think about the Navy. I'll call you in a few days. Don't call the recruiting office in Greensburg. I'll be in Pittsburgh next week. Call this number instead. Don't forget."

"Good luck, Jack. I hope to see you soon," said Cindy, as she blew a kiss at him.

Jack waved, and staggered up the steps to his dorm. Cindy's words 'You should join the Navy. You should do it soon' echoed in his head.

Over the next few days, he thought constantly about joining the Navy. He skipped his classes and hung out at the coffee shop. The whole matter of enlisting was intensified by nightly phone calls from Driggers. The lure of a paycheck, free travel, and money for college was too hard to ignore. On one of the days, Brother Vincent called Jack to his office to inform him that his tuition and fees could not be waived, and that Jack would have to take out additional loans. Brother Vincent suggested a fundraiser. Jack became increasingly distraught and unable to focus on his studies.

On the following Friday morning, a week after his dinner with Driggers and Cindy, he was in the midst of a City Planning exam, when he abruptly stood up and walked to the front of the room. He handed his unfinished test to the professor and walked out the door, not sure where he was going to go. He ran straight into his friend Dingo Jim, an exchange student from Australia.

"Rumor has it you're thinking about joining the Navy. Are you out of your mind, mate? Let me give you two words you should not ignore… Viet-Nam! You know they send people in the Navy there too?"

"Not me. The Navy is going to send me to Europe."

"I heard the department is offering a semester in Italy senior year."

"I can't pay for that, Dingo. The only way I'll see Europe is if I can get stationed there in the Navy."

"Don't do this, Jack. You need to take some time to think about this. Things will work out. I know it's been tough losing your parents and all, but don't rush into anything. Did you talk to Brother Vincent about all this?"

"Why, so he can tell me I need to pray more? Maybe I just don't give a damn about this place anymore. You know what matters… me. Numero uno. Taking care of myself for once. I'm going nowhere here, so I'm moving on."

"Let's go for a run tomorrow. We'll talk about it over a few miles on the course."

"It's no use, Dingo. I've got to do this. I'll talk to you later."

After Dingo left, Jack went straight to the payphone on his floor and called Driggers. That afternoon, Driggers drove him to Pittsburgh. At 3:00 p.m., he stood before a Naval officer in a private room in the Federal Building, and took the oath of enlistment in the US Navy.

When he returned to Saint Mark that evening, he was met at the entrance to the dormitory by Kirk Shetler, one of his other classmates.

"You old dog, what the hell did you do today? Did you really join the Navy?"

"I sure did."

"I think that's great. I wish I were doing something exciting like you. Look at me… I'm twenty-five, still in college, and don't really know what I want to do."

"Maybe you should join too," said Jack.

"Maybe I will someday. I think it sounds pretty cool. You get to see the world, girl in every port, that sort of thing. Hey, you can send me stamps from around the world for my collection. By the way, do you have any more of those New Zealand stamps? You get them on letters from Professor Mechling, right?"

"Sure, Kirk, but I'm kind of tired. I want to hit the sack."

"Mechling is your aunt, right? Have you heard from her at all?"

"No, I haven't, but I'll send her a letter when I get to boot camp."

"I'll check on your mail and forward anything that comes in to you."

"Thanks, Kirk, and I will send you postcards with stamps from the countries I visit."

When Jack returned to his room, Brother Vincent was waiting for him at his door.

"Good evening, Jack. Jim told me you were thinking about enlisting in the Navy. He was quite concerned about you. I brought you some garden books from the festival book sale. At first, I came here to try to change your mind, but then I decided not to lecture you. I have a strange feeling you are doing the right thing, and that you will one day come back to us."

"Thanks, Vincent. You and Aunt Sarah are all the family I have now. I could not have made it this far without you. I feel like I have to do this. Sometimes, I think my dad is inside my head, guiding me. Some nights, I feel like he is trying to awaken me, to tell me something. It's really weird."

"That is the voice of the Holy Spirit. You must listen carefully in order to choose the right path in life, and pray for the dedication and diligence to stay on it. Sometimes, the right path is blurred, and we don't know which way to go. When that happens, rely on your faith. I pray you will meet that challenge and stay in God's grace. Let courage and your faith guide you. Whatever you do, make sure you do it in love and service to others. Don't think only of yourself. Then, you will have the grace of God. That is Christ's message."

"You lay it all out so cleanly, Vincent."

"So what's next for you?"

"I'm leaving for boot camp in Great Lakes, Illinois next week. Then, they're sending me to radio school in Bainbridge, Maryland in December. I'm not sure what I should do with my things while I'm away."

"You can leave everything here. I'll arrange to store them in the old gristmill building. They will be safe there until you return. No one will know about it, except you and me. Hopefully, you will have an enlightening experience in the Navy. Then, you can return here to finish your studies."

Brother Vincent glanced around the room. He noticed a book on the shelf above the desk. It was a hardcover book with a colorful photograph of a

13

beautiful lake in an English-looking park on the jacket.

"What a beautiful book," he said, as he paged through the colorful illustrations.

"Where did that come from?" asked Jack. "Ah, it must be Aunt Sarah. She goes to used-book sales and finds books she thinks I might enjoy, and then they end up here. I did not notice this one though… been too busy, I guess. One of these days, I'll get around to reading all these books."

"You must come back and finish your last two years in landscape architecture. It is such a beautiful profession… to design the land for people to use and enjoy. What could be better? Do you mind if I borrow this book? It looks like delightful reading."

Jack examined the book, thumbing through the pages. The park on the cover seemed familiar to him. He gave it a passing thought, and then closed the cover and handed it to Brother Vincent.

"No, of course not. Take any book you like."

"Go forward, Jack, and find the righteous path in life. Then return to us. Have a good night."

"Good night, Brother Vincent."

On the morning of October 2, 1972, Jack stood outside the arched entrance of the 130-year-old, brick and limestone-clad Benedict Hall building. He had his duffle bag in hand, waiting for Driggers to pick him up. The brisk, autumn morning air was alive with the scent of fresh dew on the campus lawns and a crisp, earthy aroma of fallen leaves. He ran back inside to see if Dingo had come down to see him off, but he couldn't find him. A smirking, cocky-looking Driggers pulled up in the Challenger with the windows down, singing a verse of Anchors Away. He handed Jack a packet of orders.

"Relax, this is your big day. You're shoving off on a new adventure."

Jack nodded and nervously mumbled a thank you, but didn't say much else on the twenty-minute drive to the train station in Greensburg. They arrived a few minutes before the 10:00 a.m. departure, and Jack had just enough time for a quick handshake before he darted up the steps to board the train. The silver and red Amtrak engine roared to life, and the coaches jerked and swayed as the train pulled out of the station.

Jack looked back at the surrounding hills of the city, then at the empty platform, and finally to Driggers' blue Challenger parked in front of the station. There was a woman standing next to Driggers. He caught a glimpse of her red hair and gold-rimmed glasses. It looked like Cindy, but he reasoned it couldn't be her. She was supposed to be back in Italy. He got up from his seat and ran to the back of the train, but he was too late. The train was well past the station, which soon disappeared behind a bridge abutment as the train picked up speed. For a moment, he had second thoughts. He actually thought about jumping off. Then, the notion passed and he sat down, glancing at the passing scenery.

Soon, the train passed Saint Mark. He caught a glimpse of the bell towers through a gap in the woods bordering the tracks. Saint Mark was the home that he was leaving now, not his parents' house in Greensburg. Everything felt strange. He returned to thinking about his father. He wondered what kind of emotions his father felt as he left this same station and headed off to boot camp to fight in World War II thirty years ago. Was he afraid, as Jack was now? At least he would have a taste of what his father tasted... boot camp and military life, and he would walk a little on the same path. He could not imagine he was stepping into a future clouded by the dark mysteries that had been asleep in his father's past, a past soon to be awakened by the footsteps of a new Trane in uniform.

Boot camp was ten hours away, and he could not stop thinking about his father. It must have been hell to fight in a real battle, let alone dozens of them as his father did. How did a twenty-year-old kid from Greensburg do something like that? Surely, he must have been scared and thought about running away. What was it like in the heat of battle? He wished his father had told him more about his wartime experience. He wondered what really happened on Guam back in 1944. Thoughts poured into his head that he had suppressed during the turmoil of the past few weeks. Who was the officer his father despised? Who was the New Zealand scientist his parents talked about behind closed doors?

He stared out the window at the cornfields and pastures of Ohio farmlands as the train sped west. The click-clack of the rails lulled him to doze on and off. He awakened at the sound of the locomotive horn blaring a warning to the road crossing ahead. The sun was slowly slipping below the distant, amber-colored fields. The last ray of evening light beamed from the darkening western sky and flashed across the golden pastures of waving grasses. He closed his eyes and let his thoughts drift away, through the train window and over the horizon into the distant past. They came to rest on an old, worn wallet photo of his father in Marine Corps battle gear, leaning on a palm tree, somewhere in the jungles of the South Pacific, thirty years ago.

Chapter 3
A Sinister Gleam

From a vantage point on a hill overlooking the open field of tall grass dotted with sharp, angular boulders and the distant edge of the dark jungle below, the Japanese officer scanned the landscape with his binoculars. The undulating fields of switch grass stretched for 400 yards between the steep hills and the dense jungle. The misty, metallic-blue flower plumes of the grasses rose and fell in rhythmic waves in the wind. Great white clouds, floating in the azure blue sky rested on the treetops above the jungle, and then tumbled to the island coastline below. Beads of sweat dripped from the officer's forehead onto the binocular lenses. He scanned the terrain, and panned to the coastline visible beyond the edge of the hills. Puffs of black smoke rose from the distant beachhead, marking the spot where the United States Marine invasion of Guam began five days earlier, on July 21, 1944. That's where most of battle raged, on the southwestern part of the island.

The officer froze. Under the hot noonday sun, he spotted a group of olive-colored, helmeted figures bobbing in and out of the grass plumes at the edge of the jungle. He whispered to a soldier behind him that there were twelve US Marines, probably the same patrol that had been chasing them for the past day. He told his men to hold their fire and cover anything metallic that could reflect the bright sunlight. But it was too late. One of the soldiers lifted his wrist to check the time, and the sun's rays found the shiny metal trim on the watch. They had lost the element of surprise, his only hope of stopping the pesky patrol that had been hunting them. His squad of twelve Imperial Marines was the last line of defense between the Americans and the Japanese communication base where allied prisoners were being held.

As he crouched in the swaying grass, Sergeant Albert Trane signaled to his men to get down. The faint glint of reflected metal at the edge of the hills above did not escape his notice. His squad of Marines welcomed the chance to rest after the five-mile march through the dense jungle. Albert Trane was a six-foot tall, strong and athletic twenty-one-year old with a large chest and powerful arms and legs. The strain of two campaigns at Bougainville and Kwajalein and a bout with Dinghy Fever wore heavily on his robust frame, leaving him forty pounds lighter and leaner. He enlisted in the Marines because he heard they were the toughest, and the South Pacific had some inexplicable attraction to him. From the very start of boot camp in Paris Island, he gained a reputation for fearlessness and quick thinking under pressure. He had a solid feel for tactics, and his men believed in him. No one questioned his decisions, except for his platoon commander, twenty-six-year old First Lieutenant Nick Kettering.

"Leo, get the lieutenant on the horn," Albert whispered.

"Right, but he ain't gonna' be happy we're so far ahead," said Corporal Leo Blair, who had become Albert's best friend since boot camp.

16

Lieutenant Kettering was four miles back, in the middle of the jungle with fifteen men, the remainder of the 1st Platoon of Company 523. He had ordered Albert to scout the area below the highlands and secure a vantage point for the main platoon to cross the open fields.

Albert felt uneasy about the orders. Kettering had a reputation for putting his own ambitions before the welfare of his men. Since their training for the Pacific Theater began at Camp Pendleton in San Diego, Kettering had a record of abusive treatment and a thirst for power. He once forced Albert to fight another Marine, a weaker guy who Kettering thought was disrespecting him. He told Albert that if he knocked him out, the whole company would get weekend liberty. Albert knew he could really hurt the guy, so he refused. Kettering was furious, and he put the whole company on extra duty and confined them to the barracks for the weekend. Everyone was punished except for Albert, who got a pass to town that Saturday night. Kettering sent him to run errands off base for the captain. The rest of the men thought Kettering favored Albert and had given him special privileges. Kettering adeptly spread dissension amongst his men, and he maintained order through a system of rewards and fear. Most of the men didn't trust him.

"Mainline, this is A-Train," said Albert. "We're at the edge of the field, about a thousand yards from the hills. My nose tells me there are Japanese up there. Request permission to re-enter the jungle and take position on their flank, about two miles from here. Over."

"A-Train, this is Mainline," barked Kettering. "Negative. Now you listen to me. Your mission is to pursue and kill the enemy. We got them on the run, and we're not wasting any more time. We've only got one chance to rescue those prisoners, so don't screw it up. Proceed across that field and take up position below the hills. Then wait for me. Out."

"Roger. Out," said Albert, as he slammed the transmitter piece down. "Damn him. He doesn't give a shit about us. He's marching us right into an ambush. Leo, form up the men. We're going back in the jungle."

"But Sarge, Kettering will court martial your ass if you disobey his order," said Leo.

"That's the price I'll have to pay. It's suicide to hit them straight on. I'm not losing another man because of Kettering's ambitions. We're going back in the jungle, and then we'll circle around the hill. Kettering won't know how we got there. Now let's move it."

When Albert's squad reached the hill above the pass, they were exhausted from the hike in the scorching afternoon sun and sickening humidity. He had less than an hour to secure the pass before Kettering arrived at the other end of the field. From his position, he spotted two Japanese machine gun nests on either side of the pass, about 300 yards apart. It was clear that his men would have been cut to pieces had they attacked straight on. His squad dug in for an attack on the nearest machine gun nest. He prayed there wasn't a Japanese patrol nearby. Where was Kettering, he thought? He couldn't decide whether he should wait for him or attack now. Then, Japanese rifle fire erupted from

17

the silence behind his position.

"Ficco's hit," yelled Leo a split second later.

Albert had to concentrate on the Japanese patrol behind him.

"How many, Leo?" he yelled.

"I make out twelve... wait, Kettering's on the radio. He's at the other side of the field."

"Leo, tell Kettering I'm gonna' try to knock out the closest machine gun nest. Tell him to get the hell up here."

Albert's men were pinned down by the Japanese patrol, and could not advance past the machine gun nest. Kettering's squad was taking fire from the other machine gun. Albert crawled through the high grass and boulders and advanced on the first machine gun. Leo and the rest of Albert's squad exchanged fire with the Japanese, who were dug into the rocks above them. Albert hurled the first grenade at the machine gun position. It missed. A few seconds later, he threw another one. It hit the mark. One down. Now Kettering could take care of the other machine gun across the pass. But the Japanese had Albert's squad trapped. If Kettering didn't get there soon, they'd be cut to pieces.

When Albert finally caught sight of Kettering, he was kneeling in the middle of the field next to three of his dying men, frozen with his hands over his ears. Albert stared at Kettering's motionless figure. The other men in his squad screamed for instructions. Still, he cowered behind a cluster of boulders in the tall grass, unable to give an order. Four more of his men were hit. The rest of his squad was attacking the machine gun nest at the pass. Meanwhile, Albert, who was nearing exhaustion, climbed around the hill to attack the Japanese soldiers that were firing at Leo. As he hunkered in the rocks waiting to hurl a grenade, he heard Leo's faint yell in the distance.

"Sarge, we can't hold out much longer. I think it's just me and Holmes left."

Albert heard the screams of Kettering's men being cut down by the machine gun nest. If Kettering had just flanked the machine gun then they would have had a chance. What the hell was wrong with him? Albert turned his attention to the second machine gun. The Japanese gunners had been preoccupied with Kettering's squad, and did not see him sneak up behind their position. He cocked his tommy gun and sprayed the two gunners, killing both of them instantly. Then he fell to his knees, and his body began to tremble.

A horrific scene unfolded before his blurry eyes. He never felt the Japanese bullets graze the side of his head and strike his lower back, and a third tear through his left shoulder. His head and shoulder were bleeding, and he was weakening by the minute. Leo and the rest of the squad had fought a heroic battle. Neither side would retreat or surrender. When the last Japanese rifle fell silent, Leo and Holmes emerged on the other side of the pass, the only survivors of the first squad. Albert collapsed on his side in the tall grass, as blood dripped from his wounded head. He lie face down, hidden from their view, about fifty yards away. He was too weak to call out, but was still able to see them. Kettering appeared in the distance, and Leo called to him.

"Where's Al? You damn, stinking coward… a whole platoon wiped out. Holmes and me are all that's left. You did nothing, you bastard."

Kettering stood motionless in the gleam of departing evening light, staring coldly at the ground. Albert lay bleeding against a dead Japanese soldier, out of sight from Kettering. He was dizzy and groggy, barely able to make out Kettering slowly aim the 45-caliber pistol. He pointed the gun at Leo, and fired a single shot, then turned and shot Holmes in the head. Almost simultaneously, Albert dropped to the ground, unable to hold his head up any longer, and he lost sight of Kettering. A flurry of rifle shots rang out across the grassy expanse. Albert struggled to lift his head off the ground and watch the unfolding scene, but all he saw was Leo and Holmes lying face down, about ten yards from Kettering, who was standing still with the pistol at his side, pointing it toward the ground.

A cold, sinister silence descended on the field of swaying grass, as the sun's rays slowly evaporated from the field and sank behind the hills where the brave men of both armies fought and died. Kettering's squatty, emotionless figure stood in the middle of the field, surveying the carnage. He was like a vulture, his eyes streaming back and forth searching frantically for Albert. Suddenly, there was another burst of rifle fire. The distinctly Japanese rifle sound cracked from the distance in the hills. Kettering turned and nervously began to run toward the jungle, and that was all Albert remembered as he lost consciousness in the fading light of the evening.

Chapter 4
Deliverance

The early morning light quickly faded as large, threatening clouds erupted above the jungle canopy with heavy droplets of rain that pelted the lush foliage along the path. The two surviving Japanese soldiers from the firefight with Albert's platoon struggled to carry the stretcher that held Albert's body. They carried him for two hours from the grass field into the heart of the jungle.

Albert awoke to the cool sensation of raindrops soothing his head injuries. He shivered and winced in excruciating pain each time the stretcher shifted. Perhaps the soldiers grew tired of carrying him, or maybe they feared the impending US Marine onslaught. Whatever the reason, they decided to set the stretcher down and leave him in the middle of the jungle, in the pouring rain. They argued briefly, and one of them reached for his revolver to shoot Albert. But for some reason, he returned it to his holster. They both stared at Albert for a moment with a look of hopelessness, and the three of them struck a common chord, that war was madness.

After the soldiers left, he found himself lost, without food or water, weak and exhausted in the middle of the jungle. He had no compass, and the sun was hidden behind the storm clouds. Fortunately, he was able to recall the direction that the Japanese soldiers traveled when they left him, and he decided to follow it. Something inside him told him not to return to the American lines. He managed to limp through the jungle for a couple of hours, covering about a mile before resting. The sun began to peek through the clouds, and Albert noted the orientation of the sun and the direction he was walking… north, in the direction of the Japanese.

A flock of cockatoos burst from the treetops and broke the silence. Albert crouched down in the dense foliage. Japanese voices echoed from an opening in the jungle, a few hundred yards below his position. This, he thought, must be the camp where the Allied prisoners were held. There were a few dozen Japanese soldiers scurrying about and loading some kind of tracked vehicle. It looked like they were getting ready to abandon the area, and he moved closer for a better look. There were four bamboo huts on stilts, about three feet off the ground and situated around the perimeter of a clearing in the jungle canopy. He noted that an officer was repeatedly moving in and out of one of the huts, which made him think it was the operations hut. The second and third huts were barracks and mess. But what was in the fourth hut? That must be where the prisoners were held.

He struggled with the intense pain in his shoulder, while trying to crouch and hide in the dense vegetation. Wounded and without a weapon, he thought he had to be crazy to try and make a rescue. Why in the hell did he come here? He should have stayed where the Japanese soldiers left him. He would have found his way back to friendly lines. But that meant facing Kettering, the murderer. No one would believe his story. It would be Kettering's word against his. Against his survival instincts, he decided to see if there were any prisoners in that hut. He had to. It was his homage to God for plucking him from certain death on the battlefield, and then again at the hands of the two Japanese soldiers. Tonight, he would try to save whoever was in that hut.

Darkness in the jungle is deep and thick. Albert could have walked the 200 yards to the camp unnoticed, but fearing the Japanese had set booby traps, he crawled the entire way on his belly in the hot, sticky night air. By midnight, the soldiers were asleep in their tents, except for a single sentry in the center of the camp and the radioman in the command hut listening to the soft muttering of Japanese music interspersed with Morse code. Albert crawled under the hut and waited for the sentry to move out of sight. Then, he carefully and quietly lifted the latch on the bamboo door and crept inside, closing the door behind him.

He lit a match, and his first thought was that the hut was empty. He turned around to leave, when he heard moaning. He lit another match. The faint flicker of light revealed a shocking, pitiful sight of a bound, bruised, emaciated figure quivering in the corner. Albert signaled to him to keep quiet. He untied his hands and ankles and helped him crawl to the door. He waited for the sentry to enter the mess hut, and then made his move, pulling the frail body next to his. They miraculously slid down the steps, and crawled under the hut. Then, supporting each other arm-in-arm, they hobbled into the dark jungle.

Albert guessed that he had two hours before daybreak, when the Japanese would realize their prisoner had escaped. They picked their way through the dense, dark jungle, determined to get as far away from the flickering light of the camp as possible. Albert carried the man for a few hours, until his knees buckled from fatigue under the weight across his back. His head throbbed, and stabbing pain shot through his back. He feared one of the wounds was infected. It wasn't long before the light of the camp disappeared and he found himself disoriented and struggling to push forward. Pain and thirst gnawed at his will to survive and push on to save this man, and himself.

The first morning light broke through the tree canopy, revealing a steep drop-off just ahead of him. The terrain broke from the level jungle floor into a steep, rocky hillside that overlooked a stream about 100 feet below. In the darkness, he would have easily fallen to a certain death. He decided to rest for a while at the top of the hill, where they both collapsed from fatigue, and fell asleep. But within an hour, the cackle of Japanese voices echoing in the distance awakened Albert. The soldiers couldn't have been more than a half-mile away.

"Hey, wake up," he whispered. "Do you think you can walk?"

The gaunt, bearded man nodded yes.

"Come on then, we've only got a few minutes."

They inched their way down the hillside, holding on to the tangles of tree roots and vines that wove through the red clay soil. They were desperately thirsty, and could hear the rush of water, but it would be almost an hour before they drank from the stream below. The water saved them. It gave them enough energy to push on and find a cave where they could rest and hide. After another brief rest, Albert awakened his comrade.

"Hey, pal. Wake up."

"Gidday."

"You Australian?" asked Albert.

"No, Kiwi." Albert returned a puzzled look. "New Zealander. My name is Ian Moon, Lieutenant, Royal New Zealand Air Corps. How are you going?"

"Uh, okay. I'm Albert Trane, Sergeant, US Marines. How long have you been prisoner?"

"Three months."

"I thought there would be Marines in that hut."

"There were three Yanks. I'm sorry, but the Nips shot them yesterday. I was next, until you came along."

Albert tried to swallow the lump in his throat. He looked away for a moment.

"Did you know their names?" he asked.

"No. I'm sorry, mate. I was in another camp up in the hills. My plane was shot down a few months ago. I managed to save the radio, and I came ashore here on Guam. Been up in the mountains spotting for enemy ships and planes, until the Nips took me prisoner. They brought me here last week. They were going to shoot me at dawn. You saved my life. Say, what are you doing in the jungle alone, anyway?"

"My platoon was ambushed two days ago. Everyone was wiped out but me. I was hit, and the last thing I remembered was… I think I saw our lieutenant shoot two of my men. He murdered them, at point blank range. It happened so fast, in the midst of the gunfire. Then, I passed out."

"So, you actually saw him shoot them?"

"Pretty sure. No, I know he did it. He's a coward. He's ruthless."

"Despicable act. What kind of a man does that?"

"The worst kind. The kind of man you're supposed to trust."

"That wound on your shoulder looks bad."

"I didn't even know I got hit there."

"We need food. I'll try to find some soursop fruit and leaves to fight that infection and help with my dysentery."

Albert fell back to sleep, while Ian went into the jungle. He returned about an hour later with an assortment of plants and insects. He looked pale and weak, but his mind was still alert and amazingly sharp. Ian prepared a poultice with the leaves he gathered, and applied it to Albert's shoulder. Then, he divided up the insects and roots for a meal.

"How do you know about these things," asked Albert.

"It's a hobby. I'm sort of an amateur botanist. I spent a lot of time at the Botanic Gardens at Hagley Park in Christchurch. That's where I'm from."

"How do you eat these things?"

"Pull the legs and wings out and eat the thorax portion of the grasshopper… they're rich in protein. Where are you from in the States?"

"Pennsylvania. So, you want to be a botanist."

"No, I actually want to be a physicist. What about you?"

"Police work. I want to bring scum like Kettering to justice."

"Why would he murder his own men?"

"To cover up his cowardice and tactical blunders. The son-of-a-bitch sent us right into a trap."

"And you were the only survivor, and you came to rescue me?"

"I did what I did."

"It was more than that. If you hadn't rescued me, I'd most certainly be dead by now. But I couldn't die. Not yet, not after the dreams I've been having."

"What kind of dreams?"

"Last night, I had a vision. I saw things about energy and the universe that I don't fully understand, things I think no one else has ever seen. It was the culmination of ideas and theories about the universe that I thought about while I was a prisoner. There is a different matter that we don't know about, and it can be harnessed into an unimaginable source of energy. I started thinking about it while I was in the mountains. I had a lot of time to think about the horrors of war… things I saw the Japanese do to our blokes in New Guinea and other places. I fear the world will soon witness even more powerful and horrendous types of weapons. When you rescued me, you gave me a second chance and a single purpose to which to devote my life. I am indebted to you."

Albert listened intently to the fortitude in Ian's speech, despite his frail and weakened condition. He was easily as tall as Albert, but his lean, wiry stature made him look much taller. His face was wide, with the chin jutting forward in a point, and his nose sharp and prominent. He sounded like a college professor, and he spoke with conviction. His beard covered the asymmetrical lines of his mouth and cheeks, but his face had a characteristic droop to one side.

"No sweat. I'm still not sure what made me crawl to that camp last night, but something inside me told me I had to. What happened to your face? Did the Japs do that to you?"

"Ah, my face. It's been that way for a month now. I woke up with it after one of the beatings. I'm finally able to blink my eye. Some kind of palsy, I suppose. Is it still pronounced?"

"Yea. You kinda' look like Popeye, no offense."

"Who?"

"You don't know Popeye the Sailor? He eats canned spinach to make him stronger… Shhh. Listen, did you hear that?"

They had both heard the rustle of foliage in the distance, near the top of the hill… and then a voice, and one word.

"Trane! Trane, where are you?"

"That's Kettering. He's probably out with a patrol looking for me," whispered Albert.

"Or trying to kill you."

"I can't go back with him."

"Look, you need medical attention. That shoulder is badly infected, and you have a bullet in your back. You could die from that infection."

"We're both in bad shape, but I'd rather take my chances away from Kettering."

"Right-O, then we stick together. The way I see it, the Japanese are retreating north. You Yanks are pushing up from the south, and we're right here in the middle. I'm sure this stream flows either east or west to the sea. It's just a few miles from here. When we get to the coast, we'll head south until we meet up with the Marines."

"What about Kettering?"

"I'm afraid you must say nothing. If you accuse him of murder, it will be his word against yours. Without a witness, you won't have a chance against an officer. You have to find out if there were any survivors who could corroborate your story. There will be another time for justice. But for now, we have to get out of the jungle while we still have some strength."

They followed a stream for most of the day, but by the time they stopped to rest in the evening, they still had three miles to the coastline.

Early the next morning, they were awakened by the thunderous bursts of shells exploding in the distance from a Naval bombardment that signaled the beginning of a new, amphibious attack on the northeastern beaches of the island. Albert's shoulder had become so badly infected that he was in danger of developing fatal toxic shock. The trek to the coast was mostly downhill through a narrow piece of forest, followed by scrubland and dunes ahead of the beach. Their only hope for survival was to try and reach the beach before evening, and hope that a Marine patrol found them.

By the time they reached the beach, they were both delirious and dehydrated, as the effect of the Ian's herbal remedy had worn off. They struggled to cross the sandy dunes in the hot sun. Scattered blasts of distant artillery fire broke the sound of the ocean breeze fanning the dune grasses. Shear determination and the will to survive carried them to the toe of the last dune before the beach, where they both collapsed in the late afternoon sun.

"Ian, I can't go any further. Our lives are in hands of the Almighty."

"I pledge to God, with you as my witness that if we survive, I will dedicate my life to science and to finding a power to end wars like this."

"Amen."

The two men lie face down, five feet apart with their heads toward the ocean, barely alive, about seventy-five yards from the surf. Albert must have heard the voice of God that afternoon telling him to place something reflective near them, because when the two men were found in the early evening, it was his dog tags hanging from a piece of driftwood next to his body that reflected the sun's rays and signaled the lookout on the Navy Destroyer of their presence on the beach. Within an hour, a Marine patrol with a hospital corpsman found them, and by nightfall they were both in the care of doctors at a field hospital in the confines of the American beachhead.

———————————————————

They spent a week in the field hospital while awaiting transfer to a hospital ship. On one of the mornings, Albert was awakened by a corpsman, who informed him that a Marine officer had come to visit him.

"How are you doing, Sergeant Trane?" echoed a cold, shrill voice.

Albert immediately recognized it as Kettering's. His eyes opened wide with a look of terror at the sight of his expressionless face. He said nothing.

"Calm down, Trane. The doctor tells me you're unfit for combat. They're sending you to a hospital ship, and from there you'll be sent stateside. I just wanted to chat with you for a bit. I understand you saved the New Zealander's life. HQ is pretty pleased to have him back alive."

Albert nodded.

"Say, I assume you don't remember what happened after our platoon was ambushed?" asked Kettering, in a threatening tone. "You, ah, know we lost everyone. There were no survivors, except for you and me. I looked for you. I thought you had been killed trying to knock out that machine gun. I couldn't find you. There wasn't much time and the Japs were shooting at me. I had no other choice but to leave the battlefield."

"You mean, run… from the battlefield," said Albert.

Kettering's expression quickly turned defensive and angry.

"What do you mean by that, Trane?"

Albert hesitated. He glanced across the aisle at Ian, who was dozing in his cot. Ian opened his eyes and shot Albert a look of caution and a slight facial gesture motioning for him to shut up. Kettering noticed the signal, but was confused by the facial contortions that afflicted Ian's face. The horrific image of Kettering gunning down Leo and Holmes burned through Albert's gut, and his head throbbed in pain as he strained to hide his emotions behind a veil of platitudes. He turned slowly to face Kettering, his eyes penetrating his cloak of insincerity.

"I… ah, expect you had to run from the Japanese… to save your life," said Albert. "That's all."

"That's how I see it too. I expect there will be an inquiry… just a formality. I'm not sure when… but you will support my assessment of the events of that battle, correct?"

Again, Albert glanced at Ian. Kettering's eyes followed.

"You're lucky Trane survived, huh?" he sneered.

"When a man risks his life to save a stranger, I consider it to be a divinely inspired, heroic act," said Ian. "Luck is for gamblers, whose fortunes rest with the cards. Are you a gambler, Lieutenant? Are you holding the right cards?"

"Life is a gamble, Lieutenant. That's why I always try to hold the right cards. I don't like to lose. So, what happens next for you, Kiwi?"

"Going back to New Zealand… soon as I'm well enough, and after an intelligence debriefing."

"Maybe one day our paths will cross," said Kettering, as he attempted to shake Ian's hand. Ian did not reciprocate.

"Not likely," said Ian.

"Well then, Trane, I'll see you in Hawaii."

"Hawaii?" Albert blurted out.

"That's right. The hospital ship that you're being transferred to is headed for Pearl. Coincidentally, so am I. My island hopping days are over. I've got orders to a desk job there. It pays to know someone in the top brass at CINCPACFLEET (Commander in Chief, Pacific Fleet Offices), especially when you have some dirt on him, if you know what I mean. Anyway, I'm flying out of here in a few days. You see, Kiwi, you always have to hold the right cards."

Then, Kettering turned and stepped out of the tent.

Albert's head wound was more serious than the doctors originally thought. The bullet that grazed the left side of his head had slightly penetrated his skull, causing him to suffer from chronic, painful headaches. Ian's herbal remedy applied to Albert's shoulder helped reduce the severity of the infection, and probably saved his arm. But the spread of toxins in his blood stream had irreparably weakened his heart and kidneys, and the bullet lodged in his back was inoperable and caused chronic back pain. Ian was treated for dysentery, dinghy fever, and an infected foot. He recovered from all of his illnesses and injuries. However, the Bell's palsy left him with a slightly drooping left side of his face, especially in the corner of his mouth and eyelid.

Chapter 5
The Land of the Long White Cloud

Ian was given a second chance at life, thanks to Albert. Before he returned to New Zealand, he declared over and over again his pledge to dedicate his life to science. Albert, on the other hand, wished only for justice for Kettering and his men.

"Good luck at the university," said Albert.

"I hope I see you long before that day. As the Maoris says in my country, *Hei konei ra.*"

Albert looked up and smiled, though he winced in pain.

"I'm sorry?" he asked.

"Good bye, and good fortune," said Ian.

Ian spent the next month recuperating in a military hospital in Christchurch, on the South Island of New Zealand. Albert remained in the field hospital on Guam for two weeks before departing on the USS Merry, a hospital ship bound for the United States. A few days into the voyage, the ship was forced to change course to avoid a typhoon, then again toward the Solomon Islands to avoid Japanese submarine activity. By a stroke of good fortune, they headed to Christchurch for a short port-of-call.

Albert's chronic pain and headaches had begun to take a toll on his spirits. He would have slipped into the grips of depression had it not been for his warm and cheerful nurse, Marie Yeskey. She was a little older than Albert, and at first she resented his sour disposition, but as she gradually penetrated his cloak of solitude, she found a man wounded more by injustice than anything else. She also found love. Under Marie's care, Albert continued to improve, and became strong enough to take walks on the deck with her. On one morning, when they were a few days away from arriving at Christchurch, they were greeted on the upper deck by a nurse running excitedly toward them. They recognized her as Marie's friend Sarah, and she was waving a folded piece of paper.

"Marie, I have a telegram for Albert from his New Zealand friend," she said excitedly. She handed him the telegram, and he quickly scanned the short message.

"Ian says he is out of the hospital, and would love to show me and you two "sheilas" around Christchurch," said Albert.

"What's a sheila?" asked Sarah.

"Not sure, but I'd guess it refers to the fairer sex," said Albert.

"I don't know if I should go," said Sarah.

"Of course you should," said Albert. "He's just your type... kindly, deep thinking, purposeful man."

Two days later, on November 3, 1944, under a bright blue sky animated with long ribbons of white cirrus clouds, the USS Mercy arrived in Lyttelton Harbor, nestled below the majestic Port Hills that separate the harbor from

27

Christchurch. The bay and the area known as Banks Peninsula were surrounded by steep, rolling hills covered in a spring carpet of bright green grass outlined with patches of dark green pine hedgerows. The orange and red tiled roofs of the harbor village contrasted with the soft green hills dotted with thousands of sheep that looked like tiny, white flower petals scattered from the hands of the Maori gods that guarded this unique landscape.

The horrible memories of Guam weighed heavily on Albert's mind. However, on the morning of his liberty, he welcomed the freshness of the New Zealand air, the sweet taste of a land far from the battlefield. Though he was still weak, he felt a surge of energy and vitality as he approached the gangplank wearing his dress khakis. Marie and Sarah, in their dress-white uniforms, strode together on either side of him, as they all saluted the officer of the deck and walked down the gangplank.

Just as they reached the dock below, they heard a horn honk several times, and a small Austin rounded the corner and headed up the dock toward them, stopping a few yards away. A smiling, fitter Ian Moon, dressed in a gray Air Corps uniform, stepped out of the right, driver's side of the car. His face and especially his eyes were much livelier than Albert remembered, although his right eye and the right side of his mouth retained the slight droop left over from his treatment in the Japanese prisoner camp.

"Gidday, Albert. How are you going? Welcome to New Zealand. You look much better than when I left you on Guam."

Albert stepped toward Ian and stumbled. Marie caught his arm and helped him regain his balance.

"I'm not used to terra firma. The legs still feel a little rubbery. I thought I'd never see this day. How are you, Ian?"

"Good as gold. I was discharged from the hospital and assigned to a training billet at Blenheim Air Force Base here in Christchurch. I think I'll get to stay here until the end of the war. These must be your lovely friends."

"Don't you mean sheilas?" asked Albert, as he smiled at Ian. He introduced Marie and Sarah. Albert had forgotten to mention the Bell's palsy. Marie was taken slightly aback, but Sarah didn't seem to mind.

Ian guided the little Austin through the harbor town streets, past the docked freighters and fishing boats, and then turned to climb the winding road to the top of the Port Hills. Albert and Marie snuggled in the backseat, and Sarah sat in the front. She enjoyed every bit of Ian's accent as he narrated the tour. The car chugged through the gears, struggling to climb the steep, winding road. After an hour-long, scenic drive, they stopped on the Christchurch side of the Port Hills at Victoria Park.

They found a spot with large, flat boulders overlooking the Cashmere Hills section of Christchurch. After a short stroll, they sat on the boulders and lunched on fresh bread, cheddar cheese, hard-boiled eggs, apples, and beer. They relished the warm sunshine, the gentle breeze, and the striking views of the lovely neighborhoods laid out with neatly landscaped homes tucked into steep, winding streets that led to the city below. The beautiful city of

Christchurch lie in front of them, stretching from the Pacific Ocean to the flat, patch-work fields of grains and pastures of the Canterbury Plains beyond. The entire panorama was set against the snow-covered peaks of the Southern Alps on the western horizon.

"Look, do you see that large park in the center of the city?" asked Ian. "That's Hagley Park, my favorite place in Christchurch. The Botanic Gardens are gorgeous this time of year. The place simply inspires me. I can't explain it, but it's so beautiful. You will love it."

"Yes, I'm sure we will," said Sarah.

"Over there is the airport. I grew up just north of there. My dad was a pilot. He had a small airfreight business in Christchurch and New Caledonia before the war. In his spare time, he raised trotters and pacers. Trouble was, he could never find much spare time. He was always flying somewhere. He couldn't wait to retire and spend more time with the horses. Of course, the war put an end to all those plans. My parents and my little brother were killed in the Japanese bombing of Noumea in '42. I enlisted in the New Zealand Air Force shortly after that. Seems I had an aptitude for flying, so they made me a pilot."

"I'm so sorry about your family," said Sarah. "You have no other relatives, then?"

"Just some aunts and uncles, but I haven't seen them since the war started. I plan to sell the house after it's over. I want to live in the mountains." He pointed toward the Southern Alps to the west.

"The clouds seem to stretch across the sky and touch the other side of the world," said Sarah, as a warm breeze blew across their backs.

"The Maoris call New Zealand *Aotearoa*, or "land of the long white cloud." I think the clouds are our mystical connection to the rest of the world. They are sort of like the visible strands of energy that permeate all of us and reach around the world, tying us all together."

They all raised their glasses in a toast.

"To the Land of the Long White Cloud," they said together.

The wind, as so often happens in the Port Hills, shifted from breezy to gusty. Ian held his hand over the right side of his face.

"Is something wrong?" asked Sarah, as she noticed Ian grimace.

"No, it's just this palsy in my face... sort of stings in the wind." He felt her empathy, and turned to face her as she tried to comb her fingers through her tangled brown hair as it blew in the wind. For an hour-long minute, he absorbed the softness in her voice and her unselfish, deep brown eyes. Sarah felt an energy, like the clouds that Ian referenced, flow between the two of them. Her eyes sparkled in the sunlight. Ian tried not to stare at her. He reached out and held her soft hand.

"Hey, it's almost 2 o'clock," said Albert. "I thought you were going to show us Christchurch."

"Of course. No worries, we'll make it for tea time at Hagley Park."

"You're the tour guide," said Albert.

Ian picked a route down the Port Hills that took them through the tidy, landscaped neighborhoods, with orange-roofed bungalows surrounded by white picket fences and rose gardens. It was nearly three o'clock when they entered the central business district along the bustling Colombo Street, lined with all sorts of shops and cafés. The sidewalks teemed with shoppers and New Zealand servicemen in uniform. By the time they reached the entrance gate to Hagley Park, Albert was asleep in Marie's arms. He tried to downplay the headaches and dizziness that were afflicting him.

"You and Sarah go on ahead," said Marie. "Albert is feeling a little light-headed and is too tired to walk around the park. We're going to relax on the grass bank by the river."

"Right-O," said Ian. "A little rest and she'll be right. We'll see you in an hour."

They strolled hand in hand along the winding path that followed the Avon River to Victoria Lake and the Botanic Gardens.

"I'm glad you came today," said Ian.

"Me too. You really seem to come alive in this place, don't you?"

"There is so much beauty here. It's peaceful. It's easy to clear your mind and really think. That's when I see things... scientific things, about the nature of the universe. Things that I know exist, but haven't been discovered yet."

"So, professor, I hear you are going to change the world," said Sarah, as she laughed and held her arms above her head.

"It's not a joke. I told Albert when we almost died on Guam that I'm going to become a scientist. I'm going to make a great discovery that will benefit mankind."

"It all sounds very noble... very idealistic. But is it realistic?"

"There will be many discoveries in the second half of this century that will seem impossible, that will amaze us beyond our wildest dreams. Yes, I believe my ideas will change the world."

They paused to enjoy the view of a picturesque weeping willow tree at the edge of Victoria Lake, its drooping branches swaying in the breeze above the water. Ducks waddled across the manicured lawn and scurried in and out of the water. On the opposite bank, below a gnarled English Oak, two lovers embraced, their bodies partially hidden by a patch of purple and white Japanese Irises mixed with bunches of fountain grass. They were as far removed from the devastation of the war as they could possibly be. As he grasped her hand, Ian turned to face Sarah.

"Sarah, the world is on the threshold of a new age. Someday, and I think very soon, scientists will figure out how to split an atom, and that will unleash an enormous amount of energy, like nothing the world has ever known. This energy could be used for peaceful purposes, but could also be used as a weapon. If used as a weapon, it would be hundreds of times more powerful than anything we have now. I hope to God the Japanese or the Nazis don't get it first."

"Is that what you're going to study, atomic energy?"

"I'm going to start there, but I want to explore energy in the universe that is even more powerful than atomic energy. Someday, mankind will build telescopes and spaceships that can explore outer space. Then, we can unlock the secrets of universe. This is an exciting time, and I want to be part of it. There is an unimaginable universe out there waiting to be discovered. Look over there at those tulips. How many tulips do you think are in those beds? How many flowers in this park? How many on this planet? Trillions? Take the number of flowers on earth and multiply those by a million. That's probably just a fraction of the number of stars in the universe."

Sarah listened intently as Ian described his future plans to study at the university and pursue his research.

"I hope you find what you're looking for. It sounds like a tremendous commitment. So many years of study and research, how will you ever find time for a girlfriend?" Her eyes met his, and she smiled affectionately.

"Sarah, this is a very happy day for me. Happy because I'm alive, thanks to Albert, and happy because you are here."

He clasped her hand and leaned forward to kiss her. He was at least a foot taller than her, so she stood on her toes. As their lips lightly touched, Ian caught a glimpse of Marie frantically running along the path toward them.

"Ian, come quickly. Albert had a seizure. The nurse from the park is tending to him, but we have to get back to the ship."

"Of course. Don't worry, everything will be okay."

His false assurance did little to ease Marie's concern and Sarah's disappointment in the sudden turn of events. In the fading light of the early evening, Ian guided the car through the streets of Christchurch, taking every shortcut he knew. Albert was groggy but awake on the way back to the ship. He argued that he was feeling fine, and pleaded with Ian to turn back. Marie would have none of it. She was determined to make the man she loved well again. At first Albert resisted, but he eventually acquiesced to her resolute green eyes.

"I'm sorry for spoiling the weekend. I'll have to take a rain check on the pub and dinner tonight. Marie and I insist you go back and enjoy the rest of the weekend."

Marie smiled, and nodded in agreement, but Sarah sensed Marie's underlying sadness, and suggested they all play cards aboard ship instead.

"Great idea," said Ian.

By the time they reached Lyttelton, the sun was slipping behind the Port Hills, casting a magenta glow across the water and turning the white clapboard-sided houses along the wharf to a shade of lavender. Ian guided the car up the dock and stopped in front o the ship. Before Ian and Sarah could say anything, Marie hurried out of the car to help Albert walk up the gangplank to the ship.

"We're coming with you," said Sarah.

"Please, Sarah, go without us," said Marie. "We want you and Ian to have a wonderful weekend. We'll be fine. You have to be back at the ship by 5 o'clock tomorrow."

31

Marie and Albert saluted the officer of the deck, and paused to wave to Ian and Sarah, before disappearing into the darkened decks below. Ian and Sarah drove down the dock into the approaching nightfall, away from the fading lights of the harbor and into the hills toward Christchurch. Their thoughts were with their friends. They stopped at an overlook to take in the view of Christchurch, the usual glimmering lights muted by wartime light restrictions. The magnificent view heralded the beginning of a wonderfully memorable twenty hours of precious time spent together falling in love.

The next day, on the return trip to the ship, they stopped at another overlook and walked to a rock ledge at the top of the Port Hills. They could see the ship docked in Lyttelton Harbor to the east, and Christchurch to the west. The sun peaked in and out of the puffy, white clouds. The gusty winds signaled a change in weather. Ian rubbed the left side of his face.

"Does it hurt?" asked Sarah.

"A little. It's funny, I forget about it when I'm with you. Thank you for a real beaut' of a time."

"It was a wonderful time for me too. You know, there are many great universities in the States. Maybe when this war is over, you could study in America."

"This war must end, first."

"Do you think it will end soon?"

"I think whichever country builds the atomic bomb first will decide the outcome. I pray that the Allies get it first, and then I pray we never have to use it. I really do believe the world is on the brink of a new age, an age of unimaginable discoveries. Some will end diseases, generate power, explore outer space, feed the world. But some will bring even more destruction than this war has brought. I don't want that to happen. That is why I want to discover a new energy that will prevent wars, not make them."

"You make a persuasive case for studying science. You inspire me, Ian."

"Well, then we must go to university together."

"That would be lovely. I wish I could just stay here."

She glanced at the Mercy docked in the harbor.

"We must get together after the war," said Ian.

"I'll write every day," said Sarah. Tears dripped from her cheeks and into Ian's mouth as they kissed goodbye and embraced on the rock ledge high above the city.

On the drive to Lyttelton, Ian cast a cheerful façade as he tried to make pleasant conversation. Sarah felt a gnawing ache deep in her heart for the impending separation from the man she was beginning to love. She couldn't bear the thought of leaving him. The wonderful feelings of the past day transformed into worrisome thoughts of the uncertainty that lie ahead.

When they reached the dock, Albert and Marie were standing at the gangplank. Marie was waving and smiling, but Albert seemed gloomy and preoccupied. Sarah and Ian embraced in the car. They kissed a kiss that would be forever pressed in their memory by the taste of salty tears and the fragrance of Sarah's perfume mixed with the New Zealand ocean breeze. In his kiss, she felt the strength of his character, his purity of purpose and sincerity. It was as if he was completely transparent and open. Crying and smiling, they pulled apart and walked toward Marie and Albert.

"How are you, my friend?" asked Ian.

Albert forced a smile.

"I'm feeling better," he replied.

"No he is not. If you don't tell them, I will," said Marie.

"What is it?" asked Sarah.

"As soon as the Mercy gets to the States, Albert has been ordered to report to a Naval base in Bainbridge, Maryland for a military inquiry into the events on Guam."

"It's Kettering. He's behind this. It's not what it seems. This hearing is a setup. The orders say I'm to report to a special hearing regarding my conduct in battle on Guam. Kettering is going to pin the massacre on me to clear his name. Hell, I could be facing a court martial or a dishonorable discharge."

"Surely, there will be justice," said Ian. "You risked your life to save your men, and you risked your life to save mine. They will see through Kettering's lies. If there is anything I can do—"

"Yes, there is. You can go to university, become a scientist, and study that outer space energy, and save this corrupt and destructive world we live in."

"I will dedicate my life to that single purpose. You can count on that."

Sarah nodded in agreement, but deep inside she felt an underlying worry that if they stayed together that she would always compete with that single purpose in Ian's life. She glanced at Ian and smiled. The four of them exchanged embraces. Sarah sprang into Ian's arms for one final hug. Then, she and Marie and Albert boarded the ship, and waved in unison.

"Thank you, Ian," yelled Sarah. "God bless New Zealand. We'll all be together again someday soon."

"Goodbye," they all yelled together.

"Hei Konei ra!" yelled Ian. "Don't worry Albert, justice will prevail at Bainbridge."

Chapter 6
Bainbridge, 1973

A medley of the smells of spent typewriter ink, warm radio tubes, and stale coffee left over from the previous eight hours of instruction wafted through the corridors on the last day of classes at Naval Radio "A" School in Bainbridge, Maryland. A lean, fitter-looking Jack emerged from his Morse code classroom with a tired smile, relieved that he had finished his last exam. The glass panel in the door rattled as he closed it, and he strode nervously past the empty classrooms toward the lobby, where the light of the late afternoon sun emerged intermittently through the spring clouds and bounced off the pea green walls of the hallway. The dark, worn, over-waxed, wooden floors of the old World War II-era building creaked with each step of his rubber-soled work boots, the pattern broken up by a rhythmic flap of his bell-bottom dungarees. He stopped abruptly as a voice echoed from behind him. It was the chief petty officer in charge of his class.

"Hey, Jack. I forgot to tell you to check the list again. Don't give up hope. They're just taking their time trying to figure out what to do with a radioman like you."

"Thanks, Chief. I can't understand why it's taking so long…" his voice trailed off as he pressed out the red chevron and three white lightning bolts of the radioman third-class rating badge on his left sleeve. He studied the bulletin board in the middle of the lobby, grasping a folded spiral notebook and a white sailor cap between his left arm and the side of his chest, as he fumbled with the zipper on his jacket. The white corkboard full of papers, notices, and photographs was wedged between two large, glass cases that contained models of ships, bronze bells, and other naval items. As he searched the long list in the middle of the corkboard, a door opened across the hall, and the soft, familiar voice of his girlfriend arrived simultaneously and in harmony with the staccato taps of teletypes and typewriters that faded as she closed the door behind her.

"Any news about your orders? I hope it's Hawaii."

He didn't look up. His eyes were fixed on the list of twenty-eight of his classmates' names, with orders beside them. Where was the twenty-ninth name, his? Grace reached over and squeezed his arm, and he looked up at her smiling, green eyes. That was all it took to change his mood.

"Hey, Grace. Are we still on for the movies tonight?"

"Yes, of course. You know, Jack, a couple of the girls in my barracks said it's pretty unusual for the Academic Honor Man not to have orders yet. I mean, with graduation just three days away, you should be hearing something."

She glanced at the clock on the wall and spun around, her short blonde hair bouncing and shimmering in the sunbeams shining through the corridor.

"Oh, I have to go. I'll see you later." She squeezed his hand and blew him a kiss.

"Okay, I'll meet you at your barracks at 7:30."

Silence permeated the hallway. Once more, he checked the list. The name Jack Edward Trane, Radioman Third Class, was missing. His classmates had already received their orders to new duty stations… ships of all sorts, stateside and overseas bases; but not Jack, who was first in the class. For the past three weeks, he passed this bulletin board every day and dreamed of getting orders to Hawaii with Grace. He remembered Driggers telling him that he'd get the duty station he requested if made Academic Honor Man, so why hadn't he gotten orders to Hawaii yet? It was one more disappointment in a year of tragedy and suffering, except for meeting Grace. She was the one bright spot in his life, and it was killing him to not know where he was going or when he would see her after Bainbridge.

He had stopped thinking about Europe after their relationship became more serious. Maybe that was the reason for the delay, when he changed his request to Hawaii. The thought of Europe made him think about Cindy and his early hope to get stationed in Italy. From there, he could have visited Florence, Paris, and Rome, and all the great parks and gardens. How odd, he thought, that he had not heard from either Cindy or Driggers since Driggers left him at the train station in Greensburg. His letter to Cindy in Naples was returned with no forwarding address.

He glanced at his watch, and strode through the double glass doors of the main entrance, pausing on the porch to place his sailor's cap squarely on his head with a slight tilt to the right, before bouncing down the wooden plank steps and into the Maryland spring sunshine. It was 4:30 in the afternoon on Friday, April 13, 1973. He was tired of worrying about the future, and at this very moment, he felt like going for a run. A glitter of pear tree flower petals blew across his path as he strode down the sidewalk. He loved springtime. He thought about seeing Grace later that night, and his spirits lifted.

The streets of the base teemed with visitors in cars with license plates from all over the country. It was the weekend before graduation, a time for liberty and a time to celebrate with family. But there would be no family to visit him this weekend, and no celebration. He didn't even have a set of orders. There was Grace though, and she was all he needed tonight. He was about to cross at the intersection by the chapel, when a woman tapped him on the shoulder. She appeared to be a graduating sailor's mother.

"Excuse me, would you take our picture?"

"Sure, of course," said Jack. "What a lovely family photo this will make. Move a little closer, Pop. There, how's that? Have a splendid weekend." He wondered if they had caught his sarcasm. Why at this very moment did this guy with his smiling parents have to walk right across his path? Not today. No pain today. He did not want to think about how much he missed them. But then his face twitched as a wisp of cold, spring wind bit the side of his eye. And then the horrible image of the accident flashed before him, and the newspaper headline **"Local Couple Dies in Gas Explosion."**

Thoughts of his parents flashed in his mind. He was overcome by a vivid image of the last time he saw them. It was the last weekend of summer in late

August, before the start of college. He pictured his mother hugging him so closely that the paper bag full of chocolate chip cookies crushed against his back. His father, weakened from chronic pain, smiled and seemed to gain strength as he hugged Jack.

"Remember, Jack. Life will test you, and you may only get one chance. Don't run from what is right," said his father.

"And live your life to serve others," his mother followed.

Those were the last words he heard from them. Jack tossed the thoughts of his parents' deaths into the same dark room in his mind where all the painful memories were stored. His parents were dead. It didn't matter that they had no insurance. College would be postponed until after active duty. He would save what he could and make payments on his student loans. It was the right decision to enlist. Something inside him said it was meant to be. He was determined to overcome his pain. That's why he ran.

He headed down the tree-lined street toward the busy intersection in front of the administration building, a place he passed every day to and from school. It reminded him of a similar spot at Saint Mark. He stepped over the curb while quickly saluting a passing officer, who returned a mechanical, sort of half salute. He picked up his stride, focusing his gaze on an enormous white oak in the distance, its huge leafless limbs silhouetted against the puffy, white clouds. The massive tree hid from view a cluster of white, abandoned, clapboard-sided barracks.

The base was huge during World War II. There were more than 10,000 military and civilians working and training there. Now, there was probably a third of that. Something about this place intrigued him. He felt a sense of déjà vu since he had arrived in December. Bainbridge had become his home for the past four months. His new life in the Navy was starting to feel comfortable. Still, the events of the past year weighed heavily on his mind, and he struggled with bouts of anxiety.

On most days, the sidewalks teemed with a rush of dress blue, white, and khaki uniforms flowing along the sidewalks. But on this Friday afternoon, there was just a trickle of sailors, mostly dressed in civilian clothes, along with their visiting parents. He cut across the lawn at the corner in front of the officers' club. Life at Bainbridge had become comfortable and familiar. It wasn't quite like Saint Mark, but because of Grace it felt like a home.

His barracks was just ahead, the last one in a long row of barracks in front of Tome Park where he liked to run. As he approached the door to the barracks, he stopped as he always did to absorb the view of sweet gum trees and white pines that lined the perimeter of the park, just behind the gray-shingled roofs of the newly painted, white barracks. Splashes of pink and white dogwoods oozed through the dark green soft pines, a sharp contrast between the landscaped beauty of the park and the stark order of the base. Grace would often remind him that he was the only person in Bainbridge who would think of something like that. He headed for his room to change clothes. There was still time for a run around the park before chow. As he tied his worn, white

Puma running shoes, a voice came from the doorway.

"Hey, Popeye, got your orders yet?"

"No, Reggie," said Jack. "Maybe they're going to keep me here and let me take care of the park." He had a hint of actual worry in his voice.

His roommate was Reggie Ivy from Cleveland, Ohio. He was a short, powerfully built African-American, always animated and comical. He gave Jack the nickname "Popeye" after his famous visit with Commander Haskins, the day Jack first learned that he had Bell's palsy.

"My parents are here for graduation, and we're going out to dinner at the club. You want to come with us?"

"No thanks, Reggie. I'm taking Grace to the movies tonight."

Jack bounded out the door and headed for the opening in the fence between the high grass at the back of the barracks and the gravel running path that looped around Tome Park. Reggie yelled from the porch.

"Okay. Hey, I gotta' tell my folks how you got your nickname. See you later, Popeye."

"You gonna' tell them how I saved your ass from a Captain's Mast. You would have been in deep if not for my ugly face. Say hello to your parents for me."

"Okay, Popeye. You're the man. Stay cool."

Six weeks ago, Jack was not feeling cool. Six weeks ago, he was in every kind of pain. Reggie's voice faded as Jack disappeared on the worn path that led from the barracks to the park. He stopped briefly to stretch and think about how he got the nickname "Popeye."

It was the day after the Bell's palsy struck, during the eighth week of school in late February, on the day he was to visit with the commanding officer (C.O.) of Radioman "A" School. It was a privilege that he'd earned for being first in his class. The Bell's palsy attacked without warning, in the night while he was sleeping. On that morning, when reveille sounded at 5:00 a.m., he awoke to a stabbing ache and numbness on the right side of his face. His eye refused to blink, and it began to tear uncontrollably. Saliva dripped from the drooping, right side of his mouth.

Jack jumped from his top bunk and ran to the lavatory. He froze in front of the mirror, staring in shock at the strange, deformed face looking back at him. A crowd of his buddies gathered around him in curiosity, but Reggie was the first to recognize the seriousness of the malady.

"Man, you don't look right! You better forget about your meeting with the C.O. and get to sick bay."

Tears from the unblinking eye made wavy tracks down his lathered face as he tried to shave.

"I can't, Reggie. This is my only chance to ask Haskins about Hawaii."

"Are you out of your mind? Forget about that."

"Maybe it's a temporary thing."

37

"Fine," Reggie finally relented. "But if it doesn't get better, get your ass to sick bay. I'll check back with you later."

The barracks soon emptied as everyone headed for class. Jack stood alone in his room, in the silence. His good eye moved slowly back and forth between a photo of his parents, a photo of Grace, and the light reddish glow of the early morning sunlight through his window. He worried what Grace would think when she saw his face. He couldn't stand the thought of losing her. She was the best thing that ever happened to him. He never would have made Academic Honor Man, and he never would had a shot at duty in Hawaii or Europe if it wasn't for her friendship and encouragement.

Then, his thoughts turned to his father, and the suffering that he endured with his own pain. He gathered up his courage, put on his dress blues, pulled the woolen pea coat collar up to protect his face, and walked the four blocks to the administration building. The cold, morning wind stung his watery eye, and added more pain to the joyless trek to see the C.O.

This would turn out to be a memorable day, in which Jack would make a name for himself around Bainbridge. Commander Earl Haskins' office was on the second floor overlooking the front entrance steps. Jack glanced at the window of his office, but the sunlight strained his eye. Moments later, he found himself knocking lightly on Haskins' office door. A cheerful voice invited him in. On the other side of the door sat Haskins' secretary, Mildred. She was a tiny, grandmotherly-looking woman with graying, blonde hair and pink, horned-rimmed glasses. She motioned for Jack to sit. He removed his cap and sat down. She did not seem to be affected by his face at all.

"You stop here tomorrow. I'll have a dozen of my orange cookies for you... help you forget your troubles. That looks like Bell's palsy. Have you been over to sick bay?"

Jack was stunned she knew a name of his affliction.

"How did you know what this was?"

"My son had it when he came home from Vietnam. They don't know what caused it. The doctors told him it was from post-traumatic stress. He regained about fifty percent of his facial muscles. Don't worry, the younger you are the better chance you have of complete recovery from the paralysis."

Jack was beginning to enjoy talking to Mildred. She was calm and reassuring. After a few minutes, they were interrupted by the buzzer on the Dictaphone.

"The Commander will see you now. Go on, you'll be fine."

Jack knocked, and nervously opened the door. He saluted, somewhat awkwardly, forgetting to come to attention first.

"Good morning, Jack. Have a seat." Commander Haskins stood at his desk and shook Jack's hand. He was a graying, middle-aged, prescient-looking man who gave the impression he belonged more in front of a college classroom than a military command.

"What's wrong with your face?"

"I'm not sure, sir. I woke up with it this morning."

"I'll have Mildred write you a chit to miss class and get to sick bay after you leave here."

"Thank you, sir."

"You've done very well here so far. I see you have straight A's in your classes. Where have you requested to be stationed?"

"Originally, I was hoping for somewhere in Europe. But then, I changed my request to Hawaii a few weeks ago, and I was hoping—"

"Terrific. Um, I see your parents died in a house fire last year. You have my sympathy."

"Thank you, sir."

"You have no other family, then... no brothers or sisters?" Haskins continued, trying not to look Jack in the face.

"No, sir."

"You are clearly a remarkable young man... to lose your parents, to leave college and enlist in the Navy, after studying, what is it—"

"Landscape architecture, sir."

"Yes, but why didn't you finish your degree? You would have been eligible for Officer Candidate School."

The pain in his face was becoming unbearable, making him increasingly uncomfortable. His eye watered continuously.

"My parents didn't have insurance. I couldn't afford to stay in college."

"Well, then you may want to forget about landscape architecture and pursue a career in the Navy. I'll get you information on the Navy's college program and OCS."

Jack didn't reply. Then, Haskins uttered a line that hit Jack like a shot of adrenaline.

"Jack, did you know that your father was discharged from this base in April, 1945. He was assigned to Bainbridge for two months for special debriefing before he was discharged. He served in the Marine Corps, in the South Pacific. Unfortunately, I see here that he had a dishonorable discharge."

Jack's good eye widened, and he forgot about the pain in his face.

"Sir, how did you know that?"

"Someone in Washington has taken an interest in you. Your father's record was included with your background investigation and security clearance."

"But sir, my father told me he was honorably discharged in Hawaii."

Haskins looked confused.

"Did you have a good relationship with your father?"

"Yes, sir. I've always admired my father. He was wounded in the war. He suffered his whole life, but he was always there for me."

"Well, I'm not sure why this was included in your file, but I felt you should know about it. Now, before I send you to sick bay, I need to ask you some things about your barracks."

Haskins looked at him, and Jack's eyes narrowed and he fumbled with his pen. By this point, the pain in his face was distracting him. Then, Haskins asked the question that made Jack famous with Class 73-26.

"Jack, tell me—" Haskins paused. He stood up and looked out the window at the grass mall in front of the building. "What's the "grass" situation at the barracks?"

Jack sat up. His voice cracked.

"I'm sorry, sir?"

"Look, you're a bright young man. You can see that a "dirty" environment at the barracks would not look good on my record. I'm hoping for a promotion this year. You can understand that, can't you?"

"Uh… yes, sir." Jack wanted out of there in the worst way. He couldn't stand the pain any longer. There was a brief silence as the two of them stared at each other.

"Well then, tell me. What is the grass situation at the barracks?"

For the love of God, Jack thought, why is he asking me this now? With one eye watering and his cheek throbbing with pain, he shifted in his chair and turned squarely to face Haskins.

"Well, what is it?" Haskins demanded, as his pale face began to turn a shade of red.

"Sir, I wanted to tell you about this problem before. It's of special interest to me too."

"Ah, good. I knew it. Go on."

"Well, sir. Let me just say that if you were to use a slow-release fertilizer and a premium grass seed mixture, you could have the grass around the barracks looking like the grass in Tome Park next door. You know, it's really an embarrassment to the Navy to—"

Haskins' face turned three more shades of red at Jack's perceived impertinence.

"Petty Officer Trane, you know damned well what I'm talking about. You live in that barracks. You are a squad leader. You know what's going on there."

Instantly the light bulb went on in his head. Haskins was not talking about Kentucky Blue Grass. He thought about some of the guys in his barracks. He knew that a few of them smoked weed on occasion, but he never saw them do it in the barracks. The right side of Jack's mouth began to twitch, and he began to drool. Haskins was six inches from his face, and was very irritated. With everything that had happened to him this morning, Jack reacted with the first emotion that hit him. He began to laugh.

"Sir, I thought you meant—" Jack stuttered. His face resembled the pulsating back-and-forth figures of the classic masks of comedy and tragedy. The Popeye-like smile made Haskins feel like Jack was mocking him, and he was clearly upset. "I wouldn't know anything about that kind of grass, sir."

Haskins stood perfectly still, and glared at Jack. Then he threw his arms in the air and shouted "Dismissed. Get out of here and go to sick bay."

Jack quickly shook his hand and darted out the door, closing it behind him in one movement. Mildred reached out and took his hand as he passed her desk.

"Don't worry about the Commander. He likes you, but he's under a lot of stress from some intelligence agency in Washington, and he's worried about his son. He's coming home after three months at Bethesda Naval Hospital. He was shot up pretty bad in Vietnam. You stop back tomorrow for those cookies, okay. Here is your chit for sick bay."

"Thanks, Mildred. I gotta' go now." He ran out the door, turned the corner, and ran right into Grace.

"Grace, what are you doing here?"

"Reggie told me what happened to your face, so I got a pass for the morning. I'll go to sick bay with you. Mildred was kind enough to let me wait in the hall for you."

"I look like a freak, don't I?"

"Let's just say you've had better days." She kissed him. He tried to smile, but he couldn't.

"Okay, let's get this over with."

After a short bus ride, they arrived at the base hospital, and the doctors confirmed the diagnosis of Bell's palsy. Jack took the news bravely, mainly because Grace was by his side. By lunchtime, his classmates had heard about his conversation with Commander Haskins, thanks to Reggie's visit to sick bay. That's how he got the nickname.

Jack made his way along the grass path that led from the barracks to the park. Soon, he was running along the gravel path that wound through the bright, spring green carpets of lawn. Ever since the day two weeks ago, when he returned from jogging and Reggie noticed that his eye had finally begun to blink and that the Bell's palsy was regressing, he had not missed his daily run. The more he ran, the better he felt. The exercise and peaceful beauty of the park would defeat this illness and restore his smile. Even before the Bell's palsy, he would come here just to walk and think. He loved to find the views in the landscape and settle into them, like an artist about to paint a scene.

Tome Park was quiet on this evening, with only a few joggers out. He relished the silence. It allowed him to think while he was running. He pulled the hood of his sweatshirt over his head and picked up the pace. After the strains of the first mile, his strides and his breathing synchronized into a fluid movement. Now, his thoughts were lucid and flowing. He thought about his parents, and wondered if he could return to Saint Mark and visit their graves before leaving for his duty station.

He galloped along, thinking about the first time he met Grace. It was during the second week of school, in typing class. Everyone in the class was typing madly through the assignments to the sound of classical music, mostly Strauss waltzes. He struggled to limit his mistakes, but the errors mounted, and he felt hopeless. As he yanked another failed lesson from the smooth paten, her hand descended from behind him and settled calmingly on his hand.

"What kind of music do you like?" she asked.

Startled, he quickly turned around and met her smiling eyes, which were partially hidden by short and straight blonde bangs.

"Soul and R&B."

"That's my favorite too. So, you have to pretend there's a cool sax and some "boss" keyboards in that waltz. You know, change how it feels. Then you can get into the flow of it."

"Thanks," he said, returning a broad smile. "I can feel a change coming over me already. I'm Jack. Jack Trane."

"Grace Weems," she replied, as she continued to hold his hand. "You will prevail, Jack Trane. I can see it in your eyes and feel it in your hand."

She released his hand and glanced back with a smile as she returned to her seat. Jack fell for Grace right then and there. She permeated his being and warmed his soul with a passion that excited him beyond anything he had ever felt before. They had something in common too; they were both without parents. Grace's parents died in a car accident when she was thirteen years old, leaving only her grandmother at home to raise her until she joined the Navy at the age of twenty.

Then, Grace disappeared from his thoughts, and an image of the burned carnage that was once his home came into his head… the horrible scene of the charred remains of his parents flashed in front of him. He stopped running, and leaned against the trunk of an old Japanese Pagoda tree. He thought about the funeral and the days leading up to his decision to enlist after he met Driggers and Cindy. That set into place a whirlwind of events that led him to Bainbridge. What a coincidence that it was the same place that his father was discharged.

He started running again. He thought only of Grace and how excited he was about their date. He rounded a bend and headed toward the rocky bluffs overlooking the Susquehanna River where it flowed into the Chesapeake Bay. A beautiful view of the river was framed by an opening in a grove of smooth, silvery beech trees. He thought about ending the run here and walking back, but he heard a voice calling to him. He headed back in the direction of the voice that was coming from near the barracks. He turned onto a long grass field framed on both sides by tall white pines. He was on the final 300 yards of his three-mile run. His arms and legs were pumping in rhythm as he glided along the path. In the distance, in the fading light of the cool, spring evening, and with his eyes blurry from the sweat dripping from his forehead, he caught a glimpse of a female figure waving to him. He sprinted toward her. As he drew closer, he recognized the bright green and white Saint Mark hooded sweatshirt that he had given to Grace.

"Jack, hurry!" she yelled.

"What… are you doing down here, Grace?" he stuttered, as he tried to catch his breath. "We aren't going to the movies until 7:30."

"Jack, the Chief's been looking all over for you. Commander Haskins wants to see you in his office right away."

"Hold on, I have to shower and change. What the hell is going on?

Haskins is never on base on a Friday night."

"I don't know, Jack, but he's got everyone looking for you. The Chief said to get up there, pronto."

"Like this?"

"It doesn't matter… come on, I'll walk up with you." Her calm voice was reassuring, but it wasn't enough to ease the worry in Jack's eyes. "Jack, it could be about your orders," Grace said excitedly.

"Of course, it must be about my orders. They finally came in, two days before graduation… or maybe it's some kind of problem with the orders."

She squeezed his sweaty hand and led him through the opening in the fence. They passed the doors to the barracks, and ran straight into Reggie.

"Hey, Jack, Commander Haskins is looking for you," Reggie announced, with an unusually serious look on his face.

"Yes, we know," said Grace.

Jack waved to Reggie, then turned to Grace and hugged her. He stared straight into her warm, hazel eyes, the same caring, understanding eyes that accepted his ravaged face six weeks ago.

"Don't worry, Jack. We will prevail. We will be together in Hawaii."

It didn't matter what kind of orders awaited him. All that mattered to him at this moment was holding her hand, and not letting go.

Chapter 7
Orders

The last glimmer of rose-colored sunlight faded and slid behind the bell tower of the chapel, as Jack and Grace reached the large, manicured grass mall in front of the administration building. The steps leading to the entrance from the portico were illuminated by two bollard lights that stood like sentries on either side of them. The front facade of the two-story, brick building was dark, except for a single dimly lit office on the second floor, to the right of the portico.

"That's Haskins' office," said Jack, as he pointed to the window.

A handful of rowdy sailors passed, singing songs and laughing loudly. Jack stepped aside to let them pass. The reverberating purr of a slow-moving Baltimore and Ohio diesel locomotive melded with the melodious whistle of a second freight train, and the sound echoed through the Susquehanna River valley. It seemed to settle in the spot where they stood.

Soon after, a pulsating roar of helicopter blades drowned out the melody of the train whistle, and a black Marine Corps Sea King helicopter approached the base from the south. The roar grew louder as the helicopter circled the administration building, and the craft landed in the exact center of the lawn, about seventy-five yards from where they were standing. As the engine revolutions wound down and the deafening whirr of the rotor blades softened, the fuselage door opened, and the silhouette of a short, portly man in a dark trench coat emerged and headed for the steps at the entrance portico.

"What do you suppose that's all about?" asked Jack. "It couldn't be about me, could it?"

"I don't know, but another light just went on in Haskins' office."

"Maybe it's some kind of military emergency. I should probably come back tomorrow."

"Come on, Jack, you've got to face this. It's about your future... it's about our future. Listen, I want to go in there with you. I'll wait in the lobby until you come down."

Jack shuffled his feet nervously. His eyes flitted back and forth between Grace and Haskins' window, and he hastily inventoried the surrounding landscape as if he was trying to record it in his memory. He glanced at the radio school building across the street. Behind him were the lights of the dining hall and the library. Farther to the right was the familiar stately oak tree, its dark branches moving rhythmically in the evening breeze. Behind the parked helicopter, the outline of the chapel steeple faded in the darkening western sky.

"You're right, Grace. I have to do this. But I don't want you to come. I want you to go back to your barracks. I'll come and see you after I get out." He clasped both of her hands and kissed her quickly on the lips, and then turned and walked toward the bollard-lit steps. When he reached the porch, he glanced back at Grace, who was still glued to the spot where he left her.

"Good luck," she yelled.

He waved once more. She waved back, then turned and slowly walked in the direction of the women's barracks, her green and white sweatshirt still visible in the distance. Jack brushed out his wrinkled attire. Then he glanced around, stopping to glimpse the moonlit gable top of the old Barracks 523. His eye twitched as he walked through the door. He was met in the lobby by the petty officer on watch, who was one of his classmates.

"Higgins, what's going on?" asked Jack.

"Bout' time you got here," Higgins whispered. "Something's going down. Where's your uniform? They're waiting for you up there."

Jack nodded, but didn't reply. He moved quickly toward the stairs.

"Hey, you didn't sign in," Higgins yelled.

Jack continued walking. In the next instant, he was standing at the door to Haskins' office, staring at his stenciled title in black letters on the opaque glass. He knocked twice, but no one answered. Then, he remembered from his previous visit that Mildred's office was on the other side of the door. He slowly opened the door to the first office, but hesitated before knocking on Haskins' door. He stood in silence, waiting to hear a voice or a cue that would tell him when to knock.

"Come in," called a voice from the other side of the door.

He stepped forward and started to salute Haskins, who was seated at his desk. Then, Jack quickly pulled his hand back to his side when he realized he was in civilian clothes. He couldn't recall the appropriate military etiquette.

"You can still salute me, Jack," said Haskins.

"Yes, sir," he replied.

A single desk lamp illuminated the office, flooding Jack's face with the reflected light. He didn't notice the other man seated in the tall armchair in a dimly lit corner of the room behind him. He was too nervous to look around. His eyes were fixed on Haskins in front of him. He had not been particularly observant in his last visit to this office, and he hadn't noticed the dark walnut wainscoting and trim on the walls. Dark, stained bookcases flanked either side of the window behind the massive desk. The off-white venetian blinds were tightly closed now. Haskins adjusted the brass ship wheel with a clock in the center on his desk, and leaned back in his chair.

"Sit down, Jack. Did you jog over here?" he asked.

"Yes, sir. I mean, no… I was running in the park earlier, and then I walked up here. I didn't have time to change."

"Understandable. I see your face has mostly recovered. Does it still hurt?"

"From time to time."

"Well, now, you're the Academic Honor Man, first in your class," said Haskins. "I'm sure you are wondering what this impromptu meeting is all about." He looked up from a folder that he had pulled form his desk drawer with Jack's name and social security number on the yellow tab. The folder was sealed with a horizontal black band, with red letters that read CLASSIFIED. "I have your orders here. They were delivered just now on that helicopter out there. You have been ordered to a communications unit in—"

"Is it Hawaii, sir?"

"No, it's much farther away than that. You have orders to Christchurch, New Zealand, to a communications unit that supports our Antarctic Program. You leave tomorrow morning."

"But, I'll miss graduation."

"Yes, I'm afraid so, Jack," said Haskins.

Jack began to fidget with his fingers. Haskins started to address him, but before he spoke, the brief silence was interrupted by the ring of eight bells from the chapel bell tower down the street. As the last bell sounded, Jack heard the ruffling of a trench coat, as a dark figure began to stand up from the chair in the far corner of the room. Jack turned to face the sound of vinyl fabric on the chair cushion returning from its elastic limit. Haskins nervously made the introduction.

"Jack, this is Colonel Kettering. He is the Asia Pacific Director of Impossible Weapons Research, or IWR. He's flown up from Washington to meet you and personally deliver your orders."

Jack stood up and attempted an awkward salute. Kettering did not reciprocate. His short, rotund frame shuffled past Jack, as he looked him up and down.

"Good evening, Jack," he said, in a cold, arrogant tone, his thick eyebrows raised sharply. He turned to face the window, and tugged on the cord that opened the slats of the venetian blinds. "Bainbridge hasn't changed much since I was here in '45, except there aren't any Marines here now."

Jack was disturbed by his demeanor. The red strobe light from the helicopter on the drill lawn reflected off the white blinds and spilled over Kettering's balding head. His black, round eyeglasses rested on a sharp, pointy nose. A grayish rectangular piece of moustache partially hid thin, whitish lips. He pulled out a zippo lighter and lit a cigarette from a shiny, silver case. He blew a long trail of smoke over Haskins' head, and followed it with a steely stare that met Jack's nervous eyes.

"Pity about your parents. I wonder, would you still have enlisted if they had left you some insurance money? It's shocking you were left with nothing."

Jack jumped up.

"With all due respect, sir, how did you know that?"

Before Kettering could answer, Haskins stood up.

"Well, I'm afraid I will have to leave you two. Colonel Kettering has informed me that I am not cleared to listen to this conversation. Good luck, Jack. I hope everything works out for you."

Jack stood up and saluted. Haskins returned the salute with a quick motion, and offered Jack an awkward smile of good luck as he closed the door behind him. The silence in the room was broken by a rush of exhaled cigarette smoke from the last, deep drag before Kettering crushed the spent butt in the ashtray on Haskins' desk.

"Sit down and relax, Jack," said Kettering. Jack slid into the armchair in

46

an attempt to avoid Kettering's cold, black eyes. "Jack, did your father ever talk to you about the war?"

"A little, sir. He told me he was wounded. He didn't like to talk much about it."

"I see. Did he ever mention my name?"

"No, sir."

"Did he ever talk about a scientist from New Zealand named Dr. Ian Moon?"

"He might have mentioned the name from time to time. I remember seeing some letters from New Zealand... I guess around the time when I was in high school. I remember seeing the unique-looking stamps on the envelopes."

"I see... and you say he never told you anything about the war? He never mentioned anything about Guam?"

"No, sir."

"Well, I can understand why. I'm sure he wasn't proud to tell you that he was responsible for sending twenty-three Marines to their deaths. I was your father's commanding officer on Guam. Your father disobeyed my orders to fall back from a skirmish with a superior Japanese force. I was knocked out in the battle, and he led my platoon directly into an ambush. They were all slaughtered. He and I were the only survivors. When I regained consciousness, I found myself back in the jungle. I returned to our lines, and later learned that your father was taken prisoner by the Japanese. Fortunately for him, he also did something that saved him from a prison sentence. Your father rescued a New Zealand officer named Ian Moon from a Japanese prison camp."

"I don't understand," said Jack.

"The man your father rescued went on to survive the war and become a prominent particle physicist. Dr. Moon is an expert in the field of antimatter. Do you know anything about antimatter?"

"Not really, but I heard about it on *Star Trek*."

Kettering paused for a bit.

"Yes, TV. Of course you did. Anyway, antimatter is a very powerful energy. You know, life takes us on many strange twists and turns. So it was for your father. He got his platoon wiped out, but he saved a man's life, a man who we think has unlocked an unimaginable secret of the universe. Your father should have been court-martialed and sent to prison, but I testified on his behalf. I saved him from going to prison. Actually, he was discharged right here in Bainbridge, in 1945. Had it not been for me, you might never have been born."

Jack burst from his chair. He recalled Haskins' mention of his father's dishonorable discharge, but he hadn't really dwelled on it since that meeting.

"Is there some kind of report, some kind of proof of all this that I could see?" he demanded.

"Sit down, Jack," Kettering shouted, as he leaned over the desk. "Albert Trane was an insubordinate, reckless rebel who should have gone to prison.

47

Maybe he was a better father to you than he was a soldier. That doesn't matter to me. What matters now is our national security. That is why you are here. Your country needs you, and we don't have much time."

"Why me?"

"You are the one person who may be able to persuade Dr. Moon to work for us instead of the Soviets, because you are the son of the man who saved his life. Our intelligence confirms that Moon may have developed a formula for producing and storing antimatter, and we think he has laid the groundwork for an antimatter weapon... a weapon that is hundreds of times more powerful than a thermonuclear bomb. He's far ahead of our own research, and even farther ahead of the Soviets. What's most troublesome is that he's rumored to be a communist sympathizer. That's why he's of such great interest to the Soviets. They want a weapon to help them achieve world domination, and they will pay anything to get a hold of it. They want him to defect, and we are running out of time to get to him before they do."

"Have you asked him to work for us?"

Clearly annoyed, Kettering turned and shot him a menacing glare.

"Of course, but he refuses to even meet with me. He is an eccentric. He's secretive and unpredictable, and most of all, he has no loyalty to anyone or any country."

Jack sat up in his chair, his eyes open wide, and fixed on Kettering. His purple-colored hands were swollen from gripping the wooden arms of the chair so tightly. Beads of perspiration formed on his forehead.

"But, sir, I've never even met this man."

"It doesn't matter. I believe you have the best chance to persuade him to work for us. That is why I have the authority to order you to go to New Zealand with me."

"What makes you think I'll be able to get through to him?"

"The two of you share some unique ties."

"What are you talking about?"

"First off, he is indebted to your father. He will listen to you since you are the son of the man who saved his life. You also share similar interests with him. One of his hobbies is horticulture and garden design, which coincidentally, you have studied in college. Finally, there is someone in Moon's life who is very dear to him... someone you know very well."

"Come on, who in the heck would I know from New Zealand?"

"Did you know that your parents introduced Ian Moon to Sarah Mechling during the war? I believe you refer to her as your aunt, but she has no relation to you, except that she is a physics professor at Saint Mark and was a close friend of your family. They met when your father's hospital ship visited Christchurch in 1944." Kettering paused briefly, but continued before Jack could inquire further. "I believe she was smitten with him in her younger years, but they separated. Moon later married a New Zealand woman. Sarah never married."

Jack was both shocked and confused.

48

"Sir, I don't see—"

"Moon's wife died in a suspicious automobile accident about ten years ago. Your aunt reunited with Moon a few years later, and has collaborated with him on his antimatter research ever since. After the death of his wife, he became increasingly secretive, and dropped out of the public eye. Your aunt seems to be the only one who is close to him. Moon lives on a ranch in the mountains of the South Island of New Zealand."

"Where is my aunt? Is she safe?"

"I can't say. That is going to be increasingly up to you to find out. We don't know if he is holding her against her will, or if she really is devoted to him and a partner in his plans to defect."

"This is crazy. Aunt Sarah, a communist? I don't believe it. I don't want any part of this."

"Shut up and listen to me. I don't believe your parents' deaths were accidental. They may have been murdered by Soviet agents. We've known for some time that your father has been passing Moon's antimatter research to your aunt. She used the laboratory and computers at Saint Mark to process critical data. Perhaps your father was going to squeal on Moon, and the Soviets intervened to silence him. We don't know for sure, and we need to find out, so it was no coincidence that Driggers and Cindy showed up at Saint Mark after the funeral. I had to find a way to get to you. You're the only person who can help... our only hope to stop him."

Jack's face turned white, and his eye began to twitch. He sat dumbfounded in the chair, and stared at the red strobe light of the helicopter flashing across the room. He eventually composed himself and stood up.

"You mean, this was all set up? I didn't sign up for this! I want to see Haskins."

"Haskins has no authority in this matter. You belong to me. You are part of my mission now. Don't worry, when the mission is completed, you will be compensated handsomely, and you can leave the Navy and go back to Saint Mark. Or you can stay in the Navy, if you want."

"What... what's next?" Jack stammered.

"Haskins already told you. We leave tomorrow. Go back to your barracks and pack. If anyone asks you where you are going, you tell them you just received your orders to Christchurch. Do not discuss anything about this with anyone, or you will put their lives in jeopardy. Don't get any ideas about leaving the base. There's nowhere you can go. You will be briefed in greater detail when we get to New Zealand."

"What if I refuse?"

"Ha. This is not college. You can't just walk away from this, like dropping a class. You will be a deserter. You could spend a long time in prison. I'm sure you don't want that, Jack."

Kettering crushed another cigarette butt in the ashtray and turned out the light on Haskins' desk. He placed his hand on Jack's shoulder. He had large, powerful hands for a man of such short stature. He led Jack down the staircase to the first floor, before stopping on the bottom step, the wooden nosing creaking as his weight shifted. Jack stood with his back to him, facing the glass doors ahead. Farther down the hallway, Higgins sat reading a paperback novel under the dim light of a desk lamp, oblivious to their presence. Jack spun around to face Kettering, who was now slightly taller than him with the added height of the step. He felt a surge of courage, like an electric shock. Something popped into his head. He remembered something he once overheard his father telling his mother. He told her he was wounded in the war because of the cowardice of his commanding officer. Maybe Kettering was lying. Maybe Kettering was responsible for the deaths of those Marines. His father was a good man. He wouldn't have hurt his own men.

"Where is my aunt?" Jack demanded. "She is the only family I have left. If I'm the only man for this mission, then you better tell me."

Kettering grabbed Jack by the hood of his sweatshirt and pulled him against the banister. He was surprisingly strong. Kettering cocked his right arm and was about to strike him, when he suddenly pulled back. His cold, dark eyes poured into Jack. Then just as quickly, his demeanor shifted.

"I'm sorry, Jack. We must not be adversarial. That won't help us succeed. I want you to be comfortable with this mission."

"Where is my aunt?" Jack yelled. Higgins looked up from his novel.

"You'll be fully briefed in New Zealand," said Kettering. He turned and walked into the dark hallway, away from Higgins and the light in the lobby.

"I need to know now," Jack yelled.

There was only silence, except for Higgins stirring in the lobby.

"She is with him, in Antarctica." The voice faded as the door at the end of the hallway slammed shut. Jack stood frozen for a minute, trying to comprehend what he had just heard. Then, he turned and sprinted past Higgins and flew out the door into the chilly night air.

"Jack, wait," called a warm, familiar voice from behind him.

"Grace, what are you doing here?"

"I bribed Higgins with a ham sandwich, and he let me hang out in the coffee mess. I told him I was waiting for you, and I slipped upstairs. I know I shouldn't have, but I eavesdropped on some of your conversation. Jack, that Colonel sounds like a snake. I wouldn't trust him. You don't have to go. Haskins will get you out of this. Don't do this, Jack." She launched herself into his arms.

"Grace, I need time to think. Everything is happening so fast." He pulled her closer to him and tugged on the hood of her sweatshirt so that the bangs of her short, blond hair fell across her forehead. Her wide, understanding eyes glistened in the moonlight, and they pulled together in a passionate kiss. For the first time since they met, he felt a gnawing yearning for her that filled every part of his being. Leaving her tomorrow would be unbearable.

"You're going to New Zealand, aren't you?" she asked.

Jack's touched her cheek and wiped the tears rolling down. Then, he slowly traced the outline of her face.

50

"What are you doing?"

"I don't want to forget a single detail of you."

"Your hand is trembling, Jack. When do you leave?"

"Tomorrow afternoon. This is really happening, isn't it?"

"I don't want you to go. We can tell Haskins."

"It's no use. He can't help us. Colonel Kettering warned me about trying to leave. I shouldn't even be with you right now. I don't want to put you in danger."

"How would I be in danger?"

"I don't know. He just told me not to talk to anyone. Come on, I better go. I'll walk you to your barracks. Grace, I didn't ask for any of this. But somehow, I feel it's my destiny. I keep thinking of my father. He didn't have to save Dr. Moon, either."

"Who's Dr. Moon?"

"A scientist from New Zealand. Apparently, my father saved his life during the war. I mean, he wasn't a scientist then. It's too complicated... I don't know the full story. Colonel Kettering says I'll find out when I get to New Zealand. I have to see my aunt. He said she's with Moon, and that she might be in danger. That's why I have to go."

Grace felt his anxiety, and tried to calm him with light-hearted conversation as they walked swiftly through the streets to her barracks. Jack tried not to think about the next day. When they got to the barracks, they kissed again.

"Grace, I couldn't have made it here without you," he said.

She smiled.

"Jack, I have an idea. I will be at the communications station in Honolulu next week. We can send messages to each other. That way, I'll know you're safe. When all this is over, we'll be together in Hawaii."

He pulled her close to him.

"I love you, Grace."

"I love you too, Jack."

He started running, and didn't stop until he reached the barracks. It was just after 11:00 p.m. when he entered his room, where he was met with loud snoring from Reggie. Jack wanted to wake Reggie and talk about the crazy mess he was in. He wanted Reggie to tell him that somehow this all wasn't real. He even went to the payphone in the barracks and started to call for a taxi. Maybe he could get to Perryville and take a bus back to Saint Mark. But he hung up. He knew Kettering would never let him leave the base. Instead, he packed his sea bag, and then lay awake on his bunk until 3:00 a.m., thinking about Grace and how much he was going to miss her.

Chapter 8
Aunt Sarah's Letter

Long rays of morning sunlight streamed through the window and across Jack's face, as he was abruptly awakened by a loud voice.

"Wake up, Trane! Change of plans. The Colonel wants you at the chopper by 8:00 a.m. You got forty-five minutes."

"Who… what's going on?" Jack rubbed his eyes. "Driggers!"

"Yea, it's me. Come on, Trane. I got a jeep out front. Get dressed and be outside in fifteen minutes."

Reggie stirred in the bottom bunk.

"What's going on, Jack?" asked Reggie.

"I'll explain when I get back from the head. This is Stan Driggers."

Reggie extended his hand, but Driggers pulled back.

"Ha, the "new" Navy," said Driggers in a disgusted tone.

Reggie rubbed his eyes, trying to wake up. He looked at Driggers, then raised his eyebrows and glared at him in a knee-jerk reaction to his prejudiced remark.

"You better get used to it," said Reggie.

"I don't have to get used to anything, smart ass."

Reggie jumped from his bunk to face Driggers.

"Sit your ass down! I got a black belt in karate, you little squid. It was part of my SEAL training. You'll look awfully silly in the graduation photo after I rearrange your face."

Driggers towered over Reggie, but Reggie was powerful and could fight like a badger. Jack arrived at the doorway, having caught some of Driggers' remarks.

"Thanks, Reggie, but you better stay out of this. I'll explain."

"Hurry up, Trane. I'll be outside," said Driggers, as he brushed past Reggie and snickered.

"Who is that asshole?" asked Reggie.

"That's the guy who recruited me. I'm finding out that he's not the person I thought he was. But never mind that. I got my orders last night."

"That's great. I wondered where you were? What was that helicopter about?"

"Listen, Reggie. I'm leaving Bainbridge this morning. They're taking me out of here on that helicopter. I was in Haskins' office last night, and… well I can't really talk about anything."

"Are you kidding me?"

"I'm not. I've got orders to a communications unit in New Zealand. I don't have time now, but Grace can explain everything. I need you to go and tell her that I have to leave now, instead of this afternoon. Maybe she can meet me at the admin building before we take off."

"Okay, man. Hey, I found out my ship is out of Pearl Harbor. Can you believe I got the USS Bainbridge? What are the chances? Me and Grace will come see you in New Zealand." He grabbed Jack and bear-hugged him.

"That'll be great," said Jack worriedly.

"You stay cool, Popeye. Oh wait, I almost forgot. I found this letter for you. It must have fallen behind my desk when I picked up your mail back in February. It came while you were in the hospital. I got your mail that one day, but then they wouldn't give it to me after that. Sorry, man."

Jack glanced at the envelope. There was no name on the return address, just a fleet post office zip code. The letter was addressed to him at Great Lakes Naval Training Center with an original postmark of November 15, 1972, from Christchurch, New Zealand. There was a forwarding address to Bainbridge, postmarked January 5, 1973. He stuffed the letter in his pea coat pocket.

"I don't like that Driggers," said Reggie. "You watch your back."

"I will. Good luck on the Bainbridge. We had some good times here, didn't we?"

"We sure did. You take care down there." They shook hands as Jack smiled anxiously, and he strode out to the jeep. Driggers drove straight to the waiting helicopter, eliminating the possibility of Jack meeting Grace before he left. At 8:15 a.m., the turbine engines of the Sea King roared to life. The three passengers braced in their seats as the helicopter lifted off. Jack sat by a window with a view toward Main Street and the "A" School building. Driggers had the window opposite him, and Kettering sat in the front near the pilots. As the aircraft rotated above the rooftops, his view shifted 180 degrees, and he recognized two figures running down the sidewalk waving. It was Grace and Reggie. They were the only people on the street at this time on a Saturday morning. Grace blew him a kiss, and he instinctively waved back, even though he knew they couldn't see him.

As the helicopter picked up speed, Grace and Reggie and Bainbridge began to fade into the distance, and the scene from his window looked like watercolors dripping into the Susquehanna River. The black aircraft banked and glided toward the Chesapeake Bay, and then on to Andrews Air Force Base in Washington D.C, their first destination. Driggers leaned over and handed Jack a boxed breakfast.

"We will arrive at Andrews in twenty minutes," said Kettering. "Then we'll catch a C141 flight to Travis AFB in California."

"I'm not hungry," said Jack, as he set the box down.

"Suit yourself," said Kettering.

Kettering returned to reading his newspaper, while Driggers grabbed a hardboiled egg from Jack's box. Two hours later, they departed Andrews for the five-hour flight to Travis Air Force Base near San Francisco. There were a dozen or so passengers on board the C141 Star Lifter cargo plane. Jack, Kettering, and Driggers sat in the back row. The compartment was chilly, and Jack left his pea coat on. He reached in his coat for a piece of gum, and felt the letter in his inside pocket. He had forgotten about it. He carefully and quietly tore the end of the envelope, revealing a two-page letter. He started to pull it

53

out, but when he saw that it was signed by Aunt Sarah, he quickly stuffed it back in his pocket. The last thing he wanted was for Kettering to see a letter from her.

He spent the next hour agonizing about the contents. He stared at the cloud formations, while checking every few minutes to see if Driggers and Kettering were asleep. About an hour into the flight, they were both dozing, and he seized the opportunity to read the letter. He carefully placed it on his lap and proceeded to read it, looking up every few seconds to make sure he wasn't seen.

November 3, 1972

Dear Jack,

I was devastated to learn of the deaths of your parents. I just received your letter today. It was the first day in weeks that the Hercules ski planes could fly down from New Zealand to make a mail drop. I can't imagine what you have been going through. I wish I could be with you, but I'm working with a scientist named Dr. Ian Moon on some very important research, and I must stay in Antarctica with him for the next few months.

I was shocked to learn that you joined the Navy. After I read your letter, I went straight to the message center here at McMurdo. Unfortunately, the radioman refused to send a teletype message because it wasn't official business, but a scientist friend who is flying back to New Zealand tomorrow said he would mail a letter for me from Christchurch.

Ian and I think your parents may have been murdered, and the appearance of the Navy recruiter who persuaded you to enlist seems very suspicious. The last thing I want to do is worry you and cause more stress than you already have, but there are things you need to know, secrets about your parents, about Ian and I, and about a man named Kettering who may try to harm you. I wanted to tell you these things at Saint Mark, but your father insisted that he would decide when the time was right. Now, I fear I have no other choice but to warn you that your life may be in danger.

Your father was a good man. In fact, he was a hero, having rescued Ian from the Japanese. It was Kettering who was responsible for the deaths of those Marines, but your father got the blame. Unfortunately, Ian and I think that, against our advice, your father was planning to expose Kettering by going to the media. We know he needed money, but regrettably we could not help him for reasons that I cannot tell you right now.

You should also know that your father introduced me to Ian

54

during the war. In the years afterward, we both studied physics at the University of Canterbury in Christchurch. But as things go, we went our separate ways, until Ian asked me to help him after his wife died in a car accident about ten years ago.

Jack, wherever you are, you must go to your commanding officer and request emergency leave. Say that your aunt is gravely ill. Do not return to Saint Mark, and do not believe anything that Kettering tells you about your father or about Ian and me. He will try to use you to get to us. Do not try to reach me via the radiomen at McMurdo. I don't trust them. Instead, contact Ian's friend Ted in New Zealand. He will help you. His HAM call sign is ZL5YM. You can send a message to him and he will relay it to the New Zealand Scott Base in Antarctica. Ian will get it there.

I cannot tell you anything more than this until we meet and talk privately. There are very important matters you need to know about.

God Bless You,

Love,
Aunt Sarah

———————————————

As soon as Jack finished reading the letter, he hurriedly stuffed it back in the envelope and slid it into his pocket. He stared out the window at the titanium-white clouds, and agonized over his next steps. His thoughts bounced back and forth between the comfort and safety of college life, and the mess he found himself in now in the Navy. He couldn't sleep. His hands were still shaking an hour before the plane was due to land. He thought about making a run for it when the plane landed at Travis. But where would he go? How would he get back home? Besides, he would be AWOL, in violation of the Uniform Code of Military Justice, a military fugitive.

The high-pitched strain of the Star Lifter's engines at 30,000 feet easily penetrated the cargo bay where they sat. Ordinarily, the noise would have annoyed him, but instead it seemed to create an artificial separation between him and his two captors. He drifted off in thought again and pondered the revelations in Aunt Sarah's letter. What kind of things went on between his father and Dr. Moon and Aunt Sarah? He vaguely remembered his father receiving envelopes from New Zealand with colorful stamps on the packages. It would have been over the last few years, when he was in high school. But what did his father do with the envelopes? He ran it through his mind over and over again. Then, it came to him. Aunt Sarah would come to the house to visit every month or so, on Saturday mornings. She would bring cinnamon bread that the monks made at Saint Mark. On a couple of occasions, he remembered his father handing the unopened envelope to Aunt Sarah, and she would put it in the bakery bag. That's it. Dr. Moon was passing some kind of information to Aunt Sarah. Why didn't she ever open the envelopes at the house? What did she do with them after she left? He had to figure out a way to contact her.

The plane shook with a sharp shudder. The captain announced that they were beginning the descent to land in California. In that instant, it occurred to him that he might be able to call Grace when the plane landed at Travis. He could have her contact Aunt Sarah. But how? Kettering would not let him out of his sight, let alone give him time to use a payphone. Kettering and Driggers awakened at the sound of the captain's voice announcing the landing time. Kettering leaned over and whispered something to Driggers. Then, Driggers looked over at Jack.

"Hey, Trane, we'll be on the ground at Travis for a few hours," said Driggers. "Colonel says we can get chow there before our flight to Hawaii. You stay with me. Don't leave my sight. You go to the head, I'm going with you. You go up for dessert, and I go with you. Got it?"

"Yea, I got it. I got it good from you, didn't I? You took advantage of me. I should have known when I saw you and Cindy at the train station."

Then, as quickly as a cat pouncing on a mouse, Kettering slid between the two of them, and glared at Jack.

"Jack, I want you to understand something. From here on in, you will do as I say. You will carry out my orders, and you won't try anything stupid." Jack nodded, but did not reply. "Is that a yes?" Kettering asked, raising his voice. Some of the passengers glanced back at them.

"Yes, sir," Jack replied sheepishly. He sat down, fastened his seatbelt, and thought about how he could contact Grace.

After they landed, Kettering went off on his own, and Jack and Driggers went to the dining hall. Jack ate in silence, trying not to look at Driggers. As he glanced around the cafeteria, he saw a group of sailors pass the sergeant-at-arms and head for the chow line. He noticed that one of the sailors wore the three lightning bolts and single chevron rating badge, signifying he was a third-class radioman like Jack. It occurred to him that he could pass a message to him to send to Grace. He quickly devised a plan.

"Hey, Driggers, I have to use the head."

"Okay, let's go. I'll wait outside the door for you."

Jack went into the stall and locked the door. He took a small piece of paper and wrote a message.

Please trust me.
Don't say anything.
Send this to:

RM3 Grace Weems
Naval Radio "A" School
Bainbridge, MD

Grace,

> *Tell Haskins to help me. Contact Sarah Mechling via HAM call sign ZL5YM. Do not use Naval comm. to Antarctica. Tell her I arrive NZ 4-17 with CK to meet the Dr.*

JT

When Jack returned to the cafeteria with Driggers, he ate slowly, waiting for the radioman to go to the soda dispenser. When he finally did, Jack walked up and stood next to him as he began to fill up his glass. Then Jack made a series of taps on the dispenser. The radioman looked confused, so Jack glanced quickly at him with a desperate look. The radioman recognized the Morse code message "help me." Then, Jack intentionally dropped his glass. When the two bent down to clean up the mess, Jack slipped him the message. He mouthed "thank you" and walked back to the table.

"What the hell happened up there? Come on, we gotta' get back to the plane. Say goodbye to the US. You'll be in New Zealand tomorrow. Actually, in two days after we pass the International Date Line."

They headed toward the gate to the parked plane outside. Kettering was standing at the top of the portable steps, waving for them to hurry. The noise from the jet engines was deafening. A stiff, cool breeze blew across the runway. Driggers ripped the wrapper off a Zero candy bar and shoved a huge chunk of chocolate-covered nougat into his mouth. Then, the radioman from the soda machine passed Jack and bumped into Driggers.

"Watch it, asshole," mumbled Driggers.

The radioman shot back a dirty look as he walked away from them. Jack looked back, and the radioman gave him a thumbs-up sign.

"Hey, Driggers, did you know there are millions of sheep in New Zealand?" asked Jack, as he walked up the steps to the plane.

Driggers had already entered the plane, and he turned around to reply. "Yea, so what."

"Sheep are gentle creatures. The lamb is the symbol of purity and grace. I'll bet New Zealand is a beautiful, peaceful place."

"I couldn't care less—"

"Sheep are the symbol of mindless followers, of the powerless, of most of humanity," said Kettering. "Is that what you want, Trane… to be powerless, weak, and dependent?"

"I want the truth."

"Ah, yes, 'I want the truth.' The rallying cry of the pampered, idealistic student masses on campuses across this country. What is the truth, Jack? Is it religion, tuning out with drugs, free love, joining the Peace Corps, protesting everything?"

"It's faith in something good, something greater than all of us. Don't you have faith in anything?"

"I have faith in myself. The only truth I know is power and wealth. If you want that too, then you'll do what I tell you to do."

Jack couldn't stop thinking about what Kettering said throughout the five-hour flight to Hickam Air Force Base in Honolulu. Something in the dark corners of his mind was steering him toward acceptance of the idea of making lots of money. He thought about the benefits. He could give Grace a good life, pay his bills, finish college, and the two of them could travel the world. But Kettering had never mentioned what his payment would be, or what it would take for him to earn it.

Chapter 9
So Far Away

The Star Lifter touched down on the cold tarmac after the last leg of the journey, an eight-hour flight from Honolulu to Christchurch, with a two-hour refueling stop in Pago Pago, American Samoa. The jolt woke Jack from a two-hour nap, the only peaceful sleep he had since they left Hawaii. Upon waking, he peered out the tiny window to a narrow view of hedge-bordered fields and far off snow-covered mountains shimmering in the early morning light, which he reasoned were the Southern Alps Kettering told him about during the flight.

The plane taxied to a remote runway, where a black Hillman sedan was parked. Exhaust vapor trailed from the tailpipe of the idling engine and partially obscured the silhouette of a female figure sitting in the driver's seat. Kettering led Jack and Driggers down the portable stairs that a lone airman placed at the door to the fuselage. The airman was part of a small US Air Force detachment that was assigned to support the US Antarctic program, known as Operation Deep Freeze. Jack shivered in the frosty air as the three men got into the car.

"How was your flight, Colonel?" asked a female voice behind the wheel in the front seat.

"Bearable. Is the house ready?" asked Kettering.

Jack recognized the voice and sat up. He glanced in the rearview mirror. His eyes met Cindy's nervous glance as she quickly looked away.

"Yes, the ambassador informed the Kiwis of our arrival," said Cindy. "He told them that we are communications specialists, and that we have come here to evaluate our antenna facilities for the new satellite upgrade. There should be no problems."

"Good work," said Kettering. "How far is the house from the antennas?"

"About two miles—"

"Hello, Cindy. I thought you were in Italy enjoying the architecture."

"Duty calls," said Cindy, as she pulled away from the runway and drove toward an open gate that led to a stone chip service road. "Colonel needs me down here. So, I understand you've decided to help us."

"Yea, seems you already did your duty at Saint Mark," said Jack.

"Save it, both of you," said Kettering. "Did you deliver my orders to the commanding officer of the communications unit?"

"I did. He was a little huffy about us using his facilities. He questioned why we needed to stay near the transmitter site, but I explained that we needed to set up our devices close to the antennas. He started to question your authority, so I reminded him of our orders from Naval Intelligence and IWR, though he didn't seem to know what IWR was. He backed off."

"Good, and don't forget, you do not wear your uniform here. You will dress in civilian clothes every day. We are attached to Operation Deep Freeze as guests of the New Zealand government."

The sun was rising above the Port Hills to the east of Christchurch. They had been driving for about fifteen minutes in a westerly direction away from the city, along a two-lane road through the pastures and farmland of the Canterbury Plains. Cindy slowed the Hillman and turned onto a narrow lane, stopping at a locked steel gate. Driggers got out to open it. Jack had been so preoccupied with the newness of his surroundings that he did not notice that the steering wheel was on the right side, and that she had been driving on the left side of the road. The stone chip lane led straight to a one-story bungalow, about a hundred yards from the gate.

"This is your new home, Jack," said Driggers.

Cindy stopped the car, and Jack got out to look around. The house was in the middle of a field of golden pasture grass. The tips of the Southern Alps were visible to the west beyond a row of tall pine trees. A patchwork of pastures bordered with gorse stretched to the south and east. The transmitter antenna field was located a few hundred yards north of the driveway entrance at the public road, and was surrounded by a ten-foot chain link fence.

"That is where you work, if anyone asks," said Kettering.

"Tomorrow, Cindy and I will set up the monitoring equipment and portable antennas outside," said Driggers.

"Good, we must look like we are doing something real here," said Kettering. "I don't want any interference from our people, let alone the Kiwis, who I'm sure will be keeping an eye on us too. That's why no one leaves the premises unless I say so. We'll meet in the kitchen after we unpack. I want to discuss the mission with Jack. Cindy, get me a cup of coffee."

"Hey, Jack, the Colonel is going to tell you about Moon's stepdaughter, Eva," said Driggers, as he closed the trunk. "I've seen her. She's pretty good looking."

"So what?" asked Jack.

"So, he probably wants you to make it with her to get the information he wants about her stepfather."

"What information?"

"You'll find out inside."

"Coffee is ready," yelled Cindy.

"Well, maybe Cindy can give me a few pointers on seduction and deception," said Jack.

"Ha. Yea, she's pretty skilled," laughed Driggers. "Got all the tools, especially those legs."

"Shut up, you lughead! I was just doing my job. He's here, isn't he? And he's going to do his part to help his country. Nobody got hurt, which I actually care about, unlike you, Stanley. You like hurting people, don't you?"

"People get hurt all the time. That's life, babe. How bout' all those poor bastards fighting in 'Nam? The Gooks are sending them home in body bags, because the politicians back home won't let us win the war. That could have been me. I could still be on one of those damn river patrol boats on the Mekong if it wasn't for the Colonel. What's the difference between killing

Gooks and killing… well, we're all doing our job. But I'm not so sure you're committed to this mission."

"Don't worry about me," said Cindy. "You do your job and I'll do mine."

"Cindy, get us something to eat, and tell Jack to come in the kitchen," yelled Kettering.

"Yes, sir. I'll be right there."

When Jack entered the kitchen, Kettering was sitting with his back to him, hunched over an open folder, which gave him the appearance of a snapping turtle. Jack nervously glanced around the room while he waited for Cindy to put the food out. Four days ago, he had been jogging in a park at Bainbridge, thinking about getting orders to Hawaii and being with Grace. Now, he was 10,000 miles from home, unaware that he was about to step into harm's way. The screeching whistle of the tea kettle startled him. He tripped and bumped into Cindy, who dropped the plate of eggs she had prepared for breakfast. Kettering slammed his fist on the table.

"You stupid bitch!" He raised his fist as if to strike her. Instinctively, she cowered and dropped to the floor to pick up the food. Then he recoiled. He smiled at Jack, and turned to Cindy. "Bring us another plate."

"Yes. Right away, Colonel."

Jack sensed a terrible fear inside of her, and he stooped down to help.

"Leave it for her. We have important matters to discuss."

They heard the door slam in the back hallway. Heavy footsteps pounded the floor, and Driggers appeared in the kitchen. He set the object that was wrapped in a black cloth on the wooden table, and sat down.

"I was cleaning my pistol. I'm starving. Is that all the eggs you made?"

"If you want more, you can make them yourself," said Cindy.

"Make the eggs," growled Kettering.

Jack noticed a metal gun barrel poking out of the folded cloth. He thought for a moment that he should grab it and use it to make his escape. Then he came to his senses. He couldn't shoot anyone. He had no idea where he would go, anyway. All the while, he felt like Kettering was inside his head, reading his thoughts.

"Jack, let me remind you that you that you are a guest in this country, and while you are here, you belong to me. You are here because we have treaties with New Zealand that allow our military personnel to be here, but should you decide to do something stupid, like run away, then you would be considered a deserter, and you will be caught and returned to me. You don't have a passport and you don't have any money. So the only way you can leave this island country is with me. Also, if you open you mouth about anything that I consider classified, you would be guilty of espionage too. Do I make myself clear?" Jack shook his head. "I don't think you understand. If you are a deserter and you've committed espionage, you'll be court-martialed and sent to the brig."

"Okay, I got it," Jack replied, as his voice cracked.

"Smart boy. Do as I say and you have much to gain… unlike your father, who disobeyed me, and ended up wounded and dishonorably discharged. You don't want to make the same mistakes he made."

"I don't believe anything you say about my father."

"Your father hid the truth from you. Of course, I wouldn't blame him. Any father would try to hide his failings from his son. I hope you can forgive him. I want you to know that this is not about condemning your father. It's about helping your country. It's about rising above his mistakes and being brave. Quite frankly, it's even bigger than that, because if we fail to persuade Moon to work for us, then he will almost certainly sell his formula to the Soviets, or possibly even a terrorist organization. Think of the consequences of something like that."

"What exactly is this formula?" asked Jack.

"It's the plans to build an antimatter weapon. We must persuade Dr. Moon to work for us, or else—"

"Or else, what?" asked Jack.

"Or else, he will have to be eliminated... and I'm afraid that means your aunt too. Do you see now why it is so important that you succeed?"

Jack sat completely still. Kettering was painting a picture he did not want to see, and the situation was becoming more and more complex in light of the revelations in Aunt Sarah's letter. He wanted to believe that she wouldn't lie to him. He distrusted Kettering, but now a small flicker of doubt had ignited in his mind. He wondered if it was possible that his father had actually caused the deaths of his men, and whether Moon really had an antimatter formula? After all, Aunt Sarah didn't say anything about antimatter in her letter.

"What do you want me to do?" asked Jack.

"I want you to meet Dr. Moon's stepdaughter, Eva Silk. Find out what she knows about him. She lives here in Christchurch. Get her to invite you to Moon's ranch in the mountains. You will emphasize that your father rescued Dr. Moon on Guam. Also mention your interests in parks and gardens. It may help you to gain her confidence. We think his laboratory is up there, and that Eva may know about it. It's possible that you'll find some details about the formula. We only have a few days to prepare you for your meeting with her."

"And then what?"

"After you meet Eva, we will work on a time and place to confront Moon once he returns from Antarctica in mid-May."

"What happens to me if Eva doesn't reveal anything? What happens if I can't persuade Dr. Moon to cooperate?"

Kettering paused for a moment. He lit a cigarette, took a long drag, and then exhausted the smoke into Jack's face.

"You are going to persist, until I say you're done." His eyes darkened with a crazed look of pent up violence. His words penetrated Jack's thoughts of trying to escape. Cindy, sensing the sudden change in Kettering's tone, instinctively stepped back and leaned against the sink. Driggers recoiled from his slouched position on the chair and placed his hand on his revolver. "I will not tolerate failure. I have spent many years in pursuit of this formula, and I am not about to acquiesce to a mediocre effort from you. No, Jack, you will work tirelessly for me. You're going to climb a mountain for me… because you want your freedom and comfort back. You want to succeed, because you want a reward, don't you?"

"Yea, you mentioned earlier about a reward. What kind of reward?"

Kettering's tone lightened a bit, and his eyes warmed a degree.

"A reward for your hard work and service to your country. You see, Jack, if you fail, then the doomsday clock ticks faster toward world destruction. But if you succeed in persuading him to cooperate with us, then there will be a substantial monetary reward for you, say $100,000."

Jack's mouth dropped. Suddenly, the darkness surrounding Kettering began to brighten. A short, bald genie with a pointy nose emerged from a golden lamp in Jack's hand. This could be the opportunity of a lifetime.

"And if I don't succeed?"

"Then you'll be discharged, and you can go back to Saint Mark."

"Just like that? I don't understand. I don't understand any of this. Why can't I just drive to his house, introduce myself to him, and ask him to cooperate with you? Yes or no… then you'll have your answer."

"Save the sarcasm. It's not that easy. He is an eccentric, and he's unpredictable. Don't you think I've tried just about everything else? I've practically offered him the world, but he doesn't trust anyone. Except, as I said before, I think he might trust you, because you are Albert Trane's son."

"I still don't understand. Why don't you just let me talk to my aunt? Surely she could arrange for me to talk to Dr. Moon."

"I don't believe your aunt is stable either. She suffers from unrequited love. Moon jilted her a long time ago."

"How so?" asked Jack.

"He chose his work over her, and then he married a woman he barely knew. Your aunt still doesn't see that Moon is using her. She is still hoping he will marry her and the two of them will live happily ever after. She's been toiling away in the laboratory at Saint Mark for years, secretly working on his research. That's how Moon has been conducting his experiments without anyone knowing what he's up to. I don't suppose you know how she received the research material from Moon?"

Jack was pretty sure of the answer from Aunt Sarah's letter, but he pretended to be oblivious.

"I have no idea."

"For years, Moon paid your father to pass data to your aunt, who had access to the college's computers. Recently, we've learned that the money stopped. Moon succeeded in drawing your father, your mother, and your aunt into his web of deceit." Kettering's eyes met Jack's. "But not you. You're going to be the only smart one. You're going to come out of this a rich man, and all you have to do is follow my orders."

"But I still don't understand why you think he will listen to me. Just because my dad saved his life?"

"You are pure and uncorrupted. You still have the faith. You are the person Moon once was. I'm pinning my hopes on you. If I can get you face to face with him, then I believe there's a good chance he'll listen to you. But we're running out of time. I'm certain that if I confront him, he'll just sell it to the Soviets… or maybe even destroy it. You are our best chance to persuade him to cooperate with us." Jack still wasn't satisfied with Kettering's explanation, but Kettering continued on with the details. "Eva takes a gardening class at the Christchurch Botanic Gardens on Fridays. You will call her to arrange to meet her next Friday when her class is over."

"What should I say?"

"Introduce yourself, and explain that you received orders to Christchurch on short notice. Tell her that you arrived last week, and that your father was an old friend of Dr. Moon's. You will say that you phoned him several times, but no one was home, so you looked up her phone number and you are calling to arrange for a visit. You will say you have the afternoon off, and hopefully she will agree to meet. Suggest afternoon tea at the Botanic Gardens Café. Driggers will drive you to the park." Kettering could sense Jack's apprehension. "Don't try to run, and don't try to seek refuge in our embassy or go to the New Zealand government. There is nowhere you can go."

Cindy slid a 5" x 7" black and white photograph across the table in front of Jack.

"That's Eva with Dr. Moon," said Kettering.

Jack studied the photo. Driggers was right, she was attractive. He was relieved to finally put a face to Dr. Moon, the man who seemingly controlled his destiny. He absorbed the image of a lean, learned man with peaceful eyes, round, gray eyeglasses, and bushy, unkempt gray hair atop a high forehead. He fixated on his face. There was something odd about his smile.

The next day, Jack phoned Eva. She answered on the first ring.

"Are you there?" said Eva.

"Yes, I'm here," he replied.

Cindy whispered that's how they answer a telephone in New Zealand. He stumbled through the brief conversation, but made the arrangements.

"She seemed fairly agreeable about the whole thing," said Jack.

"Good. Your stock is rising, Jack," said Kettering.

The following morning, Cindy noticed a gray sedan after she returned from driving Kettering to the base for a meeting.

"It's probably New Zealand SIS," said Driggers. "I'll pretend to set up our monitoring equipment. That should satisfy their curiosity."

Jack peaked through the curtains at the sedan. What if he went to that Kiwi agent for help?

"I've got a headache, Driggers. Can I lay down for a minute?"

"Yea, go ahead."

Jack went into his bedroom and lay down on the soft sheepskins covering the bed. He sprang from the bed as the door slammed behind him. He heard muffled whispering on the other side of the door as the lock engaged.

"Colonel said it wasn't necessary to lock him in the bedroom," said Cindy.

"I don't care what he said, I'm not taking any chances. Besides, I thought you and I might have a little rendezvous while the Colonel is away."

"Well, you thought wrong. I have errands to run."

Driggers switched on the radio and turned up the volume.

"Come on, remember the time in Pago Pago when we had to stay the night at The Polynesian when the Starlifter was held up for repairs?"

Jack could make out the sound of feet shuffling, mumbling, and giggling as Driggers and Cindy stumbled down the hall. Then a door slammed, bringing dead silence. He fell back on the bed and pondered his list of woes. His parents were dead. He was working in a phony unit in the Navy in a country on the other side of the world, with no passport, no money, and no one to turn to. Surely Grace had contacted Haskins or Aunt Sarah by now. But why wasn't anyone coming to help? He felt consumed with fear that his life was in danger. He felt a pain in his right cheek from the remnants of the Bell's palsy, as a terrifying thought flashed through his mind. What if Kettering murdered his parents? What if he plans to kill him too?

Jack jumped from the bed and tried to open the window and the door, but both were locked from the outside. He flung the closet door open and saw a small plumbing chase in the corner, with a trap door to the crawl space below. While he was outside with the antenna equipment, he noticed that the crawl space was not completely enclosed. He might be able to make a run to the sedan across the road. He decided it was now or never.

He dropped into the two-foot-high crawl space and inched his way through the dark, musty cavity. He had only crawled about six feet when he realized that the vent on the outside wall was too small to crawl through. His chest was pounding. He realized he had to turn back before Driggers heard him, but as he turned around, his shirt got stuck on a water valve. He yanked hard to free it, but the valve broke, spraying cold water everywhere.

Then, the muffled, distant music on the radio stopped. He heard the key turn in the door lock. Instantly, two huge bear claws were wrapped around his legs. In one powerful motion, Driggers yanked him out of the trap door and through the closet. Like a raging grizzly, he threw Jack against the wall and held him by the neck, his feet inches above the floor. He punched Jack in the stomach so hard that he gasped for air and couldn't catch his breath. He was about to punch him again, when Cindy stepped between them.

"Stop it. Don't touch him. The Colonel will be furious if you bruise his face before he meets Eva."

"Shut up. I'm tired of tiptoeing around this little punk. For once I wish the Colonel would do things my way. We'll see how much he cooperates after I work him over."

Jack's eyes widened in horror as Driggers pulled out a pocket knife.

"Are you out of your mind?" asked Cindy. "Are you forgetting what the Colonel told us? This is it. This is the final mission, the big payoff he's been promising us. You're not going to screw this up for me. I'm going to shut the water off and get this cleaned up before he gets back."

65

Driggers pushed Jack on the bed. Then, he slowly closed the sharp pocket knife.

"Okay, punk. You got a few more weeks in this place. You try something like that again, and I will tear you up."

Jack nodded and said nothing, and Driggers slammed the door and walked away. The terrifying seriousness of his situation overwhelmed him. He was shivering uncontrollably. Cindy came in and threw him a towel.

"You'd better get cleaned up. The Colonel will be back soon. You are going to make out big if we pull this off. The Colonel really needs you."

"You're right, Kettering does need me. I'll show him I can get what he wants from Dr. Moon. I'll make this meeting with Eva work too."

"Sure you will," said Cindy.

She turned the radio back on. Jack closed his eyes and listened to the music. The Carol King song *So Far Away* was playing. Everything that was once comfortable and familiar in his life now seemed so far away. So far, far away.

Chapter 10
Hagley Park

Friday afternoon came quickly, and Jack was anxious to get the meeting with Eva over with. Kettering decided to use a decoy car to drive to Christchurch. He reminded Jack that the gray car parked along the road could be a Soviet agent, and not New Zealand SIS, and that either way, he did not want to expose Jack's meeting with Eva. Kettering arranged for Cindy to follow them in an official US Navy car.

At two o'clock, they set out on the eight-mile trip to Christchurch. Driggers drove Jack and Kettering in the Hillman, and Cindy followed in the Navy car. As Kettering expected, the gray car followed in pursuit, so he chose a route along mostly narrow, stone chip lanes. After a couple of miles, Driggers radioed Cindy to execute the diversion. When they came to the designated fork in the road, Driggers took the left road and Cindy went right toward the base to switch her car.

Just beyond the fork, Driggers stopped his car near a fenced paddock full of grazing sheep. He quickly opened the gate, and fired his revolver to excite the sheep. Within seconds, the sheep ran out, clogging the narrow lane that was bounded by stone walls on both sides. The gray car screeched to a halt, unable to get through. But to Kettering's dismay, Driggers couldn't get through either. The Hillman was completely surrounded by sheep. Like a mad man, Kettering jumped up and down, waving his arms at the furry, white mass blocking their escape, as the gray car inched forward.

"God damned sheep! Get out of the way!" he yelled.

Driggers laid on the horn in a steady rhythm of honks. Suddenly, the gray car appeared in the rearview mirror behind a mass of sheep, just as Driggers managed to clear most of the sheep in front of him. Only a few stubborn ones remained. With a crazed look on his face, he accelerated and the car jolted ahead, plowing through the defenseless sheep one by one, spraying bright red blood on the pure white fur of the scattering flock.

"Keep the hell going," yelled Kettering.

Driggers snickered as if he had just swept a spattered bug off the windshield, and he sped away. Jack glanced in the rearview mirror at the lifeless lambs scattered alongside the road. The sight sickened him. Driggers sped out of sight and headed to the designated rendezvous point at a pub in Yaldhurst near the airport, where Cindy had readied a different car for them. Then, they drove on toward the center of the city.

"What's a few sheep?" asked Driggers. "There are millions of them in this country."

"That was disgusting," said Jack.

"Pussy."

"Shut up, Stan," said Kettering.

"You're getting soft, Colonel."

"We mustn't upset Jack. Try to cheer up before we get to Hagley Park. I wouldn't want you to make a bad impression on Eva. Why don't you enjoy the scenery. Look at all these landscaped neighborhoods. That's why they call Christchurch "The Garden City." Oh, and look up ahead. What a coincidence, there is the University of Canterbury, where your aunt and Dr. Moon studied. I hope your aunt's future bodes better than that of Moon's first wife."

Driggers laughed as he took his hand and made a cutting gesture across his throat.

"Stan, please. That's not necessary."

As they drew closer to the city center, the scenic Port Hills rose from the Pacific Ocean, and the view ignited a sense of déjà vu in Jack that seemed to get stronger as they passed the Avon River and the iconic Christchurch Cathedral. The tree-lined streets of the city teemed with shoppers and office workers. Red, British-looking double-decker buses whizzed past them. Then, Jack saw the sign for Hagley Park and the Christchurch Botanic Gardens. Driggers pulled into a parking lot adjacent to the Avon River, which looked more like a meandering stream. Kettering turned to him as Driggers parked in the far corner of the parking lot.

"You must get her to trust you, and persuade her to invite you to meet Moon. Remember, we'll be watching. Don't try anything foolish."

Jack walked warily across the black iron bridge that connected the parking lot to the entrance, but the earthy fragrances of dried leaves and freshly mowed grass in the chilly autumn air offered a welcome diversion. He stopped in the middle of the bridge to watch a couple of punts pass by. The scene of the manicured lawn along the river, bordered by tall cedars and masses of fiery orange and red-colored azalea foliage reminded him of photos of Kew Gardens, and other great British parks and estates that he always wanted to see.

He pulled the collar up on his corduroy jacket, and continued toward the visitors center where the café was located. He passed the Central Rose Garden, with faded blooms of past glorious displays. Then, he came upon long swaths of flowerbeds in ribbons of yellow cushion mums and royal blue asters, still blooming in the late-autumn sun. Groups of school children in green and gray uniforms paraded along the winding paths. The beautiful sight made him think he was dreaming. For a moment, he even forgot about the mission, until he glanced back at the parking lot to find Kettering following slowly in the distance.

He passed a girl with blonde hair, who reminded him of Grace. He wondered if she had contacted Aunt Sarah. The revelations in Aunt Sarah's letter weighed heavily on his mind, especially her dire warning to avoid Kettering, who was now directing his every move. He felt a sinking feeling in his stomach. After a few minutes, he reached the steps that led to the main floor of the café. They were framed with two massive concrete pots, each planted with a spiral, close-sheared, silvery blue juniper topiary. Jack paused at the first step and glanced behind him. Kettering had moved out of sight.

He walked slowly up the steps, and stopped at the top of the porch to look around. There were groups of mostly elderly women sipping tea and conversing. The aroma of fresh-brewed tea floated across the brisk autumn air that was tinged with the fragrance of clematis vines from a nearby trellis. He walked toward the café, stopping to peer through the wooden, divided-light windows that opened to the café beyond. He did not see anyone that resembled Eva. Maybe she backed out, he thought. He scanned the room a couple of times before he caught a glimpse of a woman near the back of the café, sitting alone at a table with her back to him. Jack approached her, but then stopped when he noticed a lone, dark figure three tables away in the corner. It was Kettering, who slowly looked up from his newspaper. The headline read **"Record Storm hits US Antarctic Base."** Jack was still staring at the headline, when the woman approached him. She spoke with a New Zealand accent.

"Are you Jack?"

He turned from Kettering to face a striking woman with short, jet-black hair and a slender figure. She was wearing a brown mini skirt and a camel-colored lamb's wool top.

"Yes... and you're Eva?"

She nodded as they shook hands.

"I'm Eva Silk. How are you going?"

"Well, ah... I came by taxi."

She giggled after hearing Jack's response.

"Oh, I guess you're not familiar with Kiwi talk yet. The expression, 'how are you going' is the same as 'how are you?' Anyway, I'm pleased to meet you."

"Same. I'll remember that. I've only just arrived here a few days ago. I'm still getting used to driving on the left side of the road."

"So, what do you think of Christchurch so far?"

"Beautiful. I love this park too."

"Well, you've started in the right place. This is one of best botanic gardens in the world. I'd love to show you around if you have time."

"Yes, I'd like that very much. I studied landscape architecture in college."

"How about that, my stepfather loved gardens. When I was little, he took me here many times. I remember watching him sketch the plants and scenery. Of course, that's all in the past. I don't understand, you say you studied landscape architecture, but you're in the Navy?"

"It's a long story. My parents passed away last year, and I ran out of money and had to quit college. So, I joined the Navy and got orders to Operation Deep Freeze Antarctic Base at the airport. I was hoping to meet your stepfather. I wanted to talk to him about my father and their wartime experience."

"What was your father's name?"

"Albert Trane. That's actually why I called you so soon after arriving here. I'm trying to learn more about my father's past. He told me he saved your stepfather's life in the war. Did he ever talk about my father?"

"I don't really recall, except—" she hesitated, and then turned away to

69

look out the window. "I seem to remember years ago when my mother was alive, he mentioned an American who he was hospitalized with on Guam. He said he felt sorry for him. Something about... he was wounded and his men were killed in a battle with the Japanese. That's all I remember. I take it that was your father? Shall we order tea and scones?"

"Yea, sure... tea would be nice. But wait... are you telling me he never mentioned anything about my father saving his life on Guam?"

"I'm telling you that I have not had a good relationship with Ian... too many bad childhood memories. He was a terrible stepfather."

"What do you mean?"

"I mean, what would you say about a man who leaves his family eight months out of the year to pursue his quixotic, scientific endeavors in Antarctica? It drove my mother mad. He refused to compromise with her. Those were painful, wasted years... and for what? After my mother died, he broke off relations with the University and the rest of the scientific community."

The waitress set a steaming pot of tea on the table, along with cups and two scones with fresh whipped cream and jam. Eva filled the white china cups, then glanced at the scenery outside. The tall trees cast long shadows in the late afternoon sun.

"Oddly enough, the only pleasant memories I had with Ian happened in this park. It seemed like the only time he spent with my mother and me."

"If you don't mind me asking, how did your mother die?"

"She died ten years ago in an automobile accident. I think someone was after whatever it was she was delivering to the University that day, which made me suspicious about the whole thing. It was his fault though. He should have never sent her out alone. We lived in Akaroa, on the ocean side of the Port Hills. The roads through the hills are winding and treacherous. Her brakes failed, and the car crashed, killing her instantly. The police ruled it an accident. Ironically, the documents she was delivering were never recovered. You draw your own conclusions."

"What kind of work did he do?"

Eva pressed her lips against her teacup and paused for a few seconds, then stared earnestly at Jack.

"I don't understand the science. It involves some kind of weapon."

Jack leaned back in his chair and glanced nonchalantly around the room. He caught a glimpse of Kettering, who was still sitting by himself at the corner table. He glanced at him with raised eyebrows. Kettering acknowledged with a blink.

"I'm sorry about your mother. I understand what you are going through though. Do you have any other relatives here?"

"Not on Ian's side. His parents and brother were killed during the war. My mother was from Dunedin and I still have an aunt and uncle there. My mum first met Ian when they were in school together at Canterbury University. After mum died, I stayed with my aunt and uncle while Ian was in Antarctica.

Sometimes, he would stay down there for nine months at a time. When I was at university, I think I only saw him once a year. If he wasn't in Antarctica, he was at his ranch in the Hawkduns. That's his private laboratory… his retreat, if you will. The last time I was there was over Christmas. I came back to make amends with him and to work here for a while. I work for an import/export company in Christchurch. But I will not stay at the ranch when she's around."

"I'm sorry, you're losing me. Who—"

"Sarah Mechling, an American scientist. She came back to work with him in Antarctica."

"Yea, I know… I mean I know who she is," said Jack, trying to choose his words carefully.

"You do?"

"She's my aunt… sort of. Well, she's not really my aunt. She was a close friend of my parents, and she taught at Saint Mark College. I understand she is one of the scientists working with Ian in Antarctica."

Eva appeared to be annoyed.

"Well, now isn't this interesting? Your aunt, who isn't really your aunt, is really the other woman."

"Other woman?"

"I remember hearing my mother argue with Ian and accuse him of seeing her. I blamed Sarah for the break-up of their marriage. They had a miserable marriage, which made for a very unhappy childhood for me. As a matter of fact, they fought about her on the day my mother died. Excuse me if I offend you, but I do not care for your aunt… or whoever she is to you."

"I'm sorry to hear—"

"My visit at Christmas was the last straw. When I arrived at the ranch, I guess I upset their plans. I didn't care though. I hadn't seen Ian in two years. I swallowed my pride and offered them an olive branch. You'd think they could have postponed their holiday." Her tone grew increasingly angry. "Instead, they hurried off for their vacation and offered to put me up in a hotel in Christchurch. Hell, they were going to be together for six months in Antarctica. They couldn't spare a couple of days with me? So, we agreed to spend the day together, one miserable day. She didn't have much to say to me. She was standoffish, and acted so damn high and mighty about how she was the only one Ian trusted. Well, I don't trust her, and I don't like her either."

"I think you are mistaken about Sarah. That's not the person I knew. She was kind and considerate. She tutored me in math and physics. She was a good friend of my parents too, and was like a second mother to me."

"Did she ever mention antimatter to you?" asked Eva.

"Anti…what?" asked Jack, pretending to be oblivious.

"When I saw them last Christmas, I overheard her talking to Ian about some kind of antimatter research that she brought with her from Saint Mark. It must have been pretty important to him. He needed it for something he's doing in Antarctica, and he clearly didn't want me to know about it."

"Sorry, I don't know anything about that," said Jack.

71

"Well, all I know is antimatter and your Aunt Sarah changed Ian. I wish I knew what he is up to. He is not the same person I remember when my mother first met him. No, he's cold, bitter, and secretive. He doesn't seem to care about anything but his research, and I don't think he has good intentions for its use."

"So, you think he's working on something harmful?"

"I do, Jack, and I don't know what to do about it. Oh, listen to me. I'm burdening you with my problems, and you came to talk about your father. I'm sorry. Listen, why don't you let me show you around the gardens, and then I'll drive you back to your base."

Jack glanced around the room, and noticed Kettering leaving his table.

"Sure, that would be nice."

Eva insisted on paying the bill, and then she led Jack out a side entrance and down a path that led to the conservatories and the rose garden that he had passed on the way in. They strolled past beds of perennials, some still in bloom, and geometric, bare-soiled beds mulched for spring plantings.

"I wish you could have seen these beds in the spring, all ablaze with yellow and red tulips and violet hyacinths," said Eva.

They strolled through the woodland, water, and rock gardens that covered a large part of the park, until Eva suggested they head back before the park closed.

"Wait, what's down this path?" asked Jack.

He pointed to a gray stepping-stone path bordered with juniper-draped boulders and clumps of topiary pines.

"That's the Japanese Garden. Many of the plants in this garden were given to the city of Christchurch as a gift from the Emperor of Japan, before World War II of course. The sculpture that's dedicated to peace in the pagoda over there was also a gift from the Japanese people of Hiroshima. It is a symbol of hope for a peaceful, nuclear-free world. Ian used to take me here and we would feed the goldfish and koi in the pond over there. It was his favorite place."

Jack knew this would be his favorite place too, even before he opened the iron gate. That's when he noticed the outline of a dove on the gate, shaped in wrought iron, with an inscription **"Blessed are the Peacemakers."** They passed through the gate and followed a path along a small pond ringed with boulders, and then crossed over a wooden, arched bridge. Two stone lanterns on either side of the bridge marked the entrance to a meditation garden, with perfectly raked patterns of white and black pebbles. A group of three irregular, black basalt boulders created a focal point of the composition. There was a cedar pagoda behind the meditation garden.

"I feel like I've been in this garden before. It has a strong sense of place," said Jack. He stood and studied the composition of plants and rocks, absorbing the tranquil landscape. The pagoda was accented by groups of fine-textured junipers and shiny-leafed boxwood. A large Blue Atlas cedar and a fifty-foot-high Copper beech rose up from behind the pagoda. The pair of trees was faced by a cluster of silver-bark hawthorns with bright orange and red foliage and covered with red berries. A picturesque, fifteen-foot-tall, red-leafed Japanese maple situated in a mass of Japanese Garden juniper completed the composition. Jack stood motionless for a minute, staring at the splendor of his surroundings. He sat down on a bench facing the pagoda. He was so absorbed in the view that he did not notice that Eva, who was shivering from the brisk autumn wind, had sat down next to him.

"Simplicity, tranquility, and rejection of the straight axis line are common principles in Japanese Garden design," said Jack. "Actually, Japanese Garden design has its origins in the Chinese Garden, which in turn influenced English Landscape Gardening School in the eighteenth century."

"How interesting," she said, as she snuggled closer to him.

"What I'm getting at is that the design of Hagley Park is based on the English Landscape Gardening School, which was led by a man named Capability Brown. He designed parks and gardens in the UK that I'd like to see some day... Blenheim Palace, Stowe, Milton Abbey."

"I can't say I've heard of any of those," said Eva.

"I find it fascinating how Eastern and Western garden design look so entirely different, and yet they are linked by common design principles of harmony, balance, and unity. If my father were alive, he would have trouble associating peace and harmony with the Japanese, because of his experience in the war. I believe we all seek order and harmony regardless of social behavior or political thought. That is the basis of good design. But it's how we implement and maintain order that gets us into trouble. Gardens change with the cycles of nature. Societies change with the vagaries of politics and human behavior... and that's how friends become enemies, and enemies become friends."

Eva sat with a blank stare and her mouth open, facing him.

"What did you say?" she asked.

"I said, funny how one minute, you're friends, and the next minute, you're enemies... you know, like the relationships among countries."

"I don't believe it. That's really creepy. You sound just like Ian... that is to say, before he changed."

"What do you mean by that?"

"I mean, before Mum died, he would say the same kinds of things as you."

"I guess we have something in common."

"Yes, but I wouldn't expect him to be as altruistic as he once was. No, he's become more cynical, more extreme in his political thought. He's so far left leaning, you'd think he was a communist! That's why I'm frightened of him. I don't trust that he would do the right thing with whatever it is he is inventing. There is a dark side to him. What did your father think of Ian?"

"The few times he mentioned him, he spoke favorably of him. My father refused to talk to me about the war, but he did mention that he saved Ian's life. It was as if that was the most important thing he did. I wish I knew more about my dad. I wish I knew more about your stepfather too. That's why I would like to meet him. Do you think you could introduce me to him?"

"Yes, I suppose when he returns from Antarctica, something could be arranged, if he's willing. Come on, it's late. I'd better get you back to your base." She took his hand and walked toward her car. Jack noticed Driggers' car in the corner of the lot. Driggers was supposed to follow Jack to the base.

Eva accidentally dropped her purse, and she and Jack bent down at the same time to pick it up. They both had a hand on the purse strap as they rose from the ground. Their eyes met, just as they straightened up. Jack inhaled a wisp of her perfume. She ran her free hand through her hair, and gently moistened her lips. She shifted her stance to release the strap, and her thigh brushed against his. Then, she leaned forward and kissed him, and pulled him close to her. The strain of the burden he bore since Bainbridge seemed to leave his body. A cold gust of wind blew an assembly of dry leaves across the parking lot, scattering them across the last light of evening sky. They separated and slid into her car.

"Thanks, I really enjoyed the tour," said Jack.

"My pleasure. You know, the Operation Deep Freeze Base is where all the flights leave for Antarctica. That's the place where the scientists are outfitted before they leave for the "Ice" as they call it. I used to go there with my mother to see Ian depart for Antarctica."

About twenty minutes later, they passed the Operation Deep Freeze sign and pulled in front of a group of Quonset buildings. Jack expected Driggers to arrive soon, since he had been tailing them for the whole trip from Hagley Park.

"Thanks again," said Jack. "Don't forget, I'd really like to meet Ian. Here's my phone number." He handed her a slip of paper and started to get out of the car, but she leaned over and kissed him on the cheek.

"I was thinking, since tomorrow is Saturday, and if you have the day off, I'd like to take you to Ian's ranch. It's about three hours from here. I still have a key. There might be something there to learn about your father."

"That's where Ian did his private research, right?"

"Yes, that's the place."

"I think I would like that very much," said Jack.

"Great. Where should I collect you?"

Just then, Driggers drove past and parked down the street.

"Right here," said Jack.

"Beaut'. I'll see you here at nine o'clock tomorrow morning."

"She'll be right," said Jack.

Eva giggled.

"Ta!" she replied.

Chapter 11
Russian Gold

Jack gulped down the last spoonful of lukewarm tea, smacking his lips to remove the bitter taste from the sediment at the bottom of the cup. He buttoned his pea coat.

"The weather changes pretty quickly in the South Island, especially in the mountains," said Kettering.

"Eva will keep you warm," said Driggers, motioning an obscene gesture.

"Shut up, Stan. We should be thanking Jack for this new development. Eva inviting him up there is very encouraging. I'm confident Jack will come away from this little escapade with some useful information for us."

"What should I ask her?"

"I don't want her to think you are probing her, but find out if Moon has contacted any foreigners. Get her to talk about his work, and listen for any hints about where the formula is hidden. Use her! We don't have much time. Moon will be returning from Antarctica soon."

Around 8:30 a.m., Driggers dropped Jack off in front of the administration building. The tiny US Antarctic Program Base was unusually quiet for a Saturday morning. The US and New Zealand flags on the flagpole in the center of the circular driveway island flapped wildly in the blustery wind.

"Remember, we'll be following you," said Kettering. "The money is real, Jack. You just have to go out and earn it." He reared around to face Jack, and his eyes narrowed. "I want that formula. Find it!"

Jack stepped out of the car and walked to the front porch of the administration building where Kettering had told him to wait for Eva. The wind blew steadily from the northeast, and fought tenaciously with the remnants of the clear, sunny sky that was quickly disappearing in the west. Driggers parked the car on a side street where he could watch Jack and follow Eva after she picked him up.

As he leaned against the porch railing, Jack watched an Air New Zealand DC-10 take off and quickly disappear into the low, gray ceiling that melded into the horizon. He wondered if the plane was headed for Hawaii. He thought about Grace and what she was doing at the communications station in Honolulu. He wished he were on that plane. His eyes darted nervously from Driggers' car, back to the street, and to the airport terminal in the distance. He thought about making a run for it, but there was a large parking lot and a couple of Air New Zealand aircraft hangars that separated the base from the terminal at Christchurch International. If he sprinted the 500 or so yards, he might beat Driggers to the terminal. But then what would he do? Without money and a passport, he couldn't fly anywhere.

A sailor wearing a blue work jacket approached the porch. Jack noticed the lightning bolts of the radioman rating badge on his jacket sleeve as he passed him on the way to the door. He remembered Driggers telling him that some personnel wore their work uniforms on the base. The sailor nodded a friendly hello, and immediately the wheels began racing in Jack's mind. There had to be a message center in there. He could get a message to Grace.

"Say, I'm a radioman too," said Jack. "I'm new here, working at the transmitter site. Is this where the message center is?"

"Where's your uniform?" asked the radioman.

"Got the day off, and I'm waiting for a friend to pick me up."

The radioman nonchalantly pointed in the direction of a hallway and gave him directions. Jack glanced back at Driggers, remembering his orders not to talk to anyone. Driggers shook his fist at Jack, and was about to step out of his car, when Eva's red Mini turned the corner and approached the circular drive. She honked and waved. Jack half-heartedly waved back, and then stood frozen at the top of the steps. He glanced at the airport, then at the radioman passing through the closing door, and then at Driggers and Kettering across the street. He turned around and stretched his neck to see inside the building. Driggers started his car and inched away from the curb, toward Jack. Eva honked again. The flag flapped in a cacophony of howling wind and smacking fabric.

In the din of it all, he heard a man's voice inside his head. *"Go inside."* The voice sounded like his father's. It seemed to carry in the wind. Against his better judgment, he stepped off the porch and bounded toward Eva's car. He motioned to her to roll down her window.

"What's the matter? You look like you've seen a ghost," said Eva, as a light drizzle began to fall.

"I have to use the restroom. Give me a minute?"

The black Hillman had pulled away from the curb and was inching toward them. Then, it stopped as a group of scientists approached and crossed the street in front of them.

"We can stop at a petrol station if you can wait," said Eva.

"Can't wait. Be back in a flash."

He turned around and darted into the building. Once inside, he went straight to the message center. Teletype machines buzzed with the rat-a-tat-tatting sound in a constant hum of background noise. He recognized a similar message center set in his practical class at radio school.

"Hey, man, I only have a second. Can you send a message for me?"

"I need authorization. Do you have an ID card?"

"Here's my ID. Please, it's to my girl. She's a radioman at NAVCOMM STA, Honolulu, but I need you to send this to her via HAM radio. Use this call sign... ZL5YM. Jack scribbled a note.

4/28/73
In NZ now. Any news from Haskins or Sarah?
Watch your back.
Love, Jack

"Please hurry," begged Jack.

"Is that it?" asked the radioman.

"Yea. Oh, by the way, I'm Jack." He reached out to shake the radioman's hand.

"Phil."

"One more thing… could you keep this to yourself, including any reply you get from her. Oh, and do you have a number I could call you at tomorrow to check back with you?"

Phil wrote the number on a piece of paper and handed it to Jack.

"Thanks, gotta' run. If someone comes in here looking for me, don't tell him I was in here."

"Hey, you sure this is on the up and up?"

"You gotta' trust me. Thanks, man."

"Ah, okay… good luck."

Seconds later, Driggers appeared in the hallway, agitated and out of breath. He disappeared around the corner, and the restroom door banged against the wall. Before he could say anything, Jack appeared, drying his hands on a paper towel.

"Hey, Driggers, what's up? I had to go. What did you want me to do?"

"Don't try anything like that again."

Jack jumped down the steps. He strode to Eva's car, and jumped inside.

"Good morning," said Jack nervously. "I sure am glad to see you. So, where exactly are we headed?"

"Otago, near the Hawkdun Mountains… about a three-hour drive. It looks like we'll be heading into some rainy weather."

Jack took a deep breath and sat back in the seat, staring straight ahead. As he tried to compose himself, she reached across and touched his hand. He glanced at her from the corner of his eye, noticing her tight jeans and pink lamb's wool sweater. Before long, Christchurch faded behind them as they drove through the stormy weather along Route 1, the main north-south highway of the South Island.

They passed patchwork fields of brown and gold bordered by dark green hedgerows. About an hour from Christchurch, near the port city of Timaru, the storm began to worsen. Eva suggested that they stop and wait out the storm. She pulled in front of a small tea shop near a public park. They were drenched when they entered the deserted shop, and sat at a table facing the window, sipping hot tea and watching the howling wind and driving rain spray against the shop window. She pointed to the park across the street.

"Ian would take my mum and me to that park. We would stop here on the way to the ranch, back in happier times."

"You must really miss her."

"Yes, she was my dearest friend, and she deserved better than what Ian gave her in life."

"You really like him, don't you?"

"You sound like Ian... and I don't appreciate the sarcasm either."

"Sorry, I was just joking. I miss my parents too."

"Well, I only miss my mother." She glanced out the window. "Let's change the subject. Let's talk about you. Do you have a girl back home?"

Jack hesitated. He fidgeted with his coffee cup and glanced around the room, trying to resolve the implications of his answer.

"I didn't think it was such a difficult question." She batted her eyelashes and smiled seductively at Jack.

"Yes, her name is Grace. I met her in radio school."

"That's a pretty name. So, you've only known her for a few months? Does she know you are in New Zealand?"

"Of course she does." He looked away, puzzled by the question.

"Do you miss her?"

"I do. I miss a lot of things about her. But, ah... then again, she's not here, and—"

"Storm is letting up. We should get going."

Jack reached for his wallet, but she had already laid down a couple of bills and some change on the table. They stepped outside to find that the rain had changed to a steady drizzle, but the air had turned colder. Jack noticed the black Hillman parked across the street, but pretended not to.

Within a few minutes, they were cruising through the South Canterbury countryside, past neat farms and pastures. Soon, the flat fields morphed into rolling pastureland, with the rugged mountain peaks in the distance. Eva explained that they were leaving the agricultural region of Canterbury and nearing the sheep grazing lands of Otago. They crossed the swollen Waitaki River and climbed the winding road into the foothills of the Hawkdun Range. Huge, gleaming, gray boulders jutted from hillsides, and patches of green pasture grass filled with white specs of sheep spread out for as far as he could see.

They turned off the main road, and Jack noticed a sign on a post for **"Dansy's Pass Road."** It was a narrow, stone chip road that led into a valley surrounded by grassy hillsides. After a couple miles, the road converged on a rain-swollen stream that ran parallel to the road.

"I've only seen one house so far, and it doesn't look like anyone lives around here. Why did he pick such an isolated place?"

"Secrecy. There was something about this area and how he was able to hide his equipment from American satellites. I remember he would go up in the hills with a mule loaded with his equipment. He'd stay up there for a couple of days and then come back with notebooks full of data. Mum and I would be so excited to see him, but then he would disappear into his laboratory. They would quarrel, and then came the bitter silence. Ian could never separate his work from his family."

Eva slowed the car and turned onto a narrow lane, almost striking a dented galvanized mailbox. The name **"I.A. Moon"** was handwritten in permanent marker on the side of the box. Immediately next to the mailbox was a small wooden sign that read in stenciled letters **"Moon Mountain."**

"Moon Mountain. What's that all about?" asked Jack.

"That's the name of ranch. It's my only contribution to the Moon family legacy. I made that sign when I was thirteen. I'm surprised it's still here."

"Catchy name."

"Pity my mother never liked it here. She felt like a visitor, instead of his wife."

Jack remained silent, becoming preoccupied with the worsening weather. Eva steered the car around a sharp curve and drove cautiously along the rutted lane through the driving rain. The small tires of the Mini sunk in the rain-filled potholes, and bounced out with a jolt. About a half-mile down the lane, they came to a narrow wooden bridge. They made it across, just before the rushing water reached the bridge deck.

As they continued past the bridge, a portion of the drive had washed out, and they were forced to leave the car and walk. They headed up a rocky path that led to an overlook. Eva pointed to the ranch, a few hundred yards across a grass field. The house sat on a promontory that overlooked grassy hills and sloped to the creek below. As they neared the house, the clouds broke apart and a stream of sunlight illuminated the mountains beyond. Eva struggled to keep her footing on the slippery rocks as they made their way along the narrow path. Near the top of the hill, she let out a shriek as she slipped and appeared to twist her ankle.

"Are you hurt?" asked Jack. "Can you move it?"

"I think so, but I'm afraid to put my weight on it."

Jack started to take her arm, but stopped when he thought about Kettering, who was most likely watching them. Without saying a word, he bent down and scooped her up. She blushingly accepted his act of chivalry, which he hoped would impress her. He hadn't forgotten his mission. He carried her across the field in the cold, driving rain, not stopping until he reached the front porch.

"Thank you, kind sir, but it doesn't seem to hurt as much now," she said, as she placed her hand on his cheek.

Jack did not respond as he strained to catch his breath. He simply smiled, then bent forward and slid her across his shoulder, easing her to the porch floor. He helped her to the door. As he unlocked the door, a gust of wind flung it open with a bang, startling both of them. She reached across him to switch on the ceiling light, but it didn't work.

"Damn, the electricity is out. It must have been the storm. There's firewood out back to get a fire started."

Jack returned a few minutes later with an armful of firewood, stopping to take a mental inventory of the interior. The great room had a high ceiling with exposed timber beams. There was a large, stone fireplace and hearth on the far wall directly in front of them. The kitchen and two bedrooms adjoined the great room on one side, and a passageway led to a large addition on the other side. A set of stairs led to the second floor bedroom that opened to the loft area above the great room.

"Where did Ian do his work?"

"In the addition on the other side of the passageway. That was his laboratory. I'll show you after we eat. You're shivering. You should get that fire started, and I'll try to find you some dry clothes."

His shivering intensified with each exhaling of vapor in the cold, vacant room, as his trembling hand struck the matchstick. Soon, the crackling flames radiated heat deep into his body, especially his face, which was stinging from the cold. The fire engulfed the larger logs and the room began to warm. Eva returned with some dry clothes.

"I'll fix us something to eat. Why don't you rest?"

Jack removed his soaking wet sweater and laid down on a soft sheepskin rug in front of the fireplace. The spreading warmth felt like a sleeping potion, and he drifted off to sleep. He dreamt of Grace, embracing her as her warm lips pressed gently against his mouth. They were standing on a moonlit sidewalk at Bainbridge, the night before he left. Then Kettering appeared, laughing and sneering as he watched Driggers push Grace, and then his parents into the flames of the fireplace. Jack was helpless. He tried to stop him, but his body wouldn't move. Then it began to snow, and a man and a woman appeared. It was his Aunt Sarah, and a tall, thin, bearded man that must have been Dr. Moon. They were dark and gray in his dream. Then Grace appeared again. She was running to him, screaming "no, no."

"Jack! Jack! Wake up! What's wrong?"

"Huh, what... nothing, I'm fine." He awoke to find Eva standing over him, holding two glasses of wine and what was left of the bottle. "What time is it?" he asked.

"Half past seven. The electricity never did come back on. Here, drink some wine. It'll relax you." She had placed candles around the room.

"That dream was so real. I saw my parents dying, and Ian and Sarah were there... and Drig... it was snowing. It was a cold place. A voice was trying to warn me about something..." he paused upon noticing that Eva had changed into a short, blue dress.

"I didn't realize I left this dress here last Christmas," said Eva. "It's all I could find to wear. What do you think?"

"You look great. Your ankle seems to be much better."

"Yes, fancy that. I must be a fast healer."

Jack could not help but notice how sexy she looked as she walked across the room. He sat on the sofa and pulled up the jeans that Eva gave him, surprised that they fit so well. The roaring fire warmed the spacious room and illuminated the pine shelves filled with books in a cozy glow. The candles around the room provided enough light to see the framed paintings and many photographs composed on the walls on opposite sides of the fireplace. There was a large photograph of Dr. Moon with Aunt Sarah, and another smaller one of a much younger Eva with Ian and her mother. Jack searched for photographs of his parents, but was frustrated that he couldn't find a single one. Eva returned with plates of food and more wine. They sat close together on the sofa, devouring the quiche and drinking wine. Jack looked up at the photograph of a younger Dr. Moon accepting an award.

"What's wrong with his face?"

"Bell's palsy. He got it during the war. He never fully recovered. Some people do, some don't."

"Yea, I know. I've had it for a few months now. It still bothers me. I get pain and twitching in my face."

She turned and looked closely at his face.

"Yea, your eye still droops a little."

"It flares up now and then. Your mother was very pretty. I see where you got your good looks."

"Thank you. Flattery will get you everywhere. You know, I felt something the moment I first saw you at Hagley Park. Is the attraction mutual?"

Jack thought for a second about Kettering and his mission.

"I felt it too. You're very beautiful."

"Thank you, Jack. I think you are a man who is going places in life, destined for big things. More wine?"

He sensed the smoldering attraction between them was about to ignite. He was also beginning to feel the buzz from the wine. Thoughts of Grace and his commitment to her collided with Kettering's demands for the formula, and his own desire to learn more about his father's past. He stood up and walked over to adjust the logs in the fire.

"Do you think we can look around a bit more? I found a flashlight, or should I say, a torch."

Eva giggled.

"We have all day tomorrow. I can show you around then. Come back and sit down. Relax."

Jack picked up a photograph of Dr. Moon. He was receiving some sort of award. At that moment, it occurred to him that Kettering and Driggers had to be somewhere nearby.

"Eva, you said you thought Ian was involved in something sinister involving antimatter. What was that all about again?"

"I thought you came up here to be with me. I saw the way you looked at me when you got in the car at the base."

"I... I'm just a little confounded right now, and I did come up here to be with you. Really I did, but you have to trust me. I want to learn more about my father's past, and I really need to know about Ian and this antimatter business."

"Why do you care about antimatter? Besides, I feel like Sarah or maybe your parents already told you about the formula. Did they, Jack?"

"No, I really don't know anything. I just know that if there is something affecting our national security, then I have a duty to report it to my super heroes... I mean my superiors." He was beginning to feel light-headed. Eva filled his glass with more wine.

"Wait a minute. You came up to find out about the antimatter formula,

81

didn't you? You came up here to use me!" She began to cry.

"No, no, it's not like that. Everything is so confusing to me right now."

He reached out to hold her hand. She buried her head in his shoulder and pressed her breasts against him.

"Kiss me, Jack. I'll tell you whatever I know."

He couldn't hold back any longer. He kissed her warm, pink, lipstick-moistened lips, and kissed her deeply. They melted together across the warm sheepskin in front of the blazing fireplace. But Jack felt light-headed, and the room started to spin. Then everything went blank. That was the last thing he remembered when he awoke the next morning.

"Wake up, sleepy head," said Eva, as she shook him gently. "I made you breakfast."

Jack's head pounded each time she shook him.

"Oh, hey... good morning. I must have drunk too much wine last night. I don't seem to remember. What happened?"

"Nothing, that's the problem. You passed out like a light. You disappointed me. You left me hanging. Never mind that, though. I still owe you something."

"What do you mean?"

"The antimatter formula, I know that's what you're after. I like you, Jack, so I'll tell you this. If there is a formula, Ian has it with him in Antarctica. It's not here."

"Come on, Eva. What about in the laboratory? What about my father? There must be some evidence of their friendship, their correspondence."

"If there is anything in this house about antimatter, or about your father, then it would be in his laboratory. Ian practically lived in there. It was more than a laboratory... it was his study, his retreat, his bedroom. Grab the torch and I'll show you." She led him down a long, dark hallway that ended at a single door. Surprisingly, the door was unlocked.

"I thought for sure this room would be locked. I haven't been in here for years. I was never permitted in here. It was off limits, top secret, like so much of his life. He even discouraged my mother from going in there."

They entered the dark room. Jack flicked the light switch, forgetting that the electricity was still off. Eva opened the blinds to reveal a partially octagonal-shaped room about fifty feet long and equally wide, with a cathedral ceiling. The addition was built on the edge of a rock outcrop, providing a 180-degree view of the distant mountains and a valley below. The walls were filled with electronic equipment, files, and books, and there was a large desk in the center of the room. The stagnant air tinged with the smell of radio equipment that reminded him of his classes. In the far corner was a spiral staircase that led to a loft.

"What's up there?" asked Jack.

"A telescope. There's also a door in the cupola that takes you up to a

82

satellite dish on the roof."

They searched for an hour, examining the contents of drawers and file cabinets. Jack desperately sifted through papers and reports, hoping to find anything to take back to Kettering. He secretly hoped to find any bit of evidence of his father's past, as well as Dr. Moon's connection to his parents. He became excited by the search as he wandered around examining diplomas and photographs on the walls. He found a framed article from the Christchurch Star… **"Scientist Closes in on Dark Energy."**

Then Eva yelled from the back of the room.

"Come here! I found something." She stood in front of an old trunk that she had pulled out from the back of a closet. It was full of items and memorabilia from Ian's life. There were photos from his childhood, photos of his parents, newspaper clippings, and other mementos. "Look at this. It's a letter with a US return address. Albert Trane… isn't that your father?"

"Holy hell. Let me see that." He yanked the typewritten letter from the envelope, and read it in an instant. Then, his jaw dropped.

"What is it?" asked Eva. She bent down and picked up the letter, and began to read it.

March 5, 1972

Dear Ian,

>*Someone is watching our house. You are putting our lives in danger. Marie is terrified. She thinks you are talking to the Soviets, and I'm beginning to think she's right. I don't know what you are up to, but I'm telling you again that I desperately need the money you owe me, or I'll lose everything. I can't pass anything more to Sarah until you pay me. Why are you threatening me? I told you I wouldn't go to the FBI. For God's sake, I saved your life. Doesn't that mean anything to you?*

>*Please, I'm begging you.*

Albert

Eva stared at Jack with a look of empathy.

"I knew it. I'm so sorry, Jack. I told you Ian was up to something. I'm sure he has developed an antimatter weapon, and he's going to sell it to the Russians. We've got to do something."

"Wait a minute, don't get hysterical. I can't believe my parents were involved in something like this. I mean come on… my mother, how could she be a spy? This is probably just a big mistake. I need more proof."

83

"You're being naïve. Don't you realize the implications of all this. We are talking about World War III. This is serious! If I were you, I would give some thought to some of the strange coincidences in your life."

"Like what?"

"You said your parents were killed in a house explosion. What if Ian was behind it? What if he had Soviet agents kill your parents? According to that letter, your mother thought their house was being watched. Think about it. Ian stops paying your father. Your father stops sending Ian's research to Sarah. Maybe Ian had your parents killed to cover his tracks."

Jack stood motionless, staring out the window.

"Jack, are you listening to me? What's wrong with you?"

"I don't know what to think. Nothing makes any sense," he yelled, banging his fist on the file cabinet.

"Calm down. Let's keep looking." After a few minutes, she yelled out again. "Jack, get over here. Take a look at this. I think there is a recess behind this file cabinet."

"How'd you spot that?"

"I don't know. It just looked odd to me."

Together they pulled out the first cabinet, exposing a small, single drawer cabinet recessed in the wall behind it. Eva opened the drawer. She felt inside and retrieved a heavy, zippered canvas bag. She excitedly unzipped the bag, revealing something shiny inside.

"Oh my God, these are sixteen ounce gold bars," said Eva, as she examined each of them. "There must be twenty of them."

"Okay, so he invests in gold bars. Big deal."

"Russian gold bars. Take a look at the inscription on the back of this one. It's in Russian. He and your aunt are involved in some questionable business."

"Wait a minute—"

"Jack, I'm sorry about getting you involved. I'm sorry about your father. Seems like neither of us knew that much about our fathers."

"Well, I do feel like I owe you. As much as it sickens me, I guess I'm glad I learned about this mess."

"Oh, you're so sweet." She grasped his hand and pulled him toward her. She kissed him passionately, but he pulled back.

"Eva, are you sure the formula isn't here? Are you sure Ian has it with him in Antarctica?"

"My God, why are you worried about that right now? For the last time, I'm sure he has it with him in Antarctica. If you want to try and persuade him to cooperate, then that's where you have to go."

"Okay, thanks. I'm going to tell my commanding officer about this."

"Yes, you should—" They were interrupted by a loud tapping that progressed to a thunderous knocking at the front door. The sound echoed throughout the house.

"Who could that be?" asked Jack. "Are you expecting someone?"

Eva shrugged her shoulders. Jack stepped softly, moving toward the great room. Eva kept up with him, then whispered for him to wait while she got a gun from her bedroom. The banging continued. She tiptoed into the hallway, with both hands locked around a small revolver.

"Don't worry, I know how to use one of these. Ian was away so much, my mother and I took shooting lessons to protect ourselves."

They both peaked through the single eight-inch square glass light in the door.

"Do you recognize him?" Jack whispered.

She shook her head no. Jack unlocked and slowly opened the heavy wooden door. Eva stood directly behind him, stretching her neck around his shoulder. Jack propped the wooden screen door open with his foot. A tall, gray-haired man in rain gear and gum boots stood looking down at them.

"Can I help you?" asked Jack.

"Gidday. Mind if I ask if you're friends of the Doc?"

Eva stepped in front of Jack.

"I'm Eva, Ian Moon's stepdaughter. And you are?"

"Why, of course you are... little Eva. I haven't seen you since you were a little girl. You probably don't remember me. My name's Ted McClintock. I got a little spread just over that hill. The Doc asked me to watch the place while he was away. I saw the cars down below and figured someone might be up here. I figured you walked up, since the bridge was flooded. It's safe to cross now though. I reckon most of the area is without power too. Clive Walker... he's got a ranch on the other side of those hills over there. He says he heard the Electric Board announced that the power will probably be out for another day. That was some storm... say, you're a Yank."

Jack paused for a moment to take a mental inventory of the tall, white-haired man, with a wrinkled, weathered face. His huge hands wrapped around the porch post.

"Yep. My name's Jack. I'm a radioman with the US Navy Antarctic Program in Christchurch. I'm pleased to meet you."

Ted smiled as he reached across to shake Jack's hand, which disappeared in his huge grip.

"Pleased to meet you too. This place doesn't get too many visitors this time of year, unless of course the Doc is around. Matter of fact, you're the only ones been here in months. Except old Clive thought he saw a couple of jokers up here earlier today. Was that you two?"

"No, we came yesterday... during the storm," said Eva. "Maybe he was mistaken."

"I don't think so. Clive said they came in the same black Hillman that was parked down by the bridge. Is that your car, or are you the red Mini?"

"The Mini is mine. I don't know anything about the black car, or who drove it here. Maybe they were hikers. If you don't mind, we have to tend to the fire and find some candles before nightfall."

An ever-so-slight smirk appeared on Ted's wrinkled face.

"That's right, Miss. It's gonna' be frosty. You'll need a mighty fire tonight.

But I don't think you'll need the candles. Doc has a small petrol generator in the back shed. It's a little persnickety, but once you get her going she performs just fine. It'll run the pump, a few lights, and make you hot water for tea. Why don't you come with me, Yank, and I'll show you how she works."

"Fine by me," said Jack.

Ted led him around the house past a small kitchen garden by the back porch. It was still full of kale, turnips and carrots.

"Doc loves to garden. He and Miss Sarah planted this little patch last spring."

"Do you know Dr. Moon personally?" asked Jack.

"Right-O. Me and the Doc go way back. We served together in the war. There's no finer man than Doc Moon." He motioned Jack toward the shed. "The generator is in here." He opened the door and waited for Jack.

"So, you're saying Dr. Moon is an honorable man, not likely to betray his country."

"What in God's name are you talking about, man? I know the Doc is a bit eccentric, but he would never do something like that."

Jack breathed a small sigh of relief.

"Give me a hand lifting this. So, are you her boyfriend?"

"Well, uh… no, not really. I just met her the other day."

"I don't see you two as a match."

"Eva invited me up here to find out what I could about my father. He saved Dr. Moon's life during the war. I just arrived in New Zealand a few weeks ago. I thought I might learn something about him up here."

"So, you say your father is Albert Trane?" asked Ted.

Jack, surprised that Ted knew his father's name, dropped his end of the generator as they pulled it from the shed.

"Yes, how'd you know that?"

"I told you, I've known the Doc most of my life. I've heard him speak highly of your father, the man who saved his life and inspired him to excel in science. Matter of fact, both he and Sarah mentioned you and your folks many times, in a good light."

He placed his hand on Jack's shoulder and tipped his bush hat back, revealing a balding forehead. His deep, placid eyes scanned Jack's face. He froze for a moment and glanced across the tall tussock grass in the field behind the house. Then, he returned to studying Jack's face.

"There's something familiar about you, son. I can't put my finger on it. You bear a fairly smart resemblance to a young Ian. Your mouth is a bit crooked, too."

"It's Bell's palsy."

"What a coincidence, that's just like the Doc. Say, you're not in any kind of trouble are you?"

Jack shook his head unconvincingly.

"No, everything is okay. Why do you ask?"

"That black Hillman is coming up the drive. It'll be out front in a couple

86

minutes. It looks like there are two jokers in the front seat. I'm afraid I will have to leave you for now."

"Wait, Ted. Do you know anything about Dr. Moon's antimatter research? Do you know anything about the formula?"

"I just know it belongs to the Doc. Beware of that Colonel joker. Do not trust him."

"How did you know about Kettering?"

"I talk to the Doc and Sarah on HAM radio. But I gotta' go now."

"Wait a minute. Tell them you talked to me. Tell my aunt I need to hear from her. I mean Sarah."

"Of course, lad."

He turned and scrambled up the steep, rocky path in back of the barn. He moved nimbly for a man his age. The last thing Jack saw as Ted disappeared behind the shed was the silhouette of his huge, waving hand.

Chapter 12
Sins of the Father

Jack walked slowly toward the generator in the middle of the yard. A cold gust of wind blew across the paddock and set in motion an eddy of leaves that had fallen from a nearby Mountain beech tree. The frosty wind nipped his face. He stopped for a moment to rub a painful twinge in his cheek, and immediately sensed that he was not alone.

"Where's the old man?" asked Kettering.

The sound of the familiar, steely voice stopped Jack dead in his tracks. He spun around to the unnerving sight of Kettering and Driggers standing on the back porch on either side of Eva. For an instant, the three of them gave the appearance of an evil comic book trio. Except Eva, Jack thought, did not belong with those two.

"They said they are US military from your base in Christchurch. Do you know them?"

"I don't know," said Jack.

"You don't know these men?" asked Eva.

"No. I mean yes, I know them, but I don't know where the old man went. He said he was watching the ranch while Dr. Moon was away. He showed me how to start the generator, and then he said he had to leave. He went that way toward the valley... said he was going to walk back to his ranch." He hesitated, and pointed in the opposite direction of where Ted had headed.

"Stan, go check it out."

"Jack, what's all this about? Colonel Kettering says he has come to take you back to Christchurch," said Eva.

"Please let me explain, Miss Silk," said Kettering. "We need to take Jack back to Christchurch, because our flight to Antarctica has been moved up to tomorrow."

"Antarctica!" cried Jack. "What do you mean Antarctica? You never said anything about going to Antarctica."

"You're correct, but you understood when you joined the Navy that you go where the Navy needs you," said Kettering. "The mission has changed, and now you are needed in Antarctica."

"What does the Navy do in Antarctica?" asked Eva.

"We monitor Soviet satellite communications to verify their adherence to the Antarctic Treaty, which prohibits military activity."

"Is it dangerous?" asked Eva.

"Not typically," said Kettering.

"Is this the officer you were telling me about, Jack?" asked Eva.

"Yea, it's him."

"Maybe you should show him what we found in the laboratory."

"Right. I was planning to tell you, sir. As a matter of fact, Eva and I were searching the house today for information about my father. Eva's stepfather,

Dr. Moon, knew him during the war."

"Colonel, I think my stepfather is involved in some type of espionage, and I think it involves the Soviets. We found some Russian gold bars in the lab."

"Why are you so keen to reveal this to me?" asked Kettering. "These are very serious allegations."

As Eva hesitated to answer, Driggers stepped out of the hedgerow on the far side of the paddock and jogged toward the back porch. For a brief moment, Jack thought that the silhouette of Driggers' gangly frame against the late-afternoon autumn sky resembled Ted. Part of him hoped that it really was Ted, but he was also relieved that he had gotten away.

"There is no trace of him," said Driggers. "Either he's pretty quick for an old man, or he just disappeared into thin air."

"Forget about him for now," said Kettering. "Eva, would you show Stan the items from the laboratory. I'd like to take a look at them too, if you don't mind."

After she and Driggers left, Kettering walked in circles around the yard with his head down, saying nothing to Jack, who was sitting on the porch step. Then, he turned and looked in the direction of the far paddocks and the view into the valley beyond.

"Magnificent view up here," said Kettering. "Gorgeous country, isn't it? The Kiwis call this "God's Country." Do you feel close to God up here, Jack?"

"I suppose," said Jack, sounding rather confused. "What about Antarctica, sir? Are you serious about leaving tomorrow?"

"Yes, but don't worry about that. Antarctica will set you free. You'll learn the truth there, and then you'll be free. You are Catholic, right?"

"Uh, yes, but— "

"So, you have faith that your sacraments will connect you to God and lead you to eternal life?"

His question caught Jack off guard. He couldn't imagine Kettering as someone who knew anything about Catholicism.

"Yes, something like that."

"I don't believe in God. Do you know why? Because, I don't want to waste my time caring about something I can't see, or quantify, or possess. Right and wrong, good and evil... those things matter to religious people like you, but they don't mean a thing to me, because I don't have any faith in anyone or anything, except myself."

"That's a pity you feel that way. I happen to believe that God lives in each of us... even you."

"Ha! God certainly did not reside in me or my parents, or he would have helped me when I was a kid. Instead, I was left to figure out the world on my own." He grabbed Jack's arm, as he became increasingly aggressive. He yanked him into a sitting position on the porch step, and then coldly and emotionlessly proceeded to unwind the taut spring of misery that surrounded his childhood.

"I grew up believing that life was cruel and unfair. My father left home after I was born. My mother remarried, and I was cursed with Carl, my miserable stepfather. From the time I could remember, I hated him for what he did to my mother and me. He was a lazy, drunken bastard... a gambler and a grifter who lived in and out of every bar in South Chicago. I spent most of my childhood hoping that he would come home sober and not beat us. He never showed any emotion toward me, and he drained the life out of my mother. I went from hoping he would leave some day to hoping he would die. Do you know what it's like to watch your drunken stepfather come home from the bar, walk into the kitchen, and bash your mother's face into the table? Where was God when my bruised and bloody mother sat staring at the floor for hours, while that bastard slept off his booze?"

"I'm sorry. That must have been horrible." Jack wanted to pity Kettering, but it made him feel very uncomfortable. It was like feeling sorry for the schoolyard bully after he had just punched you.

"Don't be sorry. It helped me learn that praying or hoping leads to nothing. The only thing that matters is helping yourself. I knew my mother couldn't protect me, so I had to protect myself. I learned to do that very well. So, when I couldn't take being hit anymore, and when I saw that my mother had cracked from the suffering, I acted. I left, but not before I watched Carl trip and fall in front of a speeding subway train, killing him instantly. I think he tripped on the pant legs of a young boy standing on the platform. Yea, he tripped. My mother saw the train hit him. I thought she would be happy. Instead, shortly after that, she lost her mind and was committed to a mental institution. I never saw her again. At the age of thirteen, I became a ward of the State of Illinois, spending the rest of my youth in Chicago orphanages and juvenile detention homes."

"What happened after that?"

"I got my GED in the orphanage and finished two years of college before I joined the Marine Corps. I made second lieutenant in two years without help from anyone. You and I have something in common. We are both alone in the world... no parents, no family. The difference between you and me is you let religion control you. I would rather control people and manipulate them to get what I want. Do you know what it's like to savor the fear in someone's eyes when you have complete control over them?"

"I believe we must serve God, and that he will provide," said Jack.

"You believe that crap, after your parents left you nothing when they died? How fair is it that some kids are born with a silver spoon in their mouth and get their start in life with a check or a trust fund? Look at you. You got nothing! Doesn't that make you mad? Go ahead, be religious and see what it gets you. It'll get you shit! Wake up! Be a man! Go to Antarctica and take what is yours. Persuade your aunt to get Moon to work for us instead of the Soviets. That's all you have to do to be set for life."

Driggers interrupted from the back porch.

"Hey Colonel, she wasn't kidding. Those are real Russian gold bars."

Eva appeared in the doorway with him.

"Miss Silk, your stepfather may have committed a very serious crime," said Kettering.

"I can't believe I'm saying this, but I think I agree with you," said Eva.

Then Jack jumped up.

"How can you all judge and convict him before you even talk to him? Maybe he has an explanation. Why don't you wait until he gets back from Antarctica? Then we can hear what he has to say."

"I don't think he is planning to return on a US Navy plane... maybe a Russian plane," said Kettering.

"Wait a minute, if my aunt and Dr. Moon are at McMurdo, why don't you just radio the commanding officer there and have them detained?"

"I'm not stupid, Trane." He motioned for Jack to come closer, and whispered to him. "I have already ordered the commanding officer at McMurdo to conduct surveillance on them, but not to draw attention to it. Moon is known to be erratic, and I can't take a chance on him destroying the formula if he thinks he is being threatened." Then he turned to Eva.

"Miss Silk, I'm sorry if I've disrupted your weekend with Jack, and I feel terrible about these revelations, but I'm afraid that I have to take Jack away from you, too. We must get back to the base, right away."

"It wouldn't make any difference to me," said Eva. "I don't care what happens to Ian or that hateful Sarah."

"What if you're wrong about both of them? What if they're actually working on something that's good for mankind?"

Eva didn't reply, but instead stormed off to retrieve her things, slamming the door behind her. Kettering chuckled.

"Stan, stay here with Jack. I'm going to take another look around the lab before we leave."

He entered the dimly lit laboratory and surveyed the boxes and files scattered on the tables. He moved from box to box like a cat burglar in the midst of a big heist. After a few minutes, he settled on the old trunk that Eva and Jack had found. He opened the dusty lid, and lifted out a shoebox of photos and a stack of newspaper clippings. He shuffled through some photos of Dr. Moon in Antarctica. A few of them had dates on the back, including one of a youthful Dr. Moon and Sarah standing in front of the science building at the University of Canterbury, dated November 1951.

He set the photos down and began sifting through the stack of newspaper clippings. One clipping in particular caught his attention. It was from the Pittsburgh Press, dated June 1956. It was a short article about Sarah graduating from the University of Pittsburgh with a Masters Degree in physics. He lifted it out, and a black and white photo fell out of the folds. It was a photograph of Albert and Marie with baby Jack, dated August 1954, with the words **"Jack's Second Birthday"** written on the back. He paused to scan articles from New Zealand newspapers about Moon's accomplishments. Near the bottom of the trunk was an article from a Greensburg, Pennsylvania newspaper about Sarah taking a teaching position at Saint Mark, dated March 1962.

Satisfied that there was nothing more to be found, Kettering gathered up the clippings and photos that he had set aside, and stuffed them in his briefcase. He took one final look around the room, which ended at the framed photo of Dr. Moon with Eva and Sarah on the mantle. He stood glued for five minutes, concentrating on each figure in the photo. Then finally, his deep, black eyes widened until the whites disappeared. He bolted from the room to confront Jack, who was leaning on the back porch railing, staring at the distant valley.

"Colonel, you look like you saw a ghost," said Driggers.

Jack turned around to face Kettering, who was studying his face with a sinister gleam in his eyes.

"Jack, are you feeling better now. I couldn't help but notice your face looked, so... so strained earlier. You must relax, Jack. Things are looking up. Soon, you will know the truth. We will all know the truth. We must get back to Christchurch right away." He turned to Eva. "You will have to ride with us, Eva. Stan said your car has two flat tires, and you've only got one spare."

"I can't imagine how that happened. It must have been that oaf, Ted."

"He seemed like a nice guy to me," said Jack, glancing back at the ranch as the car descended the winding drive.

The galvanized roof reflected the last rays of the setting sun. Jack thought he saw a tall, silhouetted figure step out from behind the house. He looked again, but the figure was gone. He slept for most of the three-hour trip back to Christchurch, and they arrived at the base around 10:00 p.m. Cindy was waiting in a car to meet them. A sailor strode from the administration building and greeted Kettering with a stack of papers.

"Here are your messages, sir," said the sailor.

Jack looked up after recognizing Phil's voice, the radioman who had helped him earlier. Phil noticed that Jack looked panicky, and he purposely looked away so as to not bring attention to him.

"Is that all, sir?" asked Phil.

"Yes, that's all for now. But I will need to use the message center for a couple hours later tonight. I have classified messages to prepare, and I don't want to be disturbed."

Phil nodded, then turned sharply and darted into the building. Kettering wistfully paged through the messages, then turned to Eva.

"Cindy will drive you home, Miss Silk. I am sorry for any inconvenience. I'll arrange for the towing and repair of your car. Thank you for your help."

Eva shot a glare at Jack, then gave a curt goodnight and departed with Cindy.

"Was that the radioman who was on duty this morning?" asked Kettering.

Jack hesitated for a moment as he thought about his reply.

"Uh, I don't remember."

"Do you want me to check with him about bunking here at the base tonight?" asked Driggers.

"Yes, see to it. Get some sleep. Tomorrow, we fly to Antarctica."

The next morning, Jack and Driggers stood in the chilly morning air outside the dining hall behind a large group of Navy Seabees and scientists waiting for breakfast. The chow line was usually longer on days with departing flights to Antarctica. Driggers was characteristically impatient when he wanted to eat. When they finally entered the warm dining hall, Driggers took his anger out on the master at arms. The burly chief petty officer appeared to be in no mood for his lip, and threatened to report him if he didn't shut up.

Jack stayed in the background, hoping for a miracle, that Driggers would be put on report. Then, he could slip off to the message center to see if Phil had heard anything from Aunt Sarah or Grace. Unfortunately, Driggers calmed down and struck up a conversation with the chief about Vietnam. Jack noticed an exit door a few feet away, and was about to step outside, when someone tapped him on the shoulder.

"Hey, I got some news from your aunt," said a voice from behind him.

"Phil! Holy hell, it's good to see you. Listen, man. I can't let you-know-who over there see me talking to you."

"No problem. I just got off the midnight shift, and I got this message from the radioman at McMurdo in Antarctica. It's from your aunt."

Jack glanced at Driggers, who was still laughing and talking to the chief. Jack read the short message.

To: RM3 Jack Trane, NavCommU, Christchurch NZ
From: Sarah Mechling, McMurdo Station, Antarctica
(via RM2 Pratt)

Jack,

> *I want to come home to Saint Mark. I am afraid of Ian. It is for the best. I will explain when I return to Christchurch at the end of May. Maybe the Colonel is right.*

Love, Aunt Sarah

"Jesus, this doesn't sound right," said Jack. "Is it possible the message could have been doctored?"

"Yea, it's possible."

"Who is Pratt?"

"He's a son-of-a-bitch. I don't like him, and I wouldn't trust anything you get from him. Anyway, I saw on today's flight manifest that you are going to the "Ice." You're on the 11:45 a.m. flight this morning. I'd stay away from Pratt once you get down there."

"Thanks, I really appreciate this. Can you do me one more favor? Can you send this message to Grace like you did before?"

Jack scribbled a quick note and handed it to him.

Grace,

Have you heard from Sarah on HAM? I am leaving with CK for Antarctica today. Hopefully will see the Dr. and all will be well.

Love, Jack

"No problem. Oh and by the way, your Colonel friend was in the message center until about 3:00 a.m. last night. He made me sit in the hallway while he typed up his messages. He sent them himself... seemed pretty intent on me not seeing what he was doing. He took the teletype tapes with him too. The thing is, our machine acts up sometimes and makes duplicate tapes. I found a piece of one inside the machine."

"Do you know what it said, or who he sent it to?" asked Jack.

"The only thing I could make out was a couple of addressees on one of the messages. One was to the Social Security Administration, and the other to some hospital in Pittsburgh. Who knows what these officers are up to in their spare time?"

"Yea, that's for sure," said Jack. "You better get going. I owe you one. I'll buy you a beer when I get back."

"Good luck, man," said Phil, as he disappeared out the side entrance.

Jack began to wonder what Kettering had been doing in the message center. Why did he send a message to a hospital in Pittsburgh, and why the sudden change in Aunt Sarah's attitude toward Dr. Moon? And why hadn't he heard from Grace? As his thoughts swirled, he began to feel sick in his stomach, and his face began to twitch.

"Hey, Trane," Driggers called. "You better get your shit together. In less than ten hours your ass will be in forty-below temps. Now come on, let's eat. We got a lot to do this morning."

After breakfast, Kettering and Driggers went back to the message center, while Jack and Cindy assembled bundles of arctic gear for each of them. Each bundle had a complete outfit of insulated underwear, special insulated bubble boots, down-filled snowsuits, and goggles. Kettering sent an airman over to pick up Jack and Cindy and the bundles of gear. He drove them to meet Kettering and Driggers, who were already seated in the C-130 Ski-Equipped Hercules.

Kettering was unusually upbeat, and even joked with Jack about what to expect if he joins the "300 Club" at McMurdo, which is an honor bestowed on those hearty souls who endure a 200 degree sauna and then plunge naked into the outside temperature of 100 degrees below zero, thus enduring a temperature swing of 300 degrees.

The four-engine, propeller-driven cargo plane sat with engines idling at the far end of the runway, the same one Jack arrived on a few weeks earlier. A small group of passengers, mostly scientists, boarded the plane ahead of them. Within minutes, they were taxiing toward the runway. Suddenly, the plane braked and came to a halt a few yards from the runway. An airman opened the hatch, and Jack heard an exchange of voices. One in particular sounded familiar. It was Phil, who approached Kettering carrying a folder.

"Sir, I have an "Immediate" classified message for you that just came in. My supervisor thought we could catch you before you took off."

Kettering, who was sitting by the window, reached across Cindy for the folder. At the same moment, Phil appeared to stumble, and he dropped the folder behind Cindy. It landed by Jack's foot in the aisle, and a few of the papers fell out. Phil quickly bent over and scooped up the papers. But before he stood up, he placed a folded piece of paper under Jack's foot.

"Excuse me, sir," said Phil. "I'm so sorry."

"You clumsy idiot." Kettering grabbed the folder from Phil and signed a form on the clipboard that Phil had handed him. Phil nodded apologetically, and quickly walked away.

A few minutes later, the Navy Hercules rumbled down the runway and climbed into the cold, blue-gray sky, bound for Antarctica. Jack reached down and grabbed the folded paper, and quickly slid it into his pocket. He waited until the seatbelt light went off, then told Driggers that he had to use the head. Driggers walked back with him, as had become customary at this point, and stood outside the door. After Jack closed and locked the door, he frantically unfolded the paper. It was a handwritten message from Phil.

From: Grace via Ted on HAM
To: Jack

    Sarah says not to go to Antarctica with Kettering. It is not safe. I will try to help you.

Love, Grace

Jack quickly ripped the message in small pieces and flushed it down the toilet. He walked to his seat, ignoring Driggers' presence. What kind of plot had Kettering cooked up? He closed his eyes and thought about Grace. How was she possibly going to help in Antarctica?

Chapter 13
For Jack

Grace jogged along the beach path, glancing warily behind her to make sure that she wasn't being followed. After twenty minutes of running, she finally felt comfortable that she was alone. She relaxed and spread her arms like a sail to catch the warm afternoon breeze that gently blew off the Pacific Ocean, choreographing a cluster of nearby coconut palms to dance in the wind. The oceanfront path was part of the Pearl Harbor Park System, a place she was drawn to from the first day she arrived in Honolulu. It reminded her of being with Jack. She slowed her pace and jogged to a bench beside a huge, black boulder underneath one of the palms. Reggie was to meet her there at 5 o'clock.

She stretched her legs and glanced at her wristwatch… 4:45. She sat down and gazed far out to sea, past the inlet to Pearl Harbor where a naval ship was returning to port. She reached in the pocket of her white running shorts and pulled out the familiar photograph that Reggie had taken of her and Jack at the graduation party at the club at Bainbridge, the week before graduation. She could still feel the touch of his arm around her waist, and the long, warm softness of his kiss. She gazed at the ocean, slipping deep into thought, mesmerized by the ultramarine blue waves lapping against the rocks along the shore.

That memorable evening might never have happened if it wasn't for Reggie. He arranged for Grace and Jack to meet on their first date back at Bainbridge. He could see that Jack really liked her, but he wasn't moving fast enough to suit Reggie. So, Reggie took matters into his own hands. On an unusually mild Saturday afternoon in January, he and Jack set out for a six-mile run around the base. It wasn't a coincidence that Reggie said he had pulled a muscle in front of Grace's barracks on the last mile. Nor was it a coincidence that Reggie had called Grace beforehand to say that he and Jack would be running by, and that he could stop to show her exercises for her workout. That was all it took. Jack and Grace spent every Saturday together after that. Grace never did find the time for Reggie to show her those exercises.

The breeze was calm now, and barely moved the coconut palm fronds. The waves lapped lightly against the weathered rocks. Grace closed her eyes and listened to the rhythm of the waves, and her thoughts went right to Jack. She was terribly worried about him, and all she could see were his warm, sincere eyes full of suffering and anxiety, a pain she could feel across the ocean.

"Hey! Wake up, girl. Sorry I'm late."

"Reggie, thank God you came. I'm so glad to see you. Were you able to get it?"

"Yep. I did just what you said. My mother wasn't too happy about lying, especially about a made-up, near-death illness afflicting my dad, but the Red Cross bought it. The communications officer approved four weeks of leave.

Apparently, it was no big deal since our ship will be in Hono' for repairs for at least a month. I packed mostly civilian clothes like you said, and checked into the transit barracks. Why did you pick this place?"

"I couldn't take a chance of us being seen together, especially with both of us staying in the transit barracks."

"So you think Jack is in some kind of trouble?"

"Yes. I think it's pretty serious too. Do you remember before we left Bainbridge last month, I told you I received a message from Jack via one of the radiomen at Travis Air Force Base? He said Jack was going to New Zealand with that Colonel Kettering, and he wanted me to contact his aunt. I knew right away he was in trouble."

"Let me tell you, Jack was frightened of that dude, Kettering. He told me a little about his father and some scientist, but it seemed like he was in the middle of a puzzle that was missing a lot of pieces. I told him not to worry, and that the Navy would take care of him when he got to New Zealand."

"That's just it, the Navy is not going to take care of him. When I first arrived here in Honolulu, I went to my C.O. and told him about Jack. I asked him to send a message to the Bureau of Naval Personnel (BUPERS), inquiring on the status of RM3 Jack Trane."

"So, what'd they say?"

Grace looked Reggie in the eye. She turned pale and started to shake.

"BUPERS sent a reply. They said Jack was dishonorably discharged from Bainbridge, the same day he left in the helicopter with Colonel Kettering. I asked my C.O. to look into it, but he was convinced there was nothing he could do."

"Oh my God! So that means there's no record of Jack in this "Canoe Club." His ass is hanging out there, man. Wait, we could contact Haskins. He would have a record of Jack's transfer from Bainbridge. Although, come to think of it, I don't remember seeing Jack with a packet of orders. But everything was happening so quickly, so—"

"Reggie, he probably never had any orders… and it gets worse. I went back and begged my C.O. to contact Haskins and inquire about Jack's whereabouts. Bainbridge sent a reply that said Haskins had taken unscheduled leave, and his whereabouts were unknown. So, I decided to call Higgins, who was still in Bainbridge. Higgins, if you remember, was friendly with Haskins' secretary, Mildred, and I thought he might know where Haskins went. Well, I just don't know what to think…" she trailed off, and her voice quivered and she began to cry. "Higgins told me Haskins was killed in a car accident. His car supposedly swerved off the road and plunged into the Susquehanna River not far from Bainbridge, a few days after he left on leave. Higgins said the police ruled it an accident, so no autopsy was performed. What's more, Haskins was separated from his wife, so there was no way to find out why he took the leave or where he was going."

"Wouldn't Mildred know?"

"Higgins did say Mildred thought he was going to Washington to talk to someone about Jack, but—"

"But what?"

"Higgins said Mildred took a leave of absence too, and that no one knows where she is."

Reggie reached out and hugged Grace, and tried to comfort her.

"Grace, Jack really is in a world of shit. What are we going to do?"

"That's what I've been struggling with since I watched him leave Bainbridge in that helicopter. That's why I took thirty days leave now. I know Jack needs me."

"Jack's a pretty smart guy. Maybe he's figured a way out of this."

"Oh, Reggie, you're the eternal optimist. But let me tell you, I'm scared! Jack told me to watch my back, and he was right. Lately, I feel like I'm being watched. A new radioman transferred to our station last week, and I swear he seems to be everywhere I go. That's why I sent you that message. When I heard your ship was coming in for repairs, I figured you could take leave."

"That was pretty slick, you sending me a duplicate copy of a garbled AP Sports News to our ship and inserting your message in the recap of the Cleveland Indians game. You knew I'd surely be reading that. But what the heck do you think I did when I saw the note? I'll tell you what I did... I tore it off the teletype so fast I almost pulled the whole roll out. Luckily, no one saw me. That was so cool though! Look I saved the teletype tape."

He unrolled it and began to read it back to Grace.

RBI, #7%tak 30 dy-leave H*ono now. 4 J. train+ Sa ur mom (@sik. after Indians k8*^took the lead %%on a m.,Me+et me@ 5 eve bal Parkl&* perl Bench($2 3 ? by &4p /z pa+lm ta.//rees.

"I knew it was about Jack. So, the first thing I did was head to personnel and put in for the leave."

"Thanks, Reggie. You really are a devoted friend to Jack and me. I couldn't do this alone."

"Everything's cool. I'd do anything for Jack, especially after what he did for me. You remember the weed incident when I got in trouble with shore patrol?"

"How could I forget?"

Though Jack and Reggie often looked back and laughed about that incident, it would have been disastrous for Reggie if Jack hadn't come to his aid. Reggie would have faced a Captain's Mast and probably would have been court-martialed and dishonorably discharged, maybe even faced brig time. The Navy did not tolerate any form of drug abuse. It didn't matter that Reggie never actually smoked weed. What mattered was that he had it in his pocket.

The incident happened a couple of weeks after Jack first got Bell's palsy, and after the ordeal with his meeting with Haskins. It was a Saturday night, and Reggie and a couple of other sailors had gone to the enlisted club. Afterwards, they took a taxi to another club off base, a seedy, redneck joint that Haskins had declared off limits. A couple of local guys made a few racial slurs to Reggie, and a fight broke out. Brooks, a black friend of Reggie's, was beaten up pretty badly. The shore patrol arrived, and in the confusion, someone planted a bag of marijuana in Reggie's coat pocket, which the shore patrol found when they frisked him. They took Brooks to sick bay and put Reggie in a cell at the base security building.

Later that night, Jack got word that Reggie was in trouble. Many of the guys in the barracks said Reggie was probably guilty and deserved what he got, but not Jack. He raced out of the barracks and found Brooks at sick bay. Brooks explained what really happened. Then, Jack went to the shore patrol and asked to see Reggie. Ordinarily, they would not have allowed a visitor, but Jack knew the chief petty officer on duty. He was always asking Jack for landscaping advice.

Jack sat outside the cell bars and listened to Reggie's story. At one point, Reggie broke down and cried. He told Jack he was innocent, but that no one would believe him. Jack felt so bad that he began to cry too. After Jack heard the full story from Reggie, he took a taxi to Haskins' house on the other side of the base and waited on his front porch until Haskins came out in his pajamas to get the Sunday paper. Haskins thought Jack was drunk after seeing him sleeping against the porch column, and he almost called shore patrol. Instead, he woke Jack and demanded an explanation. Jack deftly described the incident to Haskins, and ardently defended Reggie in such a sincere manner that Haskins ended up driving Jack to base security and personally ordered the chief to release Reggie.

Reggie started to laugh as they recalled the story.

"What's funny?" asked Grace.

"I'm just thinking about Jack and me crying outside my cell. His Bell's palsy really did make him look like Popeye, like he was laughing and crying at the same time."

"You would have been in a real mess if it hadn't been for Jack."

"Now it's my turn to help him. So, what are we going to do?"

"I don't know. I'm really puzzled. Last week, I received a message from a radioman at McMurdo Station in Antarctica. He relayed a message from Jack's Aunt Sarah. She said that she and this Dr. Moon were fine and they were going to fly back to Christchurch and clear up the mess for Jack. She said that Jack would be safe, and that I shouldn't worry."

"Well, there you go. That's good news. His aunt seems to have everything under control. Maybe we're jumping to conclusions."

"I don't think so, Reggie. Jack said not to trust any communications from McMurdo. I take that to mean there could be someone hostile toward him down there."

"Is Dr. Moon the scientist that Jack talked about?"

"Yes, he and Jack's aunt are working on some kind of research together in Antarctica. I want to believe that somehow his aunt and Dr. Moon can rescue Jack from Kettering, and this nightmare would go away, but…" she pulled out a folded piece of paper and handed it to Reggie. "How do you explain this HAM message from a guy named Ted from New Zealand that was delivered to me a couple days ago."

Grace,

> *I am a friend of Dr. Moon's. Jack is in danger. He must not go to Antarctica. You must help him escape from the Colonel. Mick will fly you to New Zealand, and I will contact you there.*

Ted

"Who delivered it?"

"Mick. He's a New Zealand pilot. He flies for an airfreight company out of New Caledonia, but I had no idea who he was. I was running one afternoon last week on this path, and he came alongside me and said he had a message sent via HAM radio for me from a friend of Dr. Moon's… a man named Ted. He is the HAM Jack told me to communicate with."

Reggie looked confused. He looked at his watch, and then at the sun sinking lower in the sky, as evening approached.

"Okay, so what's your plan? Are we flying with this guy to New Zealand?"

"I don't know how much of a plan it is, but it's all I've got. Mick told me to go to the commissary and call a cab at this number tonight at seven o'clock. He said to leave our bags at the lobby of the transit barracks, and he would give me further instructions."

"That's it? That's all he said? Well hell, girl. You're right, that's not much of a plan. How do we know if we can even trust this guy? What if he's working for Kettering?"

"I'm not waiting around this base to find out. I wouldn't be surprised if we are being watched right now. Look, we have to do this tonight. Time is running out. Sometimes, you just have to have some faith. This is one of those times, Reggie. Come on, let's jog back to the commissary."

Then she held out the palm of her hand, and Reggie slapped it.

"For Jack," said Reggie.

"For Jack," echoed Grace.

The two figures strode off, side by side for a mile or so, but then they separated when they were near the front gate to Pearl. Grace arrived first at the guard shack, and showed the Marine her ID card. He let her pass. Reggie followed a few minutes behind. Streetlights snapped to life as the sun sank below the horizon, saying goodnight to the darkening ocean. A warm breeze followed them along the streets as Grace headed toward the commissary. Reggie purposely stayed a block or so behind her. It was nearly seven o'clock when Grace ran up the steps of the white stone commissary building. She found a payphone inside and dialed the number that Mick gave her. A man with what seemed to be a Polynesian-British accent answered and told Grace he would pick them up in front of the commissary in ten minutes.

Grace paced nervously up and down the hall as she waited for Reggie. A nondescript, middle-aged man in a Hawaiian shirt sat reading a newspaper on a bench at the end of the lobby area. He seemed to watch her every movement. A group of sailors exited the store, laughing and conversing as they walked past her. She followed them outside, pretending to mingle with them as she glanced behind her while passing through the door. The man was gone.

Within a minute, a blue car accelerated and streaked around the street corner, heading directly for them. The group of sailors collectively gasped as the car nearly struck a man who appeared to fly across the hood. Grace screamed in terror when she recognized that the airborne figure was Reggie. Shock led to relief when she realized Reggie had actually vaulted across the hood, never touching the car. The car continued down the street, stopping about a block away to pick up a passenger. It appeared to be the man in the Hawaiian shirt, and the driver resembled the radioman that had been shadowing her for the past week.

Reggie sprinted up the steps toward Grace, and a couple of the sailors approached him and asked if he was hurt.

"I'm fine," he said. "Did you see that though? That bastard tried to run me over."

A yellow-checkered cab passed the blue car and pulled up in front of them. Grace recognized the driver. It was Mick, signaling urgently for them to hurry. Reggie asked a couple of the sailors to walk with them to the cab. They got into the cab, and as Mick sped off, Grace glanced back and noticed that the blue car was following them.

"Where are you taking us?" asked Reggie.

"Transit barracks, to get your bags... as soon as the shore patrol stops that car," Mick replied.

"How did you know about that car?" asked Grace.

"Don't worry about that. Let's just say I anticipated a little trouble and radioed the front gate. Told them some nut was driving erratically. Look, here they come now!"

Grace looked back to find a shore patrol jeep with its lights flashing, pulling over the car. Mick continued on to the transit barracks, which was about six blocks away. They arrived to find a different-colored cab parked in front.

"Hurry, get in that cab over there. Your bags are in the trunk. I'll catch up with you in a minute as soon as I ditch this cab. They jumped in the back seat, as Grace surveyed the hulking Hawaiian-looking man in the driver's seat.

"Oh, by the way, I'm Matty," he said. "Pleased to meet you."

101

They each shook his hand.

"We only have a couple minutes," said Matty. "Here, Miss, put on this Afro wig. Don't forget the black makeup too… and you, mate, you got to put on this black wig and shawl. Hurry, Miss, help your friend with some makeup. There, you two are sisters. You came to the enlisted club for a drink, and now you're going back home. You got that?"

Reggie and Grace nodded yes. Mick returned a few minutes later after parking the cab at the loading dock behind the commissary. He climbed in the trunk and squeezed between the luggage. He tapped on the back seat, signaling for Matty to go. Within a few minutes, they were at the main gate. A snappy-looking Marine held up his hand and signaled them to pull to the side lane for inspection. Grace's knees were shaking so badly that Matty reached back and slapped her on the head.

"Get a hold of yourself, Miss. That guard doesn't know anything about us. He's just doing his job."

"Great. I'm going to the brig dressed like a lady of the night," said Reggie. "My life is over."

"Quiet, Reggie. Matty's right. We have to have a little faith."

It felt like an hour had passed before the guard walked across the exit lane and bent over to peer into the dark backseat of the cab.

"You ladies heading home early tonight?" asked the guard.

"Janet isn't feeling well," said Grace. "You're not going to vomit again, are you, Janet?"

"Aah, aah, ooh," groaned Reggie in his best female voice.

The Marine stepped back from the cab, and waved them on. Matty glanced in the rearview mirror as the car passed through the gate. He noticed one of the guards was talking into a walky-talky, while a couple of other guards ran toward the cab. Matty pulled onto the busy boulevard and quickly accelerated, but caught the red light at the first intersection. It seemed like it was the longest light in Honolulu.

Suddenly, the blue car appeared in their rearview mirror, three cars behind them. Matty immediately hit the gas, zooming through the red light at the busy intersection. They narrowly missed being broadsided by a bus. Grace squeezed Reggie's arm so hard that Reggie lost feeling in his hand.

"No worries, you two," said Matty. "I'm about to lose these blokes for good. Hang on!"

Grace thought that Matty resembled a Polynesian warrior as the wind blew through the open window, blowing his long, thick black hair into a fierce warrior headdress. Matty steered the cab into a hard right turn that sent the back end of the car skidding into a phone booth. Mick yelled from the trunk.

"I'm okay. Tell Matty to forget the airport. Make for the docks instead."

Matty knew what do. It must have been their Plan B. He turned the cab into a long alley and sped across each successive street intersection, narrowly missing crossing traffic. Every time he thought he lost the blue car, it astonishingly appeared in the rearview mirror.

"Who are those guys?" yelled Reggie.

"IWR," yelled Matty.

"IW… what the hell," said Reggie.

"Impossible Weapons Research… the Doc told us they'd be relentless. It looks like he wasn't kidding. We're almost there though."

Grace caught a faint smell of ocean breeze as they approached the fishing docks on the outskirts of Honolulu. It appeared as though they had finally shaken their pursuers. Matty stopped the car by an abandoned cannery to let Mick out of the trunk. It took both Reggie and Matty, straining with all their might, to lift the rusty garage door. Grace burst out laughing at the sight of Reggie in his Afro wig and pink lipstick, and Matty with his warrior-like hair.

The four of them picked their way through the dark, empty, corrugated steel-sided structure. They reached a door that led outside to a dilapidated wooden dock. The nighttime ocean breeze felt refreshingly cool after the hot, stagnant air in the building. Matty pointed to a motorboat tied to the end of the dock. The chrome trim of the boat reflected the little bit of moonlight cast from the quarter moon. They jumped in the boat, and Mick started the engine and quickly gunned it, speeding away just in time to escape as their pursuers arrived at a distant dock across the inlet.

It took about an hour to reach an out-of-the-way landing in a salt marsh near the Honolulu airport. They crept ashore and hid in the tall reed grass, as Matty chopped a hole in the boat and waited for it to sink. Meanwhile, Mick put on a baggage handler's uniform and headed across the tarmac toward the airport terminal. He returned after a few minutes, driving a baggage vehicle. Reggie and Grace hid under the luggage in the baggage cars, as Matty drove them to an isolated hangar where a 1950's era DC-3 was being loaded with cargo.

"We're flying to New Zealand in that?" asked Reggie, laughing nervously.

"No worries, this old girl will make it," said Mick. "Quick, follow me to your hiding place. Customs will be here any minute."

They climbed into the cargo-laden fuselage. Mick lifted a metal floor panel near the cockpit door and showed them where to hide amongst the hydraulic lines and wire crisscrossing the narrow chase. A few minutes later, Matty came running across the hangar floor wearing a pilot's uniform.

"Customs is coming. Get ready," he whispered. Then, he entered the cockpit and took his seat at the co-pilot controls. Mick, dressed in his pilot's uniform, greeted the oncoming officials. Grace could hear the muffled voices above as they walked slowly through the plane, reading items on the cargo manifest… 200 pounds of assorted magazines, 100 pounds of New England Lobsters in a tank of water, ten Xerox machines… Time seemed to stand still for Grace and Reggie. They barely had enough room to breathe. Finally, after a half-hour, the plane started to move, and within a few minutes the two propeller-driven engines roared to life, and the plane taxied to the runway. Matty lifted the access panel, and Grace and Reggie emerged and took their seats in preparation for takeoff.

"I can't believe we pulled this off," said Reggie.

"See, I told you to have a little faith," said Grace.

"Prepare for takeoff," said Mick. Then he slid the throttles forward, and the propellers whined to full force, thrusting the aged silver and black plane down the runway and into the mid-morning, bright blue sky. Before the plane turned southwest and began the climb to cruising altitude, Grace had fallen into a deep sleep. Reggie found a bundle of magazines destined for the Fiji Islands, and paged through every one of them.

"No, Jack!" yelled Grace. "Don't go. It's a trap!"

Her cries startled Reggie, and he jumped up from under his magazine.

"Wake up, Grace. What's wrong?"

She jumped up as her eyes widened with fear.

"It was so real. I tried to warn him, but he wouldn't listen… and then he disappeared in a horribly cold, blowing snow."

"Try to relax. Here, Matty brought us some coffee and sandwiches. How about Matty? He told me he's not Hawaiian. He's a Maori. They're the native people of New Zealand. We were talking sports. Get this, he once played for the All Blacks."

Grace tried to act interested, but she couldn't stop thinking about Jack.

"Do you even know who the All Blacks are?" asked Reggie. "That's the national rugby team of New Zealand, the greatest rugby team in the world."

Grace stared away, preoccupied with her thoughts.

"I'm sorry, Reggie. I'm just so scared. We are putting our trust in Ted, a guy we've never met. What if his plan stinks? What if we can't find Jack?"

"Sorry to interrupt, Miss, but I overheard you talking," said Matty, as he appeared in the doorway from the cockpit. "Don't worry, you can trust Ted, and you'll be safe with Mick and me until we can smuggle you into New Zealand. Ted will arrange to meet us in Christchurch. As a matter of fact, Mick just spoke to him a little while ago on the radio. He said Jack is safe for now."

Mick interrupted from the cockpit.

"Ted thinks the IWR is monitoring the radio frequencies. We'll have to switch to Plan B."

"Does that mean we're turning back?" asked Grace.

"No, Miss," said Matty. "We can't do that. There's too much at stake."

Reggie put his magazine down, and the two of them listened intently as Mick and Matty explained what they knew of the plan.

"We were supposed to refuel in Fiji, but we now we're going straight to New Caledonia," said Mick. "We can't take a chance on IWR waiting for us in Fiji when we land. I'll radio Fiji that we're going straight on to Christchurch, but instead, we'll sneak into New Caledonia. The whole thing will look like we crashed in the drink, and the New Zealand authorities will list us as missing at sea."

"Good thing we have those extra fuel tanks," said Matty. "We'll arrive in New Caledonia in seven hours. Mick knows the blokes in the tower there. They will see to it that we arrive unannounced."

"But how will we fly to New Zealand without IWR knowing?" asked Grace. "Don't you have to file a flight plan and go through customs? How are we going to get in without passports?"

"We are going to travel by boat to New Zealand. I have a friend who is a skipper of a fishing vessel in New Caledonia who can smuggle us into New Zealand. It's about four days sailing. He'll take us to Greymouth on the west coast. Ted will meet you there and take you to his ranch in the Hawkduns. You'll stay there until we figure out what to do about Jack."

"What do you mean?" asked Grace.

"The Doc thinks Kettering plans to use Jack as a bargaining chip to get his antimatter formula," said Matty.

"His what?" asked Reggie.

"Dr. Moon has developed a super-powerful form of energy that could change the world, and Kettering will do anything to get it, including sacrificing Jack's life. That's why the Doc thinks you ought to be in New Zealand for Jack in case something happens to any of us. You two are all Jack has in the Navy, and you may have to help him escape from Kettering."

"Oh my God! What can Reggie and I do?"

"Nothing, until we get instructions from Ted," said Matty.

"I don't understand," said Grace. "How does Ted know about Jack or about what Dr. Moon is doing?"

"He lives near the Doc's ranch, and he has HAM radio communications with him in Antarctica. Ted and his son have been helping us keep Kettering under surveillance in Christchurch, too. They've got Jack working at a transmitter site near the airport. Ted thinks Kettering is planning something, either at the Doc's ranch, or in Antarctica. He's got Jack involved with the Doc's stepdaughter. I'm not sure what that's all about."

"Oh, I see... and what is she like?"

"She's a pretty bird... older than you," said Matty. "Ted said she's a bit of a shrew. She doesn't get along with the Doc."

"Are you sure Jack is safe?" asked Grace.

"You better get some rest, Miss."

"Please, Matty. Is Jack going to be okay?"

"I won't lie to you. His life is in danger. But don't worry, the Doc always has a plan. That's all I can tell you. Now, get some rest."

Grace sat back in her seat and stared out the window at the long ribbons of cirrus clouds. The sky looked like another world to her. Reggie looked up from his Time magazine.

"Grace, did you know India is building an atomic bomb. It says here they'll be ready to test it next year. Pakistan will probably follow in a few years with its own. That is just what the world needs, more nuclear weapons! The whole world has gone crazy. Hell, the combined nuclear arsenals of the world powers have enough destructive power to destroy half the earth. Can you even comprehend that?"

"That reminds me of something Jack said to me. We were in the park at

Bainbridge. We were standing under our favorite tree, a huge, picturesque white oak. Jack pointed out the sculptural beauty of the branching, the texture of the bark, and the rhythm of leaves in the wind."

"What's that got to do with the destroying the planet?"

"Jack said there is so much beauty in one tree that it is inconceivable how God would allow mankind to destroy the earth in all its beauty."

Matty interjected.

"We have a tree, an 800 year-old tree called the Pohutukawa, at the northernmost tip of the North Island. Maoris believe that upon death, a man's spirit travels to this tree, the last place it visits before the spirit leaves from the world."

"When I was a little girl, my mother said the two hickory trees on either side of our house on our farm in Indiana were like angels watching over us," said Grace.

Matty interrupted again.

"We will be arriving in New Caledonia in a few hours. It's early morning there. You two better get some sleep."

"I wonder what Jack is doing right now," said Reggie.

"I hope there are two angels watching over him," said Grace.

Chapter 14
Rendezvous on the Ice

The wind whipped across the white, desolate plain, forming swirls of ice crystals that fell to the snowy floor and filled the fading set of footprints left by the pair of weary trekkers. Ian Moon and Sarah Mechling, clad in white arctic suits, trudged forward under the weight of their backpacks. The ice on their goggles glistened in the moonlight. Ian checked his portable radio device and pointed toward a distant ice formation. He held up two fingers to indicate that they were two miles from their destination.

They reached the hidden crevasse just after midnight. Exhausted from their trek in the frigid, blowing snow, they struggled to open the steel hatch that was disguised as an ice-covered rock. The pair slowly descended a thirty-foot long metal ladder inside the steel tube. Ian went first, stepping carefully on the narrow rungs as Sarah followed above him, barely able to bend her knees. Her fingers were so numb that she had to wrap her arms around the rungs in order to hold on to the ladder. When they reached the bottom of the dark, icy cavern, Ian shined his flashlight back and forth on the ice-covered walls until he located the brown metal wall beneath quarter-inch thick ice sheets. He located the door to a seven-foot windowless cube, and began chipping at the ice covering the handle.

Sarah was too weak to help. He worked a lever on the door back and forth until the latch disengaged and the door opened. They quickly entered the compartment. The tiny chamber was full of frozen containers of water, boxes of provisions, a cot, radios, a portable toilet, and an odd-looking heating device in the corner. That device was their only hope for survival. Exhausted and facing hypothermia from hours in the minus thirty-degree temperatures, they only had a few minutes to start the heater, or they would freeze to death. Ian had designed and built the device two years earlier, when he and Sarah began building the metal cube, unbeknownst to the McMurdo community. They kept the construction secret, and built it while they were conducting research at a nearby site. Ian had envisioned the completion of the chamber for this very day, when his research was concluded, and the two of them would disappear with the formula.

The cylindrical, finned heating device required the mixing of two chemical compounds contained in plastic packets. Ian struggled to grip and tear the packets with his frozen fingers. He hurriedly poured the contents into separate drawers one at a time, but to his dismay, nothing happened. Sarah began to pray aloud, thinking they were about to die. Then a few minutes later, they heard the cracking, plinking sound of frozen metal heating and expanding, followed by a delightful warmth that radiated from the central core in the cylinder. They thawed a container of water and drank as much as they could, before falling asleep, wrapped in each other's arms.

Five hours earlier, they had abandoned their Snow-Trac vehicle and walked five miles to their current location in the crevasse, which was located near an abandoned airstrip and weather station in the Shults Peninsula, about forty miles from McMurdo. Ian left the vehicle in gear and set it on a course 180 degrees opposite the crevasse, toward the Worcester Range, about forty miles away. The blowing snow covered their footprints, making it difficult for anyone to follow them. No one would know where they were hiding. Ian intended for the vehicle to cover twenty miles or so across the open plain before running out of fuel. He planned the getaway to coincide with a storm that was forecast for the previous afternoon when they left the New Zealand Scott Base. Tomorrow, he would raise the high-frequency antenna, and transmit a coded message to Mick and Ted.

Kettering's plane approached McMurdo in the Antarctic late-Autumn darkness, about an hour before Dr. Moon raised the antenna from his hidden chamber, deep below the ice. The captain announced to the crew and passengers that at long last, they had reached the end of their 2,000-mile journey to the Antarctic continent, and were making their landing approach to the McMurdo ice runway.

Once again, as Kettering had done every twenty minutes for the last two hours, he went to the cockpit and whispered to the radioman, each time returning more and more disgusted. Then, they were instructed to fasten their seatbelts, and Jack felt the plane rock and dip in the gusty winds as it approached the runway. The landing skis made a "plunk" sound as they struck the ice and glided forward like a huge sled, bouncing up and down as the pilot reversed the propeller-driven engines to slow the plane. Jack noticed the flashing lights on the radio antennas projecting from the cluster of ice-covered, metal Quonset huts that comprised McMurdo Station. Before the plane came to rest, Kettering once more approached the radioman.

"Nothing, sir. You best try the radio shack here at McMurdo."

The captain made a final announcement, advising everyone that they had just missed a bad storm the night before, which would have likely forced them to turn back to New Zealand. He ordered them to put on their extreme cold weather gear for the quarter-mile walk to the main base at McMurdo. The temperature was a balmy minus-fourteen degrees Fahrenheit.

Jack walked single-file between Kettering and Driggers along the snow-covered path to the administration hut. Cindy walked behind Jack, and warned him about the dangers of frostbite on exposed skin after seeing his hood partially unzipped. He felt a tingling pain on the left side of his cheek where he had left the zipper open. From the moment he stepped off the plane, he felt both amazement at the stark, white beauty of the Antarctic landscape, and intense dislike of the windy, frigid weather. He couldn't wait to feel the warmth in the building. Kettering was welcomed to the facilities by Captain Henry Minton, Commanding Officer of the US Navy Operation Deep Freeze Antarctic Program at McMurdo. Minton directed Kettering to his office, and

108

quickly shut the door ahead of Driggers.

"Colonel, I regret to inform you that we have lost contact with Moon," said Captain Minton.

"What the hell happened?"

"We followed the instructions in your message. You said it was of utmost importance not to draw any attention to our surveillance of Dr. Moon and Mechling. It is not unusual for them to take the Snow-Trac to Scott Base. It's just two miles away, and they go over there at least three times a week. They left here yesterday afternoon, a few hours before the forecasted storm. I didn't think anything of it."

"It didn't occur to you that he might try to arrange a rendezvous with the Soviets? They probably sent a helicopter from Vostok to pick them up after the storm. Need I remind you that I specifically warned you that he might try to contact the Soviets?"

"I had no idea he would try to drive a Snow-Trac in that storm. Damn it, Colonel, what is all the fuss over one scientist? Why don't the Kiwis deal with him? After all, he's a New Zealand citizen."

"The Kiwis don't want anything to do with him. He's been an embarrassment to them. A few years ago, they promoted his achievements to the world media and scientific community. Then, after all the attention and fame, he quit cooperating with everyone. The official New Zealand line was that he suffered a nervous breakdown after his first wife died. They don't take him seriously anymore. We think differently. That's why we made sure the National Science Foundation approved his research in Antarctica. That way, we could keep an eye on him. Until recently, I don't think he thought that we took him seriously either, especially after he dropped out of the world scientific community. Except now, everything is different. Now, we think he is involved in espionage. We have some very convincing intelligence that he is planning to sell his formula to the Soviets, here in Antarctica."

"Formula for what?" asked Minton.

"That's classified information, and that's all I can tell you. You just need to do as I say, and we'll get along just fine."

"I have a base to run. My men have been working eight-hour shifts on and off making repairs after the storm. You can't just come in here and—"

"I don't have time for your excuses, and I don't give a damn about your repairs. This is a matter of national security."

"I'll give you what assistance I can, but let's get one thing straight, I don't like you, Kettering. And more importantly, I would never suspect Ian and Sarah of treachery or espionage. They are a kindly, amicable couple dedicated to their research. I think the Kiwis at Scott and the Argentines at Esperanza would agree with me."

"Did it ever occur to you that Sarah Mechling is an American citizen, and that she is practically married to him? We believe that she and Moon have stolen top-secret scientific information from the United States government, and for all we know they may have already delivered the goods to the Soviets."

"They did," said Minton.

"What the hell do you mean?" demanded Kettering.

"I mean they got married, two days ago at the Chapel of the Snows, here at McMurdo. As a matter of fact, I married them. I really find it hard to believe that those two are involved in anything—"

"They have you all snowballed. The wedding was a ruse to throw you off... to make you relax your surveillance, and it looked like they succeeded."

"Look, Colonel. Our mission is to support the scientific community here. There are international treaties that govern what we can do and cannot do. I'm not equipped to handle these kinds of operations. You should have your own people down here."

"We only learned of his intentions a few days ago, when we received intelligence that sometime in the next few days, the Soviets are planning to send their personnel that aren't wintering over on an icebreaker bound for Argentina. We think Moon and Mechling will be on it. My guess is that the Soviets planned to meet them somewhere out there, and fly them by helicopter back to Vostok."

"In that storm yesterday... highly unlikely."

"We'll see about that tomorrow."

They heard a knock at the door, and a pale, forbidding-looking sailor with a goatee and dark eyes framed by black plastic-rimmed glasses, entered the room.

"Colonel, here are the latest satellite photos just off the fax."

Kettering studied them intently.

"That'll be all, Pratt. Just as I thought... these photos suggest the landing of a helicopter about fifty miles northeast of here, near the last reported location of Moon's Snow-Trac. We need to investigate the possibility that Moon did not get on that helicopter, and is still out there hiding."

"They couldn't survive in these conditions," said Minton.

"You don't know Moon. He could have a portable shelter somewhere out there. We will need to take your helicopter tomorrow to find out."

"I'm afraid that won't be possible. The rotor blades were damaged in the storm, and it will take some time to repair it. The best I can do is get you a couple of Snow-Tracs. Keep in mind, there is only a few hours of daylight each day this time of year."

"Just have the Snow-Tracs ready for us by 9:00 a.m. tomorrow."

Minton nodded, and left the room without saying anything. Kettering followed him out and met Pratt in the hallway.

"We intercepted a HAM message from Moon, sir," said Pratt. "Part of it is in some kind of code. I can't make it out."

Kettering glanced at it quickly, and crumpled it in his hand.

"It's Westport! I knew it. Send a coded message to Chin. Tell him that Trane's friends are on their way to New Zealand, and that Moon's friend Ted is planning to meet them in Westport. I want Ted and Trane's friends captured alive. Take them to Moon's ranch. Tell Nelson to take some men and meet

Eva there too, and await further instructions."

"Is that all, sir?"

"Notify me immediately when the messages from Washington that I'm expecting come in... and get Trane in here."

Jack walked alongside Pratt as they entered the room. He glanced at the rating badge of a first class communications technician (CT) on his shirt sleeve. He remembered that Phil had warned him to avoid Pratt. There was something about him that didn't seem right. CT's usually worked in surveillance and intelligence gathering. There was no reason for them to be in Antarctica. His aloof, glaring stare unnerved Jack.

"Sit down, Jack. I wanted to share something with you. It appears Dr. Moon and your aunt may have rendezvoused with a Russian helicopter. How about that, Trane... the two people who are responsible for screwing up your life may be planning a Russian honeymoon."

"Honeymoon?"

"That's right. They got married a couple days ago, right here in Antarctica, and you didn't even get an invitation. I wonder how much the Soviets are paying them? It must be more than the $500,000 that I offered them." Kettering could sense Jack's shock at the offer. "Can you believe that, Trane? They turned down a half-million dollars. Who turns down a half-million and then runs to the communists? The man is nuts, and your aunt is nuts for staying with him. That's why you are my only hope. I think the both of them just might be crazy enough to listen to you."

"But I thought you said they already went over to the Russians."

"My nose tells me they are still out there. He's got something else planned. We're going to find them, and you're going to convince him to work for us."

"I can't believe this! My aunt is not crazy. She would never do something like this."

Pratt appeared at the doorway, out of breath and waving a message printed on yellow teletype paper.

"Colonel, I have an "Immediate" message for you from IWR in D.C."

Kettering grabbed the message and retreated into another room. A few minutes later, he called for Pratt, who quickly responded and closed the door behind him. Driggers stayed with Jack in the other room.

"Tell Driggers to take Jack to chow. Then, I want you to secure the radio room. I will need complete privacy. No one is to disturb me. I want you all back here in two hours. Don't let Trane out of your sight. Is that understood?"

"Yes, right away, sir."

Driggers led Jack through a series of cold, interconnected passageways that led to the chow hall. They passed a group of Naval airmen, and Jack overheard them talking about the last flight out of McMurdo, scheduled in a few days. Driggers heard steak and lobster for dinner, a special feast before the warm season personnel returned to New Zealand.

"It's your lucky night, Trane," said Driggers. "You get to chow down on lobster before we go searching for your friends tomorrow."

"I'm not hungry."

"Suit yourself," mumbled Driggers, as he stripped chunks of plump, white meat from a pile of fire-red lobster tails, devouring them like a shark in a feeding frenzy.

Jack sat staring at black-and-white photos on the walls, a collage of scientists at McMurdo from past decades. One photograph caught his eye. It was a picture of a smiling young woman and a tall, thin man holding some kind of electronic gear in the middle of snowy, white expanse. He immediately recognized his aunt and Dr. Moon as the scientists in the photo. It made him think of his predicament. Why couldn't he connect the dots and figure out the truth? Aunt Sarah a spy? Nothing seemed to add up.

Pratt appeared in the doorway, waving for Driggers and Jack to finish eating. A few minutes later, they were standing in front of a smiling, relaxed Kettering in his office, who motioned for them to sit down.

"Did you enjoy the lobster, Jack?" asked Kettering, as he smiled smugly. "It was flown in fresh on our flight this morning."

"Wasn't hungry," Jack replied, in a disgusted tone.

"That's too bad. But I do have some good news for you. Our latest intelligence suggests that Moon and your aunt may be hiding somewhere within a fifty-mile radius of here. We think they have the formula with them. We are going out there to find them tomorrow."

"What about the money? Do I still get the money?"

"I'm impressed," said Kettering, as he snickered. "You show a spirit of self preservation. Maybe what I've been telling you has finally sunk in. After your parents' untimely deaths, after Saint Mark failed you, after your aunt betrayed you, what's left? Your own aggrandizement, that's what. Bravo, Jack. Yes, of course you will receive the money I promised."

"Good, and as soon as we get back to New Zealand, I want out of the Navy, too," said Jack.

"Of course, Jack. Stan, show Jack to his quarters. Good night then. Oh, and Jack, don't wander off. It's thirty-below zero outside. I'd hate to see you miss your rendezvous with destiny."

Chapter 15
Revelation

Early the next morning, Driggers led Jack to the motor pool, where Cindy was waiting with their gear laid out across the concrete floor. She told them that Kettering was in the radio shack with Pratt, and that they were running late. She seemed preoccupied and irritated.

"Why are you so nervous?" asked Driggers. "What's the matter with you?"

"The Colonel ordered me to go along with you. That wasn't part of the original plan. I hate this cold. I don't want to go."

"Quit complaining. Don't worry, you'll get your share."

"I don't care about the money," said Cindy. "I'm tired of all this crap. Besides, doesn't it seem odd to you that the Colonel has completely changed the original plan? I thought we were supposed to have another Snow-Trac with armed Seabees to escort us in case we ran into Soviet Marines. Honestly, I don't think this ever had anything to do with the Russians. He's keeping something from us."

"I think he still wants me to try to persuade Dr. Moon to work for us," said Jack.

"Regardless, it's not like Kettering to negotiate," said Cindy. "He usually takes what he wants."

"Shut up!" barked Driggers. "If you know what's good for you, you'll just follow orders. Now get that gear ready before the Colonel gets here."

Kettering entered the room with Captain Minton, and Pratt followed behind them. Captain Minton demanded to know more about Kettering's mission to find Moon, but Kettering refused, insisting this was his mission, and that Minton did not hold the level of security to question his orders. Cindy looked quizzically at Kettering, who simply smiled at her and acted unusually upbeat, as he and Driggers loaded M-16's and .45's in the weapons locker on the Snow-Trac.

Jack and Pratt finished loading the gear and provisions. At 9:00 a.m., the two Snow-Tracs departed McMurdo in darkness, grinding through the snow-packed streets and heading south toward the vast, icy plains of the Ross Ice Shelf. Kettering and Pratt rode in the first vehicle, while Driggers, Jack, and Cindy rode in the second.

About two miles from McMurdo, they passed a sign for New Zealand's Scott Base. They continued on, traveling for about three hours and covering forty miles across the icy plain, before Kettering abruptly ordered them to halt. He stepped from the cabin and looked around, then reached inside and picked up a portable homing device. He pressed a few buttons, and a small video screen lit up. A red dot appeared on the screen, and shortly after, it began to make a beeping noise and flash, indicating the source of a radio transmission. It stopped after a few seconds, but it was enough to give Kettering a direction.

He radioed Driggers with the coordinates.

"How far is it? Over," asked Driggers.

"About ten miles, bearing 130 degrees southeast," replied Kettering. "Once we are close, we'll wait for him to transmit again, then we will lock in on that signal. Over."

"So Kettering knows where Dr. Moon is?" asked Jack.

"Not exactly," said Driggers. "He only gets a bearing when he transmits. We know he's been transmitting on high frequency to communicate with New Zealand, and there is one thing about high frequency."

"What's that?" asked Cindy.

"You need a pretty high antenna for high frequency, which is easy to spot," said Jack.

"Smart boy," said Driggers.

"I thought Kettering said Dr. Moon was going to defect to the Russians," said Jack.

"I don't know, Trane. The Colonel thinks something went wrong. He thinks Moon wasn't able to reach them."

Jack glanced at Cindy, who met his eyes with the same dubiousness about Kettering's intentions. Meanwhile, the weather conditions began to improve as they drove further away from McMurdo. Around noon, the wind died down and visibility improved. Kettering ordered them to stop, and Driggers pulled his Snow-Trac alongside Kettering's. Under the wintry afternoon moonlight, Jack observed that they were in a great basin, surrounded by high, craggy, ice-covered highlands. They were about forty miles from McMurdo. Suddenly, the homing device in Kettering's lap began to beep. Pratt turned the dials on a range-finding instrument.

"Over there, bearing 120 degrees, about two miles," said Pratt.

They sped away toward the signal, and came to rest at the face of a huge ice and rock outcrop. Kettering jumped out and quickly scanned the surroundings with his night vision binoculars. He motioned for Driggers, leaving Jack and Cindy alone in their Snow-Trac.

"Moon probably left a decoy transmitter, and we are walking into a trap," said Cindy.

The wind picked up, blowing powdery snow across the windshield. Again, Cindy looked at Jack with a puzzled expression. She wondered why Kettering was so confident that Moon was here. Then, as the wind shifted, a silvery, thirty-foot tall telescopic antenna came into view, about 200 yards away in a fan of boulders at the edge of the icy expanse. Then, it quickly disappeared.

"Ha, I knew it. They're here, Pratt! Get Driggers," said Kettering, as he opened the gun locker and took out two M-16's and a .45 pistol.

Driggers strode over and grabbed an M-16.

"Pratt, set up the tent with the portable heater," said Kettering. "You and Cindy stay here and keep the Snow-Tracs running. Point the spotlights toward those rocks over there. I'll contact you via walkie-talkie if we need you."

Then, the three of them headed toward the rocks where they had spotted the antenna. They walked for twenty minutes as Driggers led the way, poking the ice with a long, sharp rod to check for hollow cavities that could hide deep crevasses.

"They must have some kind of shelter under the ice," said Jack.

"That's right, genius," mocked Driggers. "The Colonel had a hunch Moon had planned for this."

Suddenly, the rod plunged through a layer of thin ice. The ice collapsed, and a five-foot diameter chunk fell into the dark abyss. Driggers quickly stepped back and yelled to warn the others, after marking the spot with a flag.

"Damn. I know he's in this crevasse somewhere," said Kettering, as he looked anxiously at his watch.

"We can't go any further. It's too dangerous," said Driggers.

Upon hearing Driggers yell, Jack instinctively jumped back and got his foot stuck in the thin ice. Then, a section of ice caved in, and he felt himself slipping into the crevasse. Kettering lunged toward him and grabbed his arm. Jack gasped, and felt his body slip helplessly from Kettering's grasp. In a microsecond, he thought he saw Kettering snicker, and the thought of falling into the dark crevasse paralyzed him. Then, Kettering grabbed the hood of Jack's parka, and with two hands, firmly yanked him from certain death. Jack lay on the icy ground next to the hole, and looked up at Kettering with a mixture of disdain and gratitude.

"Uh, thanks," said Jack. In the chaos, it was all he could manage to say. Kettering did not reply. He was bent over the hole, staring into the darkness. Then, he looked up at Jack.

"I should thank you. Your foot penetrated the right spot in the ice, allowing me to see the flicker of light below. We've found the good doctor!"

Meanwhile, Driggers had worked his way back to them by cautiously keeping to the higher ground. About thirty yards away, he crossed a natural rock bridge over the crevasse. He stopped once he reached the other side, and bent over a couple of large, flat rocks that were covering an opening in the ice.

"What is it, Stan?" yelled Kettering.

"I found the antenna, and it's poking out of a pipe hidden by these rocks," said Driggers.

Kettering called Pratt on the walkie-talkie and told him to bring the tent and radio gear.

"What are you going to do?" asked Jack.

"I'm going to call your, ah… aunt on the radio and let her know you're here," said Kettering.

Pratt tuned the portable transceiver to the frequency detected on the radio device that he was operating. Kettering pulled back the tent flaps and glanced at the starlit sky. Then, he looked at his watch, and pressed the switch on the microphone to transmit.

"Dr. Moon, Sarah Mechling. This is Colonel Kettering. I'm standing atop your little den with someone I know is very dear to you… Jack Trane. Do you read me? Over."

A scratchy static broke the silence in the frigid setting. Then, a faint voice replied.

"This is Dr. Moon. We won't give you what you want."

"But Jack has come such a long way to see you. Say hello, Jack."

Jack grabbed the microphone.

"Are you alright, Aunt Sarah?"

The radio blared with a loud, horrifying scream, and Jack could hear her begin to cry.

"Oh, Jack. Yes, I'm where I must be, but you are in great danger. I'm so sorry you got mixed up in all this."

"Why are you doing this, Aunt Sarah? Why would you sell the formula to the Soviets? Just give the Colonel what he wants."

"Jack, what is he promising you?" asked Sarah. "What has he told you about us? Don't listen to anything he says."

Kettering grabbed the microphone.

"You had quite an ingenious plan, Moon... to fake your death in Antarctica and disappear with your formula. How many days were you planning to hide out here, and who was going to sneak back here and rescue you? Your Kiwi friends at Scott Base? The Argentines? Or was it the Russians? I didn't think you trusted anyone. Of course it doesn't matter now, does it? Give me the formula!"

There was no reply from the radio.

"Moon! Cooperate with me, and you can go free. And I offer you more. Pratt will confirm the deposits of $500,000 each in Swiss bank accounts for you and Sarah. I will include the same for Jack. All you have to do is come up here and surrender the formula to me. Then, we will all fly back to New Zealand. That is, unless—"

Jack grabbed the microphone from Kettering's hand.

"Please, Aunt Sarah, do as he says, or he's going to kill you," said Jack.

"Jack, we are prepared to die to prevent him from getting the formula. This shelter is wired to explode, and I will not hesitate to do it," said Dr. Moon.

"I figured as such," said Kettering. He motioned to Jack to stay quiet. "If you are prepared to die, what do I do with Jack if you don't cooperate?" There was silence, until the frigid wind whistled in sync with the static noise on the radio. Kettering waited for their reply, then pressed the transmit button. "What? You have to think about it? It's a good thing I brought Jack along as an insurance policy. I thought they cared a little more for you than that, Jack."

Pratt turned up the volume, as Dr. Moon's reply echoed from the radio speaker.

"I don't have the formula here. It's in New Zealand. I'll tell you where if you take Jack back to McMurdo, and let me speak by radio to Captain Minton."

"Do you think I'm a fool? You think I don't know you have a copy of the formula hidden in New Zealand? Eva told me. She overheard you and Sarah talking. She also told me what a devoted stepfather you were. I will not take Jack to McMurdo. Instead, you will surrender and give me the formula. I suggest you cooperate, now!"

Kettering paced back and forth, obsessively checking his watch and becoming more and more irritated. The wind had kicked up, and the temperature was dropping. He knew they only had a few more hours of fuel, barely enough to make it back to McMurdo. He did not want to contact Minton for help and risk compromising the real purpose of his mission. He signaled with his hand to Driggers, who quickly moved toward Jack. Then, Jack felt a gun barrel press against his back. He started to resist.

"I wouldn't," said Driggers, with a menacing grin.

"Moon, Mechling… I should have known I could not persuade you with money alone. That's why I've gone to so much trouble to bring Jack here. You see, I've had a hunch for quite some time… and then a revelation, you might say, after I visited Jack and Eva at your ranch. The family photograph on your mantle was quite revealing… very portending. I don't know how I overlooked the Bell's palsy connection. So you leave me no choice. Give me what I want, or you will force me to…" Kettering paused, and seared Jack with a devilish smile. "You'll force me to deprive you of seeing your only son, before he dies."

Jack's hands began to shake uncontrollably, and his body refused to move. The right side of his face twitched with a stabbing pain.

"I expect the good doctor is quite surprised with this news. But I think that you, Sarah, may have sensed a motherly bond with Jack, the son that you gave up for adoption at birth."

The radio burst to life.

"You lying bastard," yelled Sarah. "He's using you, Jack. This cannot be possible."

"I'm afraid it is very true, Sarah. Surely, it can't be that hard to remember, twenty-two years ago when you came to New Zealand to work with Ian, the only man you ever loved. That would have been springtime in 1951, right? How terrible it must have felt to be jilted by a man who loved his work more than you. So you returned to America… to Pittsburgh, pregnant with Jack. Ian would have hated you for distracting him from his quest to harness antimatter. So, you gave your baby up for adoption." Once again, he paused to savor the look on Jack's face. "But as fate would dictate, baby Jack did not go directly to hopeful parents wanting to adopt. Instead, he was kept in an orphanage until he was one year old. But then, by incredible coincidence, a couple that could not conceive, a couple from nearby Greensburg… Albert and Marie Trane, ended up adopting Jack. And you, so absorbed in your obsession with Ian, never suspected a thing."

Jack grabbed the microphone.

"Is this true, Aunt Sarah?" asked Jack. She did not answer, unable to press the transmit key. "Is it true?" he screamed.

In the meantime, Kettering had placed a folder in a pouch tied to a rope, and lowered it into the crevasse.

"Take the pouch I've lowered, Sarah. Look closely at the adoption papers. Pay particular attention to the birth certificate and the hospital records on a baby boy... no name, 8 pounds, 13 ounces, brown eyes, born August 8, 1951 at Mercy Hospital in Pittsburgh."

Driggers began to laugh. Jack stood petrified in the cold silence that seemed to last for hours while Sarah read the contents of the pouch. The radio burst to life again. Sarah began to speak.

"Oh God, Jack..." her voice quivered so violently that she turned off the microphone. Ian held her in his arms. She tried, but she could not push the transmit button. She turned to Ian. "Please, God, let Jack escape."

"Surrender, Moon. Come out of that hole, and give me the formula!" said Kettering.

After a few minutes, Ian finally replied.

"Let Jack go. Take him to McMurdo. When I know he is safely in Minton's charge, then I'll give you what you want. But I will not reveal the location of the formula until we are all safely in New Zealand."

"I'm afraid I can't do that. Instead, I have a better plan. You work for me... one happy family. You will live and work on an island in the South Pacific, with everything you need to advance your work. Money, comforts... every scientific resource available will be at your disposal. Think of the progress you will make in your research. You will work for IWR, and no one will bother you. Congress doesn't even know my branch of IWR exists."

"Forget it, Kettering. I could never work for you. You are a murderer and a mad man. You've left a trail of death and suffering going all the way back to Guam when you murdered your own men in cold blood. Let Jack go, or I'll tell you nothing."

"Doctor, my patience is wearing thin. You don't have much choice. Surrender, or you will force me to hurt Jack. Or... wait... Pratt, patch me through to Eva and Chin at Moon's ranch."

Sarah and Ian began to argue, while Kettering waited for Pratt to set up the patch to Eva. Sarah begged Ian to give Kettering the formula in exchange for Jack's life, but Ian resisted. He struggled to concentrate, using his analytical mind to dissect their predicament and find a solution.

"My beloved Sarah, I am sure Mick received our transmission. He will come. Have faith."

"But what if he doesn't come? We can't transmit with Kettering up there. We're trapped here. What will happen to Jack?"

"Kettering won't do anything to Jack. Not as long as I have the formula."

"Please let Jack escape. Please God—"

"Dr. Moon, I have a voice circuit patched through to Eva at your ranch," said Kettering through the radio.

"Hello, Ian. Hello, Sarah," said Eva. "Remember me, the little nuisance you never had time for. It's time to make amends for what you did to my mother. Chin, bring the old man in here. Tie his hands to the chair arms and connect the wires to his fingers."

118

"Don't worry, Doc. I won't talk," said Ted.

"You hear that, Moon? If he doesn't talk, Chin will turn up the electric current," said Kettering. "We'll start with his fingers, and then move to more sensitive parts."

"My God, Sarah. They've captured Ted," said Ian. "Leave him alone, he doesn't know anything," he yelled to Kettering.

"Moon, are you going to surrender? I'm going to count to ten…one, two, three, four… ten. Do it Chin!"

Ted let out a horrible scream of intense pain as Chin increased the power. Ted's body shook uncontrollably. Sarah screamed in horror, and Jack yelled for him to stop, loud enough for Cindy to hear him in the Snow-Trac with the engine running. She got out and approached the tent in the dark shadows beyond the cone of light from the spotlights of the Snow-Trac. She stood outside the tent, listening to the radio chatter between Kettering and Dr. Moon. Her eyes fixated on the gun that Driggers had pointed at Jack's back. Something deep inside her conscience made her go back to the Snow-Trac. She tried to open the weapons locker, but it was locked. She grabbed the only thing she could find, a small piece of metal pipe.

Meanwhile, Jack managed to break away from Driggers' grasp. He ran outside the tent, but Driggers caught him and threw him down. He kicked his side and pointed the .45 at his head. Cindy crouched a few yards away behind the tent. Kettering and Pratt were inside the tent, preoccupied with the transmissions to Moon. Cindy strained to listen.

"I'm running out of patience. Don't make me hurt Jack. That would be such a pity, since I think he might like to join me." He glanced outside the tent at Driggers, who was holding Jack in a headlock.

"Never!" yelled Jack.

"Moon, I can't believe you would let your only son die without ever talking to him, father to son. This is your last chance. I'll count to ten, and then Driggers will start to remove Jack's clothing, beginning with his gloves. Need I remind you the temperature is ten degrees below zero and dropping. The Bell's palsy makes your face especially painful in the cold, doesn't it, Jack? Give me what I want, and Driggers will bring him back into the warmth of this tent."

Jack felt the pinching tingling on his bare skin as Driggers pulled off the first glove. Then, he felt a painful twitch in his face, as the fear of freezing to death fell over him.

"Wait! Stop!" yelled Ian. "Alright, there is a hidden door in my laboratory at the ranch. The door is behind the shelves in the closet behind my desk. It leads to a small room. There is a safe in there that holds the formula. I will give you the combination."

"You had better not try to deceive me. Dr. Crankshaw, your old associate, works for me now, and he is at your ranch. He will verify the formula's authenticity."

As Kettering spoke, Cindy ran out from behind the shadows and clubbed Driggers on the back of the head. He dropped the gun as he fell to the ground.

She yelled for Jack to run for the Snow-Trac. Driggers rebounded from the blow and grabbed Cindy by the neck. For a brief moment, Jack thought only of himself and escaping from the madness that had swarmed over his life. He knew he could easily sprint to the vehicle and drive away to McMurdo. He would tell Minton the truth. But what about Ian and Sarah? What if they really were his parents? Kettering would kill them, and he would surely kill Cindy. What if Minton didn't believe him? A flurry of scenarios filled his head, until the words of Brother Vincent filtered through... *truth and courage abound form the righteous path.* He turned around, picked up the pipe, and struck Driggers on the back of the neck again, knocking him to the ice. Then he grabbed the gun. He had to remove his glove to hold it, and the frozen steel bit deeply into his fingers. He ran toward Kettering who was still in the tent, and yelled to Cindy.

"Take the Snow-Trac and get back to McMurdo as fast as you can. Tell Captain Minton to bring help."

Meanwhile, Pratt ran to the second Snow-Trac and tried to start the engine. By the time he got it started, Cindy was a quarter of a mile away. Jack unzipped the tent flap and pointed the gun at Kettering.

"Go ahead and shoot me. But only I know the code to stop the timer that is about to detonate the bomb that's in the crevasse."

They both heard the roar of the Snow-Trac engine ripping away. Cindy was on her way to McMurdo. Pratt ran back to the tent.

"Should I go after her?"

"No," said Kettering. "Jack is going to give me the gun. Give me the gun, or I'll kill them."

"If they die, we all die," said Jack.

"Let's be reasonable. I have money. There's $100,000 in that backpack. See for yourself. I brought it in case your father was interested."

Jack froze for a moment. He glanced at Pratt. Driggers was still lying in the snow. Far off in the distance, he could see the fading red taillights of Cindy's Snow-Trac.

"Open it up and show me," said Jack.

Kettering unzipped the sides and pulled out a pack of one hundred dollar bills. He tossed it in front of Jack. When Jack bent forward to pick it up, Kettering lunged at him and knocked the gun from his hands. They kicked and punched each other, rolling around on the hard, frigid snow. Their bulky outer gear made it difficult to fight, and in the melee, Kettering knocked over the portable heater and caught the tent on fire.

Meanwhile, Driggers had regained consciousness. Jack managed to kick Kettering hard in the groin and pull away from him, but in the darkness, he lost his balance and slipped. At the same time, Pratt dove at him, knocking him backwards into the crevasse, but not before Jack grabbed hold of the nylon ladder that Kettering had placed near the crevasse opening. He began to slide down the side of the icy wall. Then, his arm became tangled in the rope as he fell, stopping him in mid-air about fifteen feet from the bottom. His right hand was painfully numb, and his face burned with a stabbing sensation. He knew he

120

only had minutes to free his arm before frostbite set in and he would be unable to move.

As he dangled on the ladder, Kettering and Driggers appeared at the top of the crevasse. They started to pull him up at the same time that the chamber door creaked open, and a flashlight beam and the barrel of a gun rose toward the ladder. A gunshot rang out. Driggers and Kettering pulled back, releasing their grip on the ladder. Somehow, in the tangle of falling rope, enough slack opened up to allow Jack to free his arm, but he was too weak, and his frozen hands could not hold on. He dropped to the darkness below, slamming into the side of the ice wall and coming to rest about eight feet from the chamber door. Kettering shined a flashlight toward the dark depth below. He could hear Jack moaning, but the irregular shapes of the ice walls blocked his view.

"You aren't going anywhere, Jack, so spend some time with your folks," said Kettering. "This is quite a turn of events. It might even make things a little easier. Now I know what to look for at the ranch."

Pratt approached Kettering, looking confused.

"Colonel, we have to leave now or we won't have enough fuel to get back. What are you going to do about Cindy?"

"Cindy… she's about to have an accident," said Kettering. He pulled a small transmitting device with a large red button out of his pocket. He watched the red taillights of the Cindy's Snow-Trac grow dimmer in the darkness. Turning toward Driggers, he snickered as he pointed at the distant red lights. Then with cold, emotionless bearing, he pressed the button, and began to laugh as the vehicle exploded, illuminating the night sky with a bright fireball. Jack heard the explosion from the bottom of the crevasse. He grimaced in pain from the fall and the blow to his head. He closed his eyes, remembering Cindy, who gave up her life to help him. A few feet away, a door creaked open, and two sets of outstretched arms pulled him into the warmth of the chamber. Then, he lost consciousness.

Chapter 16
Reunited

Moments after the steel door closed, the radio inside the chamber blared to life.

"Dr. Moon. I'm going to destroy your antenna, so you won't be able to communicate with anyone," said Kettering.

Ian could feel Sarah's anguish as she held Jack in her arms.

"Sarah, Kettering can't stay up there much longer. They are running out of fuel. They'll have to return to McMurdo. If we can just buy a few more hours until Mick gets here—"

"What if Mick doesn't come? Jack needs a doctor."

"He will come," said Ian. He pushed the transmit button, and waited a few seconds to speak. "Kettering, bring Captain Minton and a squad of Seabees back here, and bring a doctor for Jack. Then, and only then, will I surrender."

"You are in no position to dictate terms to me. I will return in less than eight hours. By that time, Crankshaw will know if the formula is real. If it is genuine, then you will surrender, and you will agree to work for me. We will discuss terms on the plane back to New Zealand tomorrow. Do not deceive me, or you will all freeze to death in your underground coffin."

There was no response.

"Answer me," yelled Kettering. He was still furious that his plan to hold Jack hostage had failed, and that the Snow-Trac was low on fuel, which was forcing him to return to McMurdo. He had intended to leave Pratt behind to stand guard in case Moon tried to escape, but with the tent and heater destroyed, Pratt could not survive until they returned.

"God damn it, Moon. Do you want to be responsible for your only son's death?" Again, his demand was met with silence from below. "Moon! Moon! Answer me!"

Ian tried to push the transmit button on the transceiver, but hesitated.

"Ian what are you going to do? I won't let then hurt Jack," said Sarah.

"Don't worry, he's bluffing. He won't do anything to us until he figures out if the formula is real. It will take Crankshaw at least eight hours before he realizes the formula is a fake. By then, we will be on our way to New Zealand."

"But what if he radios Captain Minton to send men and equipment. Mick won't be able to land if they are up there."

"Kettering will never come back here with Minton. He can't afford to let Minton know anything about his intentions. He knows Minton would alert Washington, and Kettering's whole operation would come tumbling down on him."

"Moon, answer me!"

"Concur," said Ian.

"Bravo, Doctor," said Kettering. "I look forward to discussing our future when I return in a few hours. Until then."

A period of silence, interrupted only by the short bursts of static on the radio speaker, seemed to last an eternity. Then, the radio went dead. Ian slammed the headset against the radio unit and cursed Kettering. He glanced at the last four packets of fuel next to the heater, then touched Jack's forehead with his palm.

"How could I have been so oblivious?" asked Ian. "Why didn't you tell me about the baby?"

"I desperately wanted to, but I knew that marriage and the responsibilities of being a father would interfere with your work. I thought you would have resented me… that you would have thought I tricked you into marriage. You would have given up on your pursuit of antimatter. I didn't want to burden you, so I went back home to have the baby."

"Damn it, Sarah, why is this happening now, when I'm so close to realizing my dream. It's within my grasp! Kettering will take it all away. I'll be damned before I let my whole life's work end this way."

"Listen to you. You're thinking only of yourself. Our son is injured. His life is in jeopardy. We have to think about Jack now."

"Our son? What do you mean, our son? I didn't ask for all this. I have my work—"

"Yes, we have a son now. Think about Albert and Marie. None of this would have been possible without them. Albert saved your life! They sacrificed their lives for you."

Ian was visibly shaken by the mention of his old friend's name, and the thought that Albert and Marie had raised his only son.

"Oh my God, Sarah, what have I done? Jack is our son, and now I've put him in danger. But what can I do? I have to consider the greater good. I can't let my research fall into Kettering's hands. Damn it! If Albert had just listened to me, then Jack would have never gotten involved. I told him not to go to the media. Kettering would have never allowed him to print his story. I warned him that going public would put the antimatter project in jeopardy. For God's sake, Sarah, he chose not to listen. Why?"

"You don't know how much he suffered. Marie told me he was taking handfuls of pain pills every day. But through it all, he was a good father to Jack. They both loved him more than anything."

"You're right. I owe it to Albert to see this through. I'll figure this out. There is a logical solution. Mick should be here in four hours. We'll make a vertical stretcher out of webbing and ropes for Jack. I'll pull him up the escape ladder, while you push from the bottom. Then, when we get back to New Zealand, I'll see that Jack—"

"He's coming to," yelled Sarah, as Jack began to moan and stir. Ian jumped to his side and held his hand, while Sarah shined a flashlight in his eyes to check his pupils. Jack squinted his eyes and pulled himself up, holding his head in his hands.

"What happened?" he asked.

"Jack, thank God!" cried Sarah, as she hugged him. "Thank God! Are you hurt anywhere else?"

"I hurt all over, but I don't think anything is broken. Why is this happening to me? I just want to go home, and... where are we?"

"You fell into the crevasse," said Ian. "You are in my underground shelter. Kettering just left for McMurdo, but he'll be back in a few hours. We have to leave the shelter and climb to the surface to meet Mick before Kettering returns."

"Who's Mick?"

"The pilot who is coming to rescue us," said Ian.

"Kettering murdered Cindy," said Jack.

"Who?" asked Sarah.

"She tried to help me... oh, my head. This is all real, isn't it? You are my birth mother and..." he broke off.

"And I am your birth father," said Ian.

"I honestly don't know what to say to you," said Jack.

"I'm sorry that we must meet under these circumstances, but we find ourselves in the midst of a struggle for survival," said Ian. "Nothing else matters besides escaping and preventing Kettering from getting my antimatter formula."

"So, there really is an antimatter formula?" asked Jack.

"There are two, but only one is real. The fake one is at my ranch in the Hawkduns. That's the one I told Kettering about. We only have a few hours until he discovers it's a fake. Hopefully, Mick will be here before then."

"Where is the real formula?" asked Jack.

"In my underground laboratory. That's all you need to know for now."

"Okay, fine. But how are we going to get out of here?"

"My original plan was to die in Antarctica. That is to say, let the world think that Sarah and I died here. We were going to hide in this shelter until Mick could fly down here and bring us back to New Zealand undetected. Everything was going according to plan, until you entered the equation. I didn't expect Kettering to follow me here, let alone show up with you. Sarah and I were prepared to die to protect the formula. But now that your life is in danger, I cannot let any harm come to you."

"What do I have to do with any of this?"

"You, I'm afraid, have become key to everything. I will explain it to you when the time is right. For now, we must concentrate on leaving this shelter, and hope to God that Mick makes it here."

"Can you stand up?" asked Sarah.

"Yes, I think so," Jack replied.

The right side of his face twitched as he struggled to stand.

"Look, Ian, he inherited your palsy."

Jack looked closely at the right side of Ian's face, and noticed the slightly drooping eyelid and corner of his mouth.

"The photo on the mantle at your ranch, that's the clue that tipped

Kettering off," said Jack.

"Yes, Ted told me my stepdaughter brought you there. She hates me. She still blames me for her mother's death, and now she is aligned with Kettering. I can't believe it."

"Kettering wanted me to get her to divulge information about you."

"It's more likely he was trying to see what you knew about me, and to turn you against me."

"Well, we did find some Russian gold bars—"

"That was all a ruse. Kettering must have planted them to make you think I had some kind of involvement with the Russians. He must not have known at that time that I was your real father. He was going to use you in some other way to get to me."

"My head is spinning. This is too much."

"You must muster all your strength, Jack. Mick will be here soon. He is flying alone and below radar to make it here undetected. No one will expect a civilian aircraft en route to Antarctica at this time of year. The plane is outfitted with skis and extra fuel tanks for the 5,000 mile round trip, but there will only be enough fuel to make it back to Invercargill, on the southernmost tip of the South Island. He is making a very difficult and exhausting flight, and he has to make an extremely dangerous landing and takeoff."

"What if Mick doesn't come?" asked Jack.

"Then we will have to surrender to Kettering, and I will pretend to work for him until he is through with me. But I will never give him the formula. After that, it is up to God." He paused briefly. "There is another factor too. Mick was supposed to travel with his co-pilot, Matty."

"Who is Matty?" asked Jack.

"He works for me. He stayed back in New Zealand to try to sneak two of your friends into the country. Grace and... I can't remember his name."

"Reggie!"

"Right-O. Unfortunately, the plan went awry—"

"Are they okay? Is Grace alright?"

"Yes, as far as I know. They are with Matty. They took a boat from New Caledonia to Westport on the west coast of the South Island. The skipper of the boat, on a tip that IWR was waiting in Westport, made a last-minute decision to go to Greymouth instead. That decision saved their lives. Unfortunately, Ted was waiting for them in Westport, and he was captured."

Jack broke down and began to cry. He was overcome with emotion as he tried to grasp the magnitude of the sacrifices everyone was making for him.

"You are lucky to have such devoted friends," said Ian.

"We have to get dressed and go now," said Sarah. She handed Jack a backpack that contained portable landing lights, as she and Ian took one last look at their shelter. Ian pulled the lever to unlatch the steel door. Sarah shined the flashlight into the pitch-dark cavern. There was a metal ladder about ten yards away that extended through a large metal pipe that led to a hatch at the ground surface, about thirty feet above. The outside of the hatch was covered in solid ice. When Ian reached the top, he ignited a small propane torch and began heating the hatch. He alternated between heating and pounding at the hatch, but it wouldn't budge.

"Ian, we don't have much time," yelled Sarah.

"I'm almost out of propane. It's got to open, or we'll be trapped."

Finally, as the last bit of flame died, the hatch began to move. Then, with a loud cracking noise, a chunk of ice broke off and the hatch opened, exposing the moonlit Antarctic sky. One by one, they slowly climbed out of the hatch. Ian immediately set up the portable radio and began transmitting. Jack and Sarah went off to set the runway lights, spaced two hundred feet apart, making a 1,000-foot long by thirty-foot wide runway.

Meanwhile, Ian desperately tried to reach Mick on the radio, as he kept watch on the horizon for Snow-Trac lights and signs of Mick's plane. If he did not make contact soon, Mick would turn back. Sarah finished placing the last light, and she and Jack stood in the middle of the runway, staring at the empty, starlit sky, hoping for a miracle.

"Queens Park, this is Central. Over," Ian repeated every two minutes. Nothing but the static leaked from the speaker after the first few tries. Then suddenly, the speaker erupted with a loud, New Zealander accent.

"Central, this is Queens Park," said Mick. "I'm about twenty miles from you. Over."

"Roger that... we're ready here. Out," said Ian.

Jack could hear the distant hum of the DC-3 engines. Then, the airplane lights came into view as the plane banked around to make its landing approach. A minute later, the plane landed in a giant spray of snow as the skis glided down the flat, snowy plain. Mick reversed the engines to slow the plane, and he turned it around just before the end of the runway. The snow spray cleared, revealing three weary figures walking toward the plane.

Just as Mick opened the fuselage door, Jack yelled out that there were Snow-Trac lights in the distance, moving in their direction. Sarah and Jack climbed into the plane. Adrenaline surged through Jack as he helped load the gear. Mick yelled to Ian to inspect the JATO's (Jet Assisted Take-Off Engines) on each wing. The Snow-Trac lights were getting brighter.

"We've only got a few minutes before they block the runway," yelled Mick.

Ian finished adjusting one of the JATO's, and he gave a thumbs-up to Mick as he climbed into the plane behind Jack and Sarah. Mick guided the plane to the end of the runway and faced it directly at the oncoming vehicles. He knew he had only seconds to get airborne before the vehicles were in a position to block the runway. Ian sat in the co-pilot seat, his eyes fixed on the two Snow-Tracs only two miles in front of them.

"Strap yourselves in, mates. Here we go," said Mick. He pushed the engine throttles forward, and the plane accelerated, but they struggled to pick up speed on the rough, frozen surface. "Fifty, sixty, seventy, eighty miles per hour," he yelled.

"We're not going to make it," said Ian.

"She'll be right," said Mick, as he pushed a button that ignited the two JATO engines, lifting the plane into the air, no more than a few hundred yards in front of the Snow Tracs.

"Thank God for the JATO's," said Ian.

Mick nodded as he concentrated on piloting the old aircraft. He had just sat back in his seat, when Jack's voice rang out from the back.

"They're shooting at us."

Bursts of machine gun fire erupted from the parked Snow-Tracs. Whizzing bullets struck the wings and penetrated the fuselage, narrowly missing Jack and Sarah. Within a few seconds, they were out of range as the plane gained altitude, heading north toward New Zealand. Ian looked nervously at Mick.

"What's wrong, Ian? We beat their asses," said Mick, as he threw his fist in the air in celebration.

"I wish I shared your optimism. Kettering is not going to stand by and let us fly back to New Zealand. He'll probably go to Minton and make up some story about me passing secrets to the Soviets, and tell him I'm trying to escape to New Zealand." Ian pressed his fingertips together and looked up at the cockpit ceiling, engrossed in thought. "Then again, he might not do anything."

"What do you mean?" asked Mick.

"That's it. He won't do anything. He won't tell Minton, because if he did, Minton would surely notify the Kiwis, who would alert their Air Force and send jets up to intercept us. The last thing Kettering would want is to draw attention to us. That would be disastrous for him. No, I think Kettering will go straight back to McMurdo and take the next flight out. I'm sure his people are watching all the airports in the South Island too."

"All the airports, except the one we're going to," said Mick.

"Right. But first we must get past the New Zealand air defenses undetected."

"You leave that to me," said Mick, as he yawned and stretched his arms.

"Are you okay? You look pretty knackered. There's still a good eight hours until we land, and the last three hours you'll be flying a hundred feet above the water."

"No worries, Doc. How's Jack doing?"

"Much better. He needs to rest, but Sarah won't let him fall asleep, at least not for a couple more hours. She's worried about a concussion. Once a nurse, always a nurse."

"Did you tell Jack about his friends?" asked Mick.

"Yes, he knows. Do you have anymore news about them?"

"Only that Matty is taking them to a hut somewhere in Otago. He's going to contact us once they get there."

"They really care about him, but they are just pups," said Mick. "If something happens to us, they're all he's got."

Ian cupped his hands over his face and rubbed his forehead.

"No, there is someone else. I'm going back to check on Jack. Maintain radio silence until we hear from Matty. I'll make some tea for us."

"Primo," said Mick.

Jack and Sarah sat in the only seats near the rear of the plane. Most of the cargo area was taken up by two large tanks of precious fuel. The cargo hold was unheated, except for a small electric heater near their seats that kept the temperature a chilly fifty degrees Fahrenheit. Jack sat shivering and wrapped in a blanket, with Sarah sitting next to him, holding his hand.

"How's the headache?" asked Ian.

"Better. Where exactly are we flying to?" asked Jack.

"The South Island. We will land at an abandoned airfield near Invercargill. Ted's son will meet us and drive us to a location a few miles from my ranch."

"Won't Kettering's people be waiting for us?"

"Not where we are going. There's an underground tunnel on the other side of the mountain behind my ranch. It leads to my hidden laboratory. The formula..." he hesitated for a minute. "The real formula is hidden there. We must retrieve it before Kettering finds it."

"Are you sure Eva doesn't know about it?" asked Jack.

"She knows nothing. Only Ted knows, and he won't talk. Ted is a warrior, and he is well aware of the consequences. Excuse me, I'm going to check on Mick."

Jack looked pensively at Sarah. She reached for his hand, and squeezed it gently.

"Why did you give me up for adoption?" asked Jack.

Sarah was startled by his question, and briefly remained silent.

"I did what I thought was right at the time. Ian was totally consumed in his work. I couldn't have brought a child into his life at that time. I am convinced he would have never succeeded in discovering the antimatter formula if we had started a family back then. His work required him to be away for long periods of time in Antarctica. Marriage and a family at that time would have held him back... and it wouldn't have been fair to you. He would have had to abandon his work and take a teaching position at the University to support us. Instead, he made the greatest scientific discovery of this century. You have no idea how hard he worked."

Jack looked unconvinced.

"I couldn't keep you. I had to give you up for adoption. Ian would have found out, and would have wanted to take responsibility. I suffered greatly over my decision." She began to cry. "I take responsibility for what I did. I'm so sorry, Jack."

"It's okay," said Jack, pausing to collect himself. "There were times I felt a connection to you. Did you feel the same with me?"

"I did. First, when you were a little boy, when I would come to visit with Albert and Marie. I would read to you. Every character, every scene, every color that excited you seemed to touch a chord in me in the same manner as when I was a child. Even more pronounced was your likeness to Ian. You have a kind, non-judgmental tenderness that radiates from you, much like Ian does, and your determination and attention to detail reminded me of Ian. I remember how you worked for days without sleep on your landscape architecture projects. That is the same dogged determination that led Ian to his discovery."

"Sarah, I can't help but think about how my parents died for all this. This wasn't fair to them."

"Jack, you must know that Ian did everything he could to help them. Albert was a good man who suffered his whole life because of Kettering and because of the sacrifice he made to save Ian's life. You must understand that the antimatter formula would not have been possible if it weren't for Albert and Marie. Ian tried to warn Albert about Kettering's power and reach. Kettering would have never let Albert go to the media with the story. I'm sorry your parents had to die, but I promise, their deaths were not in vain."

Ian stepped out from behind a fuel tank and approached them.

"Feeling better, Jack?"

"My head is still sore, but I'll be alright."

"He's also hungry," said Sarah. "I think we all could do with a little supper. I'll see what Mick has up front."

"Do you think we'll make it to New Zealand, Ian?" asked Jack.

"Our fate is in Mick's hands. He has to fly low, just above the water, for at least four hundred miles. Then, he has to land this old girl in a remote mountain landing strip on the South Island. It's not going to be easy, but Kettering won't be able to watch every airfield in the South Island, and I don't think we have to worry about him alerting the New Zealand Air Force about us. So I'd say we have a good chance."

"Kettering told me you were going to defect to the Russians."

"I suppose he told you I'm crazy too."

"As a matter of fact—"

"It's all lies. Kettering is an evil man. He'll stop at nothing to get my formula."

"Why can't the US Government stop him?"

"Kettering is a master of subterfuge. He has spent years building layers between his organization and the legitimate intelligence agencies of the US Government. They don't have any idea what he is up to."

"He told me you had my parents murdered by Russian agents."

"The Russians have nothing to do with any of this. Kettering's agents killed your parents to keep Albert from going to the media and exposing him for his crimes and his rogue unit within IWR."

"If my father was so desperate, why couldn't you help him? You couldn't figure a way to get him some money? They would still be alive, and I wouldn't be in this damn mess if you had just helped him."

"I sent him money for as long as I could, but when I suspected Kettering was closing in on our operation at Saint Mark, I had to shut everything down. It was too risky to even try to contact Albert. That's when Sarah left Saint

Mark and rejoined me in Antarctica. She couldn't even tell your parents she was leaving."

"That's bullshit. You used my parents. You left them defenseless to face Kettering."

"Before you pass judgment, would you let me explain something. Thirty years ago, in a stinking hot jungle on Guam, something I can only describe as a divinely inspired vision came to me. A strikingly brilliant idea, a tiny seed, was planted in my brain. It germinated in the depths of my mind, and began to incubate while your father struggled against all odds to carry me away from certain death. He risked his life to save mine, and by doing so, inspired in me a goal to produce the most powerful form of energy known to man."

"So that's how you got the idea to study antimatter?" asked Jack.

"Yes. I devoted my life to that single goal. It was no mere coincidence that your father rescued me. He battled a platoon of Japanese Marines, and he survived Kettering's execution of his own men. Wounded and weak, he crawled through the jungle to rescue me from certain death at the hands of the Japanese. What you are doing now, and what lies ahead for you is very close to the heroic struggle that he faced to make my life possible."

"What are you talking about? What am I doing that is so important?"

"What I'm talking about is a scientific discovery that will mean an endless supply of energy and a force to prevent war, and especially prevent nuclear weapons from destroying the world. The idea came to me in that jungle. I saw bands of sub-atomic particles winding through the universe, which until that point had been undetected. I saw that these particles made up another dimension of the universe, held in balance with the symmetrically opposite sub-atomic particles that we already know to exist. I saw that by collecting the antimatter particles that resulted from collisions of sub-atomic particles in space, I could produce an incredible amount of energy. From that moment, I knew I had to devote my life to the quest to harness it. What I'm talking about is you helping me safeguard the formula—"

"Sorry, did I interrupt? Mick had some bread and cheese. I fixed us all a plate and made some coffee," said Sarah. "What were you saying?"

"I said our lives are interconnected in so many ways. We are all here because of Albert. He brought you into my life, Sarah, and like so many mysteries that unfold by the grace of God, Jack was brought into the world, and he has a destiny to fulfill."

"Destiny? Me? What do you mean?"

"I mean it was destiny that brought you here, just as it was destiny that brought Sarah and I together."

"Why didn't you two stay together?"

"Jack, does that really matter now?" asked Sarah.

"He deserves to know," Ian retorted. "When Sarah came back to see me in New Zealand after the war, she found a totally committed, self-absorbed man completely in love with his work. I loved Sarah, but I was so trapped in my own world that I couldn't find a way to express it. The only thing I could focus on was my quest to harness antimatter. Looking back, it was the biggest mistake I made in my life. I regret that I lost those years with Sarah. I can never bring them back, but God had other plans for me at that time."

"We are at peace now," said Sarah. "It was all meant to be. Look, we are together, and God has blessed us with you, our son."

"Why did you wait to get married in Antarctica of all places?"

"We were about to go into hiding, and we did not want to draw attention to our relationship," said Ian. "The Chapel of the Snows in McMurdo was the perfect place to get married, and only Captain Minton knew about it."

"It's sad that you couldn't even tell Eva you got married. What happened that made her hate you so badly?" asked Jack.

"Eva needed a supportive stepfather who was there for her all the time. I was unable to be either of those. I knew this when I married Helen, and she knew how much I was dedicated to my work. We both thought we could change each other. Poor Eva was caught in the middle. Helen and I quarreled over the time that I had to spend in Antarctica, and it wasn't long before Eva turned against me. I tried my best to be a father to her, but she resented me, and our relationship never worked. Eva blamed me for her mother's death, because we were fighting on the day Helen died."

"Did Eva stay with you then?" asked Jack.

"After Helen died, I tried to raise her and keep up with my research, but she rebelled against me and got in trouble in school. I couldn't concentrate, so I sent her to live with her mother's relatives in Dunedin. She was only fourteen. Around that time, I lost the backing of the university. I foundered for a few years until Sarah wrote me and asked if she could help. That was the motivation I needed. With a renewed zeal, I enlisted the help of your father and began to pass research to Sarah at Saint Mark. That's when the breakthrough came, in the summer of 1967, when I recorded the first fingerprint of a relativistic jet."

"Is that when Kettering began spying on you?"

"Kettering took interest in me a few years before Helen died, and in the last couple of years he watched Albert and Marie more closely. Sarah was also certain there was a spy at Saint Mark, as someone was tampering with her computers. That's when I had to stop sending money to your father. Sarah could no longer support my research from Saint Mark, so she joined me in New Zealand. It didn't take Kettering long to surmise that I was nearing a major breakthrough in my antimatter research. He had spies everywhere, even in Antarctica. That's why we spent months at the Argentine base at Esperanza. The head Argentine scientist was a good friend, and he made sure we had privacy. That allowed me to finalize my calculations. Last year, I completed the detailed specifications for the antimatter formula."

"It will be mankind's greatest hope for peace," said Sarah.

"Unless we fail to stop Kettering," said Ian.

"God help us," said Sarah.

Chapter 17
The Formula

As the aging plane flew north across the night sky, Jack listened intently to Sarah and Ian tell their stories and reveal details of their lives that opened his eyes to a world that was too unbelievable to comprehend. He admired Sarah's fierce devotion to Ian, and her strong convictions for a nuclear-free world. He knew her as a kind, caring woman who was always willing to help him, but he never knew just how strongly she cared for him and instinctively wanted to protect him. He remembered when she drove from the college in the middle of a snowstorm to sit up with him when he was nine and sick with pneumonia, because his father had to work the nightshift, and his mother was sick.

Sarah came to most of his birthdays, sporting events, and his presentations at Saint Mark. Throughout his life, she showed him the same kindness, compassion, and loyalty she showed Ian. Even more enlightening was the realization that Jack shared the same convictions to help mankind that Ian did; Jack through design, and Ian through science. Jack came to respect Ian's analytical mind, but he struggled to understand the science that Ian tried to explain to him. Ironically, Ian's understanding of landscape architecture and his shared interest in the things that Jack was studying at Saint Mark struck a common chord with him.

"A park is more than a plot of land with a collection of plants and walkways," said Ian. "It should have a sense of place, and the variety of spaces should feel like a place that has a soul. It should be a progression of spaces, with views and paths that invite and surprise the visitor. Don't you think, Jack?"

"That sounds like something right out of my second year design studio. Do you really understand design principles of landscape architecture?"

"Of course I do. I told you, it's my hobby. I'm partial to Capability Brown and the English Landscape Gardening School. Hyde Park and Blenheim in England, your Central Park in New York, and my favorite, Hagley Park in Christchurch, are fine examples of that design philosophy. But, I must say I am in awe at the power of the Palace of Versailles in France, the shear dominance of man over nature exemplified in the magnificent gardens, the great fountains and topiary, and the sheer scale of it all. I've read about these places, and someday I would love to visit them with you."

"You make me wish I was back at Saint Mark."

"And you will be. Brother Vincent is sure you will return someday."

"Wait, what? How do you know Brother Vincent?"

"He came to visit us at the Argentine base at Esperanza a couple of years ago. He is a very holy man. You should listen to him. He has helped me to strengthen my faith. I don't think I could have made it this far without him."

"Funny, I feel the same way," said Jack.

"Brother Vincent taught me how to pray to the Holy Spirit," said Ian. "I would have never figured out how relativistic jets are generated from the twisting magnetic fields if it wasn't for inspiration from the Holy Spirit. For most of my life, I believed in God. I believed in serving the greater good. But it was Vincent who explained the concept of God's grace and the power of prayer… I have so much to tell you."

"We have the rest of our lives to be a family," said Sarah. "That is, if you want that, Jack."

"Of course I want that," said Jack, even though he may have felt differently a few hours earlier. He was torn between anger at Ian and Sarah, and the peace of mind from knowing he had a family again. "But what about Kettering?" he continued. "He'll never stop hunting us to get the formula. What kind of life will we have? What about Grace? I love her… and what about Reggie? I can't turn my back on Reggie. They're risking their lives to help me. No way, I can't. Damn it, why can't you just give Kettering what he wants? Eventually, someone else is going to figure out this antimatter stuff. Let Kettering go after them. Do you really mean to tell me the United States doesn't know about it already?"

"No scientist, and no country, has made the progress that I have. And believe me, all the major powers are seeking to develop it. Carbon-based fuels such as coal, oil, and gas are polluting the atmosphere and becoming more and more costly to extract. The number of nuclear power plants is growing every year, and the risk of a cataclysmic accident grows with it. Antimatter is the answer to the world's energy crisis, and the means to live peacefully without nuclear weapons and nuclear energy."

"Why don't you work for the New Zealand Government? You don't have to work for Kettering."

"You don't know how the world works, Jack. New Zealand doesn't have the resources to go it alone. Eventually, the US and other world powers would end up collaborating with New Zealand. Then, the legitimate military establishment in the US would eventually succumb to the political hawks in the government, and there would be pressure to make it into a weapon."

"So, what's wrong with that? All the major powers of the world have nuclear weapons. Hell, there are enough nuclear weapons in the world today to destroy the entire planet, and that hasn't happened yet."

"You have no idea of the destructive power of an antimatter weapon. The world has never seen this kind of power, something much more powerful than a hydrogen bomb. I will not allow a weapon like this to be built. My formula must only be used for peaceful endeavors, and must be used to prevent war, not make it. That is why I plan to keep it secret until the world is ready. I could never work for Kettering. I could never work for any country, because I know they will eventually try to make it into a weapon."

"But wouldn't antimatter weapons in the hands of countries that have nuclear weapons today still employ the same policy of mutual assured destruction that keep us from launching nuclear weapons at each other?"

"No, I don't think so," said Ian. "My formula is unique. No one has anything close to it, so whoever has my formula will dominate the world."

"How can antimatter be this powerful? Is it possible to explain it to me in simple terms? What exactly is this formula? How can a formula alone generate such power?"

"Do you know about the Big Bang Theory, the origin of the universe?"

"Sure. I took Sarah's Intro to Physics class," said Jack with a smirk.

"Shortly after the Big Bang, the universe was composed of matter and antimatter. You know what matter is, right?" Jack nodded. "Well, antimatter is the symmetrical opposite of matter. In antimatter, there are antiparticles, where the electrons are positive and protons are negative, the opposite of matter. Neutrons are a little more complicated. All you need to know is that when antimatter particles collide with particles of matter, they annihilate each other and release an unimaginable amount of energy, because one hundred percent of the mass is converted into energy. We know this from Einstein's Theory of Relativity. In plain terms, one fifty-millionth of a single gram of antimatter would be equivalent to 4,000 pounds of TNT, or a few grams of antimatter would be thousands of times more powerful than a hydrogen bomb."

"So, if in the Big Bang, matter and antimatter particles annihilate each other, where is the matter left over to make up earth and the other planets in our solar system?"

"I believe that some matter must have been left behind to make up our universe. You see, antimatter is still being generated by relativistic jets that originate in black holes in far off galaxies, and I've shown that it's possible to capture it."

"How is that?"

"That's the tricky part. That is what I envisioned on Guam when Albert rescued me. I thought I was hallucinating, but it was a real vision. There were bands of energy crisscrossing the earth. I saw there were sub-atomic particles that were smaller than protons and electrons that clung to the jets. I noticed that these particles could be dislodged and captured. I couldn't understand how that was done, but I understood that the particles had a tremendous amount of energy. I also envisioned a means to harness and control these particle collisions."

"How soon did you start working on your research?"

"After the war, I went back to university and concentrated on the study of relativistic jets and the means of capturing antimatter from them in outer space. I discovered that relativistic jets contain antimatter particles, part of a universal, unseen energy that is everywhere, and contributes mass to everything in the universe. I knew that once I proved my theory, I had to devote my life to harnessing antimatter energy. I was even more emboldened by what I saw happening in the world after World War II. The escalation of nuclear technology for energy and weapons would increase the potential for worldwide destruction. That motivated me to find an alternative to nuclear energy and its hazardous radiation. I'm most proud of discovering how to use antimatter energy to render nuclear weapons harmless."

"That is what first brought attention to you from the United States intelligence community, and later, from the IWR," said Sarah.

"That is right, dear. It was in 1962 when I published my first paper that identified the properties of antimatter in a relativistic jet. That is right around the time Kettering began spying on me, and that's when I knew I had to take my work underground and out of the public eye."

"That's around the time Helen was killed too. Eva said that spies killed Helen, and she blamed you," said Jack.

"She was killed by spies, but not by the Soviets, or even by my own government, as I once suspected. I'm convinced it was Kettering. Before he began to spy on me, I had good relations with the New Zealand and United States scientific communities. But once Kettering dug his claws into my life, everything began to unravel. My work was discredited by my New Zealand colleagues. Even my closest associate, Dr. Merlin Crankshaw, turned against me and led a smear campaign to discredit me. I was shocked because we were such good mates. We studied together at university. I was even the best man at his wedding. He knew more about my research than anyone else. But Kettering got to him, and like a cancer, he grew on him. He planted ideas in his head, and eventually Merlin came to envy me. He became obsessed with trying to steal my research. It was no coincidence that on the day Helen died, Crankshaw was the only person who knew when and where she was going. I'm positive he tipped off Kettering."

He paused as Sarah gave him a sympathetic smile.

"I should have never given her such an important document to deliver by herself, but I was suffering from a terrible migraine headache and couldn't drive. I had to get the calculations to a professor who was leaving for the UK that evening. I would have called Merlin, but I was beginning to distrust him, and I did not want him to see these particular calculations. That's why I needed Helen to drive. God forgive me for putting her in harm's way. My headache was so bad that I didn't realize I gave her the wrong folder. So as it was, Helen did not die in vain. After the accident, Crankshaw disappeared with the bogus calculations. Kettering must have thought he finally had the breakthrough that would lead to the completion of the formula. Instead, it set him back years, and it bought me time to work in my underground laboratory and funnel the formulations to Sarah, who had access to the powerful new computers at Saint Mark. During that time, I fooled the scientific community into thinking I had a nervous breakdown and could no longer be taken seriously."

"This is unbelievable! It all sounds like the plot to a bad movie."

Ian looked Jack in the eye with a calm, deadly serious stare. Jack looked away.

"Look at me. There never will be anything more serious in your life. My formula is real, and it will change the world."

The intensity in Ian's speech seemed to finally resonate with Jack.

"Okay, I'll help. I'll try to understand all this. So tell me more. You were explaining relative jets. How do you get the antimatter from those jets?"

"Relativistic jets originate from black holes in distant galaxies. They may be hundreds of thousands of light years away. The jets are created from superheated gases, or plasma, that contains a mixture of antiparticles. As I said before, antiparticles have the same mass but opposite charges of ordinary matter. When the collisions occur between antimatter and matter in the black holes, the relativistic jets that are produced are full of positrons and antiprotons, which can be intercepted and trapped in space."

"But what does the formula do?" asked Jack.

"I have demonstrated a process to separate the antimatter from these jets by altering the magnetic fields that surround the particles, thus freeing them so they can be channeled and stored in a vessel in outer space. The particles are separated from the jets by a MASER that—"

"Hold on, what's a MASER?"

"It's a device that creates microwave emissions of radiation, which results in antimatter particles breaking away from the jets. A cluster of MASERS fire pulses of electromagnetic radiation in a geometric pattern from a specially designed spaceship or space station orbiting the earth. The pulses form a sort of fishing net, if you will. They excite the gamma rays in relativistic jets causing a change in their magnetic field. The electromagnetic radiation they produce is precisely calculated to make wavelengths that match the wavelengths emitted by antimatter particles, thus absorbing the particles into a higher energy state. The laws of thermodynamics tell us that these particles will want to move to a lower energy state. So, they must be trapped and contained in a super-low temperature vacuum by powerful electro-magnets, before they dissipate and are carried away into space by neutrinos. These traps are essentially fuel tanks full of antimatter particles. The antimatter particles are fed to a fusion reactor where they collide with matter to generate energy."

"How is that regulated? Wouldn't the whole thing blow up when the matter and antimatter collide?"

Sarah smiled at Ian.

"That's a very insightful question, Jack. The answer lies in the mountains of the South Island, and nowhere else in the world. You see, to make the reactor work, I have discovered that super-hard crystals of calcium magnesium silicate mineral emit an electromagnetic field that can be easily manipulated with MASERS to release regulated amounts of matter. That way, the collision of matter and antimatter can be controlled to produce energy."

"What is this mineral?" asked Jack.

"Look no further than Sarah's necklace," said Ian.

Sarah removed her necklace and showed Jack a beautiful jade Tiki.

"That's jade, some kind of Maori symbol, right?" asked Jack.

"Yes, we call it New Zealand Greenstone," said Ian. "The Tiki is a symbol of the first man created by the Maori gods."

"Jade crystals, MASER antimatter nets, super-cooled magnetic traps… I don't mean to sound disrespectful, but how do you know all this will work? I assume you've never been able to test your prototypes in outer space, right?"

136

"Well, sort of… that is to say, a colleague of mine, an American quantum physicist with the National Science Foundation who worked with me in Antarctica, arranged to send a small-scale device that I built into space on several of the Apollo missions. These devices tested the effects of electromagnets in a vacuum. The whole affair remains a great triumph of mine over Kettering. His agents never knew a thing about it."

"Ian, I understand that you have figured out how to capture and store antimatter, but how could you possibly design and build an antimatter engine? It sounds impossible for one man to do on his own."

"Jack, I don't mean to sound pretentious, but in my laboratory, I have designed and built prototypes of a device that simulates the use of antimatter to create fission-free explosions. These explosions produce energy that can be used to generate an endless supply of power."

"But they could also be used to create a weapon, a weapon more powerful than anything the world has ever seen," said Sarah.

Ian turned away from Jack and reached for Sarah's hand.

"Unlike Kettering, I am only concerned with using my formula to prevent nuclear annihilation."

"Ian has developed a preliminary design for an antimatter defensive shield that would vaporize nuclear missiles and bombers in the event that a hostile country launches an attack," said Sarah.

"That's right, and a space-based system could even be effective at neutralizing the lethal radiation from a nuclear blast," said Ian.

"How's that going to stop a crazy terrorist from setting off a suitcase nuclear bomb?" asked Jack.

"It probably won't. Some people don't care who they harm. They have no remorse. They do not feel the pain and suffering that is brought by death and destruction. They live only to draw others into their darkness."

"What does Kettering want with the formula?"

"Kettering operates a secret division of IWR. The Pentagon, CIA, and the NSA don't know a thing about it."

"You're saying Kettering is freelancing? You're saying he would keep the formula for himself?"

"He might, but it's more likely he has contracted to deliver the formula to another country or organization. They've probably paid him a substantial amount of money, and they are demanding that he bring it to them."

"I can't believe our government knows nothing about Kettering."

"I'm afraid that's the case. Instead, Kettering has managed to create multiple layers of confusing, useless intelligence on me."

"But your formula is safe, right?" asked Jack.

"Yes, it's hidden in the…" Ian hesitated, and glanced toward Sarah. "It's in a vault in my underground laboratory."

"Ian, you must tell Jack the truth about what we face," said Sarah.

"The truth is, that God help us if my formula falls into Kettering's hands. What's more, he will not hesitate to kill all of us once he has no more use for

us. That's why we cannot fail. We must retrieve the formula, and we must…
we must kill Kettering. I must be able to count on you, Jack."

"I don't know if I can promise you that. I don't know if I can kill—"

"It's not a matter of choice," said Ian.

"But Kettering's people are already at your ranch, and they've captured
Ted. What if he talks? What then?"

"He won't talk."

"Jack is right, Ian. Ted knows about the tunnel from the ranch, and the
one on the other side of the mountain. They'll use everything at their disposal
to make Ted talk. Oh, poor Ted."

"Stop it, Sarah! We can't dwell on that. Ted would die before he talked."

"What about Grace and Reggie? What's going to happen to them? You
haven't said anything about an escape plan for them. I won't risk their lives like
you are willing to risk Ted's."

"Matty is protecting your friends, but remember, they have willingly come
to help. I can't possibly guarantee their safety. Ted knows what's at stake. He is
willing, like Sarah and I, to sacrifice his life if necessary. Maybe I have
misjudged you."

"Maybe you have! I just want a chance to live my life with Grace. You
can't possibly fault me for that."

"Don't be foolish. Do you think Kettering will let any of us live once he
has the formula? Everything has come down to a fight for survival. It's kill, or
be killed. You will have no other choice."

Jack sat back in his seat, his hands trembling. Ian reached in a knapsack
and pulled out a .45 pistol, and handed it to Jack.

"When the time comes, you must not be afraid to use this," said Ian.

Jack stood up and paced anxiously about the plane.

"I need to know there is an escape plan, regardless of whether or not we
succeed," said Jack. "I need to know we have a chance."

Ian looked up and smiled at Jack.

"Mick and Matty are working on an escape plan. They have arranged to
take us by ship to New Caledonia."

"New Caledonia? How long would we stay there? And what about Grace
and Reggie?"

"If we kill Kettering, it won't matter," said Ian. "I will contact Captain
Minton, and he will make everything right for you and your friends."

Sarah put her arm around Ian. Jack could sense the tremendous angst that
Ian was feeling.

"Why don't you contact Captain Minton?" asked Jack. "You said he
would believe you."

"No, that is impossible. As long as Kettering is alive, there is no one we
can turn to in the United States Navy. If Kettering survives, then we will all
have to go into hiding and assume new identities. He'll never stop hunting us."

"Brother Vincent will help us—" said Sarah, as she was interrupted by the
cracking static of the cabin intercom. Mick groggily asked Ian to come up to

the cockpit. "Mick has got to be exhausted. He probably wants Ian to take over the controls for a while."

"Does Ian know how to fly?" asked Jack, looking puzzled.

"Yes, but he's a bit rusty. He probably couldn't land it, but he'll be fine while Mick gets some rest. He trained as a bomber pilot during the war."

Sarah glanced toward the cockpit, as an exhausted Mick shuffled from the pilot's seat and collapsed in the navigator's chair. He fell right to sleep. Ian called for Sarah to come to the cockpit.

"We are about 700 miles from Invercargill at the present course. We can't try radioing Calvin until we are within 200 miles." He motioned for Sarah to come closer, and whispered to her. "Everything depends on what happens at the ranch. We must get there before Kettering. Have you thought of what to tell Jack before we land in case something happens to us?"

Tears began to well up in Sarah's eyes.

"He is so young. How will he find the strength for what lies ahead?"

"He must. He's our only hope."

Chapter 18
Saint Anthony Help Us

Sarah could sense a growing anxiety in Jack. The cold cargo hold was beginning to feel like a prison cell. His mood had changed after Ian talked about killing Kettering. The thought of killing someone in cold blood unnerved him. Could he pull the trigger if he had to? Sarah watched as he tapped his foot nervously, while rocking back and forth and tugging on his painful cheek.

"You'll find the courage to do it when the time comes," said Sarah. "Albert and Ian had to in the war. Ian and I would do it to protect you, but more importantly, we would do it to stop Kettering."

"I'm worried about Grace and Reggie. If Ted talks and Kettering finds the formula, then we're no longer any use to him. What do you think he'll do? You know damn well he'll track us down and kill us. I can't let Grace and Reggie get involved in this."

"They know what they are getting into. They accepted the risks," said Sarah.

"Did they? Do they know what this is all really about? Do they know they could be killed?"

"They want to help rescue you from Kettering. They are doing this for you, Jack. Look, we may not even have to face Kettering. If we can get to the laboratory and retrieve the formula before he gets there, then we have a chance to escape and start new lives." She reached across and hugged Jack. "The hope for a lasting peace in the world depends on our success."

As she spoke, the plane lurched, and Jack was thrown sideways against the wall. Ian yelled into the intercom for Jack to come to the cockpit. Sarah undid her seatbelt and followed. When they got to the cockpit, Mick was lying on the floor unconscious, and his head was bleeding badly. Ian struggled to control the plane.

"The right engine died, and the gauge is showing we are almost out of fuel," said Ian. "I don't know what happened. The fuel level just started dropping... one of the fuel tanks must have taken a hit from the machine gun fire when we took off."

"How far are we from the New Zealand coast?" asked Jack.

"I can't say for sure. I'd say we are about seventy-five miles or less. How is Mick?"

Sarah was bent over Mick, holding his head and trying to stop the bleeding.

"He is unconscious, and barely breathing," she said. "The radio fell off the shelf and hit him in the head. His skull might be fractured."

"Jack, see if you can get the portable UHF radio working and try to contact Matty at 523 megahertz," said Ian. "Our present course was supposed to take us fifty miles west of Invercargill, but I'm not sure where we are."

Jack set up the radio and began transmitting. Ian struggled to control the plane as it flew dangerously low on only one engine, in the darkness, and less than a hundred feet above the ocean. After several minutes, Matty finally replied on the radio. Jack handed the microphone to Ian, who relayed their present course, speed, and coordinates to Matty.

"Queens Park, this is All Black. You are about forty miles off shore. Maintain your present course. You should see lights along the coast. Can you make it to LG? Over."

"I don't think so. We will be lucky to make the coast. I may have to ditch in the water. Over."

"Transmit your position when you ditch. I will pick you up by boat. Out."

"Jack, there's a cold water wetsuit in that locker," said Ian. "Put it on. There's only one."

"I'll be okay. I think Sarah should have it."

"Damn it, Jack. The ocean temperature is below fifty degrees. You'll need it to survive," Ian insisted.

"But what about you?"

"Do as I say and put it on," said Ian

"Put it on!" screamed Sarah.

Jack hurriedly obeyed. Matty's voice again reverberated from the radio.

"Keep transmitting. I'm getting a bearing on you. You are about fifty miles west of Invercargill, heading for a deserted coastline."

Suddenly, the left engine sputtered. Ian yelled for Sarah and Jack to put their life jackets and seatbelts on.

"Jack, listen to me," said Ian. "You must know the truth. If something happens to Sarah and me, you must destroy the laboratory. Kettering must believe that the formula has been destroyed. The real formula is not there. Do you hear me?"

"Yes, yes, I understand. But—"

"Listen to me. Whether or not you succeed or fail, you must kill him."

"Kill! I don't know if I can... where is the real formula?" Ian didn't answer, as he struggled to control the plane. "Where is it?" shouted Jack.

"In Hagley Park... but you cannot tell anyone, not even Grace, until the lab is destroyed. Then and only then, go to Hagley Park, and all will be revealed to you."

"Where in Hagley Park?"

"Botanic Gardens."

Ian continued to struggle with the plane. Jack could see dim lights on the shoreline far in the distance. They were still twenty miles away from the coastline in open water.

"Put the radio in the waterproof sack," said Ian. "The raft is by the door. As soon as we are in the water, open the door, then set out the raft and inflate it. That's our only hope to contact Matty."

Sarah unbuckled her seatbelt and put her arms around Jack. She kissed him on the forehead, and then removed her necklace.

141

"Take this. You'll need it once you're in the lab to unlock the destruct switch."

"Put your belt back on," Jack yelled.

"I always loved you. I would have been a good mother. Forgive me." She moved toward Ian to hold his hand.

"Stop it! We're gonna' make it," yelled Jack.

"Destroy the lab, Jack! Everything… revealed at Hagley Park," said Ian.

Jack watched in horror as the propeller slowed and then abruptly stopped, followed by an eerie silence, except for the sound of rushing air. The plane glided for a few seconds, then bounced off the whitecaps in the water. The nose struck the waves, breaking the plane in half. The force of the impact hurled Sarah against the navigation equipment with such force that she fractured her arm and crushed her rib cage. By sheer chance, her body became a protective cushion that prevented Jack from smashing his head into the cabin wall. Sarah screamed in pain as she stared at the bone protruding from her forearm. Ian sat motionless, slumped over in the pilot's seat as water rushed in from the severed fuselage. He grimaced in pain as Jack struggled to pull him from his seat. He was vomiting blood and his leg appeared to be broken.

Adrenaline propelled Jack across the cabin to unlock the escape door. He pulled frantically on the latch, as he glanced back and forth at Ian and Sarah. In one last effort, mustering all of his strength, he managed to pull the door open. At the same time, frigid ocean water poured through the opening. The surge of water pushed him back as he grabbed Ian and pulled him through the door and onto the wing. The damaged plane rocked and bobbed in the rough sea.

Jack went back for Sarah, who had started to go into shock. He grabbed her by her life jacket and towed her onto the wing alongside Ian. But as he did, the rear half of the plane separated completely, and began to sink rapidly into the ocean. At that moment, he realized he had to find the life raft if they had any chance to survive. He only had a few minutes before the wing sank. He mumbled the words of the Hail Mary, unable to finish each prayer that he started. He watched helplessly as the rough waves pulled Mick's dead body away from the plane.

Ian and Sarah were positioned precariously on the partially submerged wing, as Jack swam back through the door and frantically searched the dark cabin, guided only by the faint moonlight. He remembered from survival class in boot camp that a man would only have a few minutes to survive in forty-degree water. He yelled out as loud as he could, pleading in desperation to Saint Anthony.

"Saint Anthony, help us. You are the patron saint of lost things. Please help me find the raft. Saint Anthony, help us… Saint Anthony!"

The wing started to sink faster. Jack struggled to see through the foamy waves. Then it appeared, as if out of midair. The bright yellow canvas bundle bobbed in the water, just above the navigator's chair. He only had a minute to inflate the raft before the wing sank, with Ian and Sarah on top of it. He was shivering uncontrollably, and he was having trouble moving his fingers. He managed to pull the painter's cord that released compressed gas, inflating the raft in seconds. He pulled himself in and paddled toward the wing, then pulled Ian and Sarah into the raft just as the wing slipped quietly below the dark ocean. Then, he turned his attention to trying to stop the bleeding from their injuries. He found tourniquets in the first aid kit and applied them the best he could. Sarah and Ian were both in shock, mumbling incoherent things to each other. Jack covered them with a dry blanket that he had found inside the raft. Then, he tried to contact Matty on the portable radio that was in the raft. But to his dismay, the battery pack was wet, which only permitted a few seconds of transmitting.

"Damn it! Son of bitch! Something go right for me!" It was 4:30 a.m., two hours before sunrise. Kettering was probably preparing to take off from McMurdo, and Jack figured his agents would be listening for his transmissions and searching for them by this point. The green light flashed on the radio, indicating that he could transmit. Hopefully, Matty would get a fix on their position. Far off in the distance, he could see faint lights and the outline of the coast, and he paddled toward the light. Meanwhile, Sarah continued to moan in pain. She motioned for Jack to come close to her, and he held her in his arms.

"Jack, save yourself. I... love... you. I would have been a good mother to you." Her breathing became more and more labored, until the point that she gasped for air. Jack tried to calm her, but she was slipping away. Then Ian spoke, in a weak, broken voice.

"Destroy lab... formula is fake..." Ian coughed and choked. "You are...only hope..." He struggled to breathe. His voice grew weaker, and he looked at Sarah to help him explain. She spoke in a weak, fragmented voice.

"Hagley Park... letter explains everything... I love you..." She trailed off.

"Where in Hagley Park?" Jack pleaded. He frantically tried to adjust the radio, while moving back and forth between Sarah and Ian. Ian leaned toward Jack, and called faintly to him. He spoke in a weak, slurred voice.

"Hagley Park... Japanese... other piece... Brother Loo..." Then Ian closed his eyes, too weak to say anything more.

"Other piece of what?" Jack pleaded.

It didn't matter at that moment though. Survival depended on the radio. He adjusted the settings and tried other frequencies, and after a few tries, the radio finally erupted with Matty's voice. Jack sprang up and grabbed the microphone. Matty was in trouble.

"Queens Park, this is All Black. I got your position fifteen miles west of the city and five miles off shore. I'm going to make a run for you. Keep transmitting so I have a bearing. I got company about ten minutes behind me, and I can't shake him."

"Matty, this is Jack. Ian and Mick are—" he abruptly ended his transmission. He realized that IWR could be monitoring the radio, and he did not want them to know that Ian and Mick were dead. "Roger. Out."

He settled back and held Sarah in his arms, and he thought about Ian's last words. He felt a renewed sense of purpose in carrying out his last wish.

143

After fifteen minutes had passed, he began scanning the dark horizon for signs of Matty's boat. A faint red light in the distance grew brighter as the craft approached. Matty's voice cracked on the radio. He had them in sight, but the boat that was chasing him was closing. Jack told Sarah they were about to be rescued, but she was too weak and unable to speak. He turned his attention to the two sets of lights approaching them... Matty's boat, and the IWR boat in pursuit. He knew he would only have seconds to transfer Ian and Sarah onto Matty's boat.

He tried to contact Matty. As he tuned the radio, he didn't notice both Ian and Sarah roll off the back of the raft, leaving their life jackets behind. Within seconds, they sank in the cold, gray water. After a few minutes of concentrating on the radio, he glanced back, but to his horror, saw that they were gone. He frantically searched the water around the raft, screaming their names. Tears fogged his eyes. Matty was rapidly approaching, with the pursuing boat minutes behind. He continued to yell for them, just as Matty pulled alongside the raft.

"Where are Sarah and the Doc? Where's Mick?" asked Matty.

"All dead," shouted Jack, with tears in his eyes. "Mick died in the plane crash. Ian and Sarah died a few minutes ago. I tried to stop the bleeding... they were hurt bad."

Matty hesitated for a moment, his eyes fixed on Jack, as if he was unconvinced.

"If you are Jack, then where was Grace born?"

"What?"

"Where was Grace born?" demanded Matty.

"Are you serious... Muncie, Indiana. Now where is she? Is she okay? Is Reggie okay?"

Matty handed Jack a knife.

"Yes, they are okay. Deflate the raft and sink it, then hurry into the boat. IWR is only minutes behind us."

Jack paused for a second, and stared at the sea foam that flowed across the waves where the raft had disappeared. He wiped his watery eyes.

"I know how you must feel. They were like parents to me too. And Mick... Mick was my best mate...Ahhhhhhh!" He let out a Maori war cry that pierced the air. Then, he accelerated away from the pursuing boat, which was now just a few hundred yards behind them.

Backlit by the faint light of breaking dawn, Jack could make out three armed figures. The boat looked to be bigger and faster than Matty's. Gunfire erupted in their direction, as the pursuing boat closed. Matty threw Jack a parka and handed him a machine gun. He pushed the boat to full throttle. The bow bounced across the whitecaps of the rough sea, but the pursuing boat persisted. The cool, gusty sea air invigorated Jack, and he fired a couple of bursts at their pursuers.

"Our only chance is to lose them in the inlets. Hold on," said Matty. He steered the boat toward a rugged section of coastline along the shore. The rising sun illuminated the steep cliff surrounding the inlets.

"They're closing," yelled Jack, as bullets streamed past the boat.

Matty guided it toward a group of rocky islands with jagged shoals. One mistake in these waters would spell disaster. Matty knew that if he could lure his pursuers into the shallow waters, he might be able to force them into the rocks. As he maneuvered around the rocks, the pursuing boat accelerated toward them. This was his chance. He dashed behind a small island, and then appeared to accelerate as if to make a run for open water. The other boat took the bait and followed him, heading straight for the jagged shoals lying just below the surface. In the early morning light, the pilot of the IWR boat drove straight over the rocks, tearing the boat apart as it exploded. Matty pushed the throttle all the way open and headed east for the Invercargill harbor.

"They knew where we were," said Matty. "They knew when and where your plane crashed. I can't figure it out. Mick flew under the radar, right?"

"Yes, as far as I know."

"So how did they know? They seem to know our every move. They must have planted a homing device on you." Matty inspected Jack's wetsuit, while Jack checked his pockets. "Nothing. Wait, have you had the same boots on since you left Antarctica?"

"Yea, why?"

"Take your boots off, then take the controls." Matty examined each boot. He pushed and pulled on the soles, and felt the sides. Then, on the second boot, he felt something hard tucked in the insulation on the side. "It's in this boot... a small transmitter. That's how they've been following us." He cut the boot with his knife, then removed the transmitter and threw it overboard. "Standard IWR stuff. They could have followed us straight to your friends, and right to the Doc's lab. We have to get out of here... find a place to hide until dark."

Matty thought for a moment. He figured IWR would expect them to head west to the Fiordland, where there would be hundreds of places to hide with out-of-the-way roads. They would not expect them to head for Invercargill.

"We'll slip into Bluff Harbor in broad daylight," said Matty. "They won't be expecting us."

"What about the boat? We can't just park it out in the open. Someone will see the bullet holes."

"Don't worry, my friend has a boat repair shed. We'll take it there, and then we'll take his skiff up the New River estuary to the wharf at Invercargill. Did you say back there on the raft that Sarah was your mother?"

"That's right. I suppose I have two mothers and two fathers."

"How's that?"

"It's pretty complicated..."

"You are a very privileged man. Very blessed."

"I believe I am."

"The Doc placed his faith in you. That's what Mick told me on the radio before the plane crashed. I swore I would help take you to the laboratory. Mick told me that if something happens to the Doc or Sarah, then I'm to help you blow it up before IWR gets to the formula."

"And help get my friends home too."

"Right-O. Your friends are fine. Your sheila will be mighty glad to see you... and you should have seen Reg. I had to disguise him as a visiting rugby player from Tonga."

Jack laughed, and realized it was the first time he had laughed since he landed in New Zealand a month ago. Matty turned the boat around and sped toward Invercargill. As the boat sliced across the waves, the ocean wind inflated Matty's hair. Jack thought he resembled a Maori figure that he'd seen in a magazine, a warrior carved from the bow of a Maori war canoe. All he needed were the elaborate green markings on his face.

An hour later, they reached the mouth of the harbor. They slipped past the docks undetected, and quickly headed for Matty's friend's vacant shed. It was almost noon. Jack had fallen into a deep sleep below deck. He had only had a couple hours of sleep in the last two days. Matty knew it wasn't safe to venture out in daylight, so sleep was the best use of time until nightfall. Matty had just closed his eyes, when the radio came to life.

"All Black, this is Scrum. Over."

"Read you. Over," said Matty.

"What's going on? Over."

Matty was anxious to hear from Calvin, but he worried that IWR could be listening. Still, he had to let him know the plans had changed.

"Go to alternate. Over," said Matty.

That meant Matty and Jack were on their own to get to the next rendezvous point. Matty left a note for Jack and went out to pick up food. He returned around four o'clock in the afternoon with fish and chips, a couple of beers, and some new clothes for Jack, who was still asleep.

"Wake up, Jack. I brought some food. We have to leave right now. The police have roadblocks set up all over town. They are looking for your friends... two AWOL American sailors, wanted for assault and robbery at the US Antarctic Program Base in Christchurch. Take a look at this." He handed Jack a copy of the local newspaper. "Reggie and Grace made the front page."

"That son-of-a-bitch. Kettering set them up to get to us. He concocted some story about Reggie beating up and robbing a sailor at the base, and then running off with Grace." He continued reading. "Hmm, they don't mention me in the article."

"Of course not. Kettering doesn't want anyone to know anything about you."

"Where are Grace and Reggie right now?"

Matty held his hand up, his mouth full of fish and chips. He noticed something in the newspaper, and started paging quickly to the sports section.

"Queens Park Fish n' Chips... best fish and chips in the South Island, and my favorite place when I played rugby down here. I wonder..." he thought for a moment, then scanned the sports pages. "That's it. Friday nights are Professional Rugby Union games. Canterbury has a game here tonight. They'll be leaving on the train for Christchurch tomorrow morning. I know the team manager. He can get us a seat with the team. I'm going to make you look like a rugby player."

"Uh, okay. Where are Grace and Reggie right now?"

"They're with Calvin in a hut at the Dasher."

"Who's Calvin... and what is the Dasher?"

"He's Ted's son. He's like family to the Doc. And the Dasher is short for Mt. Dasher. It's about two hundred miles from here, just south of the Hawkdun Range."

"He must be really worried about his father."

"He is. When he found out that Kettering was holding his dad, he almost lost it. I was worried he wouldn't agree to bring your friends to the Dasher from Letts Gully."

"Letts Gully?"

"It's an abandoned Royal New Zealand Air Force airfield. Mick was supposed to land there, and Calvin was going to take the Doc and Sarah to the ranch to blow up the lab. But when the Doc told us you were on the plane, we decided to bring your friends to Letts Gully. Then, I was going to take the three of you to a safe place and wait for the Doc's instructions. Of course with the crash and all, everything changed, and Calvin had to take Grace and Reggie to the Dasher. Pass the chips. I can't think without food."

"Okay, so we have to go there right away."

"Listen, mate. I promised the Doc I would take care of you and your friends and help destroy the lab. Until we get to the Dasher, you just do as I say, okay?"

"I'm sorry, Matty. It's just that I did not want my friends to get hurt."

"We brought your friends here, because the Doc said if something happened to me and Mick, they would be your only connection back to the US Navy. Otherwise, without a passport, you are a man without a country. At least your friends can vouch for you, especially if Kettering erased your identity."

"Did Ian ever say anything to you about Hagley Park in Christchurch?"

"No, just that he liked to go there. Why do you ask?"

"No real reason. He just mentioned it before he died."

"What happened, anyway? I never asked you what went wrong."

"We ran out of fuel. They must have shot one of the fuel tanks when we took off from Antarctica. Ian was at the controls when it happened. Mick died when we hit the water. Sarah was trying to get to the co-pilot's seat to be with Ian. I screamed at her to put her seat belt on. Everything happened so fast. They were all smashed up. I did all I could, but they lost a lot of blood. They were dying, and I had to fix the radio. I didn't see them go overboard. Honest, I'm so sorry."

"It's okay, mate. Don't you see what they did? They knew if they'd stayed on the raft it would have held us up. We probably wouldn't have gotten away. They sacrificed their lives so we could finish the mission. Now, it's all up to us. We'll figure it out. She'll be right, mate. No worries."

"Ian must have really loved that place," said Jack.

"What's that you say?"

"Hagley Park."

"Oh yes, that's a beautiful place. The Doc always said it was the most peaceful place he knew. He must have wanted you to know he loved it there."

"I suppose so."

Chapter 19
Meeting at the Dasher

Early Saturday morning, Matty and Jack, wearing red and black Canterbury Crusader rugby shirts under their jackets, stepped out of the skiff and climbed a set of steps to a private dock on the south side of Invercargill. The weather was overcast, drizzly, and windy, a typical late-autumn day in the southernmost city in the South Island. No one noticed the two hooded figures dodging raindrops as they walked the six blocks to the train station.

The streets were filled with shoppers, in spite of the bad weather. They ducked into a small café near the train station, and waited for the bus carrying the Canterbury team to arrive. While Matty made a scheduled call to Calvin at 8:30 a.m., Jack sipped his coffee and stared out the window at the station across the street. He caught a glimpse of the blue and yellow passenger cars of the Southerner as it readied for boarding alongside the platform. The Southerner made a daily eight-hour journey to and from Christchurch, winding its way through the foothills of Otago, along the Pacific coast and through the Canterbury Plains. Matty returned from the phone booth a few minutes later.

"I'm going to get the tickets now," he whispered. "The team bus is here, and my friend will meet us at 9:15 when the team is boarding the train. We'll sneak in the back of the line. Calvin is going to stop the train near the town of Herbert. It's about three hours from here. I'll explain the rest to you on the train. You just do as I do and she'll be right as rain, okay?"

"Yep, no worries," said Jack.

Matty introduced Jack to his friend Eddie, who amused Jack with anecdotes about when Matty played as they walked to the train. They took seats by the manager and coaches in the last train car. Eddie told the other coaches that they were friends of his, and everything was settled, just as Matty had hoped.

The train pulled out of the station on schedule. Jack sat by the window and watched the Pacific Ocean come into view as the train crossed the estuaries and inlets around Invercargill, which were famous for the oysters that were harvested there. He thought about the last time he was on a train, when he left Greensburg for the Navy almost a year ago. He felt a twinge of pain in his cheek as a gray cast of apprehension settled over him.

"Tickets, tickets," yelled the conductor.

"Quick, take your jacket off so they can see your rugby shirt," said Matty. "Pretend you are sleeping."

As the conductor approached their seats, Eddie handed him the tickets.

"Tired from the game last night… better let them sleep," said Eddie.

The conductor nodded, and continued on.

"Thanks, Eddie. I owe you a pint at the Yaldhurst when we get to Christchurch," whispered Matty.

Matty turned to Jack, and whispered the rest of the plan that he and

Calvin had cooked up on the phone at the station. Then, Jack settled back and tried to doze off, though it was difficult to fight the urge to watch the beautiful scenery unfold from the train window... rolling hills with green and gold carpets of grass dotted with sheep, and panoramic views of the teal blue Pacific coastline. The train wound its way through the foothills along the coast, crossing bridges over clear, glacier-driven rivers. The sky cleared and the sun emerged as the train headed north past towns called Gore, Balclutha, Milton, and Dunedin, which was the second largest city in the South Island.

Matty awoke from a long nap when he heard the conductor announce that the train was nearing Dunedin. He grew increasingly anxious as the train pulled into the station. Matty carefully watched the platform, examining every figure that got on and off the train. A few minutes after the train stopped, he noticed a slightly built man mingling among the passengers on the platform, but not talking to anyone. About fifteen minutes passed before the train whistle blew and the conductor called for the passengers to board. Matty watched the man disappear behind a magazine kiosk, but as the train pulled away from the platform, he thought he saw the man leap onto the steps of one of the forward cars.

"Jack, I think one of Kettering's men is on the train. I'm going up front to see what's up."

"Are you sure?" asked Jack.

"I'm pretty sure, but we can't take any chances. I'll talk to Eddie and make sure no one comes into our car."

Most of the players were asleep, and the cabin was quiet except for the rumble of train wheels as it passed over cross tracks outside the station. Jack kept checking his watch every five minutes, remembering that Matty told him that the train would stop about forty minutes after leaving Dunedin. A half-hour had passed, but Matty had still not returned. Jack nervously fidgeted in his seat. He was about to get up and look for him, when the door opened, and Matty strode quickly toward him.

"What happened?" asked Jack.

"Someone had an accident," whispered Matty. "He fell off the train. It's too bad, because it's a long hike back to Dunedin."

"That's good. Now we don't have to worry about being tailed."

"Right. I also told Eddie we were going up to the café car, so no one will miss us when we run for it," whispered Matty. "In about ten minutes, we'll be passing through Herbert. There's a tunnel on the north side of town. The train will make an unscheduled stop in that tunnel. When the train stops, you do exactly as I say."

Right on schedule and according to plan, the train braked hard and came to a complete stop with about three-fourths of the cars still inside the tunnel. The conductor announced that some sheep had wandered onto the tracks, and it would take a few minutes to clear them off.

"Now," whispered Matty, as he and Jack got up from their seats and quietly slipped out the rear door. In the dimly lit train car, no one noticed them disappear into the even darker tunnel. They sprinted a hundred yards away from the train and emerged outside the tunnel, where Matty led them up a steep set of stone steps that ascended the hillside. About a hundred feet up the hillside, the steps turned into a steep, rocky path. From this vantage point, they could see the train slowly emerge from the tunnel as a rancher led the sheep away from the tracks. Jack watched the sheep run across the green fields like specs of white metal directed by a magnet below the ground.

"They're fun to watch, aren't they?" said a man's voice from behind a huge boulder. The voice startled Jack, and he reached for his gun.

"Put the gun down, Jack," said Matty. "It's just Calvin. Bloody hell, you scared the piss out of us."

"Sorry, mate. I told you it would work though," said Calvin, a wiry, fair-skinned man in his twenties, with bushy, sandy-colored hair. "The bloke herding those sheep down there is old Colin McGregor. He owes my dad a favor. That's pretty slick how he flagged the train down."

"The train is picking up speed," said Matty. "Hopefully Eddie covered for us and no one saw us get off the train."

"You must be Jack," said Calvin. "I'm sorry to hear about your parents... or I should say, all four of them. Truly, mate, I'm sorry."

"Thanks. All four of them went through hell. It's nice to meet you."

"I'm sure they did, like my father is now."

"I know, man. I'm sorry to hear that too. I had the pleasure of meeting your father."

"He was trying to help your friends, except he got caught."

Jack sensed a bit of resentment in Calvin's voice.

"Are Grace and Reggie okay?" asked Jack.

"They are safe at a hut near Mt. Dasher," said Calvin.

"How far is that?" asked Jack.

"About ten miles over rugged terrain... a half day's hike," said Calvin.

"This isn't good," said Jack. "Kettering will have access to live satellite photos of this area. He can follow us right to the hut."

"Don't worry, we're taking precautions," said Calvin. "Grace contacted your radioman friend in Christchurch. He told her about the satellites. Matter of fact, he knew what time of day the US satellite sweeps this area. It will pass in about two hours."

"How long have you guys been staying at the hut? Are you sure Grace is okay?"

"Whoa, slow down," said Calvin. "She's fine, except it's been unusually cold, and we've been there a couple days now. The hardest part of staying in the hut is not being able to make a fire during the day. We can't take a chance on the satellites spotting the smoke. We better head out now. We have a mile or so hike to pick up the horses."

"Horses? I can't ride a horse," cried Jack.

"I thought all you Yanks rode horses, like the cowboys in the Wild West," Matty chuckled.

"There aren't any cowboys in Pennsylvania," said Jack.

"Relax. I'll give you a ten-minute lesson, and she'll be right."

As it turned out, the ten-minute lesson in horsemanship from Calvin resulted in the loss of over an hour of travel time to the hut. A frustrated Calvin finally succeeded in setting Jack right in the saddle, and they set out on the narrow trail that headed into the windswept highlands near the Hawkdun Range. The trail paralleled the topographical contours of the steep, tufted grass hillsides as they climbed 5,000 feet to the base of Mt. Dasher. The path became too dangerous to navigate on horseback, so they dismounted and walked the horses for over an hour, before the path widened through a more gentle rolling terrain.

They finally arrived around 4:00 p.m., and they waited under a dense stand of pines. Jack could see the hut in the distance. It was a wooden structure on stilts that was used for rest and lodging, typical of huts built along hiking trails throughout New Zealand. It was set back a mile or so from the nearest gravel road in a secluded setting, tucked into the side of the massive, rocky hillside. Calvin hid the horses in the pines, while Jack and Matty cautiously approached the hut. A broad-shouldered man was chopping wood outside. His large figure was silhouetted against the light gray sky. Jack knew right away that it was Reggie, who upon seeing Jack, put his axe down and ran to meet them.

"Popeye, how in the hell are you?" yelled Reggie. Jack extended his arm to shake his hand, but Reggie picked him up and bear-hugged him instead.

"Reggie! Am I glad to see your sorry face. Man, you didn't have to do this for me. I don't know what to say, except thanks."

"Relax, everything is cool. I had to come. I couldn't leave your ass hanging out down here. Besides, Matty is going to teach me how to play rugby, and get me one of those stripped shirts too."

"Of course, mate. That is, if you think you can tackle me," said Matty, with a laugh.

"Where is Grace?" asked Jack.

"She went for a walk down that path over there. She ought to be on her way back up by now."

Jack hurried down the path. He rounded a bend that led to magnificent view of a vast valley surrounded by golden, grassy hillsides. About a hundred yards ahead, Grace stood on a rocky platform, gazing at a great, sweeping panorama. Sunlight flooded the valley. She recognized Jack's footsteps, and quickly turned around and started running toward him.

"Grace!"

"Jack! Oh Jack!" She ran into his arms, and he picked her up and spun her around. They embraced in a long, passionate kiss.

"I missed you so much, Grace. Thank God you're okay. I've been driving myself mad worrying about you and Reggie. So much has happened since I left Bainbridge. You can't even imagine."

"I've been so worried about you too. I almost lost it when Matty told us your plane crashed in the ocean. Jack, you look so tired. What is going on?

What is happening?"

"Grace, I didn't want you to do this. I didn't want to put you in danger. My parents are dead… I mean my birth parents, Ian and Sarah. I've got to carry out their last wishes."

"I couldn't believe it when I heard the story from Calvin."

"I'm still trying to process it."

"Matty says we are going to Moon's ranch to destroy the lab."

"That's the plan. We've got to get there before Kettering. But you don't have to do this. You and Reggie don't have to come."

"I'm not leaving you. Besides, you have no idea how much trouble you are in. Kettering has erased your service record. You were dishonorably discharged from the Navy at Bainbridge. Without a service record and without a passport, you are a man without a country. That's why we had to come. We are the only people who can vouch for you after what Kettering's done to you. Right now, I don't trust anyone. Reggie and I both know firsthand what IWR is capable of. They were even watching us in Hawaii. We're all in this deep. We've got to stay together."

"Oh, Grace…" he kissed her, tasting the salt from her tears that mixed with his own.

"Matty said there might be someone in the Navy who could help us. He said Dr. Moon trusted the commanding officer at McMurdo."

"Captain Minton. But he can't help us now. I don't think there are any more flights out of Antarctica for the winter."

"We better get back inside. The satellite will be passing soon."

They ran back and met Reggie at the front door. He was on his way out to retrieve the axe and the remainder of the wood that he had chopped.

"Better leave it, Reggie," said Jack. "We'll get it later."

"Are you crazy? The cameras in those satellites can photograph the color of that axe handle. Give me a hand with the rest of this wood, and then we better get inside."

"Right, and then we need to talk," said Jack.

One by one, they took their seats around a small wooden table under the light of a single candle. Puffs of exhaled vapor rose above the table as they talked.

"After the satellite passes, I'll make a fire in the stove and fix something to eat," said Grace.

"Sounds good, I'm starving," said Reggie. "So, what's our plan, Jack? What do we—"

"Damn it," said Calvin. "I just thought of something. I left one of the canteens out by the pump."

"Leave it," said Jack. "There's nothing we can do about it now. We can't take a chance going outside."

"Bugger all, it's bad enough we have to deal with this Yank madman Kettering, but now we have to deal with your bloody satellites too."

"They're up there so you don't have to speak Russian," said Reggie.

"Come on, what does it matter? We've got to focus on this mission," said Matty. "The Doc instructed Calvin and I to blow up the lab. Those were his last words to Mick, and that's what Mick told me on the radio before he crashed."

"Well, me and Grace came all this way to help Jack," said Reggie. "I don't know about this other stuff."

Jack got up and walked around the table. He was thinking about Ian's last words. He wasn't sure if Matty or Calvin knew about Hagley Park, but they all seemed to understand the implications of Moon's formula falling into Kettering's hands. He felt he could trust Matty, but he wasn't sure about Calvin. Grace spoke up.

"We should try to contact Captain Minton at McMurdo," said Grace. "You agree, don't you, Matty?"

"Yes and no. The Doc trusted him, but we are up against IWR. For all we know, they may have already silenced Minton."

"I hate to spoil the party, but the first thing we have to do is rescue my dad. And then, I say we go to the district police and let them sort this out."

"Did you know anything about Ian's work?" asked Jack. "Do you know how important it is?"

"Of course I do. I helped build that laboratory, and I know he was a brilliant scientist. I know he was working on a new form of energy in outer space. Some people even think he's crazy. But my dad loved the Doc like a brother. They were lifelong friends. They served together in the war. That's why I know the Doc would want us to rescue my dad. And after what happened to my brother, I'm sure you would agree. Right, Matty?"

"I don't know, Calvin. From what Mick told me, we're dealing with something mighty important... maybe the very future of the world. I'm sorry about your dad and your brother, but our first priority has to be to destroy the lab."

"I understand, but my dad is all I have left. Mum, God bless her, is in Sunnyside in Christchurch. She's been there ever since we got the news about Jim."

"If you don't mind me asking, what happened to your brother?" asked Jack.

"You don't know? I thought you knew my brother, Jim," said Calvin.

"Jim who?" asked Jack.

"Jim McClintock... he went to college with you at Saint Mark."

"You mean Dingo Jim...he was your brother? How is he doing? I haven't seen him since I left Saint Mark last year. I just assumed he went back to Australia."

"He's dead."

"Jesus, Dingo Jim's dead? When? And how?"

"Dad got a letter from the college last November. They said he died in a car accident... burned beyond recognition. We didn't even have his ashes to give him a proper funeral."

"Wasn't no accident," said Matty. "It was IWR. At least that's what the Doc thought."

"Why would IWR kill Dingo Jim?" asked Jack.

"He was a courier for Dr. Moon," said Calvin. "He delivered things to Sarah at Saint Mark."

"I thought he was Australian," said Jack.

"You Yanks think we're all Australian," said Calvin.

"But why kill Jim?" asked Jack.

"My dad said the Doc thought IWR had infiltrated Saint Mark. Jim was on to their agent, and was able to warn Sarah before he was killed."

"It's probably the same guys who killed my parents," said Jack.

"Maybe. It doesn't matter now. All that matters is that my brother is dead, and Kettering is holding my father hostage."

"Yes, we have to rescue Ted," said Grace.

"How do you know Ted?" asked Jack.

"He's the man who contacted Reggie and me by HAM radio. He made the arrangements for Matty and Mick to take us to New Zealand. How do you know Ted?" she asked Jack.

"He came to warn me about Eva when we were at the ranch."

"Who's Eva?" asked Grace.

"She's Ian's stepdaughter, and she works for Kettering. She set me up. She tried to turn me against Ian and Sarah, and played me to get to the formula. But somehow Kettering discovered that I am really Ian's son, and that Sarah put me up for adoption. Once he learned Ian was my real father, he held me hostage in exchange for the formula."

"So if Moon and Sarah are dead, why is Kettering still after you?" asked Reggie.

"Because he knows there is a hidden laboratory somewhere on the ranch property. He figures that I know where the formula is."

"Do you?" asked Reggie.

Jack hesitated.

"No. I just know that Ian told me to blow the lab up."

"Well, who knows how to get into this lab?" asked Grace.

"I do, Miss," said Matty. "It's built into the side of a mountain behind the ranch. There are two ways in. One is through an abandoned gold mine shaft on the other side of the mountain. The other is through a twenty-foot deep hidden manhole in the hill behind the ranch. The manhole connects to a 200-yard tunnel that runs from the house to the lab. But we aren't going in that way. We'll enter through the mineshaft. There's a steel door at the end of the shaft that leads to the lab. We'll take the horses to the foot of the mountain, then hike up the trail to the mine entrance. There'll be some tough climbing."

"Is there actually a formula there?" asked Grace.

Again, Jack hesitated. He wanted desperately to tell everyone, especially Grace, what Ian had told him about Hagley Park before he died. For now, he kept it to himself.

155

"Ian said that the destruct switch is in his vault," said Jack. "He didn't say whether the formula is in there or not. All he said was to destroy the lab. He said the combination to get into the vault is his birthday… 3-13-24." He thought about Sarah's Tiki necklace, before Reggie interrupted.

"Jack, I'm your best friend. I'll do whatever I can to help you, but I'm just throwing this out there… what if Ian hid the formula somewhere else? What if he just wants Kettering to think it's there? Or what if we can't get into the vault? Maybe we just forget it, and get the hell out of here and save our asses."

"Wait a minute, mate," said Matty. "If the Doc said to blow it up, then that's what we're gonna' do. If you don't want to help, then you should leave."

"Matty, Reggie has a point," said Calvin. "Why would the Doc want to destroy something he spent his whole life developing?"

"Jack said Ian's last words were to destroy the lab at all costs, and that's what we are going to do," said Matty.

"What if Jack is lying?" asked Calvin.

"What the hell would I lie for?" Jack yelled.

"Jack is no liar," said Reggie. "I came here to help him, and I'm not taking orders from you. When this is over, we are getting the hell out of here."

"Listen, everyone," yelled Matty. "There is probably a copy of the formula in the lab, and the Doc wants us to destroy it. It's possible he hid the real formula somewhere else. Maybe it's in Antarctica, or on the North Island, or in New Caledonia. Who knows? The point is that he wants Kettering to think we blew it up, and that's what we are going to do. Don't worry, if he wants the world to know about the real formula some day, then he's left instructions for revealing it with someone."

"Jack was the last one with him before he died," said Calvin. "He probably told him about it."

"I'm telling you, all he said was to destroy the lab. That's it," said Jack.

"Fine. I'll do anything for the Doc, but not until we rescue my father."

"So after we rescue your dad, we run to the lab, open the vault, throw the destruct switch, run out of the lab, jump on the horses, and gallop down the mountain before it blows up," said Reggie sarcastically.

"Do you have a better plan?" asked Calvin. "I'm guessing not."

"Look, I think the mission is clear… to rescue Ted and blow up the lab," said Jack. "We will fail unless we work together. Matty, you have an escape plan to get us out of the country, right?"

"It's a pretty shaky plan, but it's all we've got. After we blow the lab, we escape out the mineshaft and take the trail to Dansy's Pass Road. Clive will meet us and take us in his truck to Timaru. I can get us passage on a freighter headed anywhere at this point. I don't think we can be choosy."

Calvin stood up, and walked to the window.

"How many of Kettering's people will be there?" he asked.

"Can't say for sure," said Jack. "At least four… Kettering, Driggers, Pratt, and Chin, but there will be other heavily armed men—"

"I don't have much experience with weapons," said Grace. "They didn't

156

teach us much in boot camp."

"You know as much as Reggie and me," said Jack.

"No worries, Miss," said Matty. "Calvin and I know how to handle any weapon. You three will be along for support."

"That's comforting to know, but—"

The radio came to life with a short Morse code message from Phil— **Mildred has the files.** Grace jumped up.

"Thank you! Thank you! Do you know what this means?"

They all looked at her with the same puzzled expression.

"It means you have a service record, Jack. You're not a man without a country. Haskins must have told Mildred to keep a separate file on you and Kettering. He must have known Kettering was trying to kill him."

"Oh God, Grace. Don't tell me..." Jack quivered.

"I'm sorry Jack... Haskins is dead."

"Dead? Are you serious?"

"Yes. Before I left Honolulu, I called Higgins to see if Haskins could help you. He told me Haskins was killed a few miles from the base in a car accident the night after I left Bainbridge. IWR had to be behind that. I told him to send a message to Phil if he had any news."

"We can use this information to build a case against Kettering once we get back to the States and sort things out with the Navy," said Reggie.

"That's fantastic. We have a chance," said Jack. His face lit up, and he grabbed Grace and hugged her. "How did you set this up with Phil?"

"I didn't. He just offered to help. He is the one who relayed Sarah's message to me at Honolulu. He sent me the heads-up that you had left for Antarctica too. We've been waiting for him to radio us as soon as he heard any news about Kettering's movements."

"That's great, but what are we going to do about the police?" asked Jack. "They think you and Reggie are fugitives."

"Wait a minute, are you serious?" asked Reggie.

"Kettering set you up, probably to draw me out to try and help you. Your faces are on the front page of every paper in New Zealand. You're being accused of theft and assault."

"Don't worry, it's not likely they'll look up here in the mountains," said Calvin. "They'll be watching the main roads near the cities."

"That's for sure," said Matty.

Again, The HAM radio buzzed to life with Morse code dits and dots— **Lots of noise about a plane from the "Ice" that landed this morning.**

"Kettering was on that plane," said Matty. "He'll head straight to the ranch tomorrow. We have to assume there is someone guarding Ted. We better leave first thing in the morning."

Jack walked to the window. The sun was sinking below the snow-covered peaks of the Hawkduns. A spark of heat wafted against the back of his neck as Grace lit the kindling wood in the small cast iron stove. He thought about the last words of Ian and Sarah, before they slipped below the ocean waves just

157

two days ago, the broken sentences about Hagley Park.

Jack turned around and absorbed the presence of each person in the room. There was Matty, who felt like an older brother to him, Calvin, who was completely focused on rescuing his father, and Reggie, whose heart was almost as big as his shoulders. But out of everyone, it was Grace who gave him the strength of purpose he never imagined. He gazed at her face, aglow from the flames of the fire. If there was ever any doubt in his mind about the mission he faced, it disappeared in the presence of Grace. Jack held her hand as they sat on a cot by the warm stove. Calvin volunteered to take the first watch, while Matty assembled the explosives and timers to be used in case they couldn't get into the vault. Reggie had already fallen asleep.

"You know we had to hike six miles up some pretty rugged hills to get here," said Grace. "We didn't have horses. Calvin just got them today, and Reggie carried most of the heavy packs. He was exhausted. He really misses home. All he wants to do is get you out of here."

"I know. I owe him so much. I never imagined anything like this in my life. I still can't believe this is all real. I'm terrified that something could happen to you or Reggie."

"I'm not afraid, because love is everything and worth the risk."

"I love you more than all the beauty of this country. I'll never leave you, Grace." He kissed her gently on the lips.

"That's touching, you two, but you better get some sleep," said Matty. "If you think the hike up here was tough, tomorrow's trek will make it seem like a walk in the park."

Chapter 20
Return to Moon Mountain

"Colonel, I've got more satellite photos of the area around the plane crash," Pratt announced smugly. "And this photo shows the last reported sighting of Trane's boat heading northeast."

"Damn it, Pratt. Don't bring me any more photos of the ocean," screamed Kettering. "I'm confident that only Trane and the Maori escaped by boat. Doctor Moon and Sarah Mechling are dead! I'm sure of it, just as I'm sure that Trane and the Maori are heading to Moon's ranch. But we need to know if they've linked up with anyone else, and what route they'll take. Maybe if I had the photos around Moon Mountain that I asked for an hour ago, I might be able to answer those questions. Get me those damn photos, Pratt!"

Pratt reeled around and sprinted out the door. A few minutes later, a yeoman on Kettering's staff knocked and entered the room.

"I hope that's you with my photos, Pratt."

"No, it's Prettiman, sir. The Christchurch Police called. There's no sign of Trane's AWOL friends. They want more information on them."

"That is to be expected, but I can't be concerned with that right now. Tell our Navy Antarctic liaison at the airport that I want him to handle this. Tell him all we know at this time is that Weems and Ivy entered New Zealand illegally. Give the commander the usual "IWR Eyes Only" directive, and tell him this information is from our ambassador. I don't want any of this in the papers. Send Driggers in as soon as he returns with the vehicles I asked for. And find out where Pratt is with those photos."

"Will do, sir."

Pratt returned a few moments later with the satellite photos. Kettering ripped them from his hands and motioned him to leave. He studied the photos carefully with a magnifying glass, and then sat back in his chair to ponder a hypothesis. He occasionally glanced out the window of his temporary office in the US Air Force hangar at Christchurch International Airport. There was a knock on the door, and Driggers entered.

"I got the four-wheel drive pick-up you wanted, and I loaded Dr. Crankshaw's equipment. Are those the satellite photos?"

"Yes, Stan. Take a look at this. It's a photo of Moon's ranch. That's Dansy's Pass Road, which leads to the ranch. Over here is the town of Herbert, about fifteen miles away. That's where the Southerner passenger train made a thirty-minute unscheduled stop two days ago. Our agent on the train thought he saw Trane and the Maori sitting with a rugby team in the last car. I'm not sure what the connection is. Invercargill Station had no record of them purchasing tickets, so they must have snuck on."

"Or someone helped them. Didn't our man follow them?"

"He tried, but the Maori threw him off the train. Either way, I feel like I can sense Trane's moves. He has to link up somewhere with his friends. The

Maori is leading him to a rendezvous location somewhere between Herbert and Dansy's Pass Road. It can't be too far from Herbert, unless they are traveling by ATV."

"Or horses. ATV's would be too easy for us to track," said Driggers.

"Good point, Stan. That's all rugged terrain between Herbert and Moon Mountain. It's only passable on foot or by horse. I reckon they will head for Dansy's Pass. That's the fastest way up the mountain. It's a couple of days hike on foot, but much less by horse." He picked up another photo and scanned the terrain in the image. He paused for a moment. There was a knock on the door, and Pratt walked in.

"Eva radioed from the ranch," said Pratt. "The phones are down up there. She said it's snowing pretty hard. She said the old man had a heart attack, and he needs medical attention."

"Damn it! I need him alive. He is my bargaining chip."

After standing watch outside for the previous four hours, Calvin entered the hut around 6:00 a.m. to wake the others. A faint light above the darkened hills was all the sun would afford the band of crusaders on this cold, misty, overcast day. Matty prepared a breakfast of toast with warm, canned spaghetti on top.

"What the hell is this stuff?" asked Reggie jokingly. "I was expecting bacon and eggs."

"Quit your moaning. It's all we got," said Matty. "Try it. You'll like it, mate. There's a pot of tea to wash it down."

After breakfast, Matty and Calvin packed the explosives and loaded them on the horses. Jack and Reggie packed the rest of the rations and gear, while Grace checked over the radio.

"Maybe we shouldn't go through with this, Jack," said Reggie. "I don't know about you, but I don't see a clear plan for pulling this off... and more importantly, escaping from that mountain."

"Matty and Calvin know what they're doing, Reggie. We're all committed to this, right?" asked Jack, with a biting undertone.

"Well, yea. That's why we came all this way... to help you."

"Of course you did. I'm sorry, Reggie. I didn't mean it that way. You're right, the road ahead is full of uncertainty. But trust me, it's the right thing to do. I've never been so sure of anything in my life."

"Jack, I think Reggie is suggesting that we at least consider another option, like going to the New Zealand authorities," said Grace.

Jack quickly turned around after staring out the window, watching Calvin bring up the horses.

"And then what?" he questioned.

"We could hike back to Herbert and turn ourselves in," said Reggie. "We could ask to see Captain Minton, or the American ambassador in Wellington."

"Reggie, it's far too late for that. If we turn ourselves in now, Kettering will discredit everything we say. They won't listen to us. And what would I even say to the authorities? I can't say anything about Ian or the formula. Kettering will get to us somehow. He's relentless. He won't give up until he gets what he wants. But we can't let him get the formula, or we face cataclysmic consequences. I know what this power can do. I haven't told anyone else yet, but Ian showed me photos of the new Fermi Lab Supercollider near Chicago. He explained to me the power of just one ounce of antimatter annihilating one ounce of matter. It would be equivalent to 750,000 tons of TNT. Do you have any idea how much power that is? It's incomprehensible."

"You gotta' be kidding me. It sounds like something out of *Star Trek*," said Reggie.

"Well, it's true."

"Okay. I believe you," said Reggie.

"We have to do this... not just for Jack, but for the whole world," said Grace.

"I said I'm in," said Reggie. "Just tell me what I gotta' do."

"We'll figure it out on the way to the ranch," said Jack. "I have to let Matty and Calvin take the lead. They know the terrain and the lab, but after that it's up to us to stop Kettering from getting the formula, even if it means killing him."

Reggie was shocked by the suggestion of killing Kettering, and he walked outside. Grace put on her parka and was about to leave the hut, when the radio came to life. The dit-dots of the Morse code message from Phil said that McMurdo confirmed that Minton would be on the last plane out that was scheduled to depart for Christchurch in two days.

Kettering stared out the window at a plane that was taking off. The sky was growing increasingly dark, and light snow spit intermittently at the window. He turned abruptly to face the door, even before Pratt knocked once and entered the room.

"Colonel, I have a copy of a message from McMurdo. It says Minton will arrive by plane in Christchurch on Tuesday."

"That doesn't give us much time to find Moon's laboratory. Minton loathes me. He's coming to help Trane. We have to get up there and find the formula before he arrives. He can make a lot of trouble for me. Pratt, take a look at this satellite photo. Look here under the stereoscope. What do you suppose this gray rectangle is?"

Pratt leaned over and studied the photo.

"It looks like a hiker's hut," he said. "There are a lot of them along the trails that wind through those mountains. The government builds them for hikers to use for shelter."

"What time does the satellite pass over southern Otago?"

"2200 Zulu time."

"I want the highest resolution photos faxed to me immediately after the

161

satellite passes," said Kettering. "I don't care what it takes. I think they are staying in one of those huts. And I need those mining maps of the Mt. Domet area that I told you about."

"Yes, sir. We probably won't receive them until this evening. But I guess that doesn't matter since the weather is too bad to go up there tomorrow anyways."

"I'm not waiting for good weather. We fly there tomorrow no matter what! Now get me the damn maps!"

Reggie was falling behind the others, as he struggled to control his horse along the narrow trails on the steep hillsides. Grace stopped several times to help him, and it took a couple miles before he got the hang of it. However, the horses were the least of their worries. Another slow-moving cold front was approaching from the northeast, bringing snow showers and wind. Matty was concerned it would cost them valuable time that they needed to reach the entrance on the west side of the mountain. Jack marveled at the mountains in their snow-covered splendor. It helped him to ignore the inclement weather.

"My brother and I used to hang glide in these mountains," said Calvin. "You can stay aloft and ride the drafts all the way to the Waitaki River and the Pacific coast."

"I tried hang gliding once at the dunes on Lake Michigan," said Grace. "I actually glided for a few hundred yards."

"Exhilarating," chuckled Calvin.

"Well, at least she did it. That's more than I can say," said Jack.

"The drafts in these mountains can be deadly," said Calvin. "I've seen experienced hang gliders spin out of control and get slammed into the side of a mountain by the fickle winds in these valleys."

"I'll stick to terra firma," said Jack.

By the middle of the afternoon, after covering about seven miles, they reached a narrow, rocky path along a steep mountainside, where they had to dismount. That was as far as they could go on horseback. Calvin was the most familiar with the trails, so he led the way, while the others walked their horses single file behind him along the dangerous path.

They were heading to a fork in the trail about a mile ahead. From there, they would split into two parties. Matty and Reggie would head for the mineshaft, and Grace and Jack would go with Calvin to the ranch. Calvin would take an easterly path that followed a stream down the mountain to Dansy's Pass, where he planned to meet Clive Walker and hand off the horses. They had devised a Morse code signal on the radio to coordinate the meeting. He hoped to meet Clive before 2 o'clock in the afternoon, so they could avoid the satellites.

Matty and Reggie would take the west fork for a couple of miles to Moon Mountain. Once there, they would have to climb a steep trail to the entrance to an abandoned gold mineshaft that led to the laboratory. They were nearing the fork in the trail, when a jackrabbit darted out from behind a boulder and spooked Calvin's horse. The horse reared up and flung Calvin across the path. He stumbled and fell about thirty feet down the hillside.

"Calvin, you alright? Are you hurt?" yelled Matty.

"Yea, it's my arm. Damn it! I'm pretty sure it's broken."

Jack climbed down and tied a rope around him, and Reggie pulled him up.

"It looks bad, possibly a compound fracture," said Grace, as she examined his arm.

"Better put it in a splint and a sling," said Jack.

Matty looked at his watch.

"What do you want to do, Calvin?" asked Matty.

"I'll be okay. I'll manage."

"Are you kidding?" asked Grace.

"No, we need to rethink this," said Matty. "The hike up to the mineshaft requires stamina and know-how. I'm the only one here with climbing experience. I picked Reggie to go with me, because he is strong enough to help me if I get in a jam. But now, I think you'll need him to get Ted out of there, while Jack and Grace take care of the lab. There is more likelihood of you encountering resistance than me. It's best if I go it alone."

"It's up to you, Matty. Whatever you need me to do," said Reggie.

"Good, then it's settled. I should reach the mineshaft by nightfall, and the lab by early morning. Calvin will take you to the hidden tunnel entrance in the hill behind the ranch house. I'll meet you in the lab tomorrow morning at 8:30. When you get there, send a Morse code "OK" using the Doc's HAM radio. The rest of us will listen on our portables. If you don't make it by 9:15, then get the hell off the mountain any way you can. You got forty-five minutes after the destruct button is pressed before it blows."

"What if we don't make it... or we're late?" asked Jack.

"If you get there late, and you haven't received the go-ahead, then push the button," said Matty. "If you can't get to the destruct button in the vault, or if it doesn't work, then use your explosives. Set the timers to allow time to get out. The primary escape route is through the mineshaft, and then down the trail to meet Clive. The secondary route is back the way you came, at the manhole. Once you're out, head to Clive's place. Everything clear?"

"What if we get separated?" asked Reggie.

"Then it's every man for himself," said Matty. "Get out any way you can, and make for Timaru. There is a freighter docked there called the Kiwi Star. Tell the captain you know me. He'll get you out of New Zealand. After that, you're on your own." Matty hugged each of them, and set off up the trail.

Reggie lifted Calvin onto his horse and took the point, with Calvin directing. They headed out single file, walking with their horses down the narrow east trail that led to a wooded spot near Clive's ranch. Clive, a stocky, graying, rugged-looking man, was waiting for them.

"Where's Matty?" asked Clive.

"Heading for the mineshaft entrance," said Calvin.

"By himself? One of you should have went with him," said Clive.

"He insisted," said Reggie.

"Don't think that's a good idea. I know he can take care of himself, but now I'm gonna' worry."

"Why is he so worried about Matty?" Grace whispered to Calvin.

"Because that's his son. Clive adopted Matty. His parents were killed in the war. Ian brought Matty and his sister, Kiri back from an orphanage in New Caledonia. Of course, Ian couldn't raise them, so Clive and his wife took them in."

"So, you three Yanks are friends of Ian's?" asked Clive.

"Clive, this is Ian's son, Jack, and his friends Grace and Reggie."

Clive cast a befuddled look at Jack.

"Did you say Ian's son?"

"It's a long story. They're in the US Navy. They're going to help me rescue Dad."

"There's been a lot of activity at the Doc's place over the last couple days," said Clive.

"How many men are up there?" asked Jack.

"At least six or seven, but I've only seen one guard outside," said Clive. "He stays close to the house, so you should be able to sneak up there without being seen."

"We better get going. We'll meet you at the crossroads tomorrow," said Calvin.

"You can't go with that arm," said Clive.

"Don't try to stop me, Clive," said Calvin.

"You're stubborn, just like your pap," said Clive, as he smiled. It was a weak smile, fraught with fear and concern. He waved to them as he led the horses away in the fading light of the early evening.

Shortly before dusk, Jack, Reggie, Grace, and Calvin started out for the ranch, following a forest-covered stream for about a mile, until they reached a spot about a half-mile from the ranch. It was nightfall, and the air was still and frosty. Calvin grimaced as he tried to block the pain in his arm.

Kettering paced back and forth, waiting impatiently for Pratt to bring the latest satellite photos from the fax machine. Finally, just before chow time, Pratt knocked and strode into the office with more photographs.

"These are just in, sir. By the way, the weather forecast calls for clearing later tonight. I found a company that rents helicopters. They have one that I can pilot."

Kettering continued to study the photos, and did not look up.

"Excellent! I was right! They were in this hut near Mt Dasher. There are horse tracks leading north from the hut along this hiking trail... right here. I would estimate they covered ten miles today. We will find them tomorrow from the helicopter. They will lead us right to the entrance to the laboratory.

164

Was Dr. Crankshaw's equipment delivered to the ranch?"

"Yes, it's there."

"Good. Now we wait for Trane to lead us to the formula."

The cold, drizzly wind whipped across the rocky terrain and nipped at Matty's face. The fifty-pound backpack loaded with explosives slowed his pace, as the trail climbed up the mountainside. At 4:00 p.m., he was still a half-mile of hard climbing away from the entrance to the mineshaft. He took a fifteen-minute rest, and then pushed on. With only an hour of daylight remaining, he reached a position about a hundred feet below the mineshaft. The only way to reach the top of the rocky cliff was to climb from ledge to ledge. His body was soaking wet from sweat and sleet, and the droplets of sweat irritated his eyes, making it difficult to see. By the time he reached the entrance to the mineshaft, daylight was fading, and the temperature was dropping. He faced hypothermia if he didn't build a fire soon.

The mineshaft was littered with rocks and debris, and he soon realized it was more dangerous than he had previously thought. He walked about 300 yards before he encountered the first obstacle, a partially collapsed mine ceiling. He was too tired to move the rocks, so he decided to rest, and he built a fire using pieces of the mine timbers.

In the woods below the ranch house, Jack and the others crouched amongst the tall, sap-covered pine trees, waiting to cross the open stretch of hillside between the forest and the house. There was a light dusting of snow on the ground, but the wind had tapered off. Jack tried to fight the grip of fear that was enveloping him as he nervously stared at the house in the distance. He worried about his friends. Most of all, he feared for Grace. He couldn't bear the thought of Kettering capturing and harming her. Horrible images flooded his thoughts. His breathing intensified, and he started to hyperventilate. Then, a calming thought entered his mind.

The sky was visible above a clearing in the pines. He could see the clouds sliding past the moon, unveiling the bright, snow-capped peaks of the mountains and the steep hills beyond the ranch house. At that moment, Grace came up to him and put her hand on his shoulder. He looked back at her warm, smiling eyes. It was an otherworldly feeling, to be in the grips of imminent danger with the person you love most in the world, while completely surrounded by an almost magical sight of snow-capped peaks that looked like the spires of the basilica back at Saint Mark. Almost a year ago he was there, gazing at the stars above the basilica on the same kind of brisk, early winter night. He contemplated how much his life had changed since then.

Around 10:00 p.m., they slipped out of the woods and crept across the hillside, trying to stay hidden in the tall grasses at the edge of the field, a few hundred yards from the house. They reached the rock outcrop behind a shed and waited, watching for the guards. The door opened, spilling the lights of the room into the snow-covered yard, and a group of men appeared. They were joined by another figure. Jack immediately recognized Eva's voice; she was complaining about something.

Calvin motioned that the guards looked heavily armed. Reggie whispered that they were probably ex-Special Forces, Army Rangers, or SEALS... someone like Driggers. Then, the men walked around the ranch toward the front of the house. A stocky, Polynesian-looking man stepped in the doorway, followed by an older, gray-haired man with a beard and wire-rimmed glasses.

"Matty told me about him... that Polynesian bloke. I think they call him Chin," said Calvin. "I'm not sure who the older guy is."

They waited until the guards went back in the house before they crawled to the hidden manhole in the hillside behind the shed. Calvin motioned to Reggie to move a heavy, round stone next to the flat rock, which exposed a metal box. He opened the lid on the box and pressed a red button inside. Immediately, the flat rock slid quietly into the adjacent ledge that exposed the circular hatch. Reggie opened the hatch and went in first to help Calvin down the ladder. Grace followed, and Jack went last, quietly closing the latch behind him and listening for the fake rock to slide over the entrance. One by one, they climbed down the ladder to the tunnel floor. It was pitch dark. They switched on their flashlights and followed Calvin through the tunnel to a hidden door in the basement of the house, about 150 yards from the hatch. Dr. Moon's laboratory was 400 yards in the opposite direction.

They moved quickly through the cold, damp tunnel, as water dripped from the rocky ceiling, leaving puddles on the stone chip floor. When they reached the basement of the house, they came to another door. Calvin dialed the combination, and Reggie quietly slid the steel pocket door into the side cavity in the wall. The passageway was cleverly hidden behind a wall of shelves under the basement steps.

A gush of warm air from the heated basement escaped into the tunnel. There were voices upstairs in the house. They all stood motionless, listening to the muffled conversation. Eventually, Calvin heard Eva mention his father's name. He breathed a sigh of relief, knowing he was alive and that they were holding him in the study, which was the only upstairs room in the house that was connected to the hidden passageway. They crept silently through a side tunnel that led to the laboratory study. It terminated at a ladder, which led to a hidden first floor compartment behind a wall of bookshelves in Ian's study.

Calvin moved a blackened disc to one side, and peered through a small spyglass that provided a view of the entire room. He could see his father tied to a bed in the middle of the room. He gasped as he saw the weak and nearly lifeless body covered in dried blood, his face and hands badly bruised. Calvin struggled to contain his fury. He reached in his belt and pulled out his revolver. Then the door opened, and Eva and Chin walked in.

"The old man is through. We won't get anything more out of him," said Chin.

"You fool, why did you use so much power?" asked Eva. "His heart is failing. I can't give him anymore nitroglycerin, and Kettering wants him alive when he arrives in the morning."

"He told us all we need to know," said Chin. "The formula is hidden within this compound. That's why Trane is coming here. He's going to lead us right to it."

"I'm not so sure," said Eva. "Tell Nelson and Stark to check on the old man when they are on watch tonight."

Eva and Chin walked out of the laboratory without closing the door behind them. Calvin listened as their footsteps faded down the hallway to the other side of the house. Then, he slowly slid the concealed door that was made to look like a bookshelf into the pocket cavity in the wall. He figured that he only had a few minutes before the guard would return to check the room. Calvin signaled to Reggie to untie his father and lift him off the bed. Grace tiptoed behind Reggie and helped to untie Ted, and Reggie carefully lifted him. When he started to hallucinate, Grace quickly covered his mouth. His breathing was labored, and she became worried that he would pass out.

Reggie carried him across the hardwood floor to the hidden passageway. Calvin stopped short of closing the door after realizing the guards would notice the empty bed. So, Grace went back and arranged the covers to make it look like Ted was still in the bed. She hurried back to the door, but then stopped abruptly. She pointed to water droplets and pieces of mud on the floor where they walked. The tracks would surely give them away.

Seconds later, they heard the sound of approaching footsteps in the hallway. Grace had managed to wipe up half the tracks. She yanked off her scarf and used it to wipe the remaining traces with both hands in a frenzied motion. Then the footsteps stopped, and they heard the sound of a match striking and the puff of a cigarette. It was Nelson, the square-jawed, athletic-looking IWR man who had stopped in the hallway to take another drag.

Grace had quietly wiped the last bit of mud and slipped inside the hidden compartment. Calvin started to close the door, but stopped when Nelson took a couple of steps into the room. The room was dark except for the light from the hallway. He switched on his flashlight and shined it on the bed. Then, he turned around and walked out of the room. Grace's disguise had worked. She slid the bookshelf-covered door back in place until it locked. They retreated back into the passageway. It was now 4:00 a.m. Jack helped Calvin through the narrow passageway, while Reggie struggled to carry Ted down the ladder. Ted's breathing was labored, and he was wheezing.

"He needs a doctor. If we take him into the lab, he'll die," whispered Grace.

"It's up to Calvin," said Jack.

"No, it's up to Reggie. I need his help to carry my father to Clive's ranch. It's a two-mile hike."

Reggie glanced at Jack and Grace.

"It looks like it's just you and Grace."

Jack thought for a moment. Maybe they should all just get out of there and let Matty take care of blowing up the lab. But then, he thought about his promise to Ian.

"Yep, we can do this," said Jack. "Are you sure the laboratory is impregnable once we are in?"

"It better be like Fort Knox," said Reggie.

"Don't worry, you'll be safe," said Calvin. "It's getting you out that worries me. If something happens to Matty, you'll have to make it through the mineshaft alone." Ted moaned in pain. "We better get going. Good luck."

"What if Kettering blocks the escape route? Then what do we do?" asked Grace.

"Don't worry, Matty will be there," said Calvin.

Reggie shot a worried look at Grace.

"I'll come back to help you," said Reggie.

"No, it's too risky," said Jack. "Once Kettering finds out Ted is missing, this place will be crawling with IWR."

"We better get going. Dad is in a lot of pain."

Reggie hugged Jack and Grace.

"I'll see you tomorrow on Clive's truck," said Reggie. "Then we'll get out of here and let Captain Minton sort this out. He'll take care of Kettering, and we can go home, right?"

Jack hesitated, but Grace answered.

"Absolutely."

Reggie smiled, and gently lifted Ted in a fireman's carry, then turned and started up the ladder. Calvin followed, while glancing back at Grace and Jack and trying to mask his concern. A few minutes later, they slipped out the hatch and disappeared into the darkness.

The echo of the rock sliding across the hatch slowly died, and was replaced by a cold stillness that permeated the stale air in the tunnel. Grace grasped Jack's hand tightly. They walked hurriedly through the tunnel, twisting and turning toward the laboratory. It seemed to take an eternity to reach the stainless steel door, which looked like a bank vault with a combination dial in the center. The door was built into solid rock. Jack dialed the combination that was Ian's birthday and opened the door with a loud clank on the first try. They were both exhausted and barely had enough strength to open the heavy, ten-inch thick door. They stepped across the threshold into the dark, cavernous space.

"Where are the lights?" asked Grace.

"Calvin said we have to start the generator." He reached in his pocket and pulled out a map that Calvin had sketched for him. "The generator is in the mechanical room. Stay here, I'll be right back."

"Wait, it would probably be a good idea if we closed the door," said Grace. They pulled the door closed until it locked in place. Within a few minutes, the diesel generator came to life with a low hum. The ceiling lights flickered, and the giant cavern was illuminated.

"This place is unbelievable," said Jack. "There is enough electronic gear in here to run NASA."

Grace stood in the center of the circular space that was about a hundred feet in diameter. Electronic equipment was scattered around the room. Cables crisscrossed the floor, connecting to computers, oscilloscopes, a TV screen, and other equipment. There was a scaled model of an antimatter trap prototype in one of the rooms.

There were other spaces too; a kitchen, storage rooms, a bedroom, a bathroom, and a spacious office carved out of solid rock. A long, curved, wooden desk occupied the center of the room. On a bureau behind the desk were photos of Sarah and Jack taken at Saint Mark. There was a photo of Albert and Marie and Jack when he was a small child. There were other photos on the wall, one of Albert and Ian in sick bay on Guam, and another photo of Ted and Ian in New Zealand Air Force uniforms. There was a framed poster of the Palace and Gardens of Versailles, and another of the Rose Garden at Hagley Park. Off to the side of the office was a narrow steel door with another combination lock in the middle.

"This must be the vault that contains the formula and the destruct button," said Jack.

"Should we open it now?" asked Grace.

"No, let's get a couple hours sleep first. I'd rather not open it until Matty gets here anyway."

Grace noticed the floor and the room beginning to warm.

"Radiant floor heat… Ian thought of everything," said Jack.

They rested on the warm stone floor, as Grace laid her head on Jack's shoulder. Her soft hair felt heavenly against his unshaven face. She fell right to sleep. Jack lie awake for a moment, remembering Ian's last words… to destroy the lab, kill Kettering, and go to Hagley Park. He drifted off to sleep, with images of places in Hagley Park that he tried to remember. The images tumbled and flowed together like molten lava from a volcano, disappearing into the cold ocean.

Chapter 21
Kettering Strikes Back

The low-pitched, vibrating hum from the helicopter blades grew louder as the dark craft sliced through the magenta light of the early morning sky. Reggie was the first to hear it.

"They're coming," he yelled from Clive's front porch, as he tried to catch a glimpse of the aircraft through the distant pine trees. It was 8:30 a.m., the time that Grace and Jack were supposed to have met up with Matty. "Listen, it sounds like it's landing by the ranch," said Reggie.

Calvin was kneeling over his father, who was lying on a couch, gravely ill and falling in and out of consciousness. At the same time that Reggie walked in, Clive's daughter, Kiri, entered the room from the kitchen. She came and knelt beside Ted.

"Calvin, I think your dad is trying to say something," she said.

Ted struggled to clear his throat as he tried to swallow. Tears formed in Calvin's eyes. Ted raised his finger, motioning for Calvin to come closer.

"I am dying... I... love you son... help Jack... formula is real... Ketter... must not..." his chin dropped to his chest, and he breathed his last. Calvin began to sob. Reggie helped pull Ted's limp body, once that of a strong, robust man, to Calvin's chest, and he hugged his father one last time. Then Calvin kissed his forehead, and gently closed his eyelids. Reggie said a prayer to himself. He put his huge hand on Calvin's shoulder.

"I'm so sorry," said Reggie.

But Calvin broke down, and he started screaming.

"I want to kill Kettering. I want to kill that bastard! He destroyed my family. I have no one left."

"You got us now. You got Matty. It's gonna' be okay, man," said Reggie.

They heard footsteps on the porch, and Reggie reached for his gun.

"Whoa, put your gun down. It's just my dad," said Kiri.

"Gidday, how are you going?" asked Clive. "I heard the helicopter from the back paddock... thought I'd come see if you were okay. How's your dad?"

Calvin tried to speak, but the lump in his throat was too big.

"He passed on just now," said Kiri.

Clive removed his grazier hat and bowed his head. He extended his hand to Calvin, who was slumped over sobbing and held partially upright by Reggie and Kiri. Reggie glanced at Kiri, who met his eyes at the same time.

"Reggie, this is my stepdaughter, Kiri," said Clive.

"Hello, I'm Jack's friend. He's Dr. Moon's son...and, ah, you know what, it's a long story. Anyway, it's nice to meet you."

Clive stepped behind her and took over holding Calvin. Kiri approached Reggie and shook his hand.

"How are you going? Pleased to meet you."

He immediately felt an attraction to her. She looked to be about his age, with glowing brown eyes. He tried not to stare at her, and instead turned away to console Calvin.

"You need to see a doctor for that arm," said Kiri.

"I must stay here for my father's funeral," said Calvin.

"I'm afraid there's not going to be a funeral, son," said Clive. "Your father died in the explosion that's going to happen at the ranch this morning. That's what you tell the police, that he was watching the ranch while they were away, and he must have died in the explosion."

"My father will have a decent burial. I'm sick and tired of all this secret formula bullshit. My family has paid a tremendous price for the sake of Moon's formula, the same formula that we're going to blow up, no less."

"Ian and your father did not die in vain," said Clive. "I'm sure Ian left a plan for someone. I'm very sorry about your father and Jim, but Ian left money with me to care for your mother and help with your ranch."

"I don't care about the money," said Calvin.

"We'll bury your father on your property. I know a vicar who would perform a private service for us. I'm sure Jack would want to combine it with a service for Sarah and Ian."

"Whatever you say," said Calvin.

"Your father was a good man... the finest, bravest Kiwi in the war. Ted, Ian, and I were mates. We were like brothers. We fought together and we returned home together. After the war, we settled in these high grasslands, raising our families and running our sheep stations. We had a good life, but Ted and I knew our lives would be tied to Ian and his work. We knew Ian was a brilliant scientist, and we wanted to help him. That's why we took care of his ranch for him. We kept quiet when the SIS came around asking questions. I always feared this day would come, but now that it's here, we will see this through for the sake of Ian and Ted."

"I'm sorry, Clive. I owe you an apology," said Calvin.

"Not to worry. You've been through hell."

"I'll take you to the hospital in Timaru when this is over," said Kiri.

"Reggie and I will go pick up Matty and the Yanks," said Clive.

"What about the helicopter? We've got to try and take it out," said Reggie.

"You can't go back there. It's not safe," said Kiri.

"Is there another way up there?" asked Reggie.

"Yes, we can take the horses on the old north trail that runs by Ian's ranch," said Kiri.

"What about Calvin?" asked Clive.

"I'll stay here with the radio and listen for Jack and Matty. I'll relay their status to you on the walkie-talkies," said Calvin.

"Okay, let's do this," said Reggie.

Kettering jumped from the helicopter before it landed, and ran to the house in a fit of rage. Driggers followed behind, while Pratt remained at the

171

controls, with the engine still running. Chin and Eva met Kettering on the front porch.

"You disappoint me, Chin," said Kettering. "I leave you in charge of an old man, and you let him get away. How could you be so incompetent?" He slammed the door as he entered the house.

"Nelson was on guard duty," said Chin.

"But you were responsible. Show me where you kept him."

Chin and Eva led Kettering to Moon's study.

"He was in the bed over there at midnight when I checked, and then again at 4:00 a.m.," said Nelson. "The covers were stuffed to look like someone was sleeping in the bed. I didn't notice."

"And there were no open windows," said Eva, as Kettering paced.

"You say he didn't talk?" Kettering demanded.

"We used the sodium pentothal, but all he would tell us is that the formula exists," said Eva. "He said it was in the ranch. That's all."

"Then there is a tunnel somewhere in this house that leads to the laboratory. I'm sure of that. Stan, get everyone in here and start smashing these walls. Chin, take some men and go with Pratt in the helicopter. The satellite shows fresh tracks on the west side of the mountain. There must be an entrance there that leads to Moon's laboratory. Find it, and seal it off. No one gets in or out. Take no prisoners, except Trane. I want him alive. Don't disappoint me this time, Chin!"

The noise of the helicopter lifting off drowned out the clatter of smashing plaster and broken lumber. The pounding stopped after thirty minutes of demolition. They had come up empty, and Kettering was growing increasingly restless and impatient.

"Damn it! Enough! Get the hell out of here!" he yelled. He grabbed a sledgehammer and hurled it at the bookshelves across the room. He circled the room like a caged tiger. Then, he stopped and stared out the window, as if he was in a trance. Driggers approached, and waited for Kettering to acknowledge his presence.

"Colonel, Chin radioed confirmation of a mineshaft entrance that corresponds with the satellite images. He says there is only a single set of tracks in the snow."

Kettering remained motionless, and did not respond.

"Colonel."

"Tracks," said Kettering.

"Colonel, your orders for Chin. What should I tell him?"

Kettering turned and smiled at Driggers.

"That's it, Stan! Yes, there are always tracks if you look hard enough." He stared at the floor in front of the bookcase where the sledgehammer had landed. Then, he walked over and got down on his hands and knees.

"What is it, Colonel?" asked Driggers.

"Tracks, Stan… a spec of mud. You see over there?" He pointed, and then crawled toward the wall of bookshelves. Then he stood up and grabbed book after book, hurling them across the floor. When the back of the bookcase was exposed, he picked up the sledgehammer and swung it with full force, until it left his hand and went through the wall, landing with a clank on the other side.

"Get everyone in here and bust through this wall," said Kettering. "Tell Chin to secure that mineshaft. Find whoever is in there, and kill them, unless it's Trane. Tell Chin to radio as soon as he has found the entrance to Moon's laboratory."

"Will do, Colonel," said Driggers.

After a few minutes, they broke through the wall.

"There's your secret passageway!" exclaimed Kettering. He looked around with a devilish smile. Eva stepped inside and peered at the ladder that descended to the tunnel below. She delighted at the thought of finding the formula, and even more so at the fortune Kettering had promised her. Driggers left the room, and returned with Dr. Crankshaw a few minutes later.

"Ah, Dr. Crankshaw," said Kettering in delight. "Soon you will have the chance to examine the real formula. I'm sure your colleagues will be happy too, and I suspect your skills in that safe-cracking hobby of yours will be tested very shortly."

Kettering and Driggers entered the tunnel, followed by Eva and Crankshaw. They found the ladder to the manhole where Jack and the others had entered the tunnel.

"This is where they made their escape last night," said Kettering.

They continued on until they reached the steel door to the lab.

"So, this is where the great Dr. Moon toiled on the antimatter formula," said Kettering. "Dr. Crankshaw, you may begin cracking this combination. How long do you think it will take?"

"An hour at the most," he replied.

Grace heard a buzzing sound, like an electric drill, coming from the other side of the door. She looked at her watch. It was 9:00 a.m. Jack grew increasingly anxious as each minute passed that Matty was behind schedule.

"Jack, someone is trying to open the main door," she whispered.

Jack looked worriedly at the door, pacing back and forth.

"It's Kettering. He discovered the tunnel. Where is Matty? He should have been here by now."

"What are we going to do?"

"I don't know, but we've got to get to that destruct button. Look at the time."

"Jack, what if something happened to Matty? What if Kettering's men are in the escape tunnel? We're trapped! We can't open the escape tunnel door now, or we'll be killed." She ran to the front door, as the drilling grew louder.

"I'll think of something," said Jack. He squatted with his hands over his face, trying to concentrate. He stood up and frantically surveyed the cavernous laboratory. Then, he noticed something in the far corner of the cavern. "Look at that framework over there. I didn't see it before. I thought it was a storage area. The framework disappears in the ceiling. It's too dark to see… maybe it's an elevator. Damn, but where is the car?"

"I don't know. It must be up there," said Grace. She looked around frantically for a light switch.

"Forget it, we'll go out through the rear escape door like we planned. Matty is probably just late. We'll meet up with him."

Suddenly, there was an explosion. It sounded like a muffled bang, and a strong vibration came from the mineshaft.

"Kettering's men must be in the mineshaft," said Grace. "Oh my God, poor Matty! We're surrounded."

"We have to open the vault now," said Jack, as he ran to Ian's office. He stopped in front of the round, steel door. The drilling grew louder. He entered the combination of numbers that were Ian's birth date… 3-31-24, and there was a metallic sound of rods disengaging at the vault door, followed by a clank, as the door began to swing open.

"Aha," they both yelled together. As the door swung around, bright lights switched on, revealing a small room with computers and electronic equipment arranged on racks against the walls. File cabinets were stacked against the other walls, and a small desk and chair sat in the middle of the room. There was a leather briefcase on top of the desk, and next to it was the destruct button with a keypad mounted to the desk. Jack quickly entered Ian's birthdate on the keypad, but nothing happened. Grace pulled his hand back.

"Look, Jack. There's an impression of a Tiki in the metal face of the box. Give me Sarah's necklace." She pressed the Tiki into the top of the box, and immediately there was a click, followed by a sequence of red lights and blinking orange lights throughout the lab. Only the destruct button remained unlit.

"Should I press it?" asked Jack.

"Wait a second." Grace turned and ran from the room toward the steel door. "The drilling is getting louder," she said.

"I wonder what's in this briefcase," said Jack. He carefully popped the latches. "Look at this! The formula is right here inside the briefcase." He pulled out two, 300-page bound, encyclopedia-sized volumes. He leafed through the book of notes, calculations, illustrations, and details describing the antimatter project. There were also two unmarked cassette tapes. He quickly closed the briefcase and set it back on the desk.

"Wait, maybe we should take it with us. Ian's life's work is in here."

"He said to destroy it, Grace. He said it wasn't the real formula. I'm going to press the button."

"I know, but that briefcase could be our bargaining chip with Kettering when we get out of here."

"Grace, Ian said to destroy it, damn it."

"Jack, I admire your will, but sometimes you don't think outside the box. We have leverage with this briefcase. Without it, we have nothing. Do you understand?"

"Okay, maybe you're right. We'll take it with us."

"But what about Matty? What if he didn't make it? What if IWR is behind that door?"

"We have to take that chance. It's our only way out."

"We don't have much time."

The drilling and banging grew louder. At 9:20 a.m., Jack reached across and pressed the button. Immediately, a lighted display on the keypad began ticking down from forty-five minutes. After a few seconds, they heard a voice recording from a speaker in the room.

"Forty-four minutes until destruct."

Jack grabbed the briefcase, and they sprinted to the rear escape door.

"This is it. I'm going to open the door," said Jack. "We don't have any other choice. Matty better be waiting for us on the other side." He began to turn the combination dial, again using Ian's birthdate. But each time, the door wouldn't open.

"Keep trying," cried Grace.

"It's no use. The explosion must have damaged the door. We've wasted fifteen minutes already. Oh, Grace... I'm so sorry about all of this." He held her tightly. Then, they both heard the sound of a drill bit piercing the front door. They walked toward the center of the lab, and Jack retrieved two backpacks containing weapons and explosives.

"We're not giving up without a fight, and we don't need this damn formula now either." He took the briefcase and angrily threw it against the wall in the back corner of the lab. It struck a bank of switches, at which point an elevator car slowly descended from the dark recess in the ceiling.

"It's a miracle," yelled Grace.

Above the entrance to the mineshaft, Chin and two IWR agents rappelled one by one down the long rope from the helicopter to the narrow ledge in front the mine entrance. Chin signaled to Pratt once they were all inside, and the helicopter turned and headed back to the ranch. Chin sniffed the air, smelling the smoke from Matty's fire deep inside the mineshaft, where Matty was stuck in a ceiling collapse that blocked his way forward.

He was trying to dig through the rocks and debris, when he heard the faint sound of the helicopter, followed by the muted voices of his pursuers. The voices were growing louder. He had to act quickly. Grabbing an explosive charge, Matty raced toward the voices. Beams of light from the pursuers' flashlights bounced off the rock walls ahead of him. When he was close enough to see their faces, he tossed the explosive in their direction. Instinctively, and within seconds of the explosion, Chin sprinted toward Matty, escaping the main impact of the blast. The other two agents froze, and were crushed by the rocks and debris from the collapsing ceiling, which sealed off the shaft. Matty lay on the stone floor, stunned and disoriented. The explosion had caused a deafening ringing in his ears. He found himself in complete darkness, disoriented and trapped in a space formed by the old collapse and the new explosion, coughing and choking from the dust in the stale air.

Then, a bright flashlight suddenly switched on, and the massive, terrifying figure of Chin lunged at him. He grabbed Matty's neck and began to strangle him. Matty reached for his pistol, but Chin pried it from his hand. Matty pressed his thumbs into Chin's eyes. The two powerful men wrestled in a life and death struggle in the darkness. They were equally matched in size and strength, but Matty was weakened from his hike up the mountain, and his exhausting effort to dig through the collapse.

Matty broke free of the stranglehold, but Chin had managed to stay on top of him, and pulled a knife from his boot. He slashed at Matty's throat, but Matty caught his arm. Matty desperately felt around for a rock. He grew weaker as Chin squeezed harder on his neck, but managed to grab a sharp quartz rock, and with one desperate blow, smashed the sharp edge into Chin's head, breaking his skull. As he pushed the lifeless body aside, he began searching frantically for Chin's flashlight in the pitch-black cavity, deep inside Moon Mountain. He searched Chin's pockets and found a Zippo lighter, which provided enough light for him to find his way around the section of the mineshaft where he was trapped. He managed to find the flashlight just before the lighter extinguished.

Matty looked at his watch. It was 9:30 a.m. Jack and Grace would have surely started the failsafe countdown by now. He pondered his predicament. The tunnel leading to the lab was now completely blocked, and it would be impossible to reach the door to help them. His only hope of escaping was to find the drainage grate that he saw near the ceiling collapse. After a few minutes of searching, he found it, and he frantically lifted the heavy grate, escaping to an underground stream that flowed down the mountainside.

Exhausted and freezing, he ran down the three-mile long trail to the road below where Clive was waiting. He had only covered a couple hundred yards, when the ground began to shake, followed by a massive explosion. He looked back in horror as the flames and debris shot out of the mountain, followed by billows of black smoke. In the flaming melee unfolding before him, he stared at the mountain, nervously wondering if Jack and Grace had made it out before the explosion. At that moment, something caught his eye in the smoke-covered sky. It was an object of some sort. It can't be, he thought?

The elevator cab slowly descended to the floor.

"Jack, where do you suppose this elevator goes?"

"I don't know. But get in, we are taking it. There's no other choice."

The drilling stopped, and then came a clanking sound, like steel rods disengaging in the door. Jack grabbed his backpack, and took out a machine gun and handed it to Grace. He pushed the elevator button, and the cab slowly crept upward.

"Wait, Jack… the briefcase. We left it."

Jack stopped the elevator a few feet off the floor. He jumped out and sprinted to retrieve it. As he turned to run back, he heard the giant steel door creak, and it moved slightly.

"Grace, shoot at the door!"

"I don't remember how."

"You have to cock it. Pull the trigger!"

As she fired at the door, Jack leaped onto the slow-moving elevator. A concussion grenade shot into the middle of the room, erupting in a powerful shockwave that shook the elevator and left them stunned. Tear gas followed, and it soon filled the room. They struggled to catch sight of the attackers pouring through the door. Jack could only make out muffled commands from Kettering about finding the formula. He looked at his watch. Twenty minutes until detonation. The elevator car continued upward, nearing the ceiling about fifty feet above the floor. Driggers and Nelson opened fire at them. The car climbed toward an opening in the solid rock ceiling. Jack looked up and saw a ladder in the shaft, and daylight about thirty feet above.

"We're gonna' make it, Grace."

Then, in a terrifying instant, the car abruptly stopped, just inside the opening. Driggers had found the power switch. Grace reloaded and fired at him, but hit Nelson instead. Jack dropped his gun in the confusion.

"Surrender, Trane," said Kettering. "We've captured your friends. Give me the formula, or we kill them all."

"You're lying," said Jack.

"Are you willing to take that chance? You've got less than twenty minutes before this mountain blows. Release the brake on that cab and come down, and no harm will come to your friends."

Jack glanced at the darkened ceiling. The top part of the cab was slightly inside the shaft above them, and out of sight from below.

"You're bluffing," said Jack.

Kettering turned red with rage as he looked at his watch.

"Trane! Throw me the briefcase, or you die," yelled Kettering.

Jack looked up at Grace, who was standing on the car railing and gripping the ladder rung above her. Then, he looked down at Kettering, who was smiling wryly. Two IWR agents had their machine guns aimed at them.

"Jack, throw him the briefcase. He'll kill us one way or the other."

"Get ready to climb up that ladder," he whispered. Then, he turned to face Kettering.

"All right, Kettering. You win."

He started to throw the briefcase down, when the cab suddenly jerked and started to descend. Driggers had found the override switch that controlled the elevator. Jack managed to jump on top of the railing and leap to the ladder. He grabbed the last rung and pulled himself up.

"Shoot him!" yelled Kettering.

Bullets ricocheted off the metal cage around the elevator cab. A bullet

177

grazed his arm. He dropped the briefcase, spilling the contents on the concrete floor. Kettering and Driggers rushed to retrieve the documents, as Jack gathered all his strength and climbed the ladder, catching up to Grace.

"Trane, you stupid fool! You could have worked for me. You could have been rich! Instead, you chose your friends over fortune and power, and now you are a loser, like both of your fathers. You and your pathetic girlfriend will die in this mountain tomb, but not before I tell the New Zealand police and the US Navy that you murdered your parents and destroyed Moon's laboratory after you learned you were an illegitimate bastard. You coerced your friends into helping you, and I'll make it clear that the three of you were responsible for this... terrible tragedy."

"And we will capture and execute your friends," added Driggers.

"You have fifteen minutes to think about what a miserable failure you've been, and of everything you've lost before you die. Goodbye, Trane."

"So long, sucker," yelled Driggers, as he ran out the door.

Meanwhile, Dr. Crankshaw was studying the formula documents, while one of the other IWR agents knelt over Nelson, who was moaning in pain and bleeding from his stomach.

"Dr. Crankshaw, do we have the real thing this time?" asked Kettering.

"Preliminarily, it appears to be," he replied.

"Good, let's go. We only have a few minutes to get to the helicopter."

"I need to see the computers. I'll be along in a minute."

"Alright, we'll wait for you in the helicopter," said Kettering, as he ran out the door, clutching the formula.

A few minutes later, Crankshaw hurried from the computer room. One of the agents named Stark was trying to lift Nelson.

"What should we do with Nelson?" asked Stark.

"Leave him. There's no time," said Crankshaw, as he disappeared out the doorway.

Stark glanced back at Nelson, who was pleading for help. Then, he turned and ran through the door to catch up to Crankshaw

---

Jack and Grace made it to the observatory deck with nine minutes left before detonation. There was a contraption in the room that looked like a telescope without the lenses, with wheels that ran on a track.

"This must be the MASER that Ian mentioned," said Jack.

The track led to a steel door, with a wheel that operated like a hatch on a ship door. Together, they turned the wheel to unlock the door. As the door opened, a view of the entire valley unfolded before them. They stepped onto an outside platform, about thirty feet long. It extended to the edge of a cliff that dropped thousands of feet to the valley floor. On the opposite side of the platform was a large wooden door.

"Damn it, there's nowhere to go," said Jack.

Grace ran to the wooden door and pulled it open.

"Look, Jack, a hang glider. Remember Calvin saying they used to hang glide from here? Hurry, help me get it out! We only have a few minutes."

They unfolded it and locked the wings in place.

"Grace, there is only one harness. This isn't meant for two people."

"Don't worry, I saw a couple strap themselves together at the dunes."

"Do you know how to fly this thing?"

"We'll figure it out. We don't have much choice, do we?"

Grace positioned herself in back of Jack and strapped herself tightly around him. Jack looked at his watch. They had less than a minute. They tried to move forward, but couldn't coordinate their movements.

"Grace, you have to lift your legs so I can run with you on my back. Hurry, we're down to seconds." He ran forward as fast he could with Grace on his back, and the glider dropped off the edge of the platform. For an instant, they were descending out of control. Then, the rising drafts from the valley caught their wings, and they steadied.

Just as they began to gain altitude, a massive explosion rocked the mountain. A huge fireball erupted from the observatory, followed by a great shockwave. Billows of black smoke and debris poured out, and small rocks were turned into projectiles that pierced the nylon wings of the glider. Miraculously, they continued to fly away from the mountain. Jack looked for the ranch, but it was hidden from view by clouds of thick, black smoke.

Minutes later, the smoke cleared, as they sailed away from the horrible scene of destruction. They both breathed a collective sigh of relief. Grace tapped him on the shoulder and pointed to the glorious panorama in front of them. The Hawkdun Mountains stretched across the northwest horizon. Rolling, ochre-colored grassy hills fanned out to the south, and the Waitaki River Valley and the flat checkerboard fields of the Canterbury Plains unfolded in front of them as they glided northeast toward the Pacific Ocean.

Suddenly, Kettering's helicopter emerged from the smoke about a thousand yards in front of them. Grace pointed at the side door as it slid open. Jack watched helplessly as Driggers aimed a machine gun at them. But before he could fire, the helicopter jerked and shuddered. Jack watched it slowly descend toward the ground. The crippled helicopter crashed into the field near the burning ranch buildings. He watched four figures flee the wreckage, just before it exploded.

––––––––––––––––

Moments before the mountain exploded, Reggie and Kiri stood at the edge of the woods, where they watched the helicopter take off. Reggie knew that if he couldn't destroy the helicopter, his friends would be sitting ducks as they tried to escape in the open hills. As the helicopter slowly lifted off, Reggie sprinted into the open field and fired his machine gun at the rising aircraft, until it disappeared into the smoky sky.

"I must have missed. It looks like they got away," said Reggie. He no sooner spoke, before they both looked up to see the helicopter plummeting from the sky, and then crash in a field near the ranch. Reggie thought he saw several figures run from the smoking crash scene and get into a truck.

"Look, there's a hang glider," said Kiri, as she pointed to the sky.

"There are two people on it," said Reggie.

"That's Jack and Grace. They got away! They made it!" yelled Kiri. "Wait, but where is Matty?"

"Don't worry, he's probably with Clive," said Reggie. "We have to stop Kettering. He's going after them."

"We'll never catch Kettering on horses. It would make more sense to meet my dad at the rendezvous point. He knows all the shortcuts. Don't worry, we'll catch up to Jack and Grace."

"How long can they stay up there?" asked Reggie.

"Maybe an hour if the drafts are right, but that is not what they want. They want distance. Their only hope is to make it to Timaru where we can pick them up before Kettering or the police get to them. At least Kettering doesn't know where they are going."

Reggie looked at her with concern.

"I don't think they do either."

Chapter 22
Another Peace

Jack and Grace glided twenty miles from the ranch, far from the scene of destruction, riding the unusually warm drafts eastward toward the Pacific Ocean. The river looked like woven ribbons of turquoise and white flowing across the valley floor. If the circumstances of their flight above one of the most beautiful sights in the world had been different, Jack would have thought he was in paradise. Instead, the thought of Kettering in dogged pursuit terrified him. Mostly, he worried about Grace. His love for her made him instinctively want to protect her from the dangers they faced, the dangers he felt responsible for.

The chilly wind froze Jack's hands as he tried to grip the cold, aluminum frame of the hang glider. Grace struggled to balance herself on his back. After gliding for over an hour, the drafts had subsided and the hang glider was descending toward the coast. In the distance, they could see vehicles crossing a highway bridge over the river. Next to it was a railway bridge on the main line that ran to Christchurch from Invercargill. Jack tried to shift his weight to keep them aloft. He hoped to land well before the highway bridge, out of sight of passing motorists, and above all, Kettering and the district police.

It was hard enough for an experienced hang glider to land near a river, let alone for a novice with a person strapped on his back. The glider continued to descend faster and faster. In seconds, his feet touched the tops of the grasses, and they came to rest in a muddy, marshy area near the highway bridge. Jack quickly undid the harness, and covered the wings with some loose branches.

"How far is it to Timaru?" asked Grace. "How will we get there? We can't hitchhike. Kettering and the police will be watching the highway."

"Calm down, Grace. We'll figure this out. It looks like the railway line veers away from the road up ahead. So, the tracks will be somewhat out of sight from the highway. We'll wait under the bridge until nightfall, and then we'll follow the tracks to Timaru."

"And then what? How long before they spot us? How long will Matty wait for us?"

"Shhh. Listen, did you hear that?"

"Hear what?"

A train horn sounded in the distance.

"There it is again," said Jack. "It's a train horn. It's coming from across the river. Look, it's a freight train heading north, and it's moving slow too."

The blue and yellow locomotive, pulling a long row of boxcars, lumbered toward the railway bridge.

"We've got to get on that train," said Jack. "Hurry, we've only got a few minutes." They jumped up and sprinted along the gravelly shoreline, quickly reaching the highway bridge. They passed underneath it and headed for the railway bridge. "Just a little farther, Grace. We need to get to the east side of the bridge, where we won't be seen from the highway."

They were just about to climb up the grass bank to the tracks, when they ran into a patch of swampy mud covered with tall reeds and sedges. Grace screamed.

"Jack, I'm stuck! I can't pull my leg out of the mud."

He looked up to see the locomotive approach the bridge on the other side of the river. Frantically, he searched the grass bank for a branch or stick, anything to pull her out. He found a stick and extended it to her.

"Grab a hold, Grace!"

The ground began to vibrate as the locomotive started across the bridge. He pulled as hard as he could, but her leg wouldn't budge.

"Go on without me, Jack. You must!"

"Are you crazy? I'll never leave you." He glanced at the bridge, and could see the end of the train nearing from the other side of the river. "Grace, don't move your legs when I pull. Just go limp, and hold the branch as tight as you can."

He began to pull again, but this time, her leg slipped slowly out of the mud. They scurried up the bank, reaching the tracks as the last three boxcars approached. Luckily, the door was open on the next-to-last boxcar. They began running alongside the train, preparing to jump in the open boxcar as it approached. It was difficult to keep their footing in the loose stones of the track bed. They had one chance to make it.

"Go, Grace. Now!"

She grabbed hold of the door while Jack pushed her up to the floor, but he lost his balance on the unstable ballast. The train started picking up speed. Jack regained his footing and sprinted with one last burst of speed, grabbing the frame of the doors while swinging his leg up and rolling into the boxcar. He quickly closed the door. The train horn sounded again as the freight headed northward toward Timaru and Christchurch.

"Jack, I'm freezing. We have to get some dry clothing. Then we'll get off at Timaru and look for Reggie and Matty."

"Grace, we're not going to Timaru."

"What? But I thought that is where we were supposed to meet them."

"Grace, I don't even know if Reggie and Matty are alive. I don't even know what I'm supposed to do. Do you?"

"Reggie came to help you. He risked his life for you."

"Don't you think I know that? But we have to get to Christchurch instead... to Hagley Park."

"How long is it to Christchurch?"

"Two, maybe three hours. We'll make it, but you've got to get out of those wet clothes."

Grace shivered. Her hands shook as she tried to untie her boots. Jack helped her remove the soaking wet, muddy jeans and socks. He found some old newspapers in the corner, and covered her partially naked body, creating a makeshift insulated blanket.

"Put your feet on my bare stomach inside my jacket. Just lie back and rest."

"Come to exotic New Zealand for a romantic get-away that you'll never forget," said Grace, laughing and shivering at the same time. Jack joined in laughing with her.

"Forget Hawaii. The best I can do is whisk you away to beautiful Hagley Park in Christchurch, riding first class in a luxurious air-conditioned boxcar."

"I'd go anywhere with you, Jack Trane, but I'm so worried. Are you sure we should go to Hagley Park? Maybe, we should just go to the police."

"We can't, Grace. Not yet at least. You have to trust me. When we lifted off that platform in the hang glider and I thought we were going to die, and when I pulled you out of that deep mud and we jumped in this boxcar, I could feel the presence of someone. I'm not kidding, Grace. It's as if someone is helping me beat the odds, as if someone is guiding me to where I need to go. I feel like this is the right thing to do."

Grace stared at him, a puzzled look at first. Then she squeezed his hand. She could feel the strength of his conviction. The train whistle blew. It was a higher-pitched whistle than the Conrail locomotives made back home. The freight began to pick up speed.

"Why Hagley Park? What's in Hagley Park? What are we looking for?"

"A letter. That's all I know. Ian and Sarah tried to tell me about it before they died. They said there is a letter that explains everything about the formula and what I'm supposed to do. I have to believe this is all true. Ian died before he could tell me where to find the letter. All I know is that it's related to something Japanese. At least that is what I think he said."

"Hold me, Jack. I'm scared. What if we don't find the letter? Where do we go? Do we try to go back to Timaru?"

"We can't worry about that now. We've come this far. We have to try."

"I can feel my toes again. The warmth of your body is heavenly."

"See, I told you."

"So, what's our plan?"

"Let's think about this. We know there is a letter in Hagley Park that relates to something Japanese… or it's in something Japanese, or by something Japanese. So we have to identify everything that is Japanese in the park."

"Have you ever been there?" asked Grace.

"Yes, when I first came to Christchurch, Kettering sent me there to get information from Eva about Ian and the formula. I went there a few weeks ago, and she gave me a tour of the park and the Botanic Gardens. She also showed me a Japanese Garden there."

"What else did she show you?"

"That's not funny. I told you back at the Dasher that Eva tried to manipulate me to get information for Kettering. I think he thought I knew something about the formula, or about the research my parents were passing to Sarah at Saint Mark, when in fact I didn't. He tried to persuade me to believe that Ian was a mad scientist gone bad, and that Sarah was a misguided accomplice. I think in the beginning, Kettering was going to use me to try and persuade Ian to work for him. But when he discovered that Sarah and Ian were my real parents, he must have thought he won the lottery. He had the ultimate bargaining chip."

"I can't even imagine how you felt when you found out," said Grace.

"I was stunned. I had no idea. Believe me, Grace, I came into all of this completely blind. Eva planted false information about Ian in the ranch house. She tried to turn me against him, to make it look like he was going to defect to the Soviets. She even implied that Ian had my parents killed. Kettering promised me a lot of money if I could get Ian to work for him. I almost fell for it. Thank God I escaped from him in Antarctica, and got to spend a little time with Ian and Sarah."

"I believe you, Jack, but I still have second thoughts about going to Hagley Park. Don't you think we should go to Captain Minton at the base? You said he would listen to you. Or we could call Phil and see what he knows."

"You don't understand, Grace. I believe what Ian told me. There really is a formula! And I believe there really is a letter somewhere in Hagley Park that could affect the future of mankind. We have to find that letter before Kettering does. If we go to Minton, we may never have a chance to find it, and there is no guarantee Minton will be able to protect us from Kettering and IWR. These people are ruthless."

The train continued on to Christchurch, passing through the pancake-flat fields of the Canterbury Plains. They reached Timaru around noon. As they passed through the city, Jack pulled the door open slightly and pointed.

"Look, Grace. There are the docks where we were supposed to meet up with the others. But it doesn't matter now. This train is not stopping in Timaru. It's not even slowing down. We couldn't jump off if we wanted to."

Clive parked his stake bed truck in the public car park near the docks and adjacent rail yards. Matty and Kiri sat next to Clive in the front seat, while Reggie hid in the truck bed under a load of feed sacks and straw bales. As the train passed, Matty thought he saw the door move on one of the boxcars.

"Hey, I got a crazy thought." Matty coughed, and tried to catch his breath. "What if Jack and Grace are on that train?" He started coughing again.

"You don't look too good, Matty. Are you okay?" asked Kiri.

"Yea, fine… I think we better split up. Kiri, you and Reggie go to the ship in case Jack and Grace show up there. Clive and I will go to Christchurch. I got a feeling Jack might be…" Matty hesitated and groaned in pain. Then he slumped over, hitting his head on the dashboard. Kiri caught sight of blood on his right leg under his jacket.

"He's been stabbed!" cried Kiri. "We have to get him to a doctor! Matty, why didn't you tell us?"

"Didn't want to slow us up… didn't think Chin got me that bad. I had it bandaged."

"What's going on?" asked Reggie, poking his head out from the truck bed.

"Matty is hurt. He's lost a lot of blood. We have to take him to the hospital," said Kiri.

"No, not the hospital. They'll ask too many questions... get the police involved," said Clive.

"Take me to Doc Muldoon in town here," said Matty. "He knows me. He'll keep it on the hush."

"Okay, then," said Clive. "We'll drop you off there, then Reggie and I will go down to the ship and wait for Jack and Grace."

"Wait, I think you better go straight to Christchurch. There is something Jack mentioned to me that keeps popping into my head," said Matty, as he winced in pain. "He asked me several times if Dr. Moon ever mentioned Hagley Park to me. He seemed preoccupied with getting there. I didn't think anything of it, but you better check it out."

"Okay, then we'll go to Hagley Park," said Clive.

"Good on you," said Kiri. "We'll lay low at Doc Muldoon's until I hear from you. Be careful, the police will have roadblocks everywhere."

"No worries, I know all the shortcuts," said Clive.

"Remember, they're looking for a black man. Be safe, Reggie," said Kiri, as she reached back and squeezed his hand. *"Hei Konei ra."*

"What's that?" asked Reggie.

"It means "goodbye, and good luck" in Maori."

"Thanks, but can we leave it as just, good luck?" asked Reggie.

Two hours later, around 2 o'clock in the afternoon, Clive and Reggie arrived at Hagley Park. Clive had taken a circuitous route along back roads and trails to avoid the police roadblocks. He parked the truck on the street near one of the entrances to the park, and found a phone booth to ring the skipper on the Kiwi Star to find out if Jack and Grace had turned up there. He returned to the truck and whispered to Reggie in the back.

"No sign of them at the ship. Maybe Matty's hunch is right."

Driggers slowed the car as they approached a roadblock near the city of Ashburton, not far from Christchurch. It was 1:00 p.m. Kettering was in a foul mood ever since Dr. Crankshaw confirmed that the formula was a fake. They waited in line for a half hour before a policeman approached the car.

"Stan, I will do the talking," said Kettering.

The policeman asked to see identification.

"Good afternoon, constable. What's going on?" asked Kettering.

"You are an American?"

"Yes, we are returning to the US Antarctic Base in Christchurch. I'm Colonel Kettering, US Marine Corps, attached to the US Antarctic Program. The others are Petty Officer Stan Driggers, Dr. Merlin Crankshaw, and his assistant, Eva Silk."

"We are looking for a couple of US servicemen," said the policeman, as

185

he handed Kettering photos of Grace and Reggie. "The one's a black man, and the other is a white woman. They are wanted for a robbery in Christchurch."

"Haven't heard anything about that, but I'll keep my eyes open," said Kettering.

"I knew some Yanks during the war. I still stay in touch with a bloke from Nebraska... Tim Blare. Do you know any Blares from Nebraska?"

"No, constable, and we really need to get back to Christchurch."

"He never did find peace with the Japanese... still resentful. Anyway, do you recognize the fugitives in the photos?"

"Sorry, but I don't. Now, we really have to get—"

"Were you near Dansy's Pass? Did you hear the explosion up there?"

"No, we were near Lake Tekapo. Why, what happened?"

"One of the ranches up there caught fire... some kind of chemical explosion."

"You don't say," said Kettering. "Matter of fact, we did see something strange. There were a couple of people hang gliding. They were strapped together on one glider, might have been a black man and a woman... saw them in the Waitaki River Valley."

"Thanks for the tip. Of course, people hang glide up there all the time, but we'll look into it." He waved them through, and Driggers sped on toward Christchurch.

The freight train passed the southern suburbs of Christchurch, heading for the rail yards. Jack recalled hearing train whistles in Hagley Park when he was there with Eva. He figured the rail yards had to be close to the park. The train slowed as the tall buildings near the center of the city came into view. It was 2:30 p.m.

"Tell me exactly what Ian said to you about the letter."

"For the tenth time, Grace, he said, *'the Japanese, other piece of something, and Brother Loo.'* Those were his last words before he died."

"I can't figure out what he is talking about," said Grace. "A piece of what? It could be anything. And who is Brother Loo?"

"Hold on, the train is slowing down. We're getting close to the rail yards. We have to jump off before we're seen."

"There are some tall weeds up ahead. We could jump off there."

"Okay, take my hand. On the count of three... one, two... jump!" They jumped together and landed in some thickets. They rolled into a dry drainage ditch, and stayed there, crouching low and out of site.

"I'm pretty sure Hagley Park is east of here, by the Avon River," said Jack. He peered through the tall grass, and he could make out the train station and platforms in the distance. They crawled through a damp, muddy pipe and emerged behind a retaining wall near one of the train platforms.

"All we have to do now is walk up the steps to the train platform and make our way to the concourse," said Jack.

"Wait, we can't go up there," said Grace. "There's nobody on the platform. We'll stand out like a sore thumb."

"Then we'll have to sit here and wait for a train to come," said Jack. "That could be hours."

"No, only minutes. Listen, I hear a horn and bell. That's a passenger train coming in to this platform."

A few minutes later, they climbed the steps to the platform and tried to walk unassumingly toward the concourse, attempting to mingle with the arriving passengers. As they entered the concourse, Jack spied a policeman near the exit doors. He pulled Grace toward a newspaper kiosk.

"We have to go back. I'm sure the police have your photo, Grace. They'll be looking for you."

"I have an idea. There's a shop over there. Go buy some black shoe polish, scissors, and some tape... and hurry."

Jack returned moments later with the items.

"You stay here," said Grace. "I'm going to the restroom. I'll be back in a few minutes."

A little while later, Jack was stunned to see a short-haired brunette saunter out of the ladies' room.

"Wow, if it wasn't for your blue parka, I wouldn't have recognized you."

"I got the idea from when Reggie and I had to put on disguises in Hawaii. Here, take this."

"What is it?"

"It's my blond hair. I stuck it to the tape. Go in the bathroom and tuck the pieces of hair under your watch cap. I'll wait here in the kiosk."

Jack nodded, and went in to put on his disguise. Good fortune seemed to befall them since they jumped hand in hand from the boxcar, and it continued as they walked right past the policeman and out the main doors of the train station. They strolled up Blenheim Road toward Hagley Park, and stopped at the entrance to examine a map of the park.

"I had no idea how big this park is. It's over 400 acres. That's about half the size of Central Park in New York, but that's still huge. I thought Hagley Park was mostly the Botanic Gardens, but I see that's just a small part of it. There are sports fields, a golf course, lakes, and enormous green spaces."

"I'll bet you wish you were back in school, visiting here on a field trip?"

"Only if you were here with me."

"You're so sweet. How far is it to the Botanic Gardens?"

"Half a mile north of here."

The gray clouds began to dissipate, and the sun warmed the chilly late-autumn air. They strolled toward the crosswalk at Riccarton Avenue, passing scrums of rugby players practicing on the pitch. The feeling of normalcy as they watched joggers pass by and children play masked a growing tension and nervousness that they both felt, as every passer-by looked suspicious. They hurried across the street, and quickly entered the Botanic Gardens under a green, iron archway, walking past the car park where Kettering had kept a watchful eye on him the last time he was here. He nervously squeezed Grace's hand as they walked up the wooden steps to the visitors pavilion.

"There is a gift shop and a café here," said Jack. "I'll see if I can find a book about the park."

"Right, and I will get us some coffee and sandwiches to take with us. I'm starving. You must be too."

"Very."

Grace returned from the café a few minutes later to find Jack engrossed in a book in the corner of the shop.

"We'd better eat quickly," said Grace. "The park closes in an hour and a half. Did you find anything?"

"I bought a detailed map and this paperback about the history of the park. According to the map, there is only one Japanese Garden, the same one I visited with Eva. I think we need to start there. It's not far."

They found a secluded bench near the entrance to the Japanese Garden and sat down to eat. Grace took the paperback and paged through the section on the Japanese Garden, while Jack wrote down the various Japanese components of the park.

"Let's see," said Jack. "There's a pagoda over there at the far end of the garden, two wooden bridges, ten Japanese lanterns, two stone sculptures, a pond, and a karesansui."

"What's that?"

"It's a composition of boulders surrounded by raked gravel. In Japanese Garden design, it's intended to lead your eye to the pagoda, which acts as a focal point of the garden." He dropped his coffee cup as he spoke, and stared at the pagoda.

"What's wrong? You look like you saw a ghost," said Grace.

"That's it! How could I have forgotten? There is a stone sculpture of hands together in that pagoda. I saw it with Eva. It's dedicated to peace. She said Ian called it the Peace Pagoda, even though it's not called that on the map."

"And…?"

"Grace, don't you see? Ian wasn't referring to a "piece" of something. He meant "peace," as in no wars. The letter must be hidden somewhere in this pagoda, maybe under the sculpture."

They jumped up and ran to the pagoda. Fortunately, there was no one inside. Jack felt around the wooden pedestal that supported the Peace Bell. It appeared to be hollow.

"The letter must be inside this wooden base," said Jack. "I need a crowbar or something to pry off these planks."

"I'll see if I can find something," said Grace.

"Keep an eye out."

While Grace and Jack were absorbed in their discovery, Kettering's car pulled quietly into the parking lot by the visitors pavilion. An hour earlier, while on the way to Christchurch, Eva had a revelation. It was while Kettering was arguing with Crankshaw about where the real formula was hidden. Kettering insisted that Jack was carrying the real formula, while Dr. Crankshaw believed that Moon had hidden the real formula and told Jack about it, and that Jack and Grace were on their way to find it.

"Damn it, Merlin! If you're right, then where in the hell would Trane be going? He knows I'll find him. I'm sure Moon told him he would never have peace as long as I'm alive."

"That's it! I know where the formula is," yelled Eva. "It's in Hagley Park."

"Hagley Park? What are you talking about?" asked Kettering.

"You said "peace," and I was thinking about the policeman's comment back at the roadblock, about the Nebraska man who couldn't find peace with the Japanese after the war."

"So what?" asked Kettering.

"The word "peace" kept shooting around in my head. I thought about Ian. He used to take me to a pagoda in the Japanese Garden at Hagley Park. He called it the Peace Pagoda. He would hide presents for me there. It didn't occur to me until I remembered that Ted mentioned Hagley Park when we gave him the truth serum."

Dr. Crankshaw smiled wryly at her.

"Brilliantly done, Eva. I see you have absorbed some of your stepfather's keen insight. Nicholas, you had better hurry. Your time is running out."

Jack couldn't wait for Grace. He found a rock and tried to smash the wooden base, but the wood was too thick. He yelled for her, but she didn't answer. He stood up in frustration and looked around. She was nowhere in sight. Preoccupied with his discovery, he failed to see the dark figures approaching from the far corner of the garden.

He went back into the pagoda and continued pounding on the wooden planks of the base. The wood began to splinter. Then, he saw a section of planking on the side of the tier that looked like it was removable. He was so excited that he pulled and pried the board with his fingers, and it popped out. He quickly but carefully reached inside. Instantly, the muscles of his face began to twitch.

"Come here, Grace. I found something." It was a small, metal chest with a hasp and lock on it. He held it up to examine it.

"I'm coming," she yelled.

Suddenly, a huge hand covered her mouth, and a gun barrel pressed into her back.

"Let's go see what your boyfriend found," whispered Driggers. "Don't say a word, if you want to live." He led her to a secluded spot behind a stone wall next to the pagoda where Eva was waiting.

"So, I finally get to meet you, Grace," said Eva. "You are much plainer up close. I thought you were a blonde."

Meanwhile, Jack continued staring at the chest. He wanted so badly to open it and see what kind of secrets it revealed. At the same time, he wanted to be free of his burden. Opening it, he thought, would lead to another responsibility, another quest, when all he wanted was peace. But he had no choice. He couldn't run away, not after everything that he and everyone else working to protect the formula had gone through. He had to open it.

"Grace, I'm going to open it. Come on."

"By all means, open it."

Jack immediately recognized the sinister, deliberate voice that could only belong to Kettering. He reached for his pistol.

"I wouldn't do that, or your little Gracie will be splattered all over the cedar boards of this pagoda," said Driggers. He pressed the barrel harder into her back.

"Throw down the gun, and hand me the chest," demanded Kettering.

Jack tossed the gun in front of him. He stumbled as he nervously stood up and dropped the chest. Eva bent over and picked it up. She brushed her hand across Jack's face.

"What a pity you chose her over me," said Eva. She walked toward Grace, and took her index finger and traced across her face. Grace tried to grab her hand, but Driggers squeezed her arm harder.

"I should have known my stepfather would hide the formula in this garden," said Eva. "He sent my mother and me here so many times while he worked at the university. He used to hide stupid gifts for me in here, and I'd have to find them. We were supposed to occupy ourselves while he worked. I hate this place!" She handed the chest to Kettering.

Clive was so anxious that he dropped the meat pies and tea, and left them in the parking lot outside the visitors pavilion. He did not recognize the three men, but he was sure it was Eva he saw walking with them toward the Japanese Garden. He ducked out of sight before they could see him, and then he walked quickly to the truck to alert Reggie.

"Reggie, they're here."

"Who? Did you get the food? I'm starving?"

"Forget the food. Five will get you ten that Jack and Grace are here. I saw Eva enter the park with three men."

"It's gotta' be Kettering, Driggers, and that doctor," said Reggie. He put on his watch cap and pulled his collar up to try and cover up his skin color. They walked quickly across the street and entered the main gate. Reggie started to run, but Clive couldn't keep up with him. It was four o'clock in the afternoon. The park closed at 4:30, and people were starting to leave.

When Reggie reached the gate to the Japanese Garden, he saw Kettering at the far end, standing alone in the pagoda. He was holding a small chest. Reggie ducked down. He could see Driggers forcing Jack and Grace to walk to a remote part of the garden, while Eva and Crankshaw sat on a bench outside the pagoda, watching Kettering fidget with the chest.

"Clive, go back and get the truck, and drive down that service road. Wait for me over there, out of sight. I'm going down to get a closer look," whispered Reggie. He cautiously tiptoed toward an out-of-the-way path that led to a secluded space, surrounded by a six-foot high hedge. He crouched out of sight and tried to hear what Driggers was saying.

"This is the end of the road for you two," said Driggers. "Pity it has to end this way… a jealous American sailor and his girlfriend die in a murder-suicide. I can already see the headline."

"You won't pull this off," said Jack. "Captain Minton knows what you're up to."

"How can you be so naïve?" laughed Driggers. "You have no idea who you're up against. We can make Minton disappear forever and cover up the whole mess at Moon's ranch. You picked the wrong side, idiot."

"Reggie will go to the American ambassador," said Jack.

"He won't get near the embassy. Besides, that colored idiot is too stupid to figure anything out," said Driggers.

Suddenly, the hedge behind them split open, and Reggie exploded through it like a fullback with a full head of steam. Before Driggers knew what happened, Reggie plowed into him and knocked him to the ground. They wrestled in the karesansui, as the white and black pebbles of the raked garden flew around them like stones spitting from a lawn mower. Reggie fought to wrestle the gun from him, but Driggers' combat training countered every move, until Reggie landed one punch that snapped Driggers' neck back, knocking him unconscious. However, before the punch, there was a "pop" sound, the sound that a silencer on a pistol makes. The punch landed right after the pop. Reggie knocked the gun from Driggers' hand.

"Welcome to the new Navy," said Reggie, as he fell back, clutching his thigh. Blood trickled from his jeans.

"My God, Reggie, your leg," cried Grace. She removed her scarf and wrapped it around his wound, applying pressure to stop the bleeding.

"We've got to get you to a doctor," said Jack.

"No, I'm fine. You can't let Kettering get away. Take the gun. Really, I'll be alright."

Jack removed Driggers' belt. He tied his hands behind Driggers' back and stuffed a handkerchief in his mouth. In the mean time, Clive arrived in the truck.

"What happened?" asked Clive.

"Reggie's been shot," said Jack. "You and Grace take him to the hospital. Call Captain Minton, and call the police."

"No, I'm not leaving you," said Grace.

"I'm not going to argue with you," said Jack. "It's too dangerous here."

"No, Clive can take Reggie. He'll be okay," said Grace.

"I'll be right as rain, not to worry," said Clive.

"Okay, then let's get Reggie in the truck," said Jack.

After they helped Reggie, Jack and Grace raced back to the pagoda. They crouched behind the hedge, and they could see Crankshaw dragging what appeared to be an elderly woman's unconscious body into the bushes a few yards away.

"Are you sure the chest isn't booby-trapped?" asked Kettering.

"Yes, it was a regular lock and it opened easily," said Crankshaw.

Jack and Grace moved closer.

"Do you think anyone heard her scream?" asked Kettering.

"No, I don't think so," said Crankshaw. "She's just an old lady in the wrong place at the wrong time."

"Very well. Eva will be back shortly with the car."

Jack, who had snatched Driggers' pistol, crept toward the pagoda with Grace behind him. The late-afternoon, autumn sun that struck the tall trees around the garden cast long, dark shadows across the pagoda, making it difficult to see inside. As they approached the front of the pagoda, they were caught off guard when Kettering called out to them.

"Ah, you've returned at an opportune time. You are just in time to open the chest for me."

Jack aimed his gun at Kettering.

"I don't think so, Kettering. Put the chest down, and put your hands against the wall. Grace, take the chest."

"Jack," yelled Grace.

He turned around to see Crankshaw holding her at gunpoint.

"If you shoot me, Grace dies," said Kettering.

Jack's face began to twitch in pain.

"Let her go, or I will shoot," said Jack, his voice trembling.

"You won't kill me," said Kettering. "You won't do anything. You are too weak. You'll say a prayer and hope something happens. I told you, power is everything. Power is in that chest. I offered you a taste of it once, and you refused. You're a fool."

"You forget I'm pointing a gun at you," said Jack.

"And Driggers is pointing a pistol at you," laughed Kettering.

Driggers stuck the gun barrel in Jack's back.

"Drop the gun, Trane," said Driggers. "You are pathetic. You can't even tie a square knot."

"After all these years," said Kettering, with a devious laugh. His eyes widened as he lifted a white shoebox from the chest. He carefully removed the cardboard top. His black eyes glowed. He was like a thief standing at the threshold of an open bank vault. He pulled out pieces of white tissue. Then he froze. Jack watched anxiously. No one heard the whine of a motor in the distance becoming louder and louder. Kettering turned and stared at Jack with a loathsome scowl. It was an expression of the sociopathic essence of his being. He threw the shoebox down and howled in a maddening fit of rage.

"Son of a bitch!" The box bounced off the pavement, and a small kiwi stuffed animal fell out. Eva, who had just returned from the car, ran forward to pick it up. There was a note tied around its neck.

I'm sorry I wasn't a better stepfather to you. It's not too late to repent.

Love, Ian.

"That's my kiwi. Ian gave it to me the first year he and my mother were together," said Eva. She began to cry.

Without warning, a green truck plowed through the hedge in a trajectory at full speed toward the pagoda. It struck two of the support columns, collapsing the roof. Jack and Grace were hit by falling debris, but they suffered only light bruises. Kettering, Driggers, and Crankshaw escaped and ran toward their car.

"They're getting away," yelled Clive.

Driggers reached the car first, followed by Crankshaw and Kettering. The car started to pull out as Eva struggled to catch up. Then it stopped, and the rear window rolled down. Eva started to walk toward the car, but then hesitated, and turned for a moment, looking at Jack with an expression of remorse. She started to run toward the pagoda. Then, two "pops" sounded, and Eva dropped to the ground in a pool of blood, as the car sped away and disappeared around the bend. Jack rushed to her side. He gently lifted her head as she tried to speak. Grace knelt beside them.

"I hope... not... too... late... forgive me." Her eyelids drooped as she breathed her last.

"She didn't have a chance," said Jack.

"Jack, what about Reggie? We have to get him to a doctor."

They ran back to the pagoda to find Clive tending to Reggie near the wrecked, smoking truck. Police and ambulance sirens wailed in the distance.

"I couldn't leave you guys. Kettering would've killed you," said Reggie.

"Thank God you came back," said Grace. She was crying and taking turns hugging Reggie and Clive.

"It was Clive's idea to smash into the pagoda," said Reggie.

Within minutes, paramedics were tending to Reggie on the way to the hospital. Shortly afterward, Captain Minton arrived. He strode toward Jack, with the Christchurch Police Inspector close behind.

"Captain, Reggie was shot in the leg. They're taking him to the hospital now. And my stepsister, Eva Silk..." he struggled to contain himself. "Kettering murdered her."

"And there is an elderly woman who was hurt too. Over there, in the bushes," said Grace.

The shocked inspector looked at Captain Minton, as he directed his men to tend to the injured woman and cordon off the area.

"Captain, how did you know to come here?" asked Jack.

Minton pulled out a letter from his jacket pocket.

"From this," said Minton, as he handed the letter to Jack. "It was transcribed from a radio voice message sent by a HAM operator. The message was in my mailbox at the base here in Christchurch. No one knows how it got there."

Captain Henry Minton
U.S. Naval Antarctic Program
Christchurch, New Zealand

Dear Henry,

You will only receive this message in the event that something happens to me or I am forced to go into hiding. Please heed my warning. Colonel Kettering operates a rogue section of IWR. He will stop at nothing to steal my research on antimatter. He will kill whoever gets in his way, including you.

He lied to you about the Soviets. I have no intention of defecting. My only concern is preventing him from stealing my research and using it to make war. He had been using Jack as a hostage to get to me. Sarah and I only learned today that Jack is our son. Kettering killed Jack's parents and deceptively persuaded him to enlist in the Navy.

If we survive our escape from Antarctica, we will go into hiding for as long as it takes to thwart Kettering's plans. If something happens to me or to Sarah, I implore you to protect Jack and keep him from Kettering and his agents. I ask the same for his friends, Grace and Reggie.

Your friend,
Ian

"It doesn't mention Hagley Park. How did you know to come here?"

"An anonymous woman called me at the base a little while ago. She said Kettering was going to kill you, and to come right away. She must have called the police too."

Jack looked at Grace.

"It must have been Eva," he said.

"I've been in touch with Washington, Wellington, and Bainbridge," said Minton. "It seems our Colonel Kettering is quite a dastardly character, and he left quite a puzzle to solve."

194

"Yes, you could say that, sir," said Jack.

"I'm sorry about Ian and Sarah, and I'm sorry for the hell you and your friends have gone through. I'll do everything I can to see that the Navy sets things straight for you and your friends. For now though, I've got to concentrate on finding Kettering."

"He won't get far," said the inspector. "We have the license number and make of the car, and road blocks have been set up."

"Captain, if you don't mind, Grace and I would like to visit Reggie at the hospital," said Jack.

"I'll drive you," said Minton.

As they drove across the bridge over the Avon River, Jack looked back at the park. He finally felt a semblance of relief. Captain Minton knew the truth about Kettering, and Grace and Reggie were safe.

His calm was short-lived, however, as the police inspector's car swerved in front of them, blocking the path to the gate. The inspector jumped out of the car and yelled to Captain Minton.

"We found Kettering's abandoned car a few minutes ago on a side street off the road to Lyttelton."

Jack looked up in anxious anticipation, but he wasn't prepared for the earth-shattering news. The police inspector spoke up.

"They found two dead bodies in the car. Each one had a single gunshot to the head, from close range."

Jack stood with his mouth open, unable to speak.

"Did Kettering get away?" asked Captain Minton.

"No, Colonel Kettering and Petty Officer Driggers are the ones who were shot. Dr. Crankshaw, we presume, is missing."

Chapter 23
Such a Lovely Book

Reggie was tired and weak after his surgery. The bullet had grazed a bone in his leg, and the doctors said he would need a few days to recover in the hospital. Grace and Jack were with him throughout the day and night, sleeping on the chairs beside his bed.

Jack woke up around sunrise, and couldn't fall back to sleep. He walked to the window that overlooked Hagley Park across the street. The view of the park from three stories up was striking. He stood staring at the broad swaths of lawn framed by groves of tall trees. The first rays of sunshine glistened on the dew-covered grass that had turned to frost overnight.

Jack felt more sentient than he ever had in his life, especially after the events of the last few weeks. He recognized more and more Grace's love for him and the sacrifices Reggie and his Kiwi friends had made for him. He was becoming more observant, more conscious of signals and senses around him. He was also keenly aware of the responsibility laid upon him to safeguard an antimatter formula that he neither understood, nor was able thus far to hold in his hands. As he stood looking out the window, something caught his attention out of the corner of his eye. A man got into a car parked near the gate. He looked familiar. The driver did too, but he couldn't be sure. He heard Reggie wake up, and he looked away.

"Hey, how's the leg?" asked Jack.

"Ah, it's killing me right now… but am I glad to see you two. Where's Kiri?"

"She took Clive home, and then she's coming back here," said Jack. "I'm so sorry, Reggie. I'm sorry you had to get involved."

"Wouldn't have it any other way. Besides, if I hadn't come to God's Country, I never would have met Kiri. She invited me up to the ranch. She and Clive are going to take me trout fishing at Lake Pukaki. You guys are invited too."

"Sounds great," said Grace.

"Hey, how's Matty and Calvin?" asked Reggie.

"Matty's leg took twenty stitches, and Calvin's whole arm is in a cast," said Grace.

Jack walked back to the window. The car he had seen earlier was gone.

"How's the hero doing?" echoed a voice from outside the door.

"Phil, what are you doing here?" asked Reggie.

"How's it going, Phil?" asked Jack.

"Captain Minton sent me down to see how you all are doing. He said the New Zealand SIS is looking all over for Crankshaw. They still haven't found him yet."

Jack was taken aback, and he instinctively looked toward the window. He couldn't believe the timing of the statement, since the dark figure he had seen get into the car resembled Crankshaw, and the other figure looked like Kirk Shetler, his old classmate at Saint Mark.

"I hope they catch that bastard," said Jack.

"So far, there are no leads. Captain said Washington is sending someone to debrief the three of you this week. They are very appreciative of you uncovering Kettering's organization too."

"What about Dr. Moon?" asked Jack.

"Captain said if you testify that they died in the plane crash, then it appears IWR is going to close the files on him. It seems Kettering was barking up the wrong tree with whatever it was he thought Moon was doing."

"That's a relief," said Jack.

"Oh, I almost forgot," said Phil. "I have a piece of mail for you, forwarded from Bainbridge. It came in your name, care of the US Antarctic Program in Christchurch. The captain said to give it to you. Well, glad you're feeling better, Reggie. I better get back. So long."

"Take it easy. We'll see you back at the base."

Jack stood by the window and opened the envelope. He motioned for Grace to come over.

"It's a Christmas card from Brother Vincent. It was sent from Saint Mark, and received at Bainbridge on January 6, 1973, but it was forwarded last week."

"Why would Bainbridge hold a letter for over four months, and just forward it to you now?" asked Grace.

"Maybe they were checking your mail," said Reggie.

"Only Haskins knew that Kettering was interested in me."

"It was Mildred," said Grace. "She must have intercepted your mail when Kettering's people started snooping around. She probably forgot to give it to you when you were there."

"That makes sense," said Jack. He opened the letter and started to read it.

December 23, 1972

Dear Jack,

> *Merry Christmas! I hope you are well. The Archabbot approved my request for a sabbatical, and I'm leaving Saint Mark tonight to join a mission in South America.*
>
> *I'm sorry to have to tell you that your roommate, Jim, was killed last month in an automobile accident. Since his death and your departure for the Navy, disturbing things have been happening at Saint Mark. Frankly, I don't believe Jim's death was an accident. Jim was trying to warn me about Kirk Shetler. Kirk had been acting suspiciously, and more than a few times had followed me around campus.*
>
> *Last week, someone was in my room, and they went through*

197

my things. And just last night, I was called to the old gristmill when campus security caught Kirk snooping around in there. Kirk said he was looking for the room where your belongings were stored. He said you had written to him asking him to check on your things. I could sense he was lying when he became belligerent and threatening. He disappeared from Saint Mark shortly after that. I told the archabbot that I feared for my life, and needed to leave Saint Mark.

Beware of Kirk. I will try to contact you as soon as I can. Pray for me.

May God be with you,

Brother Vincent

Jack quickly folded the letter and glanced at Reggie, who had fallen asleep. "Let's go to Hagley Park. I'm hungry."

"Okay, we can get breakfast at the café," said Grace.

The frosty morning air felt invigorating as they strolled along the path to the café, kicking the late-autumn leaves along the way.

"Why do you suppose that guy was following Brother Vincent and going through your things?" asked Grace.

"I don't know, but I think Brother Vincent was involved in Sarah's secret work at Saint Mark. Kirk must have been searching for something related to the formula. I can't believe he's working for Kettering."

"It's only a matter of time before the real IWR catches up with Kirk and Crankshaw."

"Unless they're not working for IWR…"

"What do you mean by that?"

"It's just a hunch, but I think I saw Kirk get in a car across the street from the hospital this morning. I can't be sure, but the other person looked like Crankshaw too."

"Why didn't you say something?"

"I wasn't sure. I'm just not sure about anything. That's what I'm struggling with, Grace. I can't put the pieces together. Before Ian died, he told me all would be revealed at Hagley Park. But now, after we've come here and gone to the Peace Pagoda, we've found nothing!"

"There has to be a clue," said Grace.

"Honestly, in all that has happened to me since I left Saint Mark, I still have not seen any physical evidence of the real formula. Maybe there never was an antimatter formula. Maybe this is about something else."

"What the hell do you mean? We saw Ian's laboratory. People are trying to kill us! This has to be real. Ian said that he developed an antimatter formula. You have to have faith in him. You have to believe he told you the truth."

"But he's dead! Sarah is dead! My parents are dead! Kettering is dead! I don't know anything more now than I did six months ago."

"Don't take it out on me. I'm just trying to help you."

"I know, I know. I'm sorry. I'm just so tired of looking over my shoulder."

"Jack, something is coming, and whatever it is, we'll face it together. Stop moaning about what we don't know, and let's concentrate on analyzing what we do know. Neither of us asked for this disruption in our lives, particularly for the pain and suffering you've endured, but something beautiful has emerged from all this… you and me."

Jack squeezed her hand and pulled her into his arms. Grace smiled and kissed him.

"I'm nothing without you," said Jack.

"But together we are something else, aren't we?"

"You know it. Let's go to the café. I'm starved."

They found a little table by a window with a view to the Avon River.

"It really is lovely here. It's so peaceful," said Grace.

"This past year has felt so unreal, like the feeling I have now in this beautiful place. It's like I'm dreaming all this. But I know one thing."

"What's that?"

"I'm glad it's not a dream, because I would have never met you. You're the best thing that ever happened—" Jack stopped in mid-sentence, and pointed to an elderly couple conversing at a table across from them. "Listen. They're talking about some kind of peace bell… a future location in the Botanic Gardens for a new Peace Bell memorial. Grace, that's it. That's the "other peace" Ian was talking about. I'm going to the gift shop to ask them about it. I'll be right back."

The gift shop was empty when Jack tore through the door and began searching for anything related to the Peace Bell memorial. A kindly, gray-haired woman wearing a white woolen sweater and red bifocals on a silver chain around her neck watched Jack as he darted around the shop.

"Can I help you?" she asked.

"Yes, ma'am. I'm looking for information about the new Peace Bell memorial."

"Yes, of course." She took a map from behind the counter and opened it, then pointed to the café with a **"You are here"** sign next to an arrow. "Now then, follow this path past the Rose Garden, and then along the river to the Rock Garden, which by the way is still very lovely this time of year. Go past the Japanese Garden, and through some thick woods. It's right there," she said, as she pointed to an abandoned Greek Revival temple. "We're going to turn that old monument into the new memorial."

"Thank you, thank you. How much is the map?" asked Jack.

"Fifty cents. Would you like to donate to the new Peace Bell project? We will put you name on our mailing list, and we will send you free tickets for admission to various events."

"I don't think so, because I don't know how long I'll be in Christchurch."

"Well, you don't have to live here to be a friend of Hagley Park. If you donate a dollar, we will put you on our mailing list to receive our newsletter, wherever you are."

"Oh alright, of course. I'll donate a dollar."

"I should tell you that if you donate ten dollars, you will receive these lovely garden gloves, and if you donate fifty dollars, we have this book and audio cassette tape that is simply—"

"I would just like to donate the dollar at this time, ma'am."

"Of course, I'm sorry. The council asks us to mention the different donation levels to our patrons. Now then, what is your home address?"

Jack started to recite his street address in Greensburg, when he caught himself. He thought for a moment.

"I don't actually have a home address right now. You see, I am in the US Navy at the base by the airport, but I don't know for how long."

"Is that your girlfriend behind you? You can use her address." She pointed at Grace, who had just walked into the shop. Jack turned around to face her.

"Yes, this is Grace. She's in the Navy too."

"Gidday. Very pleased to meet you. You are beautiful. You remind me of my granddaughter Barbara. I'm Doris."

"It's so nice to meet you," said Grace.

Jack nervously tapped the counter.

"I better get you two on your way. What's your name?"

"Jack Trane, ma'am."

"And the address?"

"Put it in care of Grace—"

"Excuse me, did you say Jack Trane?"

"Yes, ma'am. If you don't mind, could you just—"

"I'm sorry. I had to ask, because I was just dusting off the shelf below the counter and remembered that there's an envelope marked **"Donation for new Peace Bell Memorial"** for Jack Trane. I remembered the name, because a gentleman dropped it off a couple days ago. He said he wasn't sure when you'd be in to pick it up, but to hold it until he returned in case you didn't come."

"Did he leave his name?" asked Grace.

"No, but he left specific instructions that it was to remain here until you personally picked it up." She reached down and retrieved the envelope.

"Excuse me, Doris, but do you remember what the man looked like?" asked Grace.

"Right. Another good question, Grace," said Jack.

Grace smiled and shook her head.

"No, I wasn't working when he came in. Another clerk was on duty, but didn't take notice. Although, there is a note about what you look like; tall, thin, dark hair, glasses, and a slight droop in your right eye. Hmm, I see that in your eye," she said, as she handed him the envelope.

"Thanks, we better get going," said Jack.

"Thanks again," said Grace.

"Ta. Good luck," said Doris.

They hurried out and found a quiet bench near the rear of the café.

"Hurry up and open it," said Grace.

"Wait, what if someone is watching us?" asked Jack.

Grace looked around. The mid-morning sky was clear and blue. The frost had disappeared under the warm sunshine. It felt surreal as they flirted with imminent danger in the midst of delightful views, the aroma of flowers and of tea from the café, and in the midst of mothers pushing babies in strollers and school children laughing and playing. It was a complete contrast to the violent events of the previous day.

"I have an idea," said Grace. She pulled out a small, folded woolen blanket from a bag.

"When did you buy that?" asked Jack.

"Doris gave it to us. You were so preoccupied with the letter that you missed her giving it to us as a gift. Put your arm around me and kiss me." Grace unfolded the green plaid blanket and draped it around them. As she did, Jack opened the envelope and pulled out a letter.

Dear Jack,

I promised Ian and Sarah that in the event of their untimely deaths, I would see that you receive this letter to fulfill what Ian told you, that 'All would be revealed in Hagley Park.' Please accept my condolences. They were magnificent people.

I have reason to believe that there exists a more powerful organization than Kettering's, called "The Circle" who will stop at nothing to obtain the formula.

After you read this letter, destroy it, and go immediately to the gift shop. Give the clerk the blue ticket that is in this envelope. She will give you instructions on what to do next. Remain in the gift shop. Do not go anywhere else. Within one hour, you will be contacted by a soccer player wearing a blue and white Christchurch United jersey. He will ask you the question, 'Do you know where the Rams play?' Tell him QE II Park. Follow him, and he will lead you to me.

Until then, I remain

A friend

"Who do you suppose this friend could be?" asked Grace.

"He must have been a friend of Ian's."

"How do we know we can trust him? What if he's with the Circle, too?"

"The note said that all would be revealed at Hagley Park. That's what Ian said to me. He must have told this ahead of time to whoever wrote the note."

"Do you think we are being watched right now?"

"I told you, I thought I saw Kirk Shetler this morning. We can't take any chances. We have to do what the letter says."

"Do you have the ticket?"

"Yep, it's right here."

"Come on, let's see what it is," said Grace.

They ran back to the café.

"Back so soon?" asked Doris.

"Doris, I have this blue ticket and I was wondering if you could—"

"Give me the ticket, please," said Doris. She quickly examined it, and then smiled at Jack. "Of course, you have one of our rummage sale tickets." She checked the number against a stub that she pulled out from under the counter. "This is an odd coincidence. The donor gave specific instructions that the item can only be picked up by Jack Trane. No one has ever done that. Wait here, and I will have someone from the storage building bring up the item for this ticket number."

"What do you think it is?" asked Grace.

"No idea," said Jack.

"They are bringing it up now," said Doris.

"Who is?" asked Jack nervously.

"One of the staff."

"Right, of course," said Jack.

Grace browsed around the shop while they waited for the item.

"Excuse me, Doris. Could you mail a gift from here to the States?" asked Grace.

"Yes, of course."

"Let me give you my Granny's address in Indiana. There are such nice things in here."

While Grace wrote down the address, a young man in a green uniform entered the shop carrying a package.

"Thank you. Here's your package, Mr. Trane," said Doris.

Jack tore off the brown paper, revealing a bound book and a cassette tape.

"It's just a book, Grace," said Jack.

"Oh my, you are so lucky. That is the First Edition *Hagley Park* book, full of colored pictures, tours of the gardens, and places in the park. It comes with narrated tours on cassette tape. I'm not sure why someone would donate this back. Such a lovely book."

"It's nice," said Jack, as he nervously flipped the pages.

"My Granny would love this book. This would make a nice gift for her," said Grace.

Jack continued to leaf through the pages.

"Jack, I don't know if I want to do this," Grace whispered.

"Do what?"

"You know, what the letter said… go off with the soccer player to meet the person that wrote that letter."

"I don't think we have a choice. He'll be here soon."

"And then what? What about Reggie? And what about Matty and everyone else? We can't just leave them without saying goodbye."

"We aren't supposed to talk to anyone."

"I don't care. We have to say goodbye to them."

"Damn it, Grace! You want to live, don't you?"

Doris looked up from the counter.

"Is everything alright?" she asked.

"Yes, we're fine," said Jack.

"And we wouldn't be alive if it wasn't for them," said Grace.

"Okay, okay. The hospital is a few blocks from here. We'll run over and see Reggie, then we'll come right back."

"Doris, there is going to be a soccer player coming here to meet us," said Jack. "If he gets here before we return, would you tell him we'll be right back?"

"Surely," Doris replied.

"Come on, Grace. Hurry."

Doris kept talking, but they had already started out the door.

"What about the book and the mailing?" Doris yelled.

"What did she say?" asked Grace, as she and Jack started across the porch.

"Something about the mailing, I think," said Jack.

"Oh, she's probably asking about the mailing list. Tell her yes," said Grace.

"Yes, go ahead, Doris. We'll be back in thirty minutes," yelled Jack.

"Okay. Ta," Doris replied.

Chapter 24
Until That Day

Jack and Grace burst into Reggie's room.

"Where is he?" asked Jack, trying to catch his breath from the run to the hospital. Grace screamed when she realized the room was empty.

"They've taken him."

"Nurse, where is the patient who was in this room... Reggie Ivy?"

"He left a half hour ago, and he wasn't ready to be discharged," said the nurse.

"Who did he leave with?" asked Jack.

"A young man. I think he was an American."

"What do we do, Jack?" whispered Grace.

"Nurse, can I use your phone?"

"Who are you calling?" asked Grace.

"Captain Minton."

"He's not there," said a voice from around the corner.

"Phil, what are you doing here? Do you know where Reggie is?"

"He's in the lounge down the hall," said Phil. "I came here to get him a little while ago. I was supposed to take all three of you back to the base, but I couldn't find you and Grace."

"Who told you to come get us? Was it Captain Minton?" asked Jack.

"No, I actually don't know where Captain Minton is," said Phil. "Someone from the base called the hospital and left a message for me that said I was supposed to bring the three of you back immediately. They paged me in the lobby after I left Reggie's room this morning. I went back to the room, but you two were gone. I've been waiting for the nurse to change Reggie's bandage, and now here you are.

"Phil, listen to me. Something is not right—"

"You better take a look out the window," said Grace. "There are two men standing by the gate to the park."

Jack ran to the window.

"Oh my God, that's Kirk."

"Do you think they know we are in the hospital?" asked Grace.

"I'm sure they do. We have to figure a way out of here and get back to the park."

"What are you two talking about? I have orders to drive you to the base."

"If you do that, we're all going to die. Phil, you have to trust me one more time. From here on in, if anyone asks, you don't know a thing about the three of us after this morning. You say you picked up Reggie, but he was missing after you came back to find us. Say you don't know where we are."

Phil looked more and more perplexed and anxious as Jack explained the plan.

"You have to tell me what this is all about," he pleaded.

"I can't, Phil. You just have to trust me. I'm sorry." Before Phil could respond, Jack turned back to Grace. "Grace, go ask the nurse if there is a back way out of the hospital."

"What's going on?" asked Reggie.

"Reggie, we can't go to the base. There are men coming to kill us."

"Who? I thought Kettering was dead. I thought we ended this."

"I wish it was that easy. There are new players now. That's all I know."

"The nurse said there is a tunnel that leads from the hospital into Hagley Park," said Grace, as she ran into the room. "She also said someone called the lobby asking questions about Reggie and his visitors."

"Phil, follow us to the tunnel, then go back and tell Captain Minton that we all disappeared. Now! No, wait… I'm sorry, man. I didn't mean to yell at you. I want you to know how much we appreciate your help. We owe you, man. I hope someday I can pay you back. Take care of yourself."

"It's okay. I had a good feeling about you guys from the beginning. Good luck," said Phil.

"There are probably Circle people in the building now," said Jack. "We have to get to that tunnel."

"Who… what are you talking about? Where are we going?" asked Reggie.

"To Hagley Park. We are going to meet someone to take us out of here," said Jack.

"Who's that?" asked Reggie.

"He's a friend of Ian's."

"It's quite a hike to the Botanic Gardens. How will we make it with Reggie in a wheelchair?" asked Grace. "Maybe we should call the police."

"Police! That's it!" yelled Jack. He walked out of the room and pulled the fire alarm. Immediately afterward, nurses and doctors ran into the hallway. Jack caught sight of a suspicious-looking man walking toward them at the end of the hall. He yelled for Grace and Phil to take Reggie to the elevator, as the man started running toward them.

"Stop that man! He pulled the fire alarm," yelled Jack.

Some nurses were able to slow him down, which gave them enough time to get to the elevator. The door closed just as the man reached for his gun. The elevator seemed to take forever to descend four floors. When they reached the basement, Jack pressed the stop button. Staff and patients were streaming out of the tunnel and walking to a waiting area across the street in Hagley Park, while a row of fire trucks pulled in front of the hospital. Phil ran ahead to get his car. As they walked down the hall, Grace noticed a storage closet and grabbed two white coats. She and Jack quickly put them on and started toward the tunnel.

"Wait," said Grace. "We can't go out there. They'll be looking for someone in a wheelchair. We'll never get past them."

"We can't leave Reggie," said Jack.

"But we can hide him here in one of these rooms in the basement, until… Reggie, did you say Kiri was coming to see you this afternoon?"

"Yes, why?"

"We'll call her and tell her where you're hiding."

"What the hell is the Circle?"

"It's an organization more powerful than Kettering's. They think we still have the formula."

"Do you?"

Jack hesitated.

"Reggie, listen to me. Grace and I have to go away. I'm not sure for how long. We were going to try to take you with us, but now that is impossible. When Kiri comes, you get out of here as fast as you can. Go to Clive's ranch with her. Stay there until you can contact Captain Minton. Reggie, the Circle will try to capture you to get to us."

"Wait, where are you going?"

"I wish I could tell you," said Jack. "Just be safe. We'll contact you when we can. I love you, man."

"I love you too," said Grace.

"You be cool. I love you guys too. Don't worry about me."

Jack closed the door, leaving Reggie in the darkened room. When he and Grace emerged from the tunnel, they mingled briefly with the crowd of patients and staff, then headed down a path toward the Botanic Gardens. They walked briskly instead of running, to avoid drawing attention.

Suddenly, a man appeared at the edge of a grove of trees, and started running across a sports field toward them. Jack and Grace broke into a sprint, but he kept pace. Whoosh! Jack felt a rush of air pass his head, as he noticed that they were in the midst of a group of soccer players practicing. Then, there was a rapid-fire thumping sound of the players powerfully kicking balls. Grace glanced back, and witnessed three soccer players attacking the pursuer. The players kicked so many balls at his head that he actually stumbled and fell down, leaving him nearly unconscious. The players disarmed him and tied him up. Then, they hid him in some nearby bushes. One of the players, a blond-haired young man in his early twenties, approached Jack, while the other two jogged away.

"Where do the Rams play?" he asked.

"Thanks for helping us. I wish—"

"That's not what you're supposed to say," said Grace.

"Oh yeah. Uh, QE II Park. Man, am I glad to see you. I'm Jack Trane, and this is Grace."

"I know who you are. I'm Zach. You were supposed to stay at the gift shop. You effed everything up."

"We couldn't leave Reggie."

"My escape plan was supposed to use a route from there, not here in the open," said Zach.

"Well, I'm sorry," said Jack. "We've pretty much been to hell and back, so you'll just have to figure something out."

"Do you have the item?" asked Zach.

"What item?" asked Jack.

"Whatever it was that you picked up with your ticket at the gift shop."

"You mean the book?"

"If that's what it was. You have it, right?"

"We left it at the gift shop," said Grace.

"Damn it! You gotta' be kidding me. Now you really screwed everything up."

"Well, how were we supposed to know that?" asked Jack.

"We can't worry about this right now. We have to get out of here. In about two minutes, the Circle will be all over this place. They know you are out here now. Here, take the pistol from by backpack and start running. We've got to get to the portal, unless you want to be captured by the Circle, and you don't want that."

"Portal? What's that?" asked Jack.

"It's our escape tunnel. It's an abandoned monument that is going to be the new Peace Bell site. It's the only way out of this park without being noticed. The Circle will be covering all the entrances."

They ran as fast as they could along a narrow path that passed through a remote wooded section of the park.

"It's just a little further," said Zach.

Suddenly, a car pulled out of a service drive and blocked their path. Two men with automatic weapons jumped out and ran toward them. Jack immediately recognized one of them as Kirk Shetler.

"Follow me," yelled Zach, as he tried to run through the woods.

Machine gun fire sliced through the tree trunks and foliage all around them. Silencers on the guns masked the firing noise. One of the gunmen blocked the path in the distance in front of them. Zach pointed to some boulders for them to duck behind, and Jack fired back at the gunmen.

"Surrender, Trane, and your friends can go," demanded Kirk.

"We're trapped. Our only chance is to make a run for it," whispered Zach.

"That's suicide," said Grace.

"Have you got a better idea?" asked Zach.

"Surrender, Trane, and—"

Then, a loud sound erupted of screeching of tires as a car darted out of a clearing and slammed into the Circle's car, pushing it into one of the gunmen. Kirk sprayed the car with machine gun fire, but the car kept going and hit a tree. Gasoline from the ruptured gas tank poured onto the pavement. The driver fell out and limped toward Jack and Grace. He was covered in blood, and he fell down a few yards from Jack. Grace screamed.

"It's Phil! Help him," she yelled.

Jack pulled him behind a tree.

"I had to come back for you guys. Aghh! My head."

"You're going to be alright, Phil. Stay down," said Jack.

"Can you cover us if we run for it?" asked Zach.

"I'm out of ammo," said Jack.

"It's the end of the line, Trane," shouted Kirk, as he emerged from the back of the smoking car and approached them with his gun pointed at them.

"You damn murderer. You'll pay for Dingo," yelled Jack.

"You should have stayed back at Saint Mark," sneered Kirk. "You have no idea what you're up against."

Just then, another car approached, and stopped about thirty yards away from them. A man stepped out and walked deliberately toward them. His face was darkened from the shade of the tall pines surrounding the clearing. Jack could see that he had gray hair and a long, thin face, and he recognized the man's gait. It was Crankshaw, who walked the same way when he left his dying comrade behind in Ian's laboratory. The driver remained in the car, with the engine running.

"Dr. Crankshaw, should I eliminate them?" asked Kirk.

"Not yet. Trane, where is the formula? Tell me, and I'll let your friends go. You have ten seconds to tell me where it is."

"Don't tell him," Grace screamed.

"Five, four, three…"

"I don't know what you're talking about—"

Then, boom! Miraculously, a spark from the car's electrical system ignited the gas-soaked pavement. The flames followed the trail of gasoline to one of the crashed cars, and it exploded in a fiery ball. The impact knocked Grace and Zach to the ground.

"Bring me Trane, and kill the others," yelled Crankshaw.

While Kirk was distracted from the explosion, Jack lunged at him and wrestled the gun from his hands.

"Run for it," he yelled to Grace and Zach.

Jack and Kirk struggled in a life and death fight, violently kicking and punching each other, as the sound of police sirens grew louder. Then, Jack landed a punch, which briefly stunned Kirk, allowing Jack to turn and run toward Grace and Zach. Crankshaw ran back to his car, with the police just minutes away.

Kirk struggled to stand up, then staggered after Crankshaw's car, which accelerated away from Kirk and abruptly screeched to a stop. The driver rolled down the window and aimed a rifle at Kirk. He fired one shot, hitting him in the neck and killing him instantly. Then, the car sped away.

"We've got to get to the portal before the police get here," said Zach.

The wailing sirens grew louder by the second. Jack helped Grace up, and the three of them limped away from the melee.

"Where's Phil?" cried Grace, as red and blue flashing lights appeared near the burning wreckage. The flames from the burning cars engulfed the dry leaves and shrubbery, and choking smoke filled the woods.

"I don't know. I thought I saw him nearby, but it was hard to see in all the smoke," said Jack.

"We've got to look for him," said Grace.

"Please, you must come with me now!" said Zach. "I can't help you if the police take you. You'll be as good as dead."

"He must have escaped. We've got to go," said Jack.

The three of them limped off, following a winding path through the woods. It led to the Greek temple, the new Peace Bell memorial site that Doris told them about. The sounds of emergency vehicles and the voices of policemen and firemen in the distance diminished as they neared the monument. Near the back wall of the monument, Zach lifted a drainage grate and removed another solid steel panel on the floor of the drain inlet.

"Hurry, follow me," said Zach. He switched on his flashlight, revealing a five-foot diameter underground storm pipe that ran below the streets. They sloshed through the trickle of flowing water in silence, hunched over for what seemed to be miles. Zach knew exactly where to turn at each manhole intersection.

"Where are you taking us?" asked Jack.

"To a place where you'll be safe. It's just a little further. Here, follow me up this ladder." Zach reached the top and pushed aside a drainage grate. The three of them emerged in what looked like another world, a subtropical-looking forest with magnificently tall trees. The mid-afternoon sunlight streamed through the high tree canopy, creating rays of bright light that illuminated the patches of lush vegetation.

"Where are we?" asked Jack. "Those look like Kahikatea trees. They must be over 150 feet tall and hundreds of years old."

"You know your trees. Follow me," said Zach.

"We can't be more than a half-mile from Hagley Park. What kind of place is this?" asked Grace.

"It's called the Riccarton Bush. It's a Historical Trust property. The bush you see here is what this land looked like when the settlers first arrived over two hundred years ago. The mature trees those settlers saw dated back to when the Maoris arrived over 700 years ago."

"It's incredible," said Jack.

They continued to follow the path to a secluded grotto.

"Wait here, I'll be right back," said Zach. He walked a few yards ahead, and bent over to retrieve a bundle covered in plastic and hidden with cut branches.

"Here, put these on."

"These are monks' robes," said Jack.

"Just put them on. There's a house up ahead called the Dean Mansion. There are tourists and visitors walking around the grounds. You can't take a chance of being recognized. Now, we wait here for him to arrive."

"Who?" asked Jack.

"Your friend who wrote you the letter."

Grace and Jack's eyes met in an expression of incredulity. Moments later, a figure appeared in a distant clearing. His face was unrecognizable in the shadows of the forest.

"He's wearing a monk's robe," said Grace.

Zach signaled to him, and the man walked toward them, taking long, slow strides. He was tall and thin, with broad shoulders despite his slender physique. He extended his hand to Jack, and then to Grace.

"At long last, greetings to you brave souls. I am so very pleased to meet you both. I am Brother Luke." He spoke with a tinge of an American accent.

"Are you a Benedictine?" asked Jack.

"Yes, I am. Where is the item?"

"What item?" asked Jack.

"The item attached to the ticket. You redeemed it at the gift shop this morning."

"It was a book... *Hagley Park*. There was a cassette tape that went with it," said Grace.

"May I see the book?" asked Brother Luke.

"They mucked up the plan," said Zach.

"I'm so sorry," said Grace.

"When I went for them at the gift shop, the elderly woman Doris said she was expecting me," said Zach. "She said she mailed a book for Grace. She said the postie had just taken the mail away."

"To whom was it mailed?" asked Brother Luke. They were interrupted by the voices of people walking on the nearby path. "Zach, why don't you run on ahead and prepare their rooms."

"Yes, Brother Luke."

"Jack, Grace. Please kneel down and join me in prayer. It's alright, people are used to seeing monks from the school stroll these grounds all the time. We mustn't look out of the ordinary. Now, to whom did you mail it?"

"To my Granny in Indiana. She lives alone on a farm outside of Muncie."

"That is most unfortunate. Your grandmother will be in grave danger."

"I just thought of something. No, she won't be in danger. I gave Doris my granny's apartment address in Muncie. During the summer months, she stays at the farm, and her neighbor picks up her mail at her apartment and keeps it for her."

"Still, this is a significant setback, and I'm still waiting for news from Brother Vincent."

Jack's eyes met Brother Luke's in astonishment.

"How do you know Brother Vincent?"

"We went to monastery at Saint Mark together."

"What a coincidence," said Grace.

"That is where I went to school. Brother Vincent is my good friend."

"Yes, I know."

"Did you know that he is on sabbatical in South America?" asked Jack.

"Yes, he fled from the Circle. It was Vincent who discovered the existence of the Circle, from a message that he found in Kirk Shetler's room at Saint Mark."

At that moment, a flock of ducks landed in a nearby pond. Immediately, the light bulb went off in Jack's head. He realized that the *Hagley Park* book he paged through in the gift shop was the same book he took from his dorm room bookshelf and gave to Brother Vincent. He remembered seeing the ducks in a photo of Victoria Lake in the book.

"That's the same book that Sarah hid in my dorm room!"

"That is correct," said Brother Luke. "Sarah was a very brave, intelligent, and resourceful woman. God help us if she hadn't hidden the book in your room, and it had fallen into the hands of the Circle. Thank God Vincent was able to retrieve it. I think that is why Ian decided to hide the formula in two books, where one is useless without the other."

"You know about the formula?"

"Yes. Ian made two coded books… one in Brother Vincent's possession, and the other that you mailed to Indiana. Both books are infused with microdots and coded text. The code for each book is locked. Ian left instructions on how to unlock the code, and when and where and to whom to reveal the formula. Both books must be safeguarded until the designated time to reveal them to the world."

"Where are these instructions?" asked Jack.

"I don't know."

"How did you know Ian and Sarah?"

"Keep your voice down," said Brother Luke. "I have much to tell you. We will discuss your future later."

"Your eye is twitching. Are you alright, Jack?" asked Grace.

"Future? I'm sick of running! Where are we going now, Luke? What new quest? Whose life is going to be ruined, or killed next?"

"Jack, have faith in the purpose God has given you and Grace. We know not why we are chosen to do God's work, but know that God gives you the grace to accomplish anything he asks of you."

"How do you know so much about me, and even more about Ian?" asked Jack.

Brother Luke looked up at the tall tree canopy above them, and then stared intently at Jack.

"Because I'm his brother."

"He never told me he had a brother."

"No one knows, except for you two and Brother Vincent. Our parents were killed in the Japanese bombing on New Caledonia during the war. I was separated from them after they were killed. I was treated like an orphan, and ended up in the care of Benedictine missionaries. Ian tried to find me after the war, but he eventually gave up the search. When I was eighteen, I decided I wanted to become a monk, so the missionaries sent me to Saint Mark. I met Brother Vincent and Sarah there. It was Sarah who researched my past and discovered that I was Ian's brother. I learned of Ian's antimatter work a few years ago, and I asked to be sent to an abbey on the North Island. I've been helping him ever since."

"So, you're actually my uncle. I have an uncle, Grace."

"That's wonderful," said Grace.

"May I also say that I am honored to have you as a nephew. Come, you need food and rest."

"May we call you Luke?"

"Of course."

"Are we staying at the Dean House?" asked Grace.

"No, we are going to that place in the distance behind the Dean House. Do you see the cross on the tower over there?"

"We are staying at a church?" asked Jack.

"A church and a school... Saint Jude. Actually, I teach science there."

"Naturally," Jack laughed.

They followed a path behind the Dean House, and continued on toward Saint Jude. Zach ran to meet them. The bell tower of the church resembled the spires of Saint Mark Basilica. A train horn echoed in the distance. It was a melodious, friendlier-sounding horn.

"Everything is ready for them," said Zach. "By the way, your friend Phil is alright. He made it back to the base, with a little help from us."

"That's great. Thanks a lot, Zach," said Jack.

"You will both stay here with me for a few days," said Brother Luke, as he led them to the rectory. The house felt warm and comfortable. The air was filled with the aroma of homemade soup simmering on the stove.

"I feel like I haven't stayed in a house that felt like a home in almost a year," said Jack.

"I feel the same way," said Grace.

"Please, make yourselves at home. I hope you will find peace here. You have both suffered so much."

"What happens next?" asked Jack.

"When can we return to the States?" asked Grace.

Brother Luke walked to the stove and began stirring the soup.

"I don't have the answers to your questions. My mission is to protect you. How shall I put this?" He continued stirring the soup. "You must go away for a while... blend in with us, like the salt in this soup broth."

"What do you mean by that, Luke?" asked Jack.

"I'm talking about you becoming like me. I'm talking about both of you joining a religious order."

"Are you kidding me? This is a joke, right?" asked Jack.

"No, I'm afraid not. It is the only way. In two days, you will end all contact with each other. Jack, you will join an abbey on the North Island, and Grace, you will join a convent here on the South Island. All the arrangements have been made."

"Absolutely not," yelled Jack. "I don't want to be a monk."

"For how long?" asked Grace.

"Until we receive the instructions that Ian left."

"When will that be?" asked Jack.

"I don't know for sure. All I have to go on is a note I received in the

212